MURDER AT LAST CHANCE COVE

KIM GRISWELL

Storm

Ebook ISBN: 978-1-83700-070-8
Paperback ISBN: 978-1-83700-071-5

Cover design: Dawn Adams
Cover images: Dawn Adams

Published by Storm Publishing.
For further information, visit:
www.stormpublishing.co

ALSO BY KIM GRISWELL

A Pacific Northwest Cozy Mystery Series

Death in the Haunted Wood

Silenced at the Book Show

For Rob, without whose love, support, and mechanical skills I would be stranded on the side of the road. Wherever we may roam, you will always be my home.

In the shallow estuary where Elk Creek dumped water, soil, and secrets into Last Chance Cove, a great egret, spindly-legged and mute, lifted one foot and then the other, knobby black knees bent, silently stalking its next meal. With one quick jab, its orange beak thrust, slicing into its catch. The silver fish struggled in desperation as the shorebird lifted its beak skyward and then tilted its head back to swallow. The pure white feathers of its throat rippled as the bird gulped and gulped again. As the egret fed, the thick white marine layer that had been waiting offshore reached across the cove; hushing all sound, it settled a thick white blanket over the body dancing with the tide at ocean's edge.

ONE

Saffi Graywood gripped the wheel of her Rambler Trek RV, eased her foot off the brake, and hissed out a breath. For the last five miles, a string of cars and pickups had been kissing her tailpipe. The lead truck weaved into the oncoming lane to try to see around her RV before whipping back into its own lane to avoid being crushed by an oncoming semi. "Dweeb," she scoffed as she wrestled her rig around a hairpin curve then wrenched the wheel in the opposite direction for the next curve. She didn't dare take her eyes off the road, but she could feel the steep plunge to the sea as a constant pull on the other side of the lane of oncoming traffic.

As her Rambler swayed around the final mountain curve, she found herself barreling down Last Chance Grade at a heart-thumpin' 50 mph. "Slow down, slow down, slow down." She downshifted and pumped the brakes. "Come on, Baby Girl, you can do it." The lumbering RV resisted, but with a few more pumps, Saffi managed to slow to a slightly more survivable 40 mph. "Good girl," she patted the dashboard just as blaring horns turned her head to the driver's-side mirror. A string of cars and pickups swept into the passing lane and blasted past, complete with the (apparently) obligatory raised fists or middle fingers drivers of lesser vehicles reserved for RVers.

"Honk all you want." Saffi flicked a silver-streaked curl of black hair out of her honey-brown eyes and waved a two-fingered peace sign. Keeping twenty-eight feet of metal monster on the road required patience and fortitude, something those stubby vehicles leaving her in their wake would never have (or need, she admitted). It also required skill. She had her late husband, Levi, to thank for teaching her how to keep the Rambler on the road. As the son of a long-haul trucker, Levi had insisted that she take turns behind the wheel, so she'd be ready if anything happened to him while they were on the road. Something had happened all right. Something that had shattered her carefully constructed world into jagged shards of pain and regret and longing.

She'd pestered Levi for years to buy an RV, to spend more time together—just the two of them—without the constant tug of the tight-knit community of students and faculty at the small private Vermont college where he taught literature. When he'd finally said yes to a year-long sabbatical she'd been ecstatic. The thrill had been real for both of them but the journey had ended abruptly with a heart attack in a campground at the foot of Devil's Tower in South Dakota. Three years had gone by, but not a day passed without reminders that threatened to tug her back to the darkness of her first year without the love of her life.

Her urge to roam the roads might have come from the fact that their life together had been grounded in Levi—his life, his career, his choices. They'd moved to Vermont for his first tenure-track position and stayed. They had lived in faculty housing—a petite Victorian on campus—socialized with his colleagues and their partners. His death hadn't just shattered her heart. It had shattered her life, ripped away her home, her friendships, her entire community.

Her desire to escape for a while had turned the Rambler rolling beneath her into her full-time home. The irony expanded with every mile.

Note to self: don't make the person you love your whole world. When Saffi had taken to the road, she'd vowed to find her own places, her own friends, her own connections to carry her through the next stage of life.

Saffi shrugged her shoulders a few times, releasing the memories along with the tension of two hours of mountain curves and switchbacks punctured by glorious views of the sapphire-blue Pacific. She'd lucked out, hitting the curviest section of Highway 101 before Last Chance Cove on a cloudless day, something twice as rare as a Sasquatch sighting. On most days, the ocean reflected a lead-pipe gray sky, with waves like molten metal surging toward the shore.

One of the things Saffi loved most about the Pacific Northwest was the feeling that something was *always* about to happen —the tide would turn, the wind would howl, the marine layer would settle in or drift out to sea, the interminable gray sky would roll back to reveal the bluest of blue days, and those blue-sky days would somehow be much colder than the gray. As a writer of books about all things weird, wicked, and wonderful, Saffi loved the shiver of menace on this rugged rocky coast. She loved the way the ocean lurked offshore as if waiting for a chance to engulf everything and drag it into its dark open maw.

Saffi had checked out of Orangeland RV Resort in Temecula, California, three days earlier and driven north on the flat, featureless I-5. Like many other "snowbirds" who drove south for the winter, she followed the geese toward cooler climes as soon as the thermometer hit 90 degrees, which, this year, turned out to be the last week of May. She'd left the interstate as soon as she could for the more scenic Highway 101, veering west through Salinas and the farm-filled flatlands of Steinbeck country, then up to San Francisco. Driving through the city turned into a lip-biter and, not for the first time, she wondered how Levi had always been so calm at the wheel, so steady, while driving what was—essentially—a bus. By the time she neared her destination, Saffi had developed calluses on both palms from death-gripping the steering wheel.

Back in Temecula, one day had been pretty much like another: blue sky blazed above. The relentless desert sun baked, browned, and, unfortunately, wrinkled the skin. Peppery breezes blew a thin film of dust over everything. It was a great place for winter hikes, bike rides, and pickleball games. One glorious day folded into another. It made Saffi feel as if there was always plenty of time for her next book to unfold. According to her Manhattan editor, Poppy Morales, that was a "big, big, big!" problem. The glorious days lured Saffi away from her keyboard and the hours of research needed to ferret out the weird-but-true stories that made each volume of *Aunt Saffi's Bedside Reader* fly off the shelves.

Summering in Last Chance Cove—a place that had no actual summer—would force her to hole up in her RV. That was just what the next edition of her annual reader needed. Her editor wanted it on her desk no later than September first and Saffi had sworn that, this time, she'd not only meet her deadline, she would beat it. To death. With a freaking halibut yanked from the bottom of the ocean, if that's what it took.

She made a mental note to write something about halibut: the fact that they started out with eyes on both sides of their heads like "normal" fish but, because they lived in the sand at the bottom of the sea, over time, one eye migrated across the fish's head so both eyes stared up through the briny deep.

When Last Chance Cove's first faded motel blurred past, Saffi slowed to a sedate 20 mph and slid open the driver's-side window. The smell of salt-soaked seaweed and rotting fish filled the driver's compartment. Breakers pounded the wide sand-

and-driftwood beach that curved along the cove. Hungry gulls squawked. Seals barked. Saffi breathed deep, her lungs a thirsty sponge, soaking up moisture after all those months in desiccated So-Cal.

As she rumbled past Driftwood Dan's rickety chainsaw sculpture hut and the collapsed remains of the aptly named Tsunami Shores Restaurant, she blocked out the blaring horns of impatient drivers. She passed the marina with its rows of fishing boats, masts rocking to the harbor's gentle chop. She squinted ahead, trying to spot the sign she'd been told to look for: a lighthouse-shaped board with the word CAMP-GROUND blazoned across it. And there it was, weathered and wind-warped, the guidepost to Last Chance Cove RV Park. Her new home—at least for the next three months.

She pulled the RV into the lane beside the office, a small building painted salt-scoured blue, a color she'd come to associate with seaside towns. On the far side of the office, a row of wind-gnarled trees separated the park from Elk Creek. As she watched, an egret rose skyward from the estuary where the creek widened toward the sea. As she turned off the Rambler's engine, the office door opened and a tall, grizzled man with a bushy beard and thick mustache stepped outside.

"Check-in's at two." He locked the door and hung up a "Closed for Lunch" sign. "There's a great chowder joint at the harbor." He pointed toward the paved harbor trail leading back in the direction from which she'd just come. "Open on Sundays, unlike a lot of places around here."

"Wait! Can't you just—"

Instead of stopping to see what she wanted, he hunched his shoulders and strode down the graveled road into the park, his bright yellow safety vest fading into the ocean mist.

So much for "The Friendliest Park on the Cove!" Saffi sighed, thinking back to the tagline on the RV park's homepage.

Still, the idea of a bowl of hot chowder made her tummy rumble. She would take the grizzled guy's recommendation, but she would leave her rig where it sat. It would hold her place in line if other rigs arrived before check-in time, or, better yet, snarl traffic and cause Mr. Safety Vest a massive headache when he returned from lunch.

TWO

The windchill coming off the harbor felt more like December than June, forcing Saffi to stretch the sleeves of her hoodie over her hands and hunch her head forward. "Brisk" described both the weather and her walk as she hurried toward the small clutch of buildings just beyond the bobbing boats. A few colorful names caught her eye: *Lady Hawke, Skipjack, Dandy Bill.* Gulls argued above the boats, dipping and diving in search of tasty fish bits left behind on decks and docks.

If not for the faded red lettering on the weathered sign near the end of the paved trail, she'd never have found the Last Chance Café. The squat white building huddled behind a large marine supply store and was squished between an apparently defunct art gallery and a chain-link fence. On the other side of the fence, massive fishing boats had been hoisted high, their rusted, barnacle-crusted hulls exposed for cleanup, or perhaps repair. A predatory screech made her look up just as a gull swooped over her head. Saffi crouched for cover. The gull landed in the parking lot and started pecking at something that looked like a crushed cookie. Soon, other gulls spotted the treat.

The flap of wings and raucous caws filled the air like something out of Alfred Hitchcock's classic, *The Birds*.

Saffi fled toward the café's turquoise-painted door. When she stepped inside, her shoulders relaxed. For one thing, she was away from the scavenging birds and out of the biting wind. For another, the café was dotted with customers, many of whom looked like locals, which meant the place was good enough to attract repeat visits. She inhaled the strong notes of artisan coffee and the fishy overtones of clam chowder. Last Chance Café had the quaint, slightly rumpled look of her favorite cafés and coffee shops—the kind that welcomed guests to stay awhile, buy that second whipped-cream mocha, and, while you're at it, sample something luscious and sweet. Here, sweetness beckoned from three glass-dome-covered cake plates stacked high with what looked like homemade cookies. Saffi walked over to the wooden counter and nodded at the sign taped to the glass dome.

"Kevin's Kook... Kook-ies?" Saffi read the sign aloud.

The forty-something woman wiping spills at the coffee bar snorted. As she swabbed the counter, the silver suns, moons, and stars on her metallic purple fingernails caught Saffi's eye. She'd never seen so much nail bling. *Were those Swarovski crystals?* The barista talked as she swiped but her bedazzled nails made it hard for Saffi to concentrate on what she was saying.

"Uhm... what?" Saffi murmured.

The barista tapped the counter with a nail. "I said, I keep telling Glenn everyone's gonna think he's a kook spelling cookie with a 'k.' But he won't listen." Her short, henna-red curls shimmied as she shook her head.

"Glenn?" Saffi raised an eyebrow.

"Yeah, Glenn. The guy who owns Kevin's Kookies. He says you're supposed to pronounce it with a *c* as in cook, not a *k* as in kook. *Pish!*" She waved that idea away, her nails flashing.

"So... why isn't it Glenn's Cookies?" Saffi dared.

The barista grinned. "Excellent question. Glenn, the cookie guy, inherited a downtown bakery from his uncle, Kevin. Business was thriving until Glenn got screwed over by the city council and lost his lease."

Saffi loved the way small-town servers spilled local gossip faster than they served up food and drinks. She nodded encouragement, hoping the barista would keep sharing. She did.

"To salvage his business, Glenn got a home-baking permit and started selling cookies made from his uncle's recipes out of his van. That's the Kevin's Kookies bit. Glenn sells here, at the natural foods store downtown, and at the Saturday Market, which happens right out there." The barista waved again, this time toward the parking lot across the street by the docks. "Every Saturday. Not to be missed."

"Thanks, I'll check it out." Saffi smiled. "And Kevin sounds like quite a character."

"Glenn," the barista corrected, then stopped talking long enough to blow a red curl off her cheek and nod toward the cake plates. "You won't find a better cookie on the coast." She tapped a sun-and-pearl-studded purple nail on the glass dome. The plate filled with fat, round, powdered-sugar-coated cookies made Saffi forget the fact that she'd come for chowder, not cookies.

"His wedding cookies are my favorites. So buttery they go right to your hips." The barista winked and slapped her bone-thin hips, which made Saffi hate her, just a tad. "But," she went on, "if you want something a bit more healthy, the Hungry Mamas are to die for." She tapped on the next dome. "Glenn throws everything in there. Oatmeal, chocolate chips, raisins, pecans."

"I'll definitely take one of those to go. But, first," Saffi pulled herself back from the edge of sugar shock, "the campground host recommended your chowder."

The barista's smile went wide. "Must have been Bill. He

can be a real sweetheart when he wants to. I don't know how many customers he's sent our way. Go ahead and have a sit." She waved toward the dining area. "I'll bring everything to your table when it's ready."

Saffi had a hard time reconciling the dismissive park host with the barista's description, but first impressions were often skewed by circumstances. The cozy café had small tables with chairs for two or three perched atop black-and-white tiled floors. The tables had been spaced to give customers the illusion of privacy. Saffi scanned the room, feeling a bit like the new kid in the cafeteria as she desperately sought a spot to sit before anyone noticed she was cringingly alone. The two tables beneath the harbor-side window had glorious views. Of course, those were taken. The only other table by a window had a view of a crusty ship's hull. Not ideal. An empty armchair beside a round table looked cozy, its wave-splashed turquoise upholstery plump and comfy. But the man kicked back in the armchair on the other side of the table stopped her mid-stride.

He'd either stepped off the cover of *Reel Sexy* magazine or the deck of a fishing boat in the harbor, she wasn't sure which. Determined jawline. Eyes as steely gray-blue as a Montana sapphire. Slate-gray hair tousled by sea breezes. He wore a bulky green hoodie over cargo work pants, with black rubber Carhartt boots. He man-sprawled in the armchair, commandeering the space. The bulk of his arms and shoulders said he could easily heft a fish the size of the one in the photo behind him. After three years alone, Saffi had to admit the hardworking man vibe sent a zing through her veins. The chair was empty. Why not take it?

She could almost hear her deceased husband's fond chuckle. *Sweetheart, really? Remember Chatham Pier?* She remembered. On their first anniversary, Levi had taken her for a bowl of what he claimed to be the best chowder in Massachusetts. By the time they finished dinner, she was wearing as much chowder as she'd eaten. Levi had found her tendency to spill soup between bowl and mouth endearing. Levi was... Levi. He had loved her, foibles and all.

But sitting across the table from a stranger who would raise her blood pressure ten notches? That was a definite no-go. She was about to turn away when the stranger stood and rolled the tension out of his muscled shoulders. "See something you like?"

If Saffi had been holding the bowl of chowder, she'd have dropped it. "What? I—"

Was he flirting? Surely not. Most men close to Saffi's age were too busy eyeballing younger women to realize that a woman with silver streaks in her black tresses had more to offer than an unseasoned youth. She had experience, and she knew how to use it. But not for someone this cocky. How dare he—

Then Mr. Reel Sexy gestured toward photographs on the wall behind him. "All mine, and all for sale."

The charcoal-gray accent wall behind the table held over-sized photos of local interest: a wave nearly engulfing a lighthouse, harbor seals snoozing on a dock, a tuna as tall as the gangly preteen girl grinning beside it.

"Oh. Of course. S-spectacular," Saffi spluttered. Was that a blush she felt rising up her neck? *Dear God, no. Please, no.* "They did catch my eye."

A tiny quirk at the corner of his mouth made Saffi wonder if he'd been flirting after all.

"Anyway," she blundered on, "much as I love the photos, I live in an RV. Small walls."

His full lips pressed together in thought. "Hmmm. Maybe I should frame up some eight-by-tens and five-by-sevens. We get tons of RVers passing through here. Thanks for the idea!" He gave her a salty nod, then turned and headed out the turquoise door.

Saffi collapsed into the closest empty armchair, the one still warm from his body. Her cheeks had just begun to cool when the chatty barista slid a steaming bowl of chowder and a glass of water onto the table, then stepped back and put her hands on her hips.

"So, you're at the RV park?"

Like most small-town servers, the woman had hearing like a moth's. Wolves, owls, elephants, pigeons... Saffi had learned a lot about animals with exceptional hearing when she researched an article for her first *Bedside Reader*. But moths? Moths could detect bats, known for their supersonic hearing, in time to avoid becoming dinner.

Saffi nodded yes to the RV park question, lifted a spoonful of chowder, and blew on it.

"Tourist, then?" The barista's eyes chilled a bit.

Saffi slurped the chowder off the spoon. Creamy, slightly buttery, and filled with tender chunks of clams, not rubbery as they were in the chain restaurants that catered to tourists. *Heaven.* She paused a sec to swipe her chin with a paper napkin, just in case she'd dribbled. For her first few years of RV-ing, she'd told people she was a remote worker to avoid the tourist label, but everyone assumed she was a techie and started asking her to help with Wi-Fi connections and computer crashes. "I plan to stay a few months."

The barista's eyes warmed again. "I'm a monthly camper, too! I had a house in Paradise until the Camp Fire burned me out. Used the insurance to buy a new place outside of Oroville. Then the Bear Fire swept through. Two fires were one too many for me. Found a double-wide on a triangle of land over here in the wet zone and scooped it up. She needs a little TLC, but nothing I can't handle myself, bit by bit. In the meantime, I'm in a vintage Terry trailer at the cove. Space nine. Right by the beach path."

Saffi put down her spoon. "You left everything you knew for a fresh start on the coast? That, my dear, is brave."

The barista shook her head. "Not really. Everyone I knew

got burned out. Most of them headed over to Chico. But urban sprawl is not my thing. Besides, they don't call this Last Chance Cove for nothing." She gestured toward the Pacific. "This is as far as you can run from your problems without falling off the continent." She wiped her right hand on the turquoise apron tied over her jeans and stuck it out, purple nails and all.

"Delilah Dunsmore."

Saffi reached across the bowl to shake her hand, promptly dunking the sleeve of her hoodie in the chowder.

"Saffi Graywood. Writer. Roamer. And all-around klutz."

"Here." Delilah pulled Saffi's arm closer and scrubbed at the wet chowder stain with the tail of her apron. "Good as new."

And just like that, Saffi had made her first friend.

THREE

Buoyed by the best bowl of clam chowder she'd had in years and some much-needed conversation, Saffi walked back to the park along the paved trail, once more tucking her chin to her chest to stay warm. When she reached the park, she found four rigs lined up behind her Rambler and congratulated herself on staking out the first spot. But when she rounded her rig to reach the office, she saw a different kind of line: four drivers leaning clipboards against the wooden porch railing as they filled out paperwork. Saffi checked her phone: 1:52 p.m. *Thanks, Bill.*

Twenty minutes later, she stepped inside to register. The grizzled park host looked up from stuffing twenties into the cash register like a pirate stashing booty. "Made it back, I see."

As Saffi saw it, she had two choices. One: she could make nice and befriend the guy. Clearly, he had the power to make her life at the park miserable if she kept rubbing him the wrong way. Two: she could channel Bill's pirate vibe and leap over the counter like Ching Shih, the bad-ass pirate queen she'd just added to a section called "Women Rogues" in her latest *Bedside Reader.* For the pirate queen, jumping over a counter to teach Bill a well-deserved lesson would be just another day at work.

For Saffi, who spent too much time planted in front of a keyboard, counter-jumping would probably end with a dislocated hip.

Saffi chose option one. That didn't stop her from enjoying the way the lines on the host's face got deeper and deeper as he watched the other rigs inch around her Rambler. Odds were good at least one of the four would end up axle-deep in the massive potholes on the other side of the drive.

"Hi, uhm..."—she glanced at his name tag to make sure—"Bill. I'm Saffronia Graywood. I have a reservation for a monthly site starting today."

Bill sat down in a rolling chair and steered it toward a computer station with a view of the driveway. "Graywood... Graywood." He clicked around the booking system. "Yep. Here you are." He tugged his beard, then smoothed his mustache. "Looks like we have you in space thirty-two. Backs right up on the estuary. Nice space. Good view." He clicked a few more times. "Got you in there for... three nights."

"Three *nights*? No!" Saffi clasped the registration clipboard against her chest. "Months, not nights." She forced her face into a smile. "Look, Bill, I drove eight hundred miles to get here."

"Congratulations." Bill grinned, showing off tobacco-stained teeth. "That's quite a feat for a girl."

Saffi had kissed girlhood goodbye far too long ago to let this piratical park host condescend to her. "This *girl* reserved a three-*month* stay. Not a three-*night* stay."

"Well..." He tapped a few keys with nicotine-stained nails. "Says here you didn't exactly reserve a space. You just applied for one."

"And was approved! I talked to the park manager—Linda, I think. She told me she would hold a space for me."

"Linda!" Bill snorted. "Probably didn't even check the bookings. S'posed to manage this place but barely sets foot in the office when I'm here."

Saffi felt instant kinship with Linda. She wouldn't make it a single day in an office with this guy.

"This park's run by the city and it's not how hard you work that matters. It's whether you got the right bait to hook the fish. Used to be a 'no pets in the office' rule, but Linda reeled the city manager in quick as crickets. Lets her bring that ragamuffin dog of hers to work. Claims he's her 'emotional support dog.'" Bill made air quotes around the words. "Doesn't give a hill of beans that I'm allergic. But don't worry." He winked. "There's more than one way to get rid of bad management."

Something in his tone sent a chill down Saffi's spine.

Bill clicked the mouse a few more times. Then his bushy eyebrows dipped. "Looks like I rented the last monthly site to that couple from Texas." He waved a hand toward the window and Saffi took in the brown-and-silver Prevost beast hulking behind her Rambler. "Super-nice folks," Bill went on. "He's a retired real-estate developer and she taught kindiegarden for twenty years. Bought themselves that forty-footer stuck behind you there. Brand-spankin' new. Worth half a mil if it's worth a dollar." His eyes gleamed with admiration.

Saffi settled into her hips, grounding her body like her tai chi instructor had taught her to do when she felt threatened. "Yes. That's quite a rig." She smiled on the outside but inside she was thinking, unlike her, those "nice folks" probably owned a multimillion-dollar estate back home. They didn't *need* a space the way she needed a space. Without it, she'd be wandering from place to place all summer. That did not bode well for her latest work-in-progress. Moving and setting up an RV gulped up at least a day, more if she had to drive any distance to find a park with an open space.

"That's all well and good, Bill." She rested the clipboard on the counter. "But Linda—who you said *manages* the park—promised me a monthly space."

He shook his head and skewed his lips as if to say, *That's Linda for you. All talk.*

"Look, dear, if we had one right now, I'd back you into it myself." His grin veered too close to a leer for Saffi's comfort. "But, like I said, I just filled the last monthly." As he talked, the park host unconsciously tucked something deeper into the pocket of his safety vest, but his hand wasn't quicker than Saffi's sharp eyes. She spotted the upper corner of a hundred-dollar bill.

Saffi stiffened. Had the Texans bribed him? Her left eyelid started to twitch like it did when she was stressed. "I'd like to talk to Linda."

"No problem." Bill stuck a finger in his ear and scratched around in the nest of hair inside. "She'll be in the office first thing tomorrow. You girls can work it out between yourselves."

Ching Shih, where are you when I need you?

Saffi had little choice. She was already here, and, despite a couple of Texans with a wad of cash, Linda had promised *her* that monthly space. "Fine." Saffi handed over her bank card. "Three nights." If Linda failed to make good on her promise, she'd have a little time to check out other RV parks.

Last Chance Cove's resident pirate ran her card and logged her into the booking database as efficiently as the desk clerk at the Waldorf Astoria in New York City. She'd stayed there once on her publisher's dime after her fourth *Bedside Reader* hit the bestseller list. Maybe Bill had worked at a place like that before rolling to the edge of the continent to lord it over an RV park.

As for working things out with Linda in the morning, Bill could not have been more wrong.

FOUR

As Saffi stalked outside, she spotted a flyer taped inside the office window: *Wanted: Volunteer Park Hosts. Free monthly site.* The last thing Saffi needed with a book on deadline was a job, but she tucked the info at the back of her mind as she climbed into the driver's seat. The Rambler's tires crunched along the gravel road. Following the grainy photocopied map Bill had given her, Saffi turned right just beyond the office and then left at the larger-than-life wood carving of a fisherman dressed in a yellow rain slicker. "He's right beside the dumpster," Bill had told her. "Can't miss him."

She could, but somebody else had not. The poor old coot had a chunk the size of an RV bumper missing from his bowed right leg.

Before making the sharp turn, Saffi braked to peruse the map. Bill had highlighted space 32, in the middle of a row that backed up to Elk Creek. The Elk Creek estuary bordered the RV park's right flank where the freshwater creek met the saltwater cove. Every six hours, the incoming and outgoing tides swished and swirled the waters together. From the creekside, the row of RVs curved left along the beachfront where a high berm protected a row of humpbacked RVs from the sea, then looped back toward the office. Straight rows lined the center of the park. Rigs of all types—from motorhomes to teardrop trailers—filled the spaces, half with their noses, half with their tails, pointed toward an ocean view usually reserved for millionaires in beachfront houses.

Saffi glanced up from the map. Across the estuary, just beyond a row of stubby wind-sculpted trees, she spotted a large, grassy beachfront park. If memory served, the park marked the area scoured clean in 1964 when a tsunami blasted the town three blocks back from its original position. Thanks to the open space, Saffi had a clear view all the way to the town's iconic lighthouse.

Saffi swung the Rambler wide to make the turn, then drove past space 32, staying left in the lane. She eyeballed the lighthouse-shaped fixture housing the utilities then backed the Rambler next to it in one try. Just like always. "Thank you, Levi," she whispered, as she did every time she used the skills he'd taught her during their too-brief time RV-ing together. Sometimes she wondered if he'd known how soon she would need them.

The hydraulic jack alarm squealed as she lowered the RV's four stabilizing jacks. Saffi cringed until the jacks thunked into place. The alarm served a helpful purpose—it kept RVers from driving off with their jacks still down and causing serious damage. Still, the silence when the alarm stopped was bliss. Next, she finagled the joystick on the floor beside her captain's chair to level her rig. Then she grabbed a pair of blue latex gloves from the box behind the driver's seat, opened the door and hopped down. She unlocked the back left basement door and pulled out two long hoses: one, thick and orange; the other, thin and white. Working quickly to avoid the stench, she hooked the orange accordion hose into the sewer line. Then she screwed the white garden hose into the fitting on her rig and connected it to the water tap beside the utility pole. Finally, she lifted the plastic protector over the power outlet and inserted the Rambler's 30 amp plug. Back inside, she checked the fridge to make sure it was humming. She chucked her used gloves in the trash can and washed her hands for good measure. Finally, she pushed the button to open the living room slide-out which made the RV feel less like a bus.

"We're home!" She grinned, hoping against hope that Linda would make good on her promise of a monthly space.

Bill had been right about one thing: she loved the view. Stretched out on the sofa with the slide-out window at her feet, she could see gulls bobbing up and down as Elk Creek surged seaward with the outgoing tide. She sipped a fresh-steeped mug of her favorite North Coast tea, a London Fog made from Earl Grey with steamed oat milk and a dash of vanilla syrup. As a nearby foghorn sighed out a rhythmic warning, she counted the seconds between its haunting hoots: thirty. The view was beyond any expectation she'd had of Last Chance Cove RV Park. Too many RV parks offered little more than views of other rigs on either side. Here, a blue heron captured her attention as it stilt-walked into view, pacing through the shallows along the opposite bank. A great egret erupted skyward from its hiding place in the reeds, white wings stretched so wide Saffi could have sworn they spanned the river. For the first time in three days, her body truly relaxed. This would be the perfect place to finish her book. No matter what it took to stay in space 32, she'd do it.

Later that evening, Saffi hefted her dirty clothes bag and trudged over to the laundry room at the back of the bathhouse. As she got closer, she heard a woman's voice, shrill and desperate, softened slightly by the deep nasal singsong of a Texas twang. "I have to pay her! What choice do I have?" A deeper male voice responded in soothing tones, but Saffi couldn't make out any words.

The door swung open, and Saffi jumped back, just in time to avoid being flattened as a thirty-something woman with long blond hair fled from the laundry room, sobbing. Saffi wedged her laundry bag in the door before it could swing shut. *Here we go.* Long-term campers know something about RV parks that tourists don't—they are filled with drama. And, if what Delilah said was true—that folks at this park had driven as far away from their problems as they could without rolling right off the continent—Last Chance Cove probably had more drama than most.

When Saffi stepped into the laundry room, she knew she'd get a look at the man behind the soothing voice. What she didn't know was that she'd be looking into the gray-blue eyes of the fisherman from the café, troubled this time instead of teasing.

"Sorry." He opened a dryer and started pulling out pastel-colored T-shirts, skinny jeans, bras, lacy thongs, and crew socks and shoving them into a cheap plastic laundry basket.

Saffi wasn't sure what the sorry was all about. *Sorry you overhead that* or *sorry all the dryers are full* or *sorry you found out I have a girlfriend?* Saffi wasn't surprised, just vaguely disappointed to find one more man hitching the second half of his life to a much younger woman.

"Just finishing up," he tossed over his shoulder.

Did he live here? At Last Chance Cove? With the blonde? *Great.*

"No worries," Saffi said. "I can wait."

"Washer number two is empty."

"Uh, oh... right," she stuttered. "Wash first, dry later. Got it."

The fisherman chuckled, stood up, and stretched to unkink his back. "Good plan."

Saffi opened washer two and started stuffing clothes in. The last thing she wanted was for him to think she'd been checking out his butt while he leaned into the dryer. She had been, but he didn't need to know that.

The last of the three dryers stopped tumbling. The now-silent room felt steamy, oppressive, and much too small. To break the silence, Saffi nodded at the laundry basket. "You should probably fold those while they're still hot. Helps with the wrinkles."

As he looked at the basket, a blush rose up his neck. "Oh, no-o-o." He held up his hands as if to distance himself from the lacy bras and thongs. "Not mine."

Saffi shrugged. "No judgment. Whatever floats your boat."

The blush rose all the way to his cheeks. It felt good to take back a tiny bit of her power. Now, if he'd just gather up his girl's itty-bitty undies and leave, she could mop the sweat off her brow and relax.

But then he said, "I do have a boat. And as far as I know it's still floating. At the marina." He nodded toward the harbor. "If you're around for a while, I could take you out on it."

Was he coming on to her, after she'd just seen him elbow-deep in a woman's lingerie? *Wow.*

Then he pulled a wallet out of his back pocket and took out a card. "I run a charter fishing service."

Ah. Saffi stared at the card. *Troy's Tours. A great time for the whole family!*

"I've been running charters here for twenty-five years. I know all the best fishing spots. Rockfish. Lingcod. Albacore. Whatever floats your boat." His gray-blue eyes sparkled.

OK. Good comeback, Saffi admitted. Smart. Confident. Hard-working. Too bad he was taken.

"So, not just a photographer, then?"

"A man can have more than one passion, can't he?"

More teasing? "Yes," she said. *And no,* she thought. *Not when it comes to women.*

She stuck the card in the front pocket of her jeans. "I'll keep you in mind," she said, then caught herself. "Your charters, I mean. Those. Uh, in mind."

"I hope you do." His smile had a little sideways quirk that made him look mischievous, like Levi had been.

Unbelievably, the temperature in the room seemed to spike even higher. Was she having a hot flash? Saffi clutched her laundry bag with both hands to keep from fanning herself. When he picked up the basket, waved, and left the laundry room, she stuck her head outside to gulp cool air. She couldn't help noticing that Troy didn't hit the paved trail toward the harbor. He headed into the park toward the front row of RVs.

When Saffi got back to her RV, she found a photocopied notice taped to the door. The top line read "**BEACH HAZARD ALERT**." It was a NOAA weather warning, something she'd seen many times when visiting parks on the northwest coast. Saffi kept reading:

What: A long period westerly swell around 5 feet will bring an increased risk for sneaker waves today. Large unexpected waves at beaches will be possible.

Where: Northern Humboldt Coast, Coastal Del Norte, and Southwestern Curry County. Alert extends from 3 PM PST this afternoon until 6 AM tomorrow morning.

Saffi knew about sneaker waves. Anyone who'd spent more than a few days on the coast heard stories about careless tourists who didn't know better than to turn their backs on the Pacific. A sneaker wave could surge onto the beach without warning, sweeping people into the sea. On top of that, every year, some-where on the coast, a weary beach walker took a seat on a sturdy driftwood log far back from the surf, oblivious to the fact that a sneaker could surge across the sand and roll it over on top of them, catching and crushing them underneath.

She'd been thinking about an evening beach walk, but the notice changed her mind. Being swept into the churning tide was not the way she wanted her first day at Last Chance Cove to end.

FIVE

The lulling sound of the foghorn sent Saffi to sleep the minute her head hit the pillow. She woke suddenly, mind-fogged, a distant scream reeling her upright. Then she heard another cry. This time, it sounded like a raven's harsh croak. Saffi sat up. *Raven.* Her totem bird. Raven often brought messages. Over the years, she had learned to pay attention. Sometimes Raven told her to slow down, take her time. Sometimes, Raven said, "Get up! Take action." Had she really heard a scream? If so, Raven might be telling her to get out of bed and see if she could help.

Saffi fumbled for her phone, glanced at the time, and groaned. It was just past midnight. She rolled her shoulders to ease the knots. After three days of driving, her muscle aches had muscle aches. The last thing she wanted to do was get dressed and traipse around an unfamiliar RV park looking for... what?

Saffi had no idea. Still, what if someone needed help? She swung her legs out of bed, stood up, and inched along the narrow space between her queen bed and the window. The movement gave her a charley horse. She clenched her teeth, rubbing her calf as she limped to where she'd dropped her clothes. Once the cramp eased, she pulled on yesterday's jeans,

T-shirt, and hoodie, and stuffed her feet into the rose-pink waterproof clogs she kept by the door. She grabbed her keys off the hook, locked the door behind her, and stood still. Listening.

Above the sound of waves, she heard the foghorn's warning. A few trailers away, country music crooned a few clicks louder than was neighborly in such close quarters. The staccato crunch of tires caught her attention as a vehicle crept along one of the park's gravel lanes, slowly, which could be suspicious if not for the posted speed limit—a turtlesque 5 mph. Not a car, though. Something weightier, like a pickup or van.

Saffi inhaled, hoping to still her vibrating nerves. The night-time air was that ocean-side combo of wet and chilly that settled like a ghostly embrace and wouldn't let go. If she stayed out too long, her hair would be a halo of frizz around her head. She wanted to go back inside, to curl under a warm blanket and let sleep take her under.

Raven croaked its disapproval.

Fine. Saffi drew her hoodie over her hair and plunged ahead, clogs stumbling on the loose gravel covering the sandy road. The afternoon mist had cleared and a waxing moon offered just enough light for her to see. The bird's call seemed to come from the beach, but the warning posted on her door told her it would be nuts to venture onto the sand after dark with a sneaker-wave warning in effect. Instead, she clumped her way to the top of the berm that protected the park from inundation.

Her first glimpse of the cove side of the berm made her hesitate. A jumble of concrete braced the berm, huge chunks with pieces of rusted rebar sticking out here and there. In some places, they looked almost like steps. Below on the beach, the tide had come in. Only a scant sliver of sand remained dry. A shiver traveled up her spine as she made out dark huddled shapes at the foot of the berm. Then her brain kicked in: drift-wood. That's all. Just as her body started to relax, something white and bedraggled caught her eye. A rumpled something lodged at the edge of the logs. Should she go down there? It would be insane to risk her life for what could very well be a soaked towel left behind by a castle-building kid. A sneaker surge could swoop in at any minute.

A raven's warning caw ripped through the air like an echo of the scream that had woken her. Saffi spotted the giant bird on the beach hopping toward the bit of white. She clenched her fists and squared her shoulders. *I hear you!*

She took the jumbled concrete "steps" carefully, arms held out for balance. The blocks were uneven. Like crooked teeth, some sloped one way, some another. Her clog hit a jutting piece of rebar she hadn't seen, and she windmilled, almost falling. She steadied herself, one hand to her pounding heart before stepping carefully over the rebar and continuing downward. The last block ended about three feet above the sand. She bent her knees, swung her arms backward and jumped, two-footed. Her hips jarred as her clogs hit the damp sand.

From the beach, the tide seemed distressingly high. Waves reached upslope toward her feet. If a sneaker came, she would be slammed against those jagged iron-spiked blocks. This was nuts. But she'd come this far, and the raven's shrill cry called her closer to look at what it had found. She headed toward the white object. The closer she got, the more it looked less like a towel and more like a small dog, deposited by a wave at the edge of the logs. Clogs aren't made for running but Saffi ran, waving her arms to shoo the raven back from the scruffy bundle. When she reached it, she knelt down to find a terrier, its white fur matted with sand, and cold. Oh, so cold. She put a hand to its belly to feel for breath and almost fell backward when the little dog turned its head toward her and whimpered. Relief washed through her. *The dog was alive!*

She unzipped her hoodie and took it off, gathering the dog into its warm folds. Then she picked it up, and swaddled it against her chest. "Relax, little fellow. You're safe." She stroked the dog's body through the hoodie as she looked back toward the concrete blocks. She'd barely made it down them without falling. No way could she make it back up carrying the dog. *Think, Saffi! Think.* She took a deep breath to still her mind and a voice echoed: Delilah, telling her that she lived in space 9, right by the beach trail. *A trail!* Was there enough moonlight to find it? She had to try. It was the only way.

Saffi would have missed the trail if the raven hadn't hopped past her and croaked, as if telling her to follow. Just as she started up the incline, she heard a roaring, grinding rush she knew all too well. A wave. A big one. Saffi sped up as much as her clogs would allow, hoping to beat the wave. She didn't. It slammed into her at knee height, nearly taking her off her feet. Freezing water surged up to her thighs, flowing past her and halfway up the trail. Her leg muscles seized. She clenched her teeth against the pain, clutching the little dog against her chest. The surge reached its apex and started to pull backward, sucking the sand from beneath her clogs. Saffi wobbled, nearly losing her footing, and the dog started to struggle. She had to hold her ground, stay upright. If she didn't...

"Shhh..." She held the whimpering dog tight. "I've got you."

She leaned forward, hard, anchoring the toes of her clogs in the sand as she fought the ocean's pull. Just as her legs began to weaken, the water sank below her knees. She yanked one foot forward, then the other. Drenched in seawater and buzzing with fear, she slogged on until her clogs hit rock on the trail and the sand released its grip.

SIX

Saffi pounded on the door of the first trailer, hoping she'd find Delilah behind it. Her body shook so hard she could barely hang onto the little white terrier. Luckily, the door opened right away, but it wasn't Delilah. It was a girl, about twelve years old, and her bright blue eyes went wide with surprise. "Archie! What are you doing out there?"

"This little guy is yours?"

The girl shook her head. "I thought I saw him running loose when my mom was talking with Lin—"

"Casey Lou!" A female voice called from the back of the trailer. "Who is that?" Her Texas twang rendered the last word in two syllables—*tha-ut*—and Saffi realized she'd heard the voice before. Her hackles rose and, for some reason, so did the terrier's. She gave him what she hoped was a comforting squeeze.

"Some lady, and she has Archie!" The girl's accent was a bit less thick but equally sweet, like honey cut with rosewater.

Footsteps pounded and the door jerked wide. "Oh, my God! What happened?" The blonde from the laundry stepped into the doorway, tying a knot in the belt of a plush white robe. Her bare legs and damp hair made it look like she'd come straight from a shower, or maybe bed.

Bedraggled, shivering, and looking like something the dog dragged in—rather than the other way around—Saffi could only hope that Troy wasn't going to come to the door next.

"I-I f-f-found him." She rested her chin against Archie, feeling the grit of sand and salt in his fur. "On. On t-th—" Saffi clenched her teeth to stop the chattering. "On the beach."

The woman's mouth fell open. "On the beach! At this time of night? Why on earth were you out there?"

Horror slammed into Saffi. From the moment she'd found the nearly lifeless dog on the beach, she'd been focused on getting him to safety. Now, she remembered. "I h-heard a s-scream." She hadn't seen anyone on the beach. Just Archie. And the ravens. Had the scream been real? Or had sleep morphed a raven's cry into something more human?

A flash of what might have been fear, shock, or disbelief, crossed the woman's face. "A scream? I didn't hear a—" She stopped, shook her head. "Maybe the shower drowned it out. But look at me, grilling you when you're frozen to the bone." The blonde stepped back and waved her inside. "Casey, honey, go get blankets. They're in that basket at the bottom of the closet. Hurry up now."

She put an arm around Saffi's shoulders and ushered her to the couch.

"I'd b-better not sit," Saffi managed. "I'm soaked."

"Hang on!" The blonde grabbed a waterproof beach cushion blooming with bright pink flowers and plopped it on the couch. "Go ahead. Sit, before you collapse," she insisted.

Archie whimpered, then struggled to free himself. If she didn't hold on, he'd roll sand and salt into the trailer's carpet, leaving behind the briny smell of seawater. She hunched forward over the swaddled dog, holding him in place. "Not yet, buddy."

"I'll get some towels." The blonde hurried down the hall.

Soon, Saffi heard muffled voices, as if mom and daughter had stuck their heads inside the closet for a chat. Saffi caught a few words. "Not supposed to…" mumble mumble. "I know, but Archie…!" mumble mumble.

Saffi couldn't remember the last time she'd felt this cold. Certainly not in Temecula. Maybe when she spent a winter at Yellowstone RV Resort in Gardiner, Montana. She could feel her whole body stiffening. Her feet wet inside her damp clogs. Her legs inside her salt-drenched jeans. Without the warmth of her hoodie, her shoulders clenched, aching with cold. She needed to go home, get into a hot shower, then curl up beneath her down duvet and not move until morning.

A blanket settled over Saffi's shoulders, and she jumped. For a minute, she'd forgotten where she was.

"I'll take Archie."

Casey lifted the sea-soaked terrier from Saffi's arms and wrapped him in a thick flamingo-pink bath towel. Working from his head to his hindquarters, she rubbed him all the way down and then back up. Archie yipped once, but after a minute, his whimpers turned to sighs and then gentle snores.

"You have the magic touch." Saffi smiled, tugging the blanket closer.

"I should. My dad's a vet."

The girl's grin reminded Saffi of someone, someone local. But who? She hadn't met any other kids yet. The thought chewed at her memory, but nothing surfaced.

"Dad lets me help with the animals. At least he did before—"

"Later, sweetheart," Casey's mom interrupted. "We need to get Miz…?" She paused and gestured toward Saffi as if trying to remember who she was.

"Graywood. Saffi Graywood."

"Miz Saffi home before she freezes like a hop toad in a hail-storm. Come on." She waved Saffi off the couch. "I'll drive you."

Saffi tried to argue. Her rig was only a few rows away. Walking would warm her up. But Casey's mom was as irresistible as a Texas tornado. She whooshed Saffi out the door and swooped her into a dark green Subaru Forester. When they reached the Rambler, she took the door key from Saffi's shaking hand, unlocked the door, then stuffed it into the pocket of her robe. Despite Saffi's protests, the blonde started the shower and stripped Saffi out of her clothes, proclaiming herself to be a mom who had, "Seen it all and a box of saltines, sweetie." Somewhere in all that, Saffi caught her name: Nicole Carmody.

Saffi wasn't sure if she was in love with Nicole Carmody or just the feel of hot water cascading down her body. First her head, then her shoulders, then her torso, legs, and feet began to thaw. Saffi yelped, realizing as she did so that Archie's little yip hadn't been joy. It had been pain. But, just like Archie, she soon felt the pain ease as her body relaxed into the warmth.

"Better hop out before it goes cold, honey!" Nicole called from the bedroom.

RV hot water tanks were notorious for running cold just when you'd lathered up for a shampoo, but that wasn't what worried Saffi. What worried her was that Nicole was in her bedroom. Why? At that moment, the water went cold.

Saffi yelped. Instantly, the glass shower door opened and one of her own navy-blue towels was dangled in front of her. She toweled off and snatched her thick terry robe from its hanger to cover herself. She was fit enough. She chose walking over driving when possible. She'd hiked trails all over the country, rode a bike when the roads were safe enough, and could play a mean game of pickleball. But she couldn't think of many women her age who would want to stand naked for too long in front of a thirty-something like Nicole Carmody.

"Now, don't you worry about Archie," Nicole said as she

tucked Saffi beneath the duvet. "Casey will take good care of the little guy until Linda comes to get him."

Saffi's head felt like it weighed fifty pounds, her body like it weighed a thousand, but her exhausted brain made the connection. Archie must be the ragamuffin Bill had mentioned, the park manager's emotional support dog. So why had Archie been wandering alone on the beach after midnight? And where, Saffi wondered as she faded toward sleep, was Linda?

She heard the door close and then lock from the outside. That could only mean one thing: Nicole had kept her key.

SEVEN

"Knock, knock!" A deep voice followed by heavy staccato rapping shook Saffi awake. Sun shone through her bedroom curtains, giving the room a rosy glow. Saffi sat up, then stretched, glad that her muscles seemed to have gotten over last night's ordeal.

"Hello?" The voice boomed and someone rapped on the window closest to her bed.

Saffi sat up and leaned toward the window, peeling back the curtain edge to look outside.

"Hey!" Troy held up a hand to wave and she instantly let go of the curtain.

What was he doing here?

"Hang on!" She scooted out of bed and into the RV's petite bathroom to check herself in the three-quarter length mirror behind the toilet. She looked like what she was: a woman who'd dragged herself back from a near drowning and flopped into bed with wet hair. Her black and silver curls looked like Medusa's vile snakes. If Troy had gotten a look at her when she opened the curtain, he'd probably turned to stone on the spot.

She'd slept in her robe, so at least she was decent, but no

way was she opening the door more than a crack. When she did, she smelled coffee. Glorious aromatic coffee with notes of chocolate wafted from the thermal mug Troy held up to the narrow opening. "Let me in. It's freezing. And the coffee's getting cold."

"Fine." Saffi let go of the door and Troy shouldered it open.

One of the things Saffi was struggling to learn as a full-time RVer was to not fret so much over looks. Out here, everyone was camping. People didn't blink twice when men walked to the bathhouse in nothing but a pair of saggy pajama pants, or when women hurried back to their sites with their freshly washed wet hair twisted up in a towel. Makeup was optional, clothes casual. Shoes scuffed and comfy.

Not yet at ease with camper casual when it came to hair, Saffi tried to shove her fingers through her Medusa curls. When Troy grinned, she realized she'd only made it worse.

"Mine would look just like that, if I didn't keep it cropped." He handed her the coffee. Once inside the Rambler, Troy looked huge—like he was scrunching down to fit into a kid's playhouse. Like yesterday, he wore work pants and a hoodie— this time, the faded green of beach grass. A few short slate-gray spikes escaped from under the hood that covered the rest of his hair.

"Thanks!" She accepted the coffee and took a small sip. She tried to keep a grimace off her face but her dislike of black coffee must have been evident.

Troy grinned. "Nicole wasn't sure how you took it, but she thought you'd need coffee, and this." He dangled a key from his index finger.

Nicole. The key. Ah. Saffi nodded. "That was very sweet of her."

"She's a sweetie for sure." Troy strode across the living room and plopped down on the sofa. "I'll just wait here while you get dressed."

Saffi squinted, confused. "For...?"

"The search. Since you found Archie, Nicole thought you'd want to help find Linda."

A tingle of fear went up Saffi's spine.

Troy pushed the hood off his head, face contrite. "Sorry. You don't know. Last night, after Nicole got you settled, she called Linda. No one answered. She figured Linda had turned her ringer off for the night. Sometimes that's the only way to keep that lunatic Bill from waking her from a sound sleep to check someone in. I think he gets a kick out of it. Nic tried again this morning. Still no answer. Linda didn't show up for work, either."

What time was it? Saffi leaned over her tiny dining table and pulled back the blackout curtains covering the window facing the cove. Outside, a sheep's-wool-thick marine layer had settled over the cove. Early morning, then. But late enough that Linda should have been at work and Saffi should have been begging her to make good on that monthly spot. Anxiety settled between her shoulders. Without Linda, she had no proof that she'd been promised a monthly spot. She would have to snag a new space or leave the park the day after tomorrow. The selfishness of that fear tugged at her conscience. Even if she lost her space, she was safe in her Rambler with a hot cup of coffee in her hand. Was Linda safe?

Troy took a sip of his own coffee. "Doctor that up," he said, nodding toward her cup.

Shaking off her worry, she took his advice, stepping back into the RV's kitchen area to grab the honey bear out of the cabinet she used as a pantry. Black coffee was way too bitter for her palate, even with hints of chocolate. She tipped her honey bear over the mug, squeezing in about a spoonful, then topped it off with oat milk, and stirred.

"Linda lives in the apartment above the office," Troy told her. "We pounded our knuckles off this morning, but she didn't answer. Bill knew where the spare key was kept, so we went in to see if she was OK."

To Saffi, that sounded like a serious invasion of Linda's privacy. "You just... went in?"

Troy shrugged. "Since Linda hadn't shown up for work, Bill thought he could justify going in."

Did he? Saffi clutched the thermal mug against her belly. "And?"

After rubbing his hand across his unshaven chin, Troy shook his head. "She wasn't there. Her bed was tucked and tidy, like no one had slept in it."

Saffi froze with the mug halfway to her lips. "So, she's really...?"

"Missing." Troy nodded.

Missing. The word catapulted Saffi back in time. The first year after Levi died had been a blur. Unable to face her loss, she'd seen the world through a waterfall of tears. Poppy, her editor, called it "the year without Aunt Saffi." At the end of that year, Poppy had encouraged her to start a blog, hoping it would help her reconnect with the world and find the wonder outside her RV windows again. As always, her editor was right. *Travels with Aunt Saffi* brought her out of the past, back into the present. She blogged weekly, highlighting the interesting places and amazing facts she found along the way. Readers responded with comments, encouragement, tips on places to go, stories to investigate. They became her first post-Levi community. She would always be grateful to all of them. All but one.

At first, she appreciated her interactions with a follower who called himself Jay GoodVender, but in time she noticed a worrisome pattern. If she mentioned finding information at a specific museum, he would recommend a nearby coffee shop. If she posted a photo, he would mention an even better photo op nearby. Over time, his comments started feeling... stalkery. To protect herself, she'd made her posts less specific. Less easy to pin on a map and track.

A follower had posted a comment asking why Jay had gone missing. Jay's response had been as quick as it was unnerving: "If Aunt Saffi went missing, would anyone care?" The implied threat skittered through her memory like a cockroach she couldn't squash.

Troy cleared away the touch of early-morning gravel in his deep voice before continuing. "Chief Duarte is working a wreck on the highway north of town. But he'll be here as soon as he can."

Saffi shook her head, bouncing her curls and bringing her thoughts back into the room. "The chief of police? Don't they wait twenty-four hours before declaring an adult missing?"

Troy chuckled. "Not in a town this small. Locals look out for each other. Besides, this place is a city park. The folks in the office are tight with the police. Have to be, with all the stuff that happens around here."

Saffi quirked a brow. "Such as?" If other women had gone missing, she'd be pulling out sooner rather than later.

"Mostly stolen bikes, but coolers go missing, too. Especially when they're filled with cold pints." His grin calmed her fears. The smile made his gray-blue eyes twinkle with mischief and Saffi found herself tamping down the zing it set off. He was taken, she reminded herself. "Then there's teens partying on the beach and homeless folks camping in the bushes," he went on. "Anyway, until the chief gets here, we're rustling up volunteers to see if Linda's somewhere on the grounds."

Saffi knew a bit about searches for missing people because of an article she'd written for *Aunt Saffi's Bedside Reader, #3*. Tons of evidence could be lost if a bunch of amateurs went bumbling through what might turn into a crime scene. Her research had taught her three things: 1) Don't pick up and examine an object, then put it back where you *think* you found it; 2) Don't put your foot down next to a footprint found at the scene to compare shoe sizes; and 3) Don't add the contents of your stomach to a crime scene.

Thinking of vomit always made Saffi queasy. "Shouldn't we just wait for the chief?" she asked.

Troy took a sip of coffee. "Too late. Bill's already tromping around in the bushes collecting 'evidence.'"

"Oh, no."

"Oh, yes. The rest of us figured it would be better to be out there looking than to just sit here and let him obliterate all the clues. Of course, Nicole thinks Linda might have just taken a day trip. Maybe down to Eureka or out into the redwoods."

"Without Archie?" If Saffi knew one thing about people with emotional support animals, it was that they did *not* leave them behind.

Troy took a slow sip of coffee, as if giving himself time to think. "Archie does put another spin on it. I don't know if I've ever seen Linda without him. Hard to miss the little guy when she always had that bright red bandanna tied around his neck. It has 'emotional support pet' embroidered across it."

Saffi shook her head. "He wasn't wearing a bandanna when I found him."

Frowning made Troy even more ruggedly handsome, if that was possible. "If a wave got him, it could have been ripped off."

Surely a wave strong enough to rip off a dog's bandanna would sweep him out to sea with it. So why was Archie lying on the beach? Saffi didn't know, but there was nothing she loved more than finding answers to interesting questions, and the questions surrounding Archie and the missing Linda were the kind of doozies she loved best.

EIGHT

Before they left her Rambler, Saffi changed from her robe to jeans, her red *Straight Outta the Bookstore* T-shirt, and her warmest zippered hoodie. She scrubbed a washcloth over her face, brushed her teeth, ran a fat-toothed comb through her snarls and called it "good enough for camping." She pulled on thick socks and shoved her feet into her clogs while Troy gave her the scoop on the search. Bill had headed into the bushes on the harbor side of the RV park, his search apparently aided by his German shepherd, Smudge. Nicole and her daughter Casey, accompanied by Archie, were scouring the beach for clues. That left the estuary side of the park for Saffi and Troy.

She wasn't sure how she'd ended up partnered with the man who seemed to be Nicole's significant other, but she had little choice but to follow as he led her behind her RV to a narrow trail. The path wound through a dense swath of ice plants and was just big enough to put one foot in front of the other. It went up and over the estuary-side berm between two of the gnarled trees she'd noticed when she first arrived. Since she hadn't had time to check out the area before dark, she was surprised to find that the short path through the stubby plants led to a sandy beach. From where Saffi stood, it was about a hundred feet to where the berm curved left around the end of the RV park. A tumble of concrete blocks spilled around the curve, shoring up the estuary edge of the park, those at the bottom half buried in the sand. The creek's outlet to the sea looked shallow enough to wade across, but the tide had started to turn and waves shooshed toward the shore. As high tide approached, the water flowing up the creek would make it dangerous to dare the crossing.

A shadow passed over and when Saffi looked up, her mouth fell open. A line of brown pelicans soared overhead, their eight-foot wingspans blocking out the faint sunlight filtering through the marine layer. The massive seabirds soared toward the mouth of the creek like a squadron of fighter planes and swooped around for a water landing.

"*Pelecanus occidentalis*," Troy said. "They look like tiny pterodactyls, don't you think?" Saffi startled. For a moment, she'd forgotten Troy was there. "Oh my gosh. They do!" Saffi shook her head. "I've never seen so many in one place."

"They like to hang out in the shallows. There's plenty of little fishes offshore here. Anchovies. Sardines. Mackerel. Stick around. You'll see pellies out here every day during summer."

She'd have taken the way Troy's warm smile lit up his eyes for an invitation if she hadn't seen him with Nicole. No matter how magnetic Troy might be—and, *darn it*, he was—it was the town itself that would either charm her into staying, or convince her to go. As the pelicans bobbed in the shallows, she filled her lungs with salty moisture-laden air. Joy soared through her veins. It wouldn't take much, she admitted, to fall in love with such a seductive place.

"Let's head up creek while we can," Troy said. "At high tide, this beach will be under water."

Saffi came back to earth with a jolt. Last Chance Cove's

wonders had almost made her forget what they were doing—searching for a missing woman.

Troy led them to the right, away from the pelicans bobbing on the cove. "From here, the wetland wildlife area goes all the way up to Jed Smith."

Jed Smith, Saffi knew from volume four of her *Bedside Reader*, was Jedediah Smith Redwoods State Park. The park had been featured in an article about possible locations for the speeder bike chase in *Return of the Jedi*.

Beyond the RV park's boundary, the sandy beach petered out and the creek disappeared into dense wetlands. Cattail spikes rose here and there between the thick, rounded green stems of tule bulrush lining the creek. Saffi's clogs sank into the sandy soil and her thick socks soaked in creek water, making each step weightier than the last. When she looked back, she saw water filling each footstep.

"Uhm? I don't think I'm wearing the right shoes for going into a marsh," she ventured.

Troy—who wore the same Carhartt boots she'd noticed the day before—stopped and looked back at her. "This is far enough. I can't imagine Linda going into the wetlands alone," he said. "In fact, I can't imagine her coming this way at all. Walking the harbor trail with Archie is more her thing."

Relief washed through Saffi. Much as she couldn't imagine wading into a marsh wearing clogs, she would have been too embarrassed not to forge ahead if Troy kept going. They wandered back toward the mouth of the creek, eyes peeled for anything unusual at the water's edge. Rows of pelicans still swayed on the incoming tide. Gulls screeched overhead.

"I don't see any sign of Linda over here," Troy said. "Let's check in with the others."

Saffi could hardly believe how quickly the beach along the creek had narrowed. As they plodded back the way they'd come, only a few feet of sand separated the berm from the incoming tide. When they reached the tumble of concrete, Troy stepped up on the lowest block and offered her a hand, then kept climbing, up and around the bend toward the main beach.

Saffi stopped to do a quick scan along the other side of the now-bulging creek. On the far side of the creek, a great egret caught her eye as it lifted skyward. Sunlight reflected off a silver fish fighting for life in the grip of the white bird's orange beak. A raucous chorus drew her attention downward, to the beach just beyond the egret's fishing spot. A conspiracy of ravens hopped toward a large bundle that rocked at the creek's edge. Saffi's throat went dry. Her chest tightened.

"Troy!" she shouted, and then she was moving, off the concrete block, into the deepening water, thigh muscles straining as she pushed against the tide to reach the other side.

NINE

Within seconds, the stream's icy water caused her right calf to seize up. She gritted her teeth against the searing pain and hobbled forward, favoring her right leg. Seconds later, the estuary's tidal surge sucked the clog from her right foot. She dug the soaked toes of her socks into her left clog, trying to hold onto it while still limping forward. It was no use. When she reached the other side shoeless, she stopped to pull off her cold clinging socks and massage her cramped calf through her soaked jeans. Where was Troy? She turned, expecting to see him crossing right behind her. He wasn't. Instead, he was racing down the beach in the opposite direction, hell-bent to intercept two figures and a frantically yapping dog.

An unexpected yearning welled up from her gut: a longing for someone she could count on, someone like Levi. Saffi shoved it down. *You've been going it alone for three years now,* she scolded herself. *You don't need Troy or any other man at your back.* Saffi straightened and turned toward the ravens skulking around the bundle she'd spotted. As it rocked gently against the shore, she ran, her bare feet slapping against the cool damp sand at the creek's edge.

The ravens had called Saffi to the right place. The bundle was a body. Small enough to be a woman, but Saffi couldn't be sure. Sand and salt had plastered clothing against the still form. Seaweed wrapped around it like a shroud though she glimpsed bits of yellow through the green. Every time a wave washed into the estuary, the body moved in a gut-punching parody of life. As it rolled, Saffi spotted what looked like a deep straight gash on the back of the head. Her gorge rose, burning the base of her throat. She pressed her palm against her chest to keep it down. *Not now, Saffi. Please!*

She had to get help. Call the police. She shoved a hand into the right pocket of her hoodie where she usually kept her phone. It was empty. Frantically, she checked the left pocket. No phone. Saffi chewed her lower lip in frustration. She must have left her phone in the RV. Saffi turned away from the body toward where she'd last seen Troy. Surely by now he would be headed her way. Wishful thinking. He was moving farther and farther away as he hurried Nicole and Casey in the direction of their trailer. Only Archie looked back. As if he knew what Saffi had found, Linda's faithful companion tugged against his long red leash, struggling to run toward where she stood. Casey held tight, pulling him in her wake.

Anger took over and Saffi started to shake. Surely Troy had known what she'd spotted. He'd dragged her out of bed to search for a woman she didn't even know. Then he'd left her to face finding a body alone. Now what? Should she leave the body and go for help? *No.* The incoming tide might push it further up the creek or pull it back into the cove as it ebbed. Saffi did the only thing she could think of. She inhaled, threw back her shoulders, and screamed out every ounce of anger and frustration, "Help! Someone, please, help! Call 9-1-1!"

. . .

Half an hour later, Saffi sat on a driftwood log, huddled beneath a Pendleton blanket someone had draped across her shoulders. It smelled of wet dog, but she didn't care. For the second time in less than twenty-four hours, she was chilled to the bone, and the thick wool was the only thing keeping the blood from freezing in her veins. The police scrambled down the bank from Beachfront Park on the lighthouse side of Elk Creek. Sirens wailed, tires squealed, doors slammed. To Saffi, the sounds seemed far away, muffled as they were by the shock of finding a body and the marine layer that ghosted across the cove and settled along the shore.

The first officer on the scene looked like a seasoned veteran. He pulled the body the ravens had been investigating from the tide's grip. Then he turned to his partner, a young woman, and spoke softly. His words, captured by the breeze, floated toward Saffi: "Could be our missing park manager." As the female officer covered the body with a tarp, Saffi shivered, wrapping the blanket around her shoulders tighter. The two officers made a quick trip to their cruiser for supplies. A white truck with what looked like a city logo on its door pulled up beside the cruiser and a tall man in a blue suit stepped out. When he called a question to the officers, the female officer stopped to have a few words with him. Then she motioned for him to move his truck away from the emergency vehicles and went back to work. Minutes later, the two officers came back with orange traffic cones and a roll of yellow police tape, cordoning off the body in a wobbly oval.

Saffi heard a siren, faint at first then louder and louder until her head throbbed with the sound of it. A few minutes after it stopped shrieking, the police chief joined his officers on the beach. He took a quick look under the tarp, then scratched the stubble on his chin. "Looks like a sneaker wave got her. Be right back," he said.

Saffi watched listlessly as he huffed his way up the bank

and walked over to the city truck parked just beyond the police cars. He leaned down as if speaking to someone inside; then he straightened, glanced back over his shoulder to the scene below and nodded. After scrambling back down to the beach, he strode over to Saffi and introduced himself. "Chief Duarte. I understand you found the body."

Saffi took in the worn police-issue jacket that barely covered his belly, gray hair thinning toward bald, and pale hazel eyes—sallow and bored. She immediately slotted him into her brain's "typical small-town police chief" file. He'd been on the job for far too long. He'd seen enough to sour him on humankind. He took the easiest explanation—"sneaker wave"—and ran with it. Would Chief Duarte step outside the stereotype? Maybe not, unless Saffi pushed him. She pulled the damp wool blanket tighter, ignoring its doggy stench.

"I'm Saffi Graywood," she gave her name. "I heard you say it was a sneaker wave. Maybe it wasn't. I saw a-a—" She stopped, allowing the image of what she'd seen back into her mind. "A gash. On the back of her head."

The police chief's lips thinned, and he pointed toward the log beneath Saffi. "Lot of driftwood this side of the estuary. Wave could've slammed her into one. Warnings went out, but you know Linda." He shook his head. "Wouldn't listen to anybody when she got a notion in her head. Probably out walking that purse dog of hers."

Saffi didn't know Linda, but she did know how men like the chief treated strong-willed women with minds of their own. As she crossed the country, she'd left behind more than one of them still waiting for her to "listen up" and do things their way, some stuck in the ditches they'd backed their rigs into when they poo-pooed her parking advice.

"I've never met Linda," Saffi said. "I've only been in the RV park for one night. But she managed the park, right? Seems like she'd know enough to stay off the beach after a weather warning." The resentment she felt must have shown on her face.

"Look." Something sparked in the chief's eyes. "We see this kind of thing all the time. Most sneakers get the tourists." Saffi heard "no big loss" behind his words. "They come here to have fun. To relax. They let down their guard and whoosh! The sea takes no prisoners, if you get my drift."

A sneaker wave was an easy solution. No crime. No foul. Sure, a wave could have swept Linda into the sea. But if that was what had happened, why didn't it take Archie, too? Would the little dog be left behind and the much bigger woman taken?

"Linda wasn't a tourist. She—" Before she could dig further, a hand rested on her shoulder and squeezed.

"You OK?"

Troy's voice made Saffi stiffen. She whirled around. "No! I'm not OK. How could I be OK when you left me alone to find —" She flung out a hand toward the draped body. She didn't think she'd ever forget what it felt like to turn to Troy for help, only to discover that he had not followed her through the creek.

Troy rubbed his face. "I know. I—" He stopped, and his shoulders heaved. He lifted a hand to squeeze the corners of his eyes, as if keeping tears at bay. "I had to warn Nicole not to bring Casey this way. She's such a sweet kid. I'd hate for her to see something like this."

Saffi's chin sank toward her chest. "No one should see anything like this," she whispered.

Chief Duarte stuck out a hand to shake Troy's. "Glad you stopped the kid from coming over. Seeing a dead body could scar her for life."

Saffi glanced up to see Troy's reaction. Somehow, he managed to look both grateful and guilty at the same time.

The police chief nodded at Saffi. "Go home and get into some dry clothes, Miss Graywood," he said. "Put some food in your belly if you can. I'm gonna need you to come down to the station to give a statement. You, too, Troy. Maybe you can give Miss Graywood a lift."

"It's Mrs.," Saffi corrected stiffly. She stood and pulled the blanket off her shoulders, folding it before handing it to the chief. "Mrs. Graywood."

"Ah." The chief nodded. "Then maybe Mr. Graywood would be so kind as to drive you."

Saffi ached to have Levi by her side right now, but he wasn't. She was on her own, her only companion a metal box on wheels that had taken her farther and farther away from their shared life, a life that had disappeared in an eyeblink. She'd fled as far from his loss as she could on four wheels, but death seemed determined to jerk her back into its shadow.

It would be easy to tumble into darkness, into depression, as she had in that first year without Levi, but Saffi had journeyed too far, both physically and mentally, to fall into that black hole. No. Numbness would not get its claws into her again. She would do what she did best: dig beyond the surface, deep enough to find the hidden layers of the story that had ended with a woman shrouded in seaweed, body swaying in the tide like a restless ghost.

TEN

"Please," Troy interrupted her thoughts. "Let me give you a lift."

"I'll just go back the way I—" Saffi turned toward the creek then stopped. The water level in the estuary had risen by several feet since she'd crossed. How long had it been since she'd waded across that stream?

"Bad idea," Troy said. "Tide's in. You don't want to get sucked off your feet, like those shoes of yours did." He pressed his lips together so tight she was sure he was holding back what he knew would be an inappropriate grin, given the circumstances.

Saffi stared down at her bare feet. She'd forgotten. She pictured her clogs churning in the waves, then washing ashore, shrouded in seaweed, to be found by some future beachcomber. The picture made her shiver.

"You're freezing."

Before she could stop him, Troy unzipped his hoodie and draped it around her. It smelled like coffee and sea breezes and still held the heat of his body. Its warmth seeped into the knots in her shoulders, loosening them slightly.

"I'm parked up there." Troy pointed toward the line of vehicles on the rise above the beach. "I really don't need anything else on my conscience today."

For a moment, Saffi wondered if he meant more than running off and leaving her to find Linda alone, but his eyes held remorse, not guilt.

"Fine," she huffed. "Thank you."

Troy nodded. They walked past the crumbling embankment law enforcement had been scrambling up and down to a set of concrete stairs further along the sand. As they climbed the stairs to Beachfront Park, the rough concrete scoured her feet like sandpaper. The city truck Saffi had noticed earlier pulled away just as they reached the top. Troy gave the occupant a wave, then strode toward a metallic-blue truck parked at the beach overlook.

"Who was that?" Saffi asked. The fact that Chief Duarte had hefted his bulk up the bank to talk to the driver had caught her attention.

"Randall Bevins," Troy said. "Best city manager Last Chance Cove ever had. No matter what happens, he's on top of it."

Saffi pulled Troy's hoodie close to keep away the ocean's chill as he escorted her to the passenger side of his truck. Had Chief Duarte shared his sneaker-wave theory with the city manager? If so, the case was probably well on its way to being closed. It was probably in the town's best interests for Linda's death to be attributed to her own carelessness, just one of those things that happened if you ignored the power of the ever-churning sea.

The metallic-blue door Troy opened for Saffi was emblazoned with a logo—a white wave with a fish jumping from the spray. *Troy's Tours* was scripted underneath in sunset orange. Her wet salt-crusted jeans scrubbed against the skin of her legs. "Your seats—"

He cut her off with a wave.

"Believe me, they've had a lot worse things than salty jeans on them."

As Saffi climbed into the truck, her body felt stiff, weighted. Exhaustion set in and she rested her head against the seatback and closed her eyes.

"I really am sorry you had to face that. Alone."

His voice sounded sincere, but Saffi couldn't muster the energy to care one way or the other. Three minutes later he pulled the truck to a stop at her RV site. Saffi nodded her thanks, climbed down, and handed back the hoodie he'd draped around her for extra warmth.

"Take care," Troy said as she closed the door behind her.

Saffi peeled her wet jeans down her legs and toweled her legs dry. She tossed the soaked pants into the bottom of the RV's shower. She looked longingly at the shower head, wanting more than anything to turn it on, step inside and warm the chill from her bones, but a shower would have to wait. Right now, she wanted something else—gossip, the kind of loose-lipped gossip she was most likely to find at the park office. Gossip, she knew from her research, had led to solving crimes more often than the police wanted the public to know.

She ran her hands over the hoodie she'd put on earlier and pulled out the tail of her red bookstore T-shirt. Surprisingly, both still felt dry. She drew on a seal-gray pair of French terry leggings to replace her sea-soaked jeans, hoping they'd be thick enough to keep her warm while biking. She wrestled her mist-curled hair into a scrunchie, not daring to look in the mirror before forcing herself back outside.

She walked her retro mint-green cruiser toward the park office and leaned the bike against a porch rail. A murmuration of voices pulsed from the open windows. Inside, Saffi found Bill standing behind the counter as if shielding himself from the surging crowd of campers. Most had heard the sirens, and some had walked to the top of the berm to watch the police at work.

"Looked to me like something washed up," someone said.

"Something big," a different voice added.

Others murmured agreement.

"Everything washes up here eventually." Bill rubbed his eyes with the back of his hand then tugged his mustache. "Agates, buoys, rope, glass fishing floats. We get a dead seal couple times a year. One time we got a rowboat from a Japanese tsunami." He backed into his office chair and sat, head down, as if reluctant to answer any more questions.

"Stop stalling, Bill. What washed up?" someone toward the back demanded.

Saffi recognized the voice: Delilah. She spotted the barista's turquoise Last Chance Café T-shirt through the crowd and squirreled her way toward her, trying to ignore the miasma of wood smoke, seaweed, twice-worn T-shirts, and mist-damp hoodies coming off the campers crowded into the room.

The wheels on Bill's office chair squealed as he shoved it back and stood. "Fine. Buncha nosy parkers," he boomed. "I'll tell ya what washed up!" The room, which had been a swirl of noise, caught its breath as everyone fell silent. "Our missing park manager, that's what." He blinked his rheumy blue eyes twice, then squeezed the corners with a shaking hand.

Gasps and groans exploded across the room. Saffi took note of the look on Bill's face: desperate, like a man on a sinking lifeboat looking for someone to throw to the sharks.

"And that one there," Bill pointed an arthritic finger at Saffi, "found the body."

Like a school of sardines, everyone turned toward Saffi.

Saffi opened her mouth, ready to flay the accusation off his face, but Delilah pulled Saffi into a side-arm hug. "Don't give that son of a sand flea the satisfaction," she whispered against

Saffi's ear. Before releasing her, Delilah gave Saffi's hand a squeeze. The barista's palm felt cold, clammy. Saffi glanced up. Delilah's face was pale as paste. Had fear, or loss, blanched the color from her skin? Saffi went with loss.

"Oh, Delilah. I'm so sorry. Did you know Linda well?"

"Well enough." Delilah sighed. "I came here with no job, no connections. Linda saved my bacon. Put me in a monthly space without a page of paperwork. I wanted to help with the search, but I had to work the breakfast shift. Then when I came home for lunch"—she flapped a hand toward Bill—"this bottom-feeder's comparing Linda to flotsam washed up on the beach."

Saffi looked beyond Delilah to the others crammed inside the office. Last Chance Cove's campers were a mix of young and old, scruffy and polished. Sport fishermen and retired couples were in the majority. She half expected Nicole to be there, but the only faces she recognized were the well-heeled couple from Texas who'd taken her monthly space.

As campers reacted to Bill's bomb, voices swelled across the room. Saffi folded her arms and listened. Now was the time for gossip. Someone might have seen or heard something suspicious. If so, she wanted to hear about it. But the comments she overheard expressed only shock and surprise.

"I can't believe it..."

"Linda? No way!"

"I read the sneaker-wave flyer, but I never thought—"

Bill waved a hand. "That's just it. People don't understand sneakers. They're rogue waves. They can run up that beach of ours and, 'Wham!'" He slammed both hands on the counter. "Game over."

Bill's lack of compassion for his recently deceased boss hit Saffi in the gut. He'd made it clear he held Linda in low esteem, but... really? Who could lose a co-worker and care so little? *Someone who'd wanted her job. That's who.*

"Followed her trail myself earlier," Bill went on. "Found

this in the bushes on the harbor side." He held up a crumpled red bandanna and Saffi thought back to when she'd found Archie, minus his colorful identifier. "Dog droppings everywhere." Bill crinkled his nose like he smelled something foul. "I keep telling folks to use the puppy poo bags, but you know how *some* people are. My guess?" Bill continued. "Linda snuck Archie into the bushes to do his doodle and then took him for a walk on the beach. Silly thing to do, but that was Linda." He sniffed, rubbed his nose, then stuffed the bandanna into the front pocket of his yellow safety vest.

"Please." Delilah clenched her hands into fists. Barely concealed fury came off the barista in waves. "Having to pick up after other people's dogs was one of Linda's pet peeves. She would never let Archie do his business without picking up."

Saffi glanced around in time to see the Texas couple sharing a guilty glance. She made a mental note to talk to the Texans. Did they have a dog? More than half the campers in the park seemed to have at least one. If they'd taken a dog out before retiring last night, they might have seen something.

"As for walking Archie on the beach last night?" Delilah continued. "The Linda I knew would never have put Archie in danger like that. That dog was her everything."

Bill's nostrils flared, his eyes tightened, and his face darkened. "So I've heard." He turned away from the counter, pulled his chair back in front of the computer, and sat down.

If Archie was Linda's everything, how *had* he ended up on that beach bedraggled and alone? Whatever had happened to Linda, sneaker wave or something more sinister, it had probably happened near where she'd found Archie, not on the other side of the estuary where she'd found Linda's body.

"Alright folks." Bill waved a hand in the general direction of the door. "Some of us got work to do."

From the look on Delilah's face, the barista had a few more

choice words for Bill. It didn't take long for her to lean toward Saffi to whisper exactly what she thought of his conclusions.

"Bill's got the wrong end of the toilet brush on this whole 'walking Archie on the beach' bit. Linda knew better."

"What do you think happened?"

Delilah looked like a woman determined to set things right, even if it meant ripping a fingernail in the process. "I wish I could talk, but I ran out in the middle of the lunch rush. If I don't get back soon I'll be out on my tuchus. Come by the café when you can, OK?"

Chief Duarte had told Saffi to eat something if she could, so why not? She hadn't eaten a bite since she'd been rousted out of bed, and she desperately needed coffee to drive away the shock and make the numbness dragging her down fade. A detour to the Last Chance Café before she headed to the police station might give her a few facts to start filling in the puzzle of how Linda ended up shrouded in seaweed and sand.

Saffi gave Bill the stink eye as she made her way through the crush of campers to the front counter. "That bandanna's evidence." She pointed to the vest pocket that held the red cloth. "I'm heading over to the station to give a statement. I'd be happy to turn it over to the police for you."

Bill sniffed. His eyes looked redder and waterier than ever. "Doing it myself right after work, aren't I?"

Saffi shrugged. "Suit yourself."

He'd suit himself, of that Saffi was certain. The story of "silly" Linda's tragic accident would spread through the RV park like a tidal wave after an earthquake. Maybe that was just what Bill wanted. After all, his "there's more than one way to get rid of bad management" comment sounded a lot like a threat in Saffi's book.

ELEVEN

Biking the half mile to the harbor barely warmed the chill from her leg muscles but the cool, moist ocean air was just what Saffi needed. She breathed it in and slowly exhaled, releasing as much of the morning's tension as she could. When she reached the café, she swung out of the wide saddle, perfectly fitted to her very female butt, walked her bike to the wave-style rack, and hefted her cruiser into an empty trough. After losing two bikes in as many years, she'd bought a heavy-duty chain. Its hardened steel links kept her from worrying that she'd be a victim of the bike bandits Troy had warned her about. It added nearly four pounds of weight to her rides but every time she clicked the chain into place, she felt secure that the retro cruiser she loved so much would still be there when she came outside.

She hustled into the café through the turquoise front door, rubbing her hands to warm them. On the northwest coast, there was no such thing as a warm bike ride. Today's high temp should have been 60 degrees, but the lingering marine layer made it feel more like 40. Last Chance Cove's coastal water flowed down from the Gulf of Alaska. When air coming off the cold water met warmer surface temperature air—*presto puffo!*—

a layer of clouds formed where water met land causing what locals called "June Gloom." She had discovered the term, as well as "May Gray," "No-Sky July," and "Fogust," while researching the world's most depressing weather. She liked the rhymes a whole lot more than the reality.

As Saffi shut the door behind her, Delilah looked up from pulling an espresso shot. "Be with you in a minute, duck." The barista nodded at an empty stool at the end of the counter and Saffi hoisted herself onto its round padded seat. Delilah poured oat milk into the stainless steaming-pitcher. Soon, the wand began to hiss, then whistle as steam rose to moisten the air. Twirling sideways on her stool, Saffi glanced around the room. She spotted two familiar faces at the table by the window—Casey and Nicole, bent head-to-head. They kept their voices low, as if they didn't want to be overheard, but Saffi detected tension in Nicole's terse words and Casey's mumbled answers. Were they talking about Archie being found on the beach below their RV? Or were they discussing this morning's grisly find? Whatever it was, they weren't sharing their worries with Troy. He had not joined them at the café.

Saffi felt both relieved and disappointed. She had not forgiven him for deserting her at such a critical moment, but was that fair? They'd barely met before this morning's search. Sharing a brief conversation in the RV park laundry while he folded another woman's undies and thinking they'd had a "moment"? *Lame,* Saffi admitted. Still, she felt herself wishing he'd walk through the door and glance her way. What was it about Troy? The mischievous half-grin that reminded her of Levi, or something about the man himself—like his sexy hard-working vibe—that drew her?

A tap-tap-tapping returned Saffi's attention to the counter. Delilah added a grin to her nail-tapping. "I've heard writers live in their noggins, but I've never seen it up close like this."

Saffi laughed. "Scary, huh? So, what did you want to tell me?"

Just as Delilah opened her mouth to speak, the door swung wide. Ocean-chilled wind swept a slight figure into the café. The two stacked boxes he held wibbled and wobbled as he lost his footing. "A little HELP!" he yelped as the top box started to tumble.

Saffi hopped off her stool and grabbed the box just before it hit the floor.

"Oh, honey!" the thirty-something man gushed. "You saved my cookies!"

Saffi slid the box onto the counter, raising a brow at Delilah.

The barista laughed. "He means that literally."

Saffi glanced at the label on the box: *Kevin's Kookies*. Was this the infamous Kevin (aka Glenn)? He reminded her of someone. But who? From the straight floppy brown hair that framed his face to the green crushed-velvet shirt he wore over a pair of vintage bell-bottom jeans, the slight young man tugged at a memory. When it hit her, she smiled. Davy Jones! Not the octopus-faced Davy Jones from *The Pirates of the Caribbean*, but the sweet-faced lead singer from the 60s pop band, The Monkees. She'd developed a bit of a crush on Davy while writing an article about TV-show bands for *Bedside Reader, #5*.

The Davy Jones lookalike held up a finger, then put his hands on his hips and bent forward to catch his breath. When he stood, he flipped his hair out of his face before capturing her gaze with cheerful brown eyes.

"You have just earned yourself a free cookie, young lady."

Now you've gone and spoiled it. She'd earned every silver stripe in her black locks and each swoop in her crow's feet through a lifetime of tears and laughter. Being called young by a younger person—as if it was flattering rather than condescending—tripped her trigger every time. "I'll take the cookie, but you can keep the left-handed compliment."

The younger man had the good grace to blush.

Delilah peered around the boxes. "Glenn, stop embarrassing yourself and meet my new friend, Saffi."

"Hi, Saffi. Sorry. My mouth bumbles along without my brain sometimes." His eyes had lost their twinkle and for a moment Saffi regretted taking him down a notch.

"No worries." Saffi gave him a genuine smile. "Just hand over the cookie and we're square."

"Well!" Glenn's twinkle came back, and he took the top box off the stack. "Today, I've got Hungry Mama and Sea Salt Chocolate Chip. What's your passion?"

"Cookies in general." Saffi grinned. "But since I've already tried a Hungry Mama, I'll go for the Chocolate Chip."

"Already a fan?" Glenn asked as he pulled apart the folded-over top of the first box.

"Thanks to Delilah here." Saffi opened the self-sealing cellophane bag he handed her and took out the fat round chocolate-chip-filled cookie. "Yum!" she said after taking a crumbly bite. "All is forgiven."

Glenn clapped like a schoolkid receiving a gold star. "Welcome to Kevin's Kookie Klan!" he crowed.

Saffi widened her eyes. "Please tell me that is NOT spelled with a *k*."

Glenn clapped a hand over his mouth.

"I told you those *k*'s were going to get you in trouble." Delilah hoisted the boxes off the counter and carried them to the back room.

"You really pay attention to words, don't you?" Glenn scooted onto a barstool and Saffi reclaimed the one she'd been sitting on before rescuing the Kookie guy.

"Words. Weirdness. Details most people don't have time for. The perils of my profession."

"Which is?" Glenn leaned toward her, brown eyes wide, as

if she was about to reveal the secret to life, the universe, and everything.

"I'm a writer." No matter how many times Saffi said those words, she felt like a pretender, even now that her *Bedside Readers* were bestsellers.

Glenn made a gimme gesture with his hands, trying to coax more information from her.

"I put together collections of quirky and cool true stories and facts I happen to stumble on. You know, for people to read when they're in bed trying to fall asleep." She laughed nervously.

Glenn perked up.

"Like *Aunt Saffi's Bedside Reader?*"

Delilah came back to the counter, ready to take their coffee orders. She raised both eyebrows at Glenn and tilted her head toward Saffi. When it hit him, he smacked himself in the forehead. "Oh, my stars and stockings! You can't be *the* Aunt Saffi!"

Being recognized gave Saffi a boost of the confidence she often lacked when it came to her writing. "The one and only." She chuckled.

Delilah clicked her purple nails on the counter in front of Glenn. "Four-shot sixteen-ounce mocha with extra whipped to go?"

Glenn tried to wave her away. "I'm meeting someone famous here and you're talking coffee?"

Saffi winked at Delilah. "When it comes to writing, coffee is everything. A mocha sounds good to me, but make mine twelve ounces, one shot, with oat milk, half sweet."

"Those are very precise preferences," Glenn teased.

"Says the guy with the four-shot extra-whip mocha," Saffi shot back.

"Ooh. She's good. I approve." Glenn nodded toward the cookie Saffi was gobbling down. "And you?"

"Oh, yes. I approve." Saffi grinned. "Just what I needed after—"

Out of the corner of her eye, Saffi saw Delilah freeze, glance toward Glenn, and shake her head.

"After that cold bike ride."

Glenn looked from Saffi to Delilah. "My driver's ed teacher once told me I had exceptional peripheral vision. Dish, you two."

"Oh, for shark's sake, Glenn." Delilah shook her head. She swirled a mountain of whipped cream on top of Glenn's mocha, and then sprinkled a touch of cayenne on Saffi's. "That'll warm you up."

Glenn sucked the peak off the whipped cream Delilah had just handed him. "Thank you, young lady." His gaze darted toward Saffi. "Uhm... oops?"

"Glenn here was raised by his uncle. The original Kevin behind the cookies." Delilah leaned her elbows on the counter. "Makes him act, and talk, like he's eighty."

"It's true. I'm an old man in a young man's body." Glenn sighed.

Saffi lifted her brows. "If those clothes are from Uncle Kevin's closet, he couldn't have been *that* old. I mean, you've got that whole Monkees vibe going on, right?"

Glenn squealed. "I knew I liked you!"

"And if Davy Jones was still alive, he'd only be about..."

Glenn started laughing and could barely manage to spit out, "Eighty!"

"Sheesh!" Saffi took a tentative sip off the top of her mocha, then licked the fire from her lips. Delilah was right. The cayenne sent an instant burst of heat down the center of her body.

"Now." Glenn put both hands, palm down, on the counter, either side of his to-go cup. "What is it that you don't want me to know?" He pinned Delilah with a serious brown stare.

The barista sighed. "I guess you'll find out soon enough. It's Linda."

Glenn blinked. His lips tightened and the tendons in his neck stood out. "Whose life has that harpy ruined now?"

Well, well. Saffi sat her cup down. Maybe Bill wasn't the only one in town with a motive to murder Linda. If it was murder, as Saffi suspected, and not a sneaker wave.

"I knew you'd say something like that." Delilah's eyes darted to Saffi, as if sorry she'd heard Glenn's outburst. Was she trying to protect him? "Look, Glenn. Now's not the time to spout off about Linda."

Glenn grasped his mocha and stood. Saffi noticed that his hands were shaking.

"How can you say that? You know what she did to me."

"Well, she won't be doing anything like that again."

"Why? Did she find Jesus or something?"

"No, Glenn." Delilah touched his shaking hands with her still one. "Linda's dead. Her body was found this morning on the beach by the estuary."

Saffi had never seen a man swoon before, but that's just what Glenn did. All the blood drained from his face, he swayed, and then his bottom hit the stool, and his mocha flopped forward as if his muscles could no longer hold it. Milky brown liquid flowed down the left leg of his bell-bottoms.

Saffi grabbed the dribbling cup out of his hand and sat it on the counter. "Put your head down." She placed a hand on the back of his head and guided it toward his knees. "You're OK. You're OK," she mumbled over and over, remembering how her body reacted when she'd lost Levi.

When Glenn was able to speak, his voice was bitter as day-old black coffee, and his words shocked Saffi to the core. "Too bad it didn't happen a year ago."

Delilah clutched the counter. "You don't mean that."

"Don't I?" Glenn looked up. His eyes had darkened. All the

boyish charm Saffi had seen in him earlier had disappeared. Then he slid off the stool, paid for his mocha, and saluted Saffi and Delilah. "I'd better be off. Deliveries to make and cookies to bake!"

It wasn't the air coming through the door as Glenn left that chilled the back of Saffi's neck. It was the cold calculation in his eyes as he fumbled his cellphone from his pocket and punched a number that must have been on speed dial.

"What was that about?"

Delilah let out a breath. "You remember I told you that Glenn used to have a bakery downtown?"

Saffi nodded. "He lost his lease, right? Something to do with the city council."

Delilah nodded. "Yes, ma'am. That bakery had been on the corner of Third and G for forty years. Every time the lease came up for renewal, the council rubber-stamped it. But when Kevin left the whole kit and caboodle to Glenn, Linda was livid."

Small towns were notoriously weird, but Saffi couldn't get her mind around this one. "I'm sorry. I must have missed something. Why would Linda care if Glenn's uncle left him his bakery?"

"Because Kevin was her uncle, too."

Saffi felt like her head might spin around. "Linda and Glenn are cousins?"

"Linda moved back to the cove about a year ago, hoping to cozy up to her uncle and get a piece of the pie. Ha!" Delilah's eyes sparkled at her bakery joke. "But Glenn never left. Kevin took care of him as a kid and Glenn stuck with Kevin, and the bakery, till the end."

Saffi frowned. "So, a family feud." Family feuds were notorious for body counts. Saffi had written about some doozies, including a feud that started in 1911 when a Texas ranch-wife left her husband for a neighboring rancher. Before it was all over, there had been a kidnapping, a murder, a riot that killed four, two more murders, and a suicide. The idea of such a thing playing out on this tranquil coast made Saffi's gut clench.

"How did the feud between Linda and Glenn spill over into the town council decision?" she asked.

"Hang on." Delilah stopped to take a coffee order and steam a latte before answering.

"After Uncle Kevin's will was read, Linda went down to the probate court to contest it. Said Kevin had promised that he would leave the bakery to both of them. She'd been blabbering on to me about inheriting the bakery, so she tried to pull me into it." A bell rang behind her and she held up a finger to pick up a steaming bowl of chowder and hurry it over to a table.

When Delilah slid back behind the counter, Saffi prompted her. "Linda tried to drag you into it?"

Delilah scowled. "Wanted me to swear that I knew Kevin planned to leave her a cut of everything. Just because she'd *told* me he did." The barista blew a red curl off her cheek. "Got all het up with me when I told her that was hearsay, not direct evidence. As if I hadn't watched enough *Law and Order* to know the difference! But when Linda set her mind on something," Delilah continued, "she was like a puppy with a toy. She'd chew that thing to pieces before she'd let go."

"What did she chew to pieces this time?"

Sadness washed over Delilah's face. "Glenn's reputation. She dug around for something to prove she had legal standing and came up with 'undue influence.' Started whispers. Why would Kevin have left Glenn everything, ignoring his niece? Maybe there was more to Kevin's relationship with Glenn than anyone knew. Maybe Glenn used that 'something,'" Delilah put air quotes around the word, "to persuade Kevin to cut Linda out of his will."

A queasy feeling came over Saffi and she pushed away the

cooling remains of her mocha. "But Glenn *did* inherit, right? The bakery was his when he lost his lease."

"Yes—" Delilah's eyes flicked over Saffi's shoulder, and she turned to see a customer whose pursed lips and narrowed eyes set the barista's feet on fire. "Be right there!" Delilah yelped as she grabbed an order pad and rushed to the table.

After she handed the order to the chef, Delilah made her way back to Saffi. Much as she wanted to get to the bottom of Glenn's animosity, Saffi didn't want to cost Delilah her job.

"You're busy. We can talk about this later," she said, starting to slide off the stool.

Delilah clicked a nail against Saffi's cup. "You finish your mocha, I'll finish the story."

Saffi took a sip, holding back a grimace as she swallowed the cold coffee remains.

"Too many people in this town knew Kevin too well and he'd told quite a few of them, including his lawyer, exactly why Glenn would inherit, and Linda would not. 'Family is a verb,' Kevin used to say. 'It's something you *do*, not something you *are*.'"

Saffi's eyes widened. "Wow. That's genius. So, Linda's probate petition failed."

"It did!" Delilah grinned, then her smile faded. "But she still had that chew toy between her teeth. I tried to get her to drop it, but she wouldn't let go. If she couldn't get Kevin's bakery, she'd get Glenn. She took that first rumor she'd started and gave it a twist. Played up the idea that Glenn hired a lot of teenaged boys to work at the bakery, but none of them seemed to stay very long. Almost like they felt... uncomfortable... working for him."

Poor Glenn. No wonder he felt such animosity toward Linda. Apparently, she'd earned it. Saffi had done enough time as a waitress during summer breaks in college to see how pernicious Linda's rumor must have been. "Teenaged boys aren't the most reliable of workers," she said.

"Exactly. Around here, they come and go with the height of the waves." Delilah grabbed a towel and started scrubbing the counter hard enough to take off the stain.

It took a minute for the comment to click.

"Surfers."

"Yes, ma'am. Linda's rumor had a hank of truth in it, so it spread fast. At the time, one of the town councillors had a son working for Glenn. Linda's lie bored into him like a sand flea. He got it into his head that voting against the lease would protect his son from a pedophile. The city manager, Randall Bevins, tried to head that rumor off at the pass. I mean, he would. Wouldn't he? Given—" Delilah's eyes went wide. She grabbed a rag and started swabbing the counter.

"Given?" Saffi nudged.

"Given, uh, what a draw the bakery was for the downtown area."

Saffi had a feeling that wasn't what Delilah had first intended to say, but it seemed too soon to push her new friend on details she might not be ready to share. "So, Glenn lost his lease... and the bakery." Saffi slipped a bank card out of her pack and handed it to Delilah to keep herself from saying what she thought: Glenn had a very good motive for murder.

TWELVE

Fueled by nothing but caffeine and sugar, Saffi buzzed along the harbor trail, past the park, over the pedestrian bridge and through the downtown grid toward the police station fast enough to work up a sweat. After locking her bike outside the squat concrete-block building, Saffi hurried inside. The desk sergeant standing behind the front counter held a phone receiver between shoulder and ear as she scribbled on a notepad. She held up a finger for Saffi to wait. When the call ended, she looked up. "How can I help you?" she asked.

Saffi had a sudden case of nerves compounded by the lack of actual food. Her mouth went dry, her hands clammy. "I'm here to make a statement, about th-the woman found on the beach."

"Ah." The officer nodded. After a quick call to an internal number, she ushered Saffi down a linoleum-tiled hallway past Chief Duarte's office to a room crowded with desks. The chief had passed the grunt work to a junior officer, she supposed. Decades of bitter coffee and sweat permeated the stale air. That, combined with the flicker of fluorescent ceiling lights, made Saffi feel slightly dizzy and more than a little queasy.

"Wait here," the desk sergeant said, waving Saffi toward a worn padded office chair beside a desk.

To take her mind off how she was feeling, Saffi scrutinized the desk. The plastic stacking trays on one corner held a mix of loose papers and folders. On the opposite corner, a stack of blue binders alternated spines-out and spines-in which kept the binders from sliding like the ones on other desks in the crowded room. The work surface was clear, waiting for the next case file. Highly organized, she decided, if not downright OCD.

A few minutes later, a Native man wearing a starched blue suit with a crisp white shirt set a steaming cup of coffee on the desk and took a seat in a rolling chair. He looked young enough to have just graduated from the police academy, but the designation "detective" on the brass name plate at the edge of his desk told her he had a few years policing under his belt. Chief Duarte must be taking the case seriously after all—either that or covering his butt. Saffi unzipped her hoodie, squeezed her knees with her hands, and squared her shoulders.

Detective Richards pulled up a form on his computer screen and started firing questions, AK style. *Name. Birth date. Marriage status. Place of residence.* Short, sharp, clear bursts, slammed into her chest like a hammer. Reason for being in town? How long did she intend to stay? Why had she been on the beach? Who was with her? *Bam. Bam. Bam.*

Saffi's hands started to sweat. She rubbed them on her leggings, then stretched out her fingers.

Once Detective Richards had punctured the basics out of her, he rubbed his hands together and returned his fingers to the keyboard. "How did you come to discover the body, Mrs. Graywood? Please include as much detail as you can remember."

Saffi had a head for details. In her line of work, she had to. She started with the scream, moved on to finding Archie, then explained how she'd ended up scouring the banks of Elk Creek with Troy, looking for the missing park manager. When she described the gash she'd seen on the back of Linda's head, Detective Richards startled like a spooked elk. He opened a green file on his desk and flipped through a few papers, then pulled one out to read. One eyebrow quirked up and his full lips twisted sideways.

Saffi sat up straighter, trying to see what had spooked him. *Accidental death, pending ME findings.* ME. Medical Examiner, Saffi guessed. Detective Richards caught her looking and quickly closed the file.

"Not in the notes, but if it's there, my auntie Val will find it."

"Your auntie?"

The young detective's cheeks pinked. "Sorry. That wasn't very professional, was it?"

Saffi waved away his apology.

"My aunt is the medical examiner. Sharp eye, that one. Whenever me and my cousins tried to step out of line when we were kids, she was right there to stop us. She's Tolowa, like me."

Tolowa. Saffi just managed to stop herself from gasping. She had written about the "Tolowa Dee-ni' Holocaust" in her *Horrible History Bedside Reader*. In the mid-1800s, the government of California had allocated $1.4 million—about $3.4 billion in today's dollars—to pay mercenaries. Their job? The complete extermination of the peoples who had made this land their home for thousands of years. They'd come far too close to succeeding. The look on her face must have been a mix of shock and ancestral guilt. Luckily, Detective Richards was too intent on asking questions to notice.

"The mom and daughter who helped you after you found Archie, they were awake when you knocked?"

"Yes, I think they were awake. Casey, the daughter, came to the door right away. It took her mom a few minutes more. She might have been showering."

"And the time would have been approximately…?"

Saffi sat back. She'd heard the scream around midnight. "Maybe twelve thirty?"

"Did the scream wake them up as well?"

Saffi searched her memory. "No. Nicole said she didn't hear it."

Detective Richards glanced at her, face blank, then looked back at the screen and typed in a few words. Was he thinking the same thing she was? That if they were awake, how had they not heard a scream she heard from across the park? At the time, she'd wondered whether sleep had morphed Raven's cry into a human scream, but she wasn't about to tell the detective that.

He'd mark her down as an unreliable witness, a nutcase, or, more likely, a murderer spinning a web of lies.

Saffi understood. To local law enforcement, she was an outsider, a complete unknown. She'd been on the outside looking in since she'd driven away from Vermont College, trying to make and hold onto tenuous connections in the towns she visited, increasing her RV stays to months instead of the weeks she'd spent at each destination during her first year on the road. Her blog offered a cyber-community with a self-selected group of 'friends'—and one increasingly unnerving stalker she wished would go away. As for real-world connections? She'd pushed herself to make friends on the fly, like Delilah, here in Last Chance Cove. But in moments like this, when she found herself under suspicion for something anyone who really knew her would know she'd never do? The yawning hole between herself and the communities she visited became so dark and deep she feared she might topple in.

The detective's voice rose as if he'd been trying, and failing, to regain her attention. "The, uhm, gash you observed. Bloody?"

Saffi felt herself jerked back to that horrible moment when the ravens led her to the seaweed-shrouded corpse. Her body reacted viscerally. Her hands went cold, then clammy, and the room started to spin. Why hadn't she eaten when she had a chance? "I-I... no." Saffi put a hand to her forehead. "No. No. I don't think so. Just—" A white wave washed over her, and she clutched at the desk.

Detective Richards shoved his chair backward and knelt in front of her, putting one hand on each shoulder to steady her as she swayed. "Des!" he called. "Can we get some water over here?" He looked down at her hands then into her eyes. "May I?" He held his hands out, waiting for permission. When she nodded, he took her hands between his and rubbed the chill from her skin.

A female officer came over with a paper cup filled with water. Saffi took it with shaking hands and chugged it down.

The young officer's eyes narrowed. "You said you didn't know Linda."

Had her physical reaction to the memory of finding Linda made her look guilty? Saffi rushed to correct the impression. "I didn't know her. I spoke to her on the phone when I made my reservation, but I never even saw her in person. Except when I... when I—" Saffi waved a hand toward the floor as if indicating the body on the beach.

Detective Richards stood, looking down on Saffi. "Finding her must have been a shock."

Saffi looked up, hardening her eyes as she stared into his. "Death is always a shock, Detective."

"Of course. Of course." Detective Richards sat back down in his chair and tapped a few keys. "I think that's enough for now. I'll give you a call if we need more information." He looked up at Saffi, eyes dark with what might have been suspicion, concern, or curiosity. "Is someone here to drive you back to the park?"

Saffi shook her head. "I rode my bike. I'll be fine."

Detective Richards rolled back his chair and stood. "I couldn't possibly let you bike home. I'll drive you." Before she could argue, Detective Richards had walked her outside, waited for her to unlock her bike, and then hefted it into the back of his police SUV. "Up front's fine." He gestured toward the passenger door.

To be honest, Saffi was grateful for the lift. She felt weary. Boneless. Exhausted in a way she hadn't felt since the darkness after Levi died. All she wanted now was to fall into bed and sleep until the rest of this dreadful day was over, but before she did, she needed to tell the detective one more thing.

"The park host, Bill? He has a red bandanna like the one Archie always wore. Claims to have found it in the bushes during this morning's search. If you'd like to interview someone who actually knew Linda and had a grudge against her, you might want to give him a call."

THIRTEEN

Saffi slept long and hard, waking just in time to watch the early-morning marine layer disperse. It left behind a rare blue-sky summer day. Gulls rode the breeze, and, out on the cove, a wetsuit-clad kite surfer bounced off a wave, caught air and soared for what looked like fifty feet. *Sweet!*

She took a seat at the small rectangular dining table that doubled as her writing desk and opened her laptop. Her mind churned as she sipped purple jasmine tea and stared out the window toward the cove. She should have been biking around town in search of local gems for her next *Bedside Reader*. Small-town historical societies and museums almost always pointed her toward fresh stories to share, stories that hadn't already been told a bazillion times before. Instead, her brain kept pecking like a raven at the juicy jetsam surrounding Linda's death.

What did she know so far? Almost without thinking, she opened a new document and started typing a list.

Grudges: (Bill, Glenn)
Raised voices in laundry: (Nicole, Troy)
Midnight scream: (Linda?)

Bedraggled dog on the beach: (Archie)
Campers awake at midnight: (Casey, Nicole)
Bandanna found: (Bill)
Sneaker-wave theory: (Chief Duarte)

The whole list amounted, at this point, to a great big nothing-burger. Linda's death had been labeled "accidental." Unless the medical examiner came to a different conclusion, Saffi's amateur investigation—no matter how strong the pull to keep the police from letting the tide sweep the truth away—put her brain-deep in that age-old writer's favorite pastime: procrastinating.

Saffi shut her laptop firmly, stood, and stretched the kink out of her neck. She could either sit here stewing and tank the tight schedule for the next book, or she could hit the harbor trail and head over to the visitor center, her first research stop in any new town. Today was... what... Tuesday? As things stood, she had one more night in space 32. Without Linda to stop him, Bill would gleefully give her the old heave-ho tomorrow afternoon. If she was going to dig up nuggets about Last Chance Cove, today might be her only chance. Saffi slurped the last warm dregs of jasmine tea and headed outside.

A brisk walk later, the wind swirled her inside the angular redwood building that housed the visitor center. The small tourist-focused center consisted of an information counter and a tiny shop. She quickly scanned the shelves, finding the usual fare: books by local authors (mostly self-published), crafts by Native artisans (handmade), and touristy trinkets (made in China). Two things immediately rang her "weird-but-true" chimes: a brochure on movies made in and near the area and a book titled *Haunted Lighthouses of the Pacific Northwest*. Saffi did a little happy dance as she scooted between the shelves to reach the white-haired woman behind the register.

"Ooh! That one was written by my late husband!" She beamed at the book Saffi placed on the counter.

Late husband. So, probably a few years out of date, Saffi noted. But ghosts were timeless and if she was any judge of spousal pride, the author's widow would be more than happy if she cited her husband's book in a bestseller. Saffi introduced herself as the writer of *Aunt Saffi's Bedside Readers* and was gratified by the smile of recognition that lit up the volunteer's face.

"How exciting! Welcome to Last Chance Cove!"

Saffi had learned long ago that speaking exclusively in exclamatory sentences was a requirement of visitor center volunteers. She found it endearing.

"Do you know of any other books about local hauntings?" Saffi asked. "I'm looking for sources with lots of local color."

The widow closed her eyes and tilted her head as if it helped her think and then nodded. "The Historical Museum has a few more books on the topic. It's just a few blocks from here." She tapped a finger on her husband's book. "But this one's the most authoritative. Look!" She pointed to a list of sources at the back of the book. Short, but helpful.

Saffi grinned. "Lucky for me that I found this one first."

She left with the book and a fistful of brochures tucked inside her mist-blue shoulder sling. Most of the brochures would be useless in her work, but if by some miracle her three days turned into the three-month stay she'd booked with Linda, she'd have plenty of time to explore the area's wonders. Instead of heading straight to the Historical Museum, she turned left into Beachfront Park. From here, the harbor trail looped along the beach and then back into town. She hadn't had a good walk since she arrived and the aches in her back and shoulders told her she needed one.

She passed a wooden play structure just inside the park. A few kids slid, swung, and climbed, their squeals and shouts bringing the park to life. The young voices lifted her spirits, as did the dogs barking as they chased after frisbees and sticks. Blue-sky days brought towns like Last Chance Cove to life. It didn't surprise her to see joggers wearing shorts instead of sweats. It also didn't surprise her that those shorts were topped with hoodies. Despite the sun, sea-salted wind chilled the air.

Saffi lengthened her stride and picked up her pace, hoping to warm her muscles. Up ahead, a gull pecked at a fast-food wrapper, probably stolen from one of the trash cans spaced out along the trail. As it gulped down the remains of a burger, a whole flock of friends showed up, darting in, one by one, to snatch away scraps. The first gull lifted off, trying to protect the bit of bun in its beak. Saffi sidestepped the squawking food fight and nearly tripped over a pair of Converse-style high-tops stretched out from a bench beside the trail.

Saffi stumbled to a stop. The high-tops belonged to a young woman who could have emerged full-blown from a Frida Kahlo self-portrait. Dark thick eyebrows above intense brown eyes, pert red lips, and... *her clothes!* Scarlet-red roses entwined with thorns burst from the seafoam-green background of a vintage shirtwaist dress. A trim black jacket with belled sleeves topped the color explosion. Artfully torn red fishnet stockings emerged from the black high-tops Saffi had nearly tripped over. A red beret crowned the young woman's thick, shoulder-length black hair.

If she'd dared, Saffi would have snapped a photo. The young woman was a work of art.

"You found her."

The woman's voice startled Saffi out of her reverie. She blinked. "Sorry. What?"

"You found Linda. Down there." The young woman used a celery stick filled with nut butter to point toward the beach.

In slow motion, Saffi turned to face the cove. She stepped across the paved trail and looked twenty feet down. She stood above the exact spot where Linda's body had come to its final rest. No tarps today. No ravens. No evidence that a woman had died here, but a shiver of memory swept over Saffi and settled into her bones. The dog walkers, stroller pushers, and bench sitters sharing the trail this glorious blue-sky morning could be oblivious, but she could not. Apparently, neither could the young woman whose stretched-out legs had jarred her to a stop. Saffi turned back toward the bench, expecting to see a haughty Frida Kahlo glower on the young woman's face. Instead, she saw inquisitive brown eyes sparkle above a pensive smile.

"Can I sit?" Saffi nodded toward the bench.

The young woman pulled in her legs, sat upright, and scooched over. Her plank-straight posture once again reminded Saffi of Frida, but it seemed natural, comfortable, unlike that of the world-renowned artist. Kahlo's stiffness, Saffi had learned while writing an article called "Tragic Transformations," was the result of a horrible accident. The bus on which she was riding cut in front of a streetcar. When the two behemoths crashed, an iron handrail drove through Frida's back and out her pelvis. For months she lay in bed, encased in a full-body cast, enduring excruciating pain. Then, she picked up a paintbrush and transformed her agony into art.

Saffi wondered what past pains had turned the young woman sitting beside her into a living masterpiece.

"How do you know?" Saffi asked. "That I found Linda."

"I was up here listening to the ravens. You screamed for help. Raven told me to flag down a copper, so I did. Against my better judgment, I might add." The young woman pursed her red lips and turned her body toward Saffi, tucking her right high-top under her left knee.

"Thank you, Raven, and...?" Saffi met the woman's dark eyes and waited to see if she would share her name.

The Kahlo lookalike crunched the last bit of nut-butter celery stick and stuck out a hand. "Mellie Blue."

"Saffi Graywood." Saffi grasped her hand. Her shake was warm, firm, certain. Saffi wasn't surprised. It would take a massive amount of certainty to dress the way Mellie dressed, to stand out, when most people, Saffi included, preferred to step back and try not to be noticed.

The raven comment might have scared off others, but when her totem bird showed up, Saffi knew to listen. "What do the ravens say, when you stop to listen?"

The young woman's grin dimpled her cheeks. "Last summer, when I was out of work, the ravens told me to open my own art gallery."

She gestured toward a line of trees about fifteen feet behind the bench. Saffi shaded her eyes from the sun climbing over the coastal mountain range and caught sight of an improbable contraption: a wooden box-trailer hitched behind a sunflower-yellow electric adult trike. The box had been painted the gloss black of a raven's wings. Its hinged sides folded down to reveal white pegboards hung with seaside scenes that pulsed and swirled and exploded, as if Van Gogh's impressionistic swirls had met Kahlo's Mexican-bright colors and fallen in love with life. Small wire baskets filled with cards featuring images from Mellie's paintings hung alongside the art. A pegboard shelf held sunflower-yellow ceramic mugs, each branded with a raven. Saffi's gaze went to the raven glued to the top of the box. The bird would have looked real if it hadn't been twice the size of a normal raven. A sign hung from the bird's neck.

"Raven Mad Art." Saffi laughed. "Wicked! I love it."

Mellie's cheeks pinked. "Hand-built and foot-powered."

"You have quite the view from up here. Did you see...?" Saffi hesitated.

Mellie looked at her with eyes wise beyond her years. "Anything suspicious?" The artist closed her eyes, and then murmured, "*L is for Linda* who was swept out to sea."

A ghostly wind traced icy fingers across the back of Saffi's neck. She recognized the line from Edward Gorey's ABC book, the one with an alphabet of ways to die, though Mellie had changed Gorey's original *M is for Maud* to fit the current calamity.

"Unless," Mellie turned her deep-brown gaze on Saffi, eyes sparkling, "she wasn't."

Was Mellie saying that Linda hadn't been dragged into the cove by a sneaker wave? Saffi stuffed down her instinct to flood the emptiness with questions. Instead, she opened a space for the artist to share what she'd seen. It worked.

"I saw a white van parked down there." Mellie pointed in the direction of the lighthouse, to an unpaved parking lot with a view of the cove. "Spun out the minute the sirens got close."

"A white van? Anything identifiable?"

"Like a logo?" Mellie chuckled. "Yeah. It was the Kevin's Kookies van."

Saffi froze. *Oh, no! Glenn?*

Something tickled her memory: a sound she'd heard when she'd gone outside to see if someone needed help—the crunch of gravel. A vehicle had been creeping through the RV park that night. It could have been a van, and the cookie maker in crushed velvet clearly had a motive. Linda had done her best to destroy his reputation and his business. But could anyone have faked that visceral reaction to her death? The near faint. The spilled mocha. If so, Glenn could win an Oscar for that performance. It all seemed such a stretch.

"Oh!" Mellie jerked Saffi out of her thoughts. "I also saw Troy's tour boat. Anchored offshore."

Saffi shook her head. "No. Troy was searching for Linda. With me." What was Mellie implying? That Linda had been killed elsewhere, her body dumped on the beach to make it look like an accidental drowning? That Glenn might have done the ghastly deed? Or Troy? Saffi's stomach soured.

Mellie took a zippered plastic sandwich bag out of her

jacket pocket, took out another stuffed celery stick and crunched into it. After a few chews, she swallowed. "You know, you asked what I *saw* but you left out a whole lot of other senses. Hearing, for example."

Saffi could have smacked herself in the head. For a writer, all six senses mattered. Relying on just one—usually sight—was a surefire way to bore a reader. Sight, sound, touch, taste, smell, and the ever-present but often discounted sixth sense: intuition. "Good point. Did you hear something?"

Mellie crunched into her celery stick again and then turned slightly to wave the stub toward the parking spaces that had quickly filled after Linda's body had been found. "Chief Duarte talking to the city manager. Blame a sneaker, move along, keep the city's coffer strong," she sang.

First the police chief, now the city manager. She understood. Most tourist towns would do anything to avoid having their reputations sullied. And murder in an RV park? That would make plenty of people rethink their vacation plans. But what about Linda's plans? When she'd moved back to her hometown she must have had hopes, dreams... pictured herself becoming part of the cozy community by the sea. Uncle Kevin's will had blown her dreams out of the water and her vindictive response could as easily have put her in the path of a killer as of a sneaker wave.

"Mellie, you need to tell the police what you saw."

The artist's dark eyes turned stormy, determined. "Right. Maybe I'll do that, next time they stop by to roust me out of here. Or maybe not."

She gave the celery stalk a vicious crunch, stood and headed for her mobile art gallery. She lifted the plywood sides to cover the pegboard panels and locked them into place. "*Hasta la pasta*, Saffi Graywood." She waved. Then she pedaled away without a backward glance.

Saffi wasn't sure what to do. Should *she* tell the police what

Mellie had seen? If she did that now, while Linda's death was still labeled an accident, she'd be spreading innuendo about two men who might not have done anything wrong. That seemed to have been Linda's style, but it wasn't hers. No. She would wait. If the medical examiner found evidence of foul play, then she'd try again to get Mellie to tell the police—if she could find her—or she would tell Detective Richards and let him do the legwork.

The chance encounter with Mellie had given her more details to add to her list of things she knew, but it also left her with more questions and no answers.

FOURTEEN

Though her talk with Mellie left her mulling over Linda's death, Saffi needed to concentrate on the reason she'd come to Last Chance Cove. Not to play amateur detective but to complete a *Bedside Reader* on deadline. She sped up, concentrating on the uneven sidewalk instead of trying to collect clues as she looped out of Beachfront Park and headed downtown toward the Historical Museum. She passed a tiny library, an even tinier post office, and a massive red-roofed building housing Mimi's Attic, a typical small-town antique store crammed with glassware, furniture, and erstwhile objets d'art.

Most of the downtown buildings were dressed in cedar shingles painted beachside blue. The quaint rustic vibe made her want to stop and shop. She lingered for a minute in front of Last Chance Mercantile. She still needed to replace the clogs she'd lost to the tide. *Keep walking, Saffi! Today is about research, not shoes.* If she hadn't spent so much time talking to Mellie, she might have told the voice in her head to stuff it.

Around the corner and a few blocks north, she stopped in front of a faded, gray, two-story clapboard building. The Historical Museum's exterior wasn't in any way memorable, but the elderly volunteers seated at a long desk just inside the double doors were. One was short and pudgy with white poufs of hair above his ears and a bushy white mustache: *Walter*, according to his nametag. The other, *Martin* she noted, was tall and lean with a gray unibrow and a gray fringe above his ears. They reminded her of someone, but she couldn't grasp the wispy memory.

"That will be five dollars." Martin nodded toward a dented metal cashbox.

"I don't really have time for the museum," Saffi started, "I just—"

"Same fee, whether you have time or not." Walter tapped the box.

Martin looked at Walter and wiggled his unibrow. "She thinks we're trying to fleece her."

Walter smoothed his bushy mustache. "Why would we fleece her? She doesn't look anything like a sheep."

Martin gave a grumpy rumble that might have been a laugh. "Just trying to keep the lights on." His faded brown eyes twinkled as he shook the cashbox in her direction. It didn't make a sound. "Nothing." He gave an exaggerated sigh.

"Bupkes." Walter put a hand to his brow.

Their melodramatic flair and cranky banter smacked Saffi's memory awake: Waldorf and Statler! The cantankerous puppets from *The Muppet Show*. It was as if the elderly Muppets had left New York City for LA, turned right onto the Ventura Highway, and kept the pedal to the metal until they ran out of gas in front of this quaint, musty seaside museum.

Saffi thought she might be falling in love with these two. "Well, you can't have an empty cashbox at this time of day," she said, handing over a five. "That would be tragic."

"No." Martin shook his head. "An empty bottle of Glenfiddich is tragic. This is just sad." He laid the bill inside the cashbox and made the sign of the cross over it like a priest putting a beloved parishioner to rest.

Walter handed Saffi a brochure. "Self-guided tour. Free with your generous donation." He gave her a saucy wink.

"Thanks." She tucked the brochure into her pack. "But I'm not here for the tour. The lady at the visitor center thought you might have books about local history and hauntings." Saffi gestured toward a book-filled table between the front desk and the inner door she assumed opened into the museum's exhibits.

Waldorf sniffed. "I'm surprised she didn't force that dreck her husband wrote on you."

Saffi patted her sling bag and offered a rueful smile. "I chose that one all by myself."

Martin clicked his tongue. "Really, Walter. Hubert's book isn't half bad."

Walter snorted. "True. It's all bad."

Martin drummed his fingers on his dimpled chin, and then walked over to the book table, selected *Ghosts of the Coast*, and handed it to Saffi. She thumbed through the thin book. It looked vaguely promising. "Worst-case, I write off the cost on my taxes and call it good."

"Oh!" Walter jumped up from the desk. "If you can write off the cost, I'm sure we have others that are simply filled with thrills."

He raced across the lobby with surprising speed to rustle through the books. He picked up one after another, argued with Martin over each one's attributes and failures, and then put it down. At one point the elderly men seemed on the verge of fisticuffs. In the end, Walter recommended a book about haunted lighthouses and Martin chose one about a tragic shipwreck.

"Apparently, crates of gold bars and coins are littering the ocean floor." He waved vaguely in the direction of the coast north of town. "Right out there."

Saffi felt as if *she'd* struck gold. That bit of information would tie in nicely with an article she'd been developing called "Shipwreck Booty."

She left Walter and Martin happily counting their takings and nearly sprinted back to the RV park, ready to read and, hopefully, write, but the police SUV parked in front of the office brought her to a stop. The door stood open and two familiar voices—Bill's and Detective Richards'—ping-ponged back and forth.

"You can't do that!" Bill boomed.

"I wish I didn't have to, but I do."

"You don't and you can't!"

"I can and, I assure you, I will."

"I'm calling the city manager!"

"Feel free, but Randall's authority only goes so far. I answer to Chief Duarte."

When she couldn't stand the suspense any longer, Saffi headed up the ramp and strode inside. "Oh!" She stopped just behind the officer as if surprised to see him. "Detective Richards! What brings you here?"

Bill sat down in his office chair. He pressed the phone receiver to his ear with a glare clearly meant to send Saffi packing, but she smiled and stood her ground.

Detective Richards stepped back from the counter to bring her into the conversation. "I'm afraid I've brought bad news."

Saffi raised her eyebrows and waited.

"Ms. Oates' cause of death has yet to be determined, but homicide can no longer be ruled out."

Ms. Oates? For a second, Saffi had no idea who he was talking about, then it hit her. Linda had been Linda Oates. And Linda Oates might have been murdered. Bad news indeed, but, for Saffi, not totally unexpected.

"Come off it!" Bill spun his chair away from the computer and stood, nearly pulling the phone off the desk before he slammed the receiver back into the cradle. Angry red blotches spread up his neck. "That new medical examiner was probably too busy puking up her lunch to recognize an accident when she saw one."

Detective Richards bristled. "If she ever had that tendency —and I know for a fact she did not—six months at the Body Farm would have cured it."

Saffi whistled softly. Just writing about the forensic anthropology research center at the University of Tennessee, Knoxville, had soured her stomach. At any given time, more than a hundred corpses lay decomposing around the grounds. Future medical examiners and law enforcement officers could see for themselves *exactly* what happened to human remains left in the elements.

Inadvertently or not, the detective had let a clue slip through. At this stage of the investigation, the only way the medical examiner would know that foul play might have been involved was if Linda's death was *not* due to drowning.

"The medical examiner didn't find water in her lungs." Saffi widened her eyes. "If a wave took her, she'd have been gasping for air. Her lungs would have been filled with water."

Detective Richards scowled. "That's right."

Bill was still shaking his head.

Had the gash on the back of her head killed Linda? Saffi might have asked if Bill hadn't been hovering so close. For now, she tucked that info into her pocket. Keeping something back gave potential suspects—of which Bill was one, as far as Saffi was concerned—the chance to blurt out something they shouldn't know. That was one of the main reasons police didn't divulge findings to the public.

"So, she was murdered?" Saffi ventured.

Detective Richards gave Saffi a stern look. "It would be premature to say she was murdered, Mrs. Graywood."

Bill flapped a dismissive hand toward Saffi. "Murder shmurder. If this was a murder investigation, Chief Duarte would be here, not some—"

The look Detective Richards gave Bill instantly tied his tongue. "The chief sent me to question everyone who was in the park at the time of Linda's disappearance. So, if you'll have a seat, we'll get started."

"Me?" Bill squeaked. "What makes you think *I* was here?"

Saffi snorted but managed to keep from actually saying anything. Better to give the pirate king enough rope to swing his own neck from the yardarm.

"You took part in the search, did you not?" asked Detective Richards. "And found a..." He pulled a small notepad from his shirt pocket and glanced at it. "A bandanna, possibly belonging to the deceased's emotional support dog? Let's start there, shall we."

Bill fumbled for the desk chair behind him and sat.

Detective Richards turned to Saffi. "If you'll excuse us?"

Saffi contained her fist bump until she was out of sight of the office. She hoped Detective Richards grilled Bill like a cheese sandwich.

At the thought of grilled cheese, her tummy rumbled. *Lunchtime!* Saffi stretched the kinks from her legs as she hurried down the gravel lane to her RV. Once inside, she slid up the cove-side window to ventilate the kitchen before she lit her propane cooktop. The forward part of the RV warmed as she grilled her favorite sandwich—sharp cheddar and sauerkraut. When cheese oozed out of the butter-toasted sandwich, she turned off the burner. She plated the sandwich alongside two petite dill pickles and a single thin chocolate mint to aid diges-tion. She'd read the advice online and decided any tip involving chocolate had to be believed. Then she carried her plate to the front of the Rambler and slid into the passenger-side captain's chair.

Saffi loved kicking back in the cockpit. The windshield gave her a 180-degree view of the park with row after row of RVs spreading out in either direction. Mounted RV flags bristled from many of the rigs, their colors waving in the breeze. Saffi balanced her plate in her lap and reached for the small travel binoculars she kept on the dash. A few flags made her chuckle: *RV there yet?; I go where I'm towed; It's all fun, until someone burns their wiener!* One made her sigh: *Life is good, at the beach.* Life usually *was* good at the beach. But not for Linda. Not anymore. Linda's life at the beach had come to a bloody, violent end.

Was the person responsible inside one of those RVs with the snarky flags, confident that a sneaker wave would be blamed for what they'd done? Chief Duarte and the city manager were all too eager to write Linda's death off as an accident. Their response seemed callous, but she feared it was typical. After all, more than half of all violent crimes in the U.S. went unsolved every year and many of those were crimes against women. The thought settled over Saffi like a death shroud.

Her last blog post had been about a ghost tour in Old Town Temecula. "If you ghost me, one of those ghosts could be you," her stalker had promptly posted. At the time, she'd shrugged off the comment, but Linda's death made the threat feel more real. If her online stalker followed through on any of the threats he'd made, she would want somebody to find the bastard and make him pay.

Saffi sipped a glass of water, thinking about what might have made that gash on the back of Linda's head. The berm with its jagged concrete blocks seemed likely. Would the medical examiner find evidence in the wound? A careful examination always revealed clues, not just to the cause of death, but to where the crime took place.

A brisk rat-a-tat on her RV's metal door made Saffi jump and almost dump her plate on the floor. She hadn't seen anyone approach. Whoever it was had either cut across the empty space on the right-hand side of her rig or come in from the path to the estuary beach behind the Rambler, the perfect path, she realized, for a stealthy killer. She resisted the childish instinct to duck under the table. Instead, she leaned across it and peered out the window.

"It's me, Mrs. Graywood!" A familiar figure saluted with what looked like a small black notepad. "Detective Richards."

Saffi's muscles relaxed. "Coming!" she called, stepping into the stairwell to swing open the door.

Detective Richards dipped his head in greeting. "I'm sure you know why I'm here."

"I would, if you hadn't already interviewed me at the station."

His expression was hidden behind dark sunglasses, but his full lips pursed, then slowly drifted toward a grin. "Ah, yes. So I did. May I come in?" He nodded toward the interior of her rig.

Saffi stepped back into the living room. "If you're looking for clues, I've already gotten rid of anything that might be the slightest bit incriminating."

As he stepped up into the RV, Detective Richards slumped slightly, as if worried that his head might hit the ceiling. He was taller than she remembered, but not tall enough for that, which he seemed to realize. He straightened, opened his notepad, and then used the pen he pulled from his front shirt pocket to point toward the row of RV-safe bookshelves above her couch. Saffi loved the fact that the wooden crossbar a few inches above the bottom kept books from sliding out while she drove.

"*The Complete Guide to Poisons*," Detective Richards mumbled. "*True Crime: Conmen, Creeps, and Killers. Fatal Attractions.*" He slid his glasses down his nose and looked her in the eyes. "Just what *are* you doing here in Last Chance Cove, Mrs. Graywood?"

A warm rush that probably looked like guilt rose up her neck and into her cheeks. "Writing," she said. "I'm uh..." She hesitated, wondering if telling him about her series would help, or hurt, her chances of ending up on his list of prime suspects. "Have you ever heard of *Aunt Saffi's Bedside Reader?*"

Detective Richards made a few notes in the small black pad. When he shook his head, Saffi's hope for an easy explanation melted away. "They're anthologies of intriguing true stories. Here." She pulled one of her readers off the shelf and handed it to him.

He glanced at the front, then turned it over to read the back cover copy. "You write about murder?"

Saffi chewed her lip. "Sometimes, but I write about almost everything." She waved toward the bookshelves where the next group of books included *The Ghost Hunter's Guide to Haunted Castles, Carnivorous Plants: Nature's Silent Predators, The Ugliest Animals on Earth,* and *Bigfoot Exposed.* "Nature. Pop culture. Unexplained phenomena like cryptids. Politicians. Science. History—especially the kind of history I can only find by going on the road to places like Last Chance Cove. And, to answer your question, I'm here to do research."

Detective Richards' eyebrows furrowed. "What's a cryptid?"

A touch of relief washed over Saffi. If she piqued his curiosity, he might see her as a writer, not a murder suspect. "It's a creature that people claim to have seen, but science doesn't recognize as real."

"Like Bigfoot?" He pointed his pen toward the book.

Saffi nodded. "Bigfoot, the Loch Ness Monster, Thunderbirds."

It was Detective Richards' turn to nod. His voice deepened into storytelling mode. "Many, many years ago, before white people came, a Diné boy went out at sunrise to collect mussels along the shore. The Thunderbird that nested on Whale Island, right out there"—he pointed across the cove to the humped outcrop just beyond the harbor—"swooped out of the fog and scooped him up." The detective chuckled. "The elders tell that tale often. It's how they teach us *never* to turn our backs to the sea."

"Exactly!" Saffi beamed. Now that the young officer had warmed a bit, Saffi decided to dig a little. "So, is there anyone I should keep an eye on? In the campground, I mean." Her lame attempt to find out what he'd discovered drew a scowl.

"As in, have I developed a list of suspects, and will I share their names so you can play amateur sleuth? No." Detective Richards shifted his gaze from Saffi to other parts of the RV, all easily seen from where he stood. The cockpit with her abandoned lunch on the dash, the spice rack above her gas cooktop (which held chili, curry, garlic, and onion powders—none of which were poisons), the bathroom separating her tiny living room from a bedroom slightly bigger than her queen-sized bed (no bloodstained clothes in the hamper, no blunt instruments lying about, other than hardcover books). "You're an interesting woman, Mrs. Graywood," Detective Richards said as he put his sunglasses on. "Can I keep this?" He held up the *Bedside Reader* she'd handed him. Despite knowing that he would use it as evidence against her if he could, she nodded. "Of course."

"One more thing. Please, don't leave town unless the department gives you permission."

Saffi's hands turned cold as she shut the door behind him. He'd put the fear of small-town policing in her, but, in the process, she'd learned two useful things: 1) Detective Richards wasn't the type to share confidential information, and 2) she was definitely on his list of suspects.

Saffi headed back to the cockpit. Her grilled cheese had gone soggy. She choked it down, then let the chocolate mint melt on her tongue to soothe her frayed nerves. Then she opened her laptop and logged into her webpage. *Today, a Tolowa Dee-ni' man shared a story his elders told to warn kiddos about turning their backs on the sea.* She described the humpbacked island between the harbor and the Pacific, the bark of seals, the hunched trees protecting themselves from the relentless wind, and the people whose wealth had once been measured in tusk shells and bird scalps. Half an hour later, the latest adventure in *Travels with Aunt Saffi* was on its way to her followers.

What next? Saffi closed her laptop and slid out of the captain's chair. Since Detective Richards wouldn't share details, maybe his auntie Val, the medical examiner, would. She might be open to a professional writer inquiring about her work for an upcoming book. Over time, Saffi had found that being the brain behind the *Bedside Reader* series could open doors. Most experts were never asked about their work, not even by journalists. When she showed genuine interest in their knowledge, they were usually more than happy to dish up details. Saffi pulled her cellphone from her pack. With one call, she found someone who knew her books and, a few minutes later, she had an appointment with the medical examiner for the next morning.

As the afternoon sun streamed through the windshield, Saffi drifted toward sleep. Just before her eyes completely closed, she spotted Casey walking Archie on his long red leash. She shook the sleep away, opened the passenger-side window and called out, "Hey! I see you still have the little guy." Saffi nodded toward the white terrier.

Hearing her voice, Archie tugged Casey into site 32. Saffi extricated herself from the passenger seat, hurried outside and knelt to greet him. The terrier put both paws on her knees and slathered her face with dog kisses, his tail beating back and forth with joy.

"I have Archie for now." Casey ruffled the terrier's fur. "But Mom says I can't keep him, even though Linda's, you know, dead and all."

Saffi acknowledged the scruffy dog's loss with an extra scratch between his ears.

"Besides, Archie's not crazy about my mom. She can be a bit..." Casey hesitated for a second but then tilted her head, "shrill?"

Saffi tightened her lips, but a smile managed to squeeze through. Casey grinned in return.

"I mean, I get it," Casey went on. "She has a lot on her mind, what with the custody case and all. I know Dad would let me keep Archie, but I can't even tell him where I—"

Casey's eyes widened as if she realized she'd said too much. "Yeah. No. I mean, we gotta go. Uh. Mom told me to stay in the trailer while she went to the store but..." She waggled a bulging doggy poo bag at Saffi and gave Archie's leash a little tug. "A dog's gotta do what a dog's gotta do." For a second the smile came back, then Casey tugged Archie's leash. "Uh. See you later, I guess."

Saffi watched the pair scurry toward the dumpster beside the wooden fisherman carving. *A custody case!* And a dad who didn't know where his daughter was. What had Nicole said during her laundry room freakout? "I have to pay her." Could she have been talking about Linda? If the park manager was a blackmailer and Nicole had decided not to pay, she had a whale of a motive for murder.

FIFTEEN

Nicole had joined Glenn at the top of her list of suspects, but Saffi still needed to figure out Troy's role in the whole thing. After all, according to Mellie his boat had been anchored offshore yesterday morning when he'd pounded on her door to join the search. A picture flashed through her mind: Troy dumping Linda's body from his boat and then sauntering up to her trailer with a cup of coffee. The wave of horror that swept over Saffi nearly took her breath away. Could Troy be a cold-blooded killer? *No.* Surely she had enough life experience to spot a guy that dangerous. A protector? Yes. She could see that. When she'd run toward what turned out to be Linda's body, he'd instinctively raced away, determined to protect Nicole and Casey from the grisly find.

She had too many questions and too few answers, but she knew two things for sure: Troy had carted a load of laundry toward Nicole's trailer the evening Linda disappeared. He could have been there, keeping his presence quiet, when Saffi stumbled off the beach with Archie. Clearly, he'd been on the grounds first thing the next morning. With red warning flags waving like crazy, it was time to ask Mr. Reel Sexy a few questions.

She found the Troy's Tours card he'd given her marking her page in *Girls with Guns*, the paperback resting on her bedside table. She'd picked up the historical thriller at Eureka Books, just off the 101 in Old Town Eureka, California. As someone who relied on book sales for her living, she made a point of checking out bookstores as she traveled between RV parks. Quirky indies were her favorites, and she always bought at least one book. Saffi pulled Troy's card out of the paperback and slipped in a bookmark. Troy's Tours, the card said, was located at 130 Seal View Way, which she knew from her visits to the Last Chance Café was at the harbor.

Biking over was more of a struggle than she'd expected. An onshore wind kept trying to tip her to the left. By the time she turned onto Seal View Way, her shoulders had a serious burn going on. Worse still, the front window of Troy's Tours showed her hair sculpted sideways like a coast cypress. *Great!* Saffi tried to finger-brush some hair back toward the right side of her head. The result was comical, at best.

Troy's Tours had four parking spaces but no bike rack, so she walked her bike around the corner and locked it to the rack in front of Last Chance Café. On the way back, she spotted Troy's metallic-blue pickup with the wave-and-fish logo on its doors parked behind the building. That boded well for finding him at work.

Saffi hurried back to the front of the business and noticed a fish-shaped sign hanging in the door: "In Port." A jaunty bell jingled as she pushed the door open. She glanced at the other side of the sign, not surprised to read "Out to Sea." Saffi still had a smile on her face when she turned toward the sturdy oak desk anchoring the room. When the man hunched behind the desktop computer looked up, Saffi's heart lurched as if she'd fallen headfirst into the gray-blue sea. His short, slate-gray hair still looked wind-tossed, but so did everyone else's in Last Chance Cove, including Saffi's, although hers looked more wind-wrecked. He'd rolled up the sleeves of his green-and-blue flannel shirt far enough for Saffi to admire the Celtic fish tattoo on his muscular right forearm.

"Well, well. I wondered if you would stop by." He smiled, that little sideways quirk of his mouth reminding her once again of Levi.

Saffi's heart did a hop-skip. *Come on,* she chided herself. *You're way too young for palpitations.* Or was she too old? Saffi shook her head. Troy wasn't Levi. He was someone she barely knew, and, despite his charming mischievous smile, he might be a murderer, or in cahoots with one. Before things got too weird, she broke eye contact to take in the front room. A couple of modern blue chairs with chrome legs flanked a low glass table with brochures fanned out across it. On one wall, framed photos of giddy fishermen beside their catches spread outward on either side of an antique fishing rod. Mounted fish of various sizes and species adorned the opposite wall. Very male. Very minimalist. Very fishy. Saffi approved.

Troy pushed back from the desk and rose to greet her. "Ready to book a charter?"

"To be honest, I'm not much of a fisherman. Fisher... woman?" Saffi felt a blush rising. "Person? Fisherperson?" *Great. She'd reverted to stuttering like a high schooler with a crush.*

The corners of Troy's eyes crinkled. "These days we go with fisher. But the fish bite just as fast and fight just as hard, no matter what you call the person on the other end of the rod."

"So do you fish in the cove or...?" Saffi wanted to know if Mellie could have really seen Troy's boat near the beach on the morning of the search.

"My inshore excursion is the most popular with families and, uhm, less experienced fishers." Troy walked over to the table and gestured her toward one of the blue chairs. He took the other chair, picked up a brochure and unfolded it on the glass tabletop, forcing her to lean toward him to see it. He pointed to a map of the coast. "We head south out of the cove down to Sister Rocks." He drew a finger down the coastline. "The reefs here," he tapped a spot on the map, "are a great place to snag rock cod, lingcod, maybe a copper rockfish or a vermilion. Easy to hit your ten rockfish limit."

"Ten fish?" Saffi looked up, astounded. "What would I do with ten fish?"

Troy laughed. "Eat them? At least, that's what most people do."

Saffi's face went hot. Something about this guy made her brain go soft as tofu.

"Don't worry. I'll make it easy on you. You catch 'em. I'll fillet 'em and bag them up for freezing."

"You'd do that for me?"

Troy leaned across the table, his face turning serious. "I would."

Saffi felt special for the half second it took her to look down and catch sight of the text on the brochure's final page. *At the end of the charter, we will fillet and bag your catch.* She glanced up at Troy, then back down at the brochure. "Me and everyone else, I see."

"Of course. People who've never filleted fish..." He gave an exaggerated shiver followed by a grin. "It's a massacre."

Just as it had before, his banter drew her in, despite her misgivings about thirty-something girlfriends and possible murderous inclinations. Saffi checked herself. She'd written about the world's most charming serial killers for *Bedside Reader,* #10. The "Casanova Killer"—described as a cross between Ryan O'Neal and Robert Redford—had used his rugged good looks to lure more than eighteen women to their deaths. Too often, looks, charm, and murder went hand in hand.

Saffi held in a shiver as she forced her thoughts back to fishing charters. "What about equipment?" she asked. "I mean, I don't have any."

Troy pointed to the next paragraph. "I've got everything you need. Bait, tackle, rod, reel, life jacket."

Life jacket. Those two words reminded Saffi of why she'd come here. Not to book a fishing charter, but to learn more about Troy. To dig deep enough to figure out his relationship with Nicole and if his boat really had been anchored in the cove while they'd searched for Linda. Would going fishing give her answers? She imagined spending hours together on his boat while he attended to her every need. Those strong work-hardened hands baiting her hooks, those muscular arms helping her reel in a catch. She'd have plenty of time to pose questions. But the wrong questions, she cautioned herself, might earn her a quick shove overboard. She'd never gotten a dangerous vibe from Troy. But the vibes she *had* been getting were no doubt skewing her perception.

Maybe it would be safer to ask potentially triggering questions with her feet on terra firma. Saffi went for it. "Someone mentioned seeing your boat anchored in the cove before we went out searching for Linda. That's why I thought you might fish in the cove."

Troy drummed his fingers on the table, his brows furrowed. "Oh, right! Crab pots."

"Crab pots?"

"Casey had a hankering for some Dungeness for dinner. I was out there anchoring a couple of pots."

Casey.

"You seem... close. To Casey and, uhm, Nicole." Saffi picked up a brochure and pretended to focus on the pictures.

Troy laughed. "I should hope so. Nicole's my sister."

Saffi unconsciously crunched the brochure, and then tried to smooth it out. *Lame!*

"So, Casey's your niece?"

Troy held back a grin. "I'm pretty sure that's how it works, yes."

Something within Saffi released and before she could stop herself, she blurted, "But you're so much older than Nicole!"

"I guess they don't have stepfamilies on your planet," Troy teased. "The kind where divorced dads who are *way* past their prime remarry and start new families with women young enough to be their daughters?"

Saffi blushed so hard she could feel it to the roots of her hair. "Oh, *those* kinds of families. No." She looked up, daring to meet his gaze. "Where I come from, that is strictly taboo."

"Ah. One of those retro planets."

Saffi nodded. "I feel terribly out of place here on Earth."

"Don't worry. Once I teach you to fish, you'll fit right in." Troy's mock-pitying look made her laugh.

When she'd thought Troy and Nicole were a couple, she'd barely held herself in reserve. Now, she felt herself melting toward the quirk in his smile and the teasing in his gray-blue eyes. She'd already discovered what she'd come fishing for—the relationship between Troy and Nicole and why his boat had been in the cove the morning Linda's body was found. Maybe a different kind of fishing was in order after all. "So, when's your next available booking?"

"It's your lucky day. I just had a cancellation for tomorrow's charter. We head out at six." Troy folded up the brochure and handed it to her. "Unless the weather turns."

Saffi was already shaking her head. Tomorrow morning, she had an appointment with the medical examiner.

"Anything later in the week?"

Troy frowned. "I'm pretty booked up. We're in the middle of the rockfish season. Let me check."

Troy walked back to his desk and started tapping computer keys. He pressed his lips together and shook his head. "I don't see any openings until next Tuesday, a week from today." He looked up. "Will that work for you?"

"I'd rather do it sooner. Before I chicken out."

"I'm sorry." Troy pushed his chair back and stood. "How about this? Let's book you for the Tuesday tour, and if I get another cancellation, I'll call you."

If that was the best she could get, Saffi would take it. "Sure. Thanks!"

As she turned to leave, Troy called out. "Your phone number?"

He wanted her phone number? She glanced back, a question in her eyes.

"In case there's a cancellation." His eyes twinkled.

Oh, God. There she went again. Tofu for brains. She dug in her pack for a card and handed it to him. As he read it, his eyes widened. "*Bedside Reader?* That's you?"

"Yep." Saffi zipped her pack.

"If I take you out, I won't end up in your next book, will I?"

"Take me out?"

His left brow quirked upward. "On the boat?"

"The boat." Saffi clutched her pack like it was a life preserver. "Depends on how many strange and interesting secrets I uncover."

Troy flicked the edge of her card with his thumb. "So, I can expect you to be fishing, while you fish."

"Always."

The bell jingled as she pulled the door open. Saffi gulped in fresh ocean air as she stepped outside. It cooled her skin and calmed her jangling nerves. Behind her, she could feel Troy's presence, imagine his thumb still flicking her card as she ducked around the corner toward Last Chance Café. She hurried past her bike without a glance and pushed open the turquoise front door.

SIXTEEN

The minute Saffi stepped inside, the café's warmth wrapped her in a hug. The robust aroma of coffee made her salivate. She glanced at the comfy wave-splashed turquoise chair beneath Troy's photos. It was empty, but right now she needed girl-talk more than a comfortable tush.

"Hey, sweet pea!" Delilah wiped down a spot at the counter and Saffi slid onto a stool. "Oat-milk mocha?"

Saffi grinned. "How do baristas do that? Remember everyone's favorites."

"Like a mousetrap." Delilah tapped her forehead with a bejeweled fingernail. Coral today, Saffi noted, wondering how much time her new friend spent on those exotic nails.

"I'll have one of those, too." Saffi wiggled her fingers toward the glass-domed plate loaded with wedding cookies. Powdered sugar rained down the front of her hoodie as she bit into the buttery, pecan-studded treat. Brushing at the mess smeared it into the fabric, but Saffi didn't care. Kevin's Kookies were worth it.

As she waited for her mocha, Saffi twirled her stool toward the dining area. This late in the afternoon, the café was quiet.

An elderly couple sat at a table by the window, staring out at the choppy harbor as they sipped their coffees. The man turned her way, almost as if he'd felt her gaze, and she recognized him as the Texan behind the wheel of the Prevost that took the last available monthly space, the one she still thought of as "her" space. His brisk nod told her he recognized her, too. He leaned toward his wife and whispered something.

She still needed to ask the Texans if they'd been out walking a dog the night they arrived, in case they'd seen Linda out walking Archie. She rapped her knuckles on the counter. "Be right back."

Delilah looked over from pulling coffee shots and nodded.

Saffi made her way to the table by the window, offering her friendliest *I know you took my space, but I'm trying not to hold it against you* smile. "I guess I'm not the only one from the RV park to discover this place. I'm Saffi Graywood." She held out a hand and the Texan took it, gripping hers a little too tightly at first but backing off when she returned the squeeze. She'd attended too many faculty meet-and-greets with Levi to not know that being taken seriously required a firm handshake. Saffi started to offer her hand to the woman, but she was hurriedly scooping postcards into her purse. Saffi recognized the local lighthouse on the front of one.

"I'm Jeff," the Texan drawled. "This is Eliza."

His accent made her neck hairs bristle. She'd heard one just like it, and recently. But who? She also didn't miss the fact that he hadn't offered his surname. Maybe he had something to hide. Something worse than letting his dog do its business in the bushes.

"Hope you aren't too unsettled by this whole Linda thing," Jeff went on. "Eliza thinks we should put the chairs in the wagon and head home, but I'm not afraid of a little whodunit."

His callous attitude toward a woman's death set Saffi's teeth on edge and seemed to hit his wife the same way. She shot him a look meant to squelch, but he paid her no attention, going on about their favorite BBC murder mysteries and how exciting it was to find themselves boot-deep in one.

"Now that you mention it, I've gotten a bit caught up in the whole thing myself and I was wondering..." Saffi paused long enough to watch his reaction and Jeff didn't fail to offer one: his faded blue eyes went from excited to wary. *OK. Time to push a bit.* "I don't know if you heard, but I found Linda's dog alone on the beach the night I arrived."

"You were on the beach with a sneaker-wave warning in place? Daring or—"

He didn't say the word "dumb," but she heard it loud and clear.

"Daring? No." Saffi ignored the implied insult. "I was up on the berm staying safe when I spotted him." She wasn't about to tell this stranger the details of how she'd come to be there—the scream, Raven. "Anyway, I've been thinking about what Bill said—that he'd found Archie's bandanna in the bushes, along with some dog droppings. You don't have a dog, do you?"

Great, Saffi. Way to be subtle.

Jeff grinned. "We do."

Saffi squeezed her hands into fists at her sides and waited. Had he seen something? Would he tell her if he had?

"Prince Charlie. Sweetest little Jack Russell you ever saw."

"I'd love to meet him." Saffi smiled, glad that she could be sincere about one thing.

"Well, you'd be welcome to do that, but it's a long way to Lubbock. We left him home with our son. He's a veterinarian, and he's always railing about people who keep pets cooped up for days inside RVs."

So, no dog. Why, then, did Jeff and Eliza give each other those guilty looks when Bill mentioned finding dog poo in the bushes? Or maybe it wasn't the droppings. Maybe what they'd found was the bandanna, and maybe they'd tossed it into the bushes after they'd...

Good grief! Saffi shook her head to clear the gunk. Even she couldn't suspend disbelief long enough to make up a story about a couple of Texas boomers pushing a total stranger and her dog off the berm the night they arrived at a campground three states from home.

When Jeff started rambling about his Jack Russell's lineage, Saffi tuned out. So did Eliza. With a politely bored sigh, she let her gaze roam over her husband's shoulder to the photos on the wall behind the armchairs. An instant later, she let out a small gasp. Eliza, Saffi noted, was staring at the photo of the kid with the big fish. Jeff stopped mid-word, glanced over his shoulder at the photo, and then leapt to his feet, nearly knocking over the table in his haste. "Look at me, blustering on about murder TV and Jack Russells. Eliza, I'm sure you're ready to head on out of here." He grabbed his wife's hand and pulled her firmly to her feet. "Miz Graywood, my apologies. We'll see you 'round the park. Maybe tonight, at the campfire? I promise the only offensive thing I'll do is sing too loud if someone brings a guitar."

Saffi wandered back to her stool at the counter, shaking her head. Something about Troy's photo had freaked the Texans out and something they'd said was buzzing around her brain like a fly trying to find a place to land. Something about their son? Maybe the mocha she'd ordered would jolt her brain into gear.

Whatever was going on with the Texans, she had no business digging into another mystery. She'd already let herself be drawn into a potential murder investigation. In the process, she'd been drawn away from what she'd come here to do—write. For the first time, Saffi was forced to examine how she'd spent her three days at Last Chance Cove. She'd found a body, talked to the police, made lists of which RV park denizen might have killed Linda, but for what? She wasn't a sleuth. She was a writer, and a writer who was about to find herself without a space to park her RV. Without a space, meeting her book dead-line might be impossible.

As the reality of the situation hit her, Saffi's shoulders slumped. She'd spent her day playing amateur sleuth while she should have been calling every RV park within driving distance to find a new place to stay.

"What's wrong, chicken?" Delilah asked as she placed a mocha topped with a whipped-cream mountain on the counter.

Saffi stuck her finger in the mound, licked off the sweet creamy goodness, then indulged in a tragic sigh. "There was a screwup over my RV space. Linda promised me a monthly rental but when I arrived, Bill had rented the last available monthly to the couple that just left."

Delilah glanced toward the table where the Texans had been sitting. "Jeff and Eliza? There's something about those two I just can't put my finger on." She tapped her coral nails on the counter. "They spend a lot of time walking circles around the park. Every time I look out my window, there they are." Delilah shook her head, and her red curls bobbed. "Creeping around like they're searching for something. Or somebody."

Saffi stopped slurping whipped cream and sat up straight. *The photo!* How had she missed it? Casey's smile had seemed familiar when she met her because she'd seen it in Troy's photo. Jeff's accent reminded her of Nicole. Jeff and Eliza's son was a veterinarian, and Casey had said her dad was a vet. The Texans were Casey's grandparents, and they were trying to find her.

"They're watching Nicole's trailer!" she blurted.

Delilah's brows shot up. "Now why would they do that?"

Saffi turned and pointed at the photo of Casey. "When Eliza saw that photo, she froze like a possum in headlights."

"Did she?" Delilah took a long slow look at the photo, then sucked on her bottom lip. "Now that you mention it, the kid does look familiar."

"It's Casey. A bit younger, though."

Delilah squinted at the photo. "Well, butter my bum and call me a biscuit. You'd think I'd recognize a kid who's been living within spitting distance for weeks. Quite the coincidence. Troy taking a photo of a random girl who ends up at the park years later."

Saffi took a sip of mocha. "Not a coincidence and not random. She's Troy's niece."

Delilah's eyes popped wide open. "Wait! Are you saying what I think you're saying?"

"Yep. Nicole is Troy's half-sister. Same dad. Different moms."

That one rocked Delilah so hard she clutched the counter. "I had no idea. Troy and Nicole have been in here so often lately, I thought he was pulling a DiCaprio."

"A what?"

"You know, dating a woman young enough to be his daughter. Like Leonardo DiCaprio. Not that Troy's said a thing one way or the other. That one keeps his motor running quiet, if you know what I mean."

Saffi chuckled. "He does, indeed."

"So, the Texans are watching Nicole." Delilah whistled softly.

"And Casey." Saffi leaned her elbows on the counter. "I'm pretty sure they're her grandparents."

Delilah's eyes went wide. "If Casey is their grandkid, why don't they just knock on the door and say howdy?"

"Why indeed?" Saffi tapped her finger on the rim of her mug.

"I knew there was something odd about those two." Delilah squinted. "They're lousy tippers, you know. Rich folk usually are. That Eliza would rather squeak out a fart in public than let a dollar slip through her fingers."

Besides making her laugh out loud, Delilah's description of Eliza reminded her of an idea she'd had for a *Bedside Reader* article. Much as she'd love to spend the rest of the day speculating about the Texans, it was time to steer the conversation in a more profitable direction.

"While you're on the subject of tipping, I've been thinking of writing an article about weird ones."

Delilah's eyes lit up. "Ooh-wee! Have I got some doozies for you!"

"Hang on." Saffi rummaged in her bag for the notebook and pen she always carried, "OK. Dish!"

"Let's see." Delilah chewed her lower lip as she thought. "Troy tipped me a rockfish once. Filleted and everything. Left it on the table in a freezer bag filled with ice. Then Mellie—have you met her yet?"

Saffi nodded.

"She brought one of those raven mugs of hers to use for coffee. After she finished, she left the dirty mug as my tip."

Saffi stopped scribbling long enough to make eye contact. "She didn't just forget it?"

"Nope. Said it was worth more than the twenty percent she'd have given me, if she had it."

Saffi laughed.

"Don't laugh. Raven's my good luck mug. I use it every morning."

Saffi put down her pen to sip her mocha. "Anything else?"

Delilah drummed her nails on the counter. "Oh, yeah! This kid came in with his parents. Doodled all over a paper placemat, then signed it 'The Doodle Boy.' That's all they left on the table."

"Wait." Saffi looked up, eyes wide. "If it was the real Doodle Boy, he's kind of famous. Did you keep it?"

"Oh, shoot." Delilah frowned. "No. I spilled a glass of water on it. Blurred the whole thing."

She waved a hand and tugged Saffi's empty cup away from her. "No use crying over spilt water, is there? Now, before we got distracted, you were sharing your RV park woes. Old Mustache Mouth gave your monthly space to those Texans, did he?" Her eyes narrowed.

Saffi had a feeling Jeff and Eliza were in for some cold cups of coffee. No one could ignore a customer like a pissed-off barista.

"He did. He said he could only give me three nights in my space and tonight's the third. I got so caught up in what happened to Linda, I totally forgot. By eleven a.m. tomorrow, I'll have to check out."

Delilah's face lit up with news to share. "Guess you haven't heard."

Saffi raised both brows. "Heard what?"

"That adorable detective—Richards, I think?—went trailer to trailer telling everyone that if they were in the park the day Linda disappeared, they can't leave without police permission. Bill's had to cancel a slew of incoming campers for the week and he's over in the office pulling the last hairs out of that mustache of his."

Canceling reservations? Maybe one of those would open up a monthly space! Saffi spun herself off the stool. "I need to get over there." She was halfway to the door when she remembered: she hadn't paid. She turned on her heel, marched back to the counter, and smacked down a twenty and a five beside her cup.

"Just a sec. I'll get your change." Delilah picked up the bills and headed for the cash register.

"Oh, no. That's your tip. For the service, the stories, and the best news I've had in three days."

SEVENTEEN

As it turned out, by the time she pedaled back to the park, Bill had his chin pressed against the phone receiver, canceling incoming reservations. From what Saffi could tell, his current call concerned a monthly site. The park host was using his most affable tone to persuade the camper to postpone for a few days instead of canceling. Saffi's heart thrummed. *No, no, a thousand times no.*

"Bill!" She waved, hoping he'd realize that someone eager to fill a monthly site was standing right there in the office. Bill ignored her, continuing to pour on the charm. A few seconds later, the camper at the other end of the line sent the park host into full-blown pirate mode.

"You even think about doing that, I'll come through this phone line and murder you myself!" Bill slammed down the phone.

Saffi took a step back. "Whoa. You might want to rethink your customer service skills."

Bill's face went redder than Archie's missing bandanna. "Do you know what that knucklehead said? 'Thanks, but I'll skip my last chance to be murdered.'"

A chill washed down Saffi's spine. Despite her suspicions, Linda's death hadn't, to her knowledge, been declared a homicide. "Did Detective Richards tell you that?"

Bill shoved his fingers through his beard and tugged, grimacing. "No. He did not. It was an accident! But someone wrote a freaking social media post called, 'Last Chance for Murder!' The guy on the phone said he was going to share it with everyone he knew."

A flimsy excuse for threatening to murder the caller, in Saffi's opinion, but she couldn't resist giving Bill a nudge.

"Let's hope that post doesn't go viral."

She regretted it immediately. Bill spiraled into a rant about how unfair it was that some lazy unemployed couch muffin could spread crap on social media and tank the park, thereby costing a hard worker such as himself his job.

Saffi held up a hand. "You could fill that monthly slot right now, if you'd give me a chance to talk."

Bill's monitor-fried eyes looked so desperate she'd have felt sorry for him if he hadn't been on her list of suspects. He rolled his chair closer to the computer and pulled up a screen that showed a lot of green spaces where red had been the day she pulled into the park.

"You like it over there by the estuary? You can keep that spot as long as you want," Bill said. "Or I can get you closer to the beach. View of the lighthouse?"

For a second, she considered making him describe the pros and cons of every open space, but her better nature prevailed.

"I'm fine where I am," she tapped her credit card on the counter, "as long as I can stay there for the three months I originally booked."

Bill couldn't print out the paperwork fast enough. Within ten minutes, she'd signed, paid, and strode out of the office with a much springier step than she'd entered.

Back at her RV, Saffi put together a quick dinner of peanut

butter noodles, savoring the subtle flavors of fresh ginger root, garlic, honey, and chili paste. Over time, she'd learned the exact amount of chili her tongue could tolerate before zing turned to burn. It felt good to be home, seated at the RV-sized wooden dining table, and absorbing the evening's view from the cove-side window.

In RV parks, your view kept changing, sometimes daily, sometimes weekly... and sometimes not soon enough. It was all about your neighbors and their rigs. Saffi had been neighbors with all types: preppers, glampers, retirees, gun toters, hippies. She'd camped beside quiet families who waved shyly but kept to themselves, and boisterous families who raised a ruckus and overflowed into her space.

The more she camped, the more Saffi realized that America's RV parks and campgrounds made neighbors out of people who would never mingle in the "real world." Sometimes, they forged friendships that lasted for years. At her last park, she'd camped between two good-old-boys who kicked back every day under their awning bogarting cold beers, and a gay couple who lounged every evening under a fringed boho umbrella, sipping pomegranate martinis. Within a week, the bros and bohos were hosting a nightly "barbecue and brews" and had coaxed Saffi into the fun. When the two couples—one a couple of lifelong friends, the other a happily married couple—left for home, they exchanged phone numbers and vowed to return in a year for a grand reunion.

Saffi's current driver's-side neighbor was clearly a fisherman. He'd crammed a boat into his site beside a massive toy hauler—AKA rolling man cave. The Toyota Tundra parked in front of his rig nosed into the gravel road, challenging other campers to complain. Thankfully, the cove-side space next to Saffi's rig was empty, and the cove-front spot in her direct line of vision held a tiny teardrop trailer pulled by an SUV. That gave her a million-dollar view of the cove and the rolling ocean beyond. As the sun sank toward the sea, the angle of its rays layered the sky like a watercolor painting. Violet brush strokes lapped across pink. Pink wavered over yellow. Like thick, thirsty artist's paper, the sea drank in the colors. As she watched the sky shift toward scarlet flames, Saffi felt the day's tension melting away. The undercurrent of fear and uncertainty that had jangled her brain and body since she'd arrived to find her monthly space taken gave way to the peaceful in-and-out of the ocean's breath.

As Saffi finished off the last bite of savory noodles, she saw first one, then another, and then a trickle of campers exiting their rigs and wandering toward the berm. *The bonfire!* She'd forgotten all about it in the rush to secure her space. Should she go? Leaving her cozy rig for a chilly evening around a fire did not appeal. The bonfire would blow smoke in her face, no matter where she sat. Before she knew it, she'd be shivering and coughing and wishing she was back inside her tiny home on wheels.

On the other hand, if she went, she'd meet more of her neighbors. She'd have a chance to observe their behavior. See firsthand whether any of them seemed nervous or uncomfortable being out there on the berm where Linda might have died. Before she could stop herself, Saffi grabbed her warmest hoodie and pulled it over her curls, patting down the fluffy halo she'd given herself in the process.

She stepped outside to the nearly human sound of gull laughter and the woodsy smell of an early-stage bonfire. Misty ocean air caressed her cheeks and reminded her how much her skin needed moisture after months in the southern California desert. As she wandered past the trailer two spaces down, a birdlike elderly man dressed in jeans and a red-and-black plaid flannel shirt hopped down the steps of a vintage, yellow-and-white Shasta trailer. His hop-step reminded Saffi of a raven's gait. Unlike crows, ravens didn't simply stride.

They had their own special dance. They hopped, and then strode, hopped, then strode. She half expected her neighbor to do the same once he cleared the steps, but he hurried forward and matched his pace to hers. The man had a sailcloth bag slung over his right shoulder. A wine bottle peeked out of the top.

"Going to the bonfire?" His acorn-brown eyes sparked with interest.

Saffi smiled and nodded. "I am. You?"

Starting with a question that stated the obvious was common when greeting other campers. "Bit chilly today, isn't it?" or its companion "Hot for this time of year, don't you think?" were among the most familiar campsite hellos.

"I've met a lot of interesting people at bonfires." His eyes went from sparkle to twinkle. "Usually because I bring an extra glass for sharing. I see you're empty-handed."

Widower, Saffi deduced. Used to having a partner to enjoy an evening glass of wine and a chat. A bit cocky, she decided, as their age difference was likely as big as that between Troy and Nicole. But typical. Since Levi died, men old enough to be her father had been drawn to her like bumblebees to lavender. She treated them with kindness; after all, their attention was a compliment, despite the age span. She did her best not to lead any of them on, but that rarely stopped her from saying yes to a glass of wine.

"I'm Aaron, by the way," her walking companion informed her. "When the kids moved out, my wife and I bought our rig and hit the road." He pointed a thumb back toward the Shasta. "Traveled the whole country. North, South, East, and West. Last Chance Cove was one of our favorite spots." His bright eyes dimmed, and Saffi knew she'd been right. Aaron was a widower. "I was expecting my grandson to join me next week, but now I don't know. With what happened to Linda, this place doesn't seem so safe."

"It could have been an accident," Saffi said. "That's what Bill keeps saying."

Aaron shook his head. "My son's in law enforcement. When that young officer came by to tell me everyone needed to stay put until further notice, I called my son. He said they wouldn't do that unless Linda's death looked suspicious."

What Aaron said jibed with what Saffi had been thinking. Asking people to stay was a big deal. Campers could be irate about having their freedom curtailed. Law enforcement wouldn't make a call like that unless they had to. Whoever had made that "Last Chance for Murder" post must have thought the same thing.

Just as they passed Nicole and Casey's trailer, Aaron waved Saffi up the sandy trail to the berm. She paused at the top, taking in the wide, flat, scrub-grassy space. A circle of folding camp chairs surrounded a teepee-shaped fire which had already gone from smoking to blazing. Four-foot-high flames danced and crackled, shooting sparks toward the darkening sky.

She turned to Aaron with a frown. "Looks like we should have brought chairs."

"Most people do, but the park provides a few extras for those of us on the forgetful end of the spectrum." He leaned closer and whispered, "Or those who remember but don't want to lug chairs across the camp."

A familiar figure waved from the far side of the fire. "I saved you a seat!" Delilah called.

"Is there an extra chair for my new friend?" Saffi put a hand on Aaron's shoulder, and he grinned his thanks.

"I brought wine!" he said.

"In that case, get on over here!" Delilah waved.

Delilah had reserved Saffi's chair with a plaid throw, cool greens woven with warm yellows and reds. Saffi picked up the blanket to hand it back to her friend. "Oh, my gosh. This is so soft. I may have to steal it."

Delilah snagged the throw and snuggled her face into it. "I like you, sugar. But if you steal my lambswool blankie, I'll hunt you to the ends of the earth." That said, Delilah tossed it across both of their laps.

Between the fire, the friends, and the blanket, Saffi soon felt as content as she had while watching the sun set from inside her RV. The sun had now sunk below the horizon and with darkness came a temperature drop that would have made her shiver if not for the lambswool across her lap and the flames a few feet from her knees. Aaron opened a musky Bordeaux, dark red with just a hint of black raspberry. "Lovely." Saffi nodded after he poured her a sip. He filled her glass halfway, then held out the bottle for Delilah's glass.

She tapped a coral nail on the lip. "Fill 'er up!" she coaxed with a beguiling smile.

Aaron obliged, and as he turned his attention to Delilah, Saffi took a moment to check out the other campers around the bonfire. Notably, despite the bonfire being just uphill from their trailer, neither Nicole nor Casey had shown up, at least not yet. Troy wasn't there either, but, being a local businessman, and *not* —Saffi smiled at the thought—Nicole's boyfriend, he probably didn't live at the park. She spotted the Texans across the fire and waved. Jeff tipped the brim of the Stetson he was wearing in acknowledgment, but Eliza kept turning her head, glancing side-eyed, this way and that, like a skittish deer.

Saffi's skin prickled when Bill showed up with his German shepherd, Smudge, at his heels and carrying a banged-up guitar case. He took a seat on the opposite side of the fire, opened the case, pulled out what looked like a vintage Martin acoustic, and tuned the pegs. Then he broke out a booming bass voice worthy of North Cornwall's Fisherman's Friends to lead a sea shanty. You could have knocked Saffi off her chair with a gull's feather. Almost against her will she found herself singing along with choruses of "Haul Away Joe" and "The Wellerman" and laughing until she snorted wine and nearly choked. By the time the bonfire had burned down to sun-hot coals, the last knots of tension she'd been holding in her belly loosened. Here by the fireside, lulled by the music, she felt at home for the first time since she'd pulled into Last Chance Cove.

As the fire started to die down, campers drifted away in twos and threes, some to the beach, others back into the park. The Texans headed down the path. She lost sight of them as they rounded the front of Nicole's trailer, but a few seconds later, she saw movement in the faint glow of light from windows on the opposite side. Saffi stood, trying to get a better look, and made out a figure crouched beneath the living room window. Between one eyeblink and the next, the figure popped up as if trying to get a look inside and Saffi saw the unmistakable shape of a Stetson. Jeff? She thought back to Eliza's reaction to the photo of Casey. And then there was Delilah's observation about Jeff and Eliza being outside her trailer every time she looked, or her own guess that they might be watching Nicole's trailer. And now... that Stetson beneath the living room window.

Before caution got the better of her, she threw a hasty goodnight toward Delilah and Aaron and darted toward the trail. Just as she reached it and started down, a rock rolled beneath her right boot, and she yelped, barely catching herself before she fell. She slowed then, hoping whoever she'd seen hadn't been alerted by her cry. Her hiking boots hit gravel at the end of the trail, and she slowed even more, trying to quiet the crunch beneath them. She passed in front of Nicole's trailer, and then ducked down the other side, hoping to surprise the lurker she'd seen from the berm. No one was there. Saffi walked around the back of Nicole's trailer and had just started up the other side when light spilled from the front door, and someone cleared their throat.

"What in the name of tarnation do you think you are

doing?" Nicole stood just inside the door, arms folded, glaring at Saffi.

"I, uh—" Saffi turned toward the back of the trailer and then back to Nicole. "I was up on the berm, and I-I thought I saw someone down here. Outside your window. Big guy." She stretched her arm above her head to about Jeff's height. "Wearing a cowboy hat."

Nicole's eyes went wide. Without saying a word, she slammed the door closed and thunked the bolt into place. A second later the lights in the trailer went dark one by one, from the front all the way to the back.

"OK...?" Saffi shook her head. Nicole's startled reaction—like a rabbit racing into its burrow to hide—confirmed her guess. Casey's grandparents had stalked Nicole from Lubbock to Last Chance Cove and they had not come for a friendly "knock-on-the-door" kind of visit.

But how had the Texans found Nicole? Who would have known where she'd landed? Troy, but she didn't think he would rat out his sister. Nicole and Casey themselves, but if they were hiding, why would either of them spill the beans? That left one person who might have known: the park manager. "I have to pay her," Nicole had wailed. If she'd paid Linda for her silence, why kill her? Maybe the boomers had a stronger motive. If Linda had seen them skulking around the park in the dead of night, maybe they had silenced the park manager before she could warn their daughter-in-law of their arrival.

So much intrigue. So few facts. Saffi sighed. If she was lucky, tomorrow's meeting with the medical examiner would settle the issue of whether Linda had been murdered... and how.

EIGHTEEN

After Detective Richards' visit to the park yesterday, and the admonition for campers to stay put, Saffi felt a buzz of anticipation as she strolled the few blocks downtown for her appointment with the medical examiner. Not surprisingly, the medical examiner's office was close to the police station in a drab flat-roofed concrete building that also housed the sheriff's station and the jail. The scraggly junipers huddled against the building did little to brighten its prison-gray vibe. Clearly, Saffi mused, the building was no one's happy place. Beyond the double front doors, the interior wasn't any better: faded linoleum tile, fluorescent lights, dingy blue walls that cried out for a new coat of paint, the sour smell of mop water with overtones of formaldehyde.

Saffi couldn't help comparing these work surroundings with her own. Her "office" views had included some of the country's most dramatic scenery: the ever-rolling Blue Ridge Mountains, the colorful striated Badlands, the other-worldly Craters of the Moon, and, here, Last Chance Cove blending into the endless Pacific. Even with Linda's death clouding her days, gratitude welled up when she thought about the thousands of miles of beauty she'd experienced since Levi's untimely death.

Gratitude laced with regret. The RV sabbatical had been Saffi's idea, a trial-run for a possible future, when, and if, Levi retired. Saffi shook herself. Who had she been kidding? Herself, she supposed. Levi had loved being a professor. He loved the picturesque Vermont campus where he taught with its red-brick buildings nestled against rolling hills. He loved the mahogany faculty lounge lined with bookshelves where he could sip wine and indulge in jargon-filled academic discourse with colleagues. Most of all, he loved watching the bored faces of students who thought they already knew everything light up as history's most brilliant authors exploded their preconceptions, from Austen to Atwood, Bulgakov to Bukowski, Chaucer to Cather, and on and on. To Levi, literature *was* human history: the sum total of who we are and what we've done, what makes us tick, what opens our hearts and what rips our hearts to shreds, at least since humans began to put pen to paper. She pressed her hand to her chest, feeling the weight of Levi's loss while acknowledging that the urge to ramble had been hers, not his.

"Can I help you?" A perky voice jerked her attention back to the now. A young woman with an undercut hairstyle—shaved on the bottom, long and tinted blue on top—stood behind a counter dividing the entrance from a clump of computer-topped office desks. As soon as Saffi introduced herself, the young woman's questioning smile broadened. "It's you!" Without another word, she pulled a well-thumbed *Bedside Reader* from beneath the counter, then hesitated before sliding it forward. "I hope you don't mind."

This, Saffi decided, must be the fan who'd arranged the appointment with the medical examiner. Despite her lingering heartache, Saffi mustered a genuine smile. "Are you kidding? I usually have to beg readers to let me sign these."

The young woman leaned her elbows on the counter and

Saffi glimpsed a raven's wingspread tattooed across her collar-bone in the open "v" of her white, button-down cotton shirt. She noticed Saffi's gaze and tapped two fingertips on the tattoo. "Raven's been with me for five years of recovery." The young woman held out a hand. "Hi, I'm Laurie."

"Hi, Laurie." Saffi gave her hand a warm squeeze. "It's nice to meet another Raven mentee."

"Ah. You know her." Laurie gave a sage nod.

"Oh, yes. When Raven talks, I listen."

Saffi took a Sharpie from her bag and wrote: *For Laurie, friend of Raven and fan of Bedside Readers.* She sketched an outline of Raven, then signed *Saffi Graywood* in a calligraphic style she'd practiced for hours before getting it right.

"Thank you SO much!" Laurie clutched the signed book to her chest. "These are my only addiction now."

Saffi beamed. "I'd better keep 'em coming, then!" And she would, as long as fans like Laurie kept reading and her publisher kept the contracts coming.

Laurie tucked the signed volume beneath the counter and waved a hand toward an inner door. "Dr. Boardman is expecting you." She led Saffi through a maze of corridors to an office with *Dr. Valerie Boardman, Medical Examiner* etched into the door's frosted glass. Laurie rapped her knuckles on the glass and a soft voice called, "Come in!"

"Good luck!" Laurie winked.

Saffi nodded her thanks, then turned the knob and stepped inside. Behind a U-shaped brown laminate desk sat a woman about Saffi's age with straight jet-black hair and rose-brown skin a shade paler than her nephew's, as if she spent much of her time indoors under fluorescent lights. Saffi could see the family resemblance, but the medical examiner had a seasoned look her nephew had yet to acquire. Deep furrows crossed her brow and laugh lines crinkled in the corners of her auburn eyes.

"Dr. Boardman? I'm Saffi Graywood. Author of the *Bedside*

Reader series." Saffi held out a hand and the medical examiner rose to give it a tight squeeze. "I'm adding more science to this year's reader," she went on. "So, when Detective Richards mentioned that his aunt was the local medical examiner, I could not pass up the chance to interview you."

Dr. Boardman beamed. "That nephew of mine is making the whole family proud."

"Looks like he's following in your footsteps. Medical Examiner! That's quite a feat."

Dr. Boardman rubbed a finger across the badge she wore on her white lab coat. "You mean, for a woman? Or for a Native?" She put air quotes around the word "Native."

"Without offending, I hope, I mean both." Saffi scrunched her lips together, raised her eyebrows, and waited for the medical examiner's reaction.

After a click, Dr. Boardman burst out laughing.

"Call me Val," she said, motioning for Saffi to pull up a chair to face her desk.

Val turned out to be far more forthcoming than her nephew, especially after Saffi took the liberty of implying that he had sent Saffi her way. As she had hoped, Val seemed delighted to discuss her chosen profession, but skeptical about whether the average reader would want to read about it.

"Most of my job is paperwork." Dr. Boardman waved at the tower of metal stacking trays overflowing onto her desk. "Most days it's *dead* boring."

Saffi gave the lame pun a respectable snort.

"Gallows humor." Val wiggled her eyebrows. "It's how I make it through the day."

Saffi rummaged through her bag for a notepad and gel pen. A page of dark comedy would make a good companion to an article about Dr. Boardman's job.

"So, besides the jokes, what's the most interesting thing about your job?"

"Surprises."

"Surprises?" Saffi coaxed.

Val twined her fingers together and bopped her hands on the desk. "One day, this decedent comes in after a car accident. Officer on the scene's notes say the young woman had rear-ended the car in front of her. Air bag deployed. Driver is transported to the ER. Should have been fine, but no. She's DOA."

"Dead on arrival." Saffi nodded.

"Maybe the air bag killed her. It happens. But when I took a closer look, what do you think I found?"

Saffi scribbled "Disturbing DOAs" followed by two question marks on her notepad. "I have no idea."

"I spotted the first clue right away. Cyanosis."

Saffi looked up.

"Blue discoloration of the skin," Val explained. "The second clue was in her eyes. Petechial hemorrhage. That's tiny burst blood vessels." She gestured toward her own eyes before Saffi had time to ask. "Asphyxiation seemed likely, but was it the air bag?" She waited for Saffi to stop writing and look up. "Nope." She shook her head and grinned. "When I opened her throat, I found a vape pen lodged in it. She must have been puffing away when the air bag deployed. Shot the pen down her throat and cut off her airway."

Val's story was exactly the kind Saffi's readers would devour. She'd need at least six more to flesh out a good *Bedside Reader* article. Val spilled them out for the next hour until the last story—about a swimmer whose cause of death was murder, not accidental drowning—reminded her of the real reason she'd come to see the medical examiner: to find out what the autopsy had revealed about Linda's death. It was past time to plunge in.

"Anything, uhm, unusual about the death of the RV park manager?"

Val's auburn eyes widened. "That's an active investigation. You can't write about that."

"I won't," Saffi assured her. She drew a line beneath the title she'd scribbled earlier, then smiled. "Unless it fits with the others."

Val sputtered, but Saffi held up a hand. "And *only* if it has been solved before my manuscript's due."

"Hmm." Val's brow furrowed, deepening the grooves even more. "OK. My guess? The victim died on the RV park side of the creek, somewhere along that ridiculous jumble of concrete that keeps all those rigs from washing into the cove."

"So, a sneaker wave didn't drag her out?"

Val chewed her lip. "Could have done. The body clearly spent time in the water. Puckered flesh. Evidence of pincer marks."

Saffi shuddered. "Pincers?"

"Crabs, probably. Also, seaweed in her hair. Sand weighing down her clothes. But water didn't kill her."

"And you know that for sure?"

"No water in her lungs," Val said.

Saffi nodded. "Detective Richards told me as much."

"Did he now?" Val licked her lips then pulled a photo out of the file, a close-up of the vicious gash Saffi had glimpsed when she'd found Linda's body. "Look closer." Val pointed at the photo.

Saffi didn't want a closer look, but if she wanted to know what had killed Linda, she had to.

"See these whitish bits in the wound?"

Saffi felt herself going green.

"The victim's head came into contact with a block of concrete, forcefully enough to cause her demise."

"Murder?" Saffi ventured.

Val flicked the edge of the photo as she thought. "Possibly an accident. A backward fall on unstable concrete. I've categorized the death as 'blunt force trauma, cause not determined.'"

Saffi paused her pen. "Isn't blunt force trauma the cause?"

Val shook her head. "No. In forensics, 'cause' refers to whether the death is an accident or a murder. In this case, I can't be certain which. But I can establish the time of death. A few hours either side of midnight."

Saffi raised her brows. *Midnight.* When Raven called. But was it murder? It would take more digging, but Saffi spent her days chasing stories. The story of Linda's death was out there and, no matter how twisted the plot, she wouldn't stop until the mystery had been solved.

NINETEEN

After thanking Val for the interview, Saffi waved goodbye as she opened the office door, not noticing the man standing just outside until she'd slammed into him.

"I'm so sorry, I—" Saffi put up her hands and backed away.

"My fault. Lurking out here like an eavesdropper."

She'd been thinking the exact same thing but the fact he'd said it aloud reassured her that, if he was eavesdropping, it wasn't for nefarious reasons. Though she'd only seen him from a distance, Saffi thought the tall man in the blue suit might be the city manager. What was his name?

"Randall Bevins. City Manager." He held out a hand and Saffi shook it.

"Saffi Graywood."

"Ah. The famous Aunt Saffi!"

How on earth did he know who she was? Her eyes must have held a question, because Bevins answered.

"Glenn. He's been gushing about you."

"Really?"

The compliment and the source came as a surprise, but something tickled at the back of her mind. Something about

Glenn and the city manager? Yes. Saffi tugged at the memory. Delilah had told her that the city manager came to Glenn's defense during Linda's smear campaign. She'd started to say more about why, but she'd stopped herself. Saffi gave Bevins a closer look. He had the patina of a politician. Bespoke blue suit. Polished loafers. Shirt as white as teeth in a toothpaste commercial. His smile didn't quite reach his eyes, but that was often the case with people who had public-facing jobs. If she had to smile at everyone in town to keep her job, she would run screaming for the hills. Randall Bevins had serious blue eyes, Cupid's bow lips, and a chin cleft, like Matt Damon with dark hair, Saffi realized. A bit taller, though. Could Davy Jones and Matt Damon be more than friends? Not a question Saffi wanted to blunder into on a first meeting.

"Here to see Val?" she asked instead, tilting her head toward the still-open door.

"Yes. I was hoping she'd have an update on the accidental drowning. The sooner Val wraps this up, the better off we'll be. The town, I mean." He adjusted his tie, then glanced at his watch. "I'd better get moving."

"Same here." Saffi nodded. "It was a pleasure to meet you, Mr. Bevins. Give Glenn my best."

"Of course!" he said without thinking, then seemed to catch himself. "Next time I run into him, I'll do just that."

So, Saffi mused as she made her way down the linoleum hallway to the exit, the cookie maker and the city manager just might be an item. But if they were, they also might be keeping their relationship hushed.

Saffi didn't know how a meeting that involved photos of deadly injuries could make her stomach grumble with hunger, but as she walked through Last Chance Cove's downtown area, she realized it had. She was trying to remember what was in her tiny fridge when she noticed the Kevin's Kookies van parked in front of a Thai restaurant. Though the Texans had been taking up a lot of sleuthing bandwidth, her encounter with Randall Bevins reminded her that Glenn had a motive for murder and, so far as she knew, the Texans did not. Linda had smeared Glenn's reputation and made sure the city canceled his lease on the bakery he'd inherited from his uncle. The chance of reconnecting with the cookie maker gave her a perfect excuse for indulging in Thai food. She spotted him through the window, dining on what looked like seafood pad Thai at a table half hidden behind a sprawling banana plant.

After ordering massaman curry at the counter, she pasted on a smile and strode up to the cookie maker's table, greeting him like an old friend. "Glenn!"

Glenn stopped mid-slurp and accidentally bit through the noodle dangling from his mouth. He glanced down, plucked the noodle length from his lemon-yellow turtleneck, then shook it in her direction. "Aunt Saffi!"

Saffi laughed. "You're the second person today to call me that."

"Really? Your fame must have preceded you."

"May I join you?" She pulled out a chair and sat without giving him the chance to say no.

Glenn's left eyebrow twitched upward, but he picked up his teacup and saluted. "Sure. Be my guest."

"Actually, I interviewed Val Boardman, the medical examiner, this morning for a *Bedside Reader* article."

"Do tell." Glenn put down his fork and wiped his mouth with his white cloth napkin.

"Nope." Saffi shook her head. "You'll just have to buy the next book."

Glenn picked up his fork, stabbed a prawn and bit it in half. "So unfair," he mumbled around the prawn he was chewing.

Saffi laughed. "I ran into the city manager as I was leaving Val's office. Literally."

Glenn kept chewing. "Hmm-uhm…"

"He's the one who called me Aunt Saffi. Told me you'd been talking about me."

Glenn gulped before he should have. His eyes bugged out and he coughed into his napkin. "S-sorry," he murmured after he'd cleared his throat and slurped a mouthful of tea.

Hoping to keep him off-kilter, Saffi cut to the chase. "He seemed anxious to have the medical examiner close the case on your cousin's death. Any idea why?"

The sip of tea he'd just taken almost came back out, but Glenn clamped his lips and forced it down. After taking another sip he looked her in the eyes. "You're a mystery hound, aren't you? Those books of yours are filled with intrigue. Whodunits. How they dunit. Why they dunit."

Saffi clenched her teeth and looked down at her hands clasped in her lap. "Guilty as charged," she admitted.

"I love mysteries, but I'm afraid you won't find anything *Bedside Reader* worthy in our sleepy little cove. Stay here long enough and you'll understand why Linda's death isn't anything to write about. People die out there"—he pointed his chopsticks toward the cove—"all the time. Randall's just doing his job. Taking care of our town."

Saffi heard the emphasis on the word "our" as a reminder of her outsider status. But was Randall truly taking care of the town, or was he taking care of Glenn, the way he'd done when the town council rose up against him?

A change of topic might garner more information, or at least flatter Glenn enough to get him to open up. "Cookies like yours must require a mastermind."

He held up a finger. "As you already know, Uncle Kevin was the master. I merely inherited his business, and his recipes."

"And Linda?" Saffi paused to let his cousin's name toll in the silence. "What did she inherit?"

Glenn forked a mass of noodles into his mouth, chewing slowly, as if hoping she'd forget her question before he finished.

She put her elbows on the table and folded her hands to rest her chin as she waited… and waited.

"Fine." He parked his fork at the edge of his plate and patted his lips with his napkin. His dark brown eyes narrowed to slits. "Linda inherited exactly what she gave Uncle Kevin in life. *Nothing.*"

"She wasn't too happy about that, or so I've heard."

Glenn tossed his napkin on the tabletop. "Delilah Dunsmore, Mouth of the Cove, strikes again. I love that woman to death, but someone needs to tie a knot in that tongue of hers."

Saffi quirked a brow. "Harsh much?"

Glenn leaned forward. "Harsh? My cousin, who ruined my business, is found dead, possibly *murdered.* Thanks to Delilah, the author of a series that includes many a true crime story is asking questions that lead me to believe she sees *me* as a suspect."

Saffi sat back in her chair. "OK. I deserve that. Sorry. Sometimes I just can't help myself." She shot him what would have been a winsome smile on a younger woman but, on her, probably looked like she had a leg cramp.

A young waitress with sleek black hair spun into a bun with chopsticks brought Saffi's curry and sat it in front of her. "Careful. Plate's very hot." The waitress glanced at Glenn, eyes worried as if she'd observed all the choking he'd been doing. "Everything fine?"

"Excellent. As always." Glenn pushed his plate away. "But I need to go, so if you don't mind?" He nodded toward the Pad Thai starting to congeal on his plate.

"Go box? I thought you were expecting—"

"No." Glenn cut her off. "Just me."

Glenn *had* been expecting someone. She could see it in the way his eyes shifted away from the server when he cut her off. Randall? Maybe they'd planned to discuss what the city manager learned from Val over lunch, until Saffi and her questions intruded.

When the waitress left, Saffi apologized again. "You don't have to leave. I'll get another table."

Glenn scooted his chair back and rose. "No. No. Cookies to sell and all that." His gaze softened and he looked Saffi in the eye. "Be careful, Aunt Saffi. Not everyone in this town will be as understanding of a writer's need to dig deep as I am."

After Glenn left, Saffi picked up her fork and spread her napkin across her lap. He was right. She'd been in town for less than three days. She didn't *really* know anyone in Last Chance Cove. Not even Delilah, much as she liked the feisty barista. Was she a reliable source, or not? The first time she met Delilah, she'd said Bill could be a sweetheart. Bill! Really? Later, she'd defended Linda even though she knew how horrible the park manager had been to Glenn. Saffi was beginning to think Delilah might be the worst judge of character she had ever met.

She took a bite of curry, savoring the creamy flavor of spiced potatoes and chicken. Her tongue detected cardamon, anise, and lemongrass, blended to perfection. *Mmm.* She was glad her sleuthing had brought her in here, but she regretted pouncing on Glenn. He seemed like such a nice guy. On top of that, he seemed genuinely upset about Linda. Not about her death. About the possibility of it being *murder* and Linda's spiteful treatment of him being common knowledge. That, he would certainly know, made him the prime suspect. Whether Saffi sniffed about or not, if he was guilty, she'd made a big mistake cornering him as if he was one of her *Bedside Reader* subjects. Prodding a porcupine, she knew all too well from writing about nature's defense systems in book #11, could result in a face full of quills.

Chiding herself for her folly, Saffi turned her focus to her food, wanting to relish every bite before the curry cooled. She and Levi had loved dining out, discovering new restaurants together. Now that she was on her own, she usually tossed together meals from whatever she had in her staples cabinet or small fridge. Her tiny RV kitchen meant she had to limit the ingredients she kept on hand and, all too often, she found herself munching on spinach wraps or brown rice crackers with hummus. As her belly filled, she decided to take half the curry home in a to-go box for tomorrow's lunch.

A short walk later, she tucked her leftovers into the fridge. The shelves needed filling. She'd spotted a natural foods market between the Thai restaurant and the RV park. A quick trip would do the trick. But first, she needed to clear her head of murder, mystery, and a mishmash of clues before she sat down to write. Every minute she spent away from her computer put her further behind on her manuscript. If she didn't settle in this afternoon and pound out pages, Poppy would be on the phone demanding to know why.

Saffi took her favorite hoodie off a hook in the stairwell and headed toward the beach path. As she passed Aaron's trailer on her right, she spotted him kicked back in a gravity chair, asleep with a book on his belly. Saffi smiled and kept walking, glancing toward the Texans' gleaming Prevost mid-row to her left. She spotted Jeff wrestling his long legs out of what must have been a rental car. The Prevost had not been towing a vehicle when they arrived. Curiosity bubbled in her gut. After all, a few well-crafted questions might get to the bottom of what he was doing outside Nicole's trailer after the bonfire.

Keep walking, Saffi! She could almost hear her editor's voice. Sometimes she pictured Poppy as a tiny figure, standing on her shoulder and carping in her ear. Just as she tucked her head down to continue, a raven swooped across her path. It flew along the row, passing Jeff as he opened the car's trunk and stuck his head inside. The raven perched on the Wi-Fi tower at the other end of the row and cocked its head her way. Saffi's steps stilled. Kicking herself for being an A-plus writing procrastinator, she put her hands in her pockets and strolled toward the Prevost. By the time she reached the site, Jeff was tugging a box out of the rental's trunk. When she cleared her throat, Jeff stumbled backward. The two-pound box of potato chips he'd been manhandling popped out of his hands and landed at her feet.

Saffi raised an eyebrow. "Throwing a party?"

Jeff's face had the guilty look of a man cheating on his heart-healthy diet. "Couldn't resist those grocery outlet prices."

"Your kitchen must have a lot more storage space than mine." Saffi tossed out the compliment, hoping Jeff would invite her inside for a look. He didn't. He just picked up the box and gave her a nod and a wink that said, *Oh, yeah, little lady. You bet it does.*

Saffi stood for a moment, taking note of how bare the Texans' site looked. Some campers with luxury RVs circled chairs around a fancy propane-fueled fire ring and set up an outdoor bar and grill. Others didn't put out a thing, preferring to spend all their time inside. Jeff and Eliza seemed to belong to the latter type.

As she walked past the Wi-Fi tower, the raven squawked and then pointed its beak back toward Jeff. Saffi looked back. She couldn't help herself. All she saw was Jeff wobbling up the steps with his massive box of chips. Saffi grimaced, embarrassed that she'd let a common beach raven divert her attention. Obviously, this was not *the* Raven.

As she turned beachward, the cool wind she'd been hoping would clear her head slapped her cheeks as if to say, "Wake up! Remember why you're here." Saffi hunched inside her hoodie and pointed her sneakers toward the beach path. She scurried past Nicole's place without a glance. *No more sleuthing today,* she promised herself, *except the kind required for writing Aunt Saffi's Bedside Reader.*

As she emerged from the RV park onto the beach, the wind

hit her full force, blowing her hoodie off her curls. Saffi yanked it forward, clutching it against her face. In the summer, a brisk wind often meant blue skies, especially in the afternoon. Beyond the sandy expanse of beach, the cove sparkled. Gulls strained against the stiff breeze, bobbing backward then pushing forward, sometimes frozen mid-air for a fraction of a second by the wind's force. Whitecaps raced atop the blue-gray water. On the other side of the cove, a white kite, string taut, struggled in the blue sky above the aptly named Whale Island. Perhaps Thunderbird nested there still and had swooped down on Linda as she stood on the berm, her back to the feckless sea.

Near the marina, restless seals barked as they jostled for space on the floating docks. As Saffi looked that way, a sport-fishing boat roared into the cove, nose out of the water, white spray kicking up in its wake. A few seconds later, the captain pulled back on the throttle and glided into the no-wake zone. Hoots and cheers echoed in the sudden silence. The faint hint of diesel fuel wafted toward her, and she turned her face until the air cleared, wondering if Troy was behind the throttle, heading in with a deck-load of tourists and their morning's catch.

To keep the wind out of her hoodie, she turned away from the harbor, walking the cove's half-moon beach toward Elk Creek. When the estuary's stream lapped at her shoes and she looked up, her gut clenched. Her steps had taken her to the spot from which she'd spotted Linda's body bobbing with the tide. Her thoughts went to what Val had told her earlier. Linda had died from blunt force trauma, not from drowning. The blow could have happened by accident or been delivered with deadly intent.

Despite how much she liked him, for obvious reasons Glenn still topped the list of potential suspects. The Texans were acting suspicious, but their focus seemed to be on Nicole and Casey. They'd arrived the day Linda died and, as far as Saffi knew, hadn't even met the park manager. Then there was Troy. Had he rushed off to protect his sister and niece from news of Linda's death? Or had he run to alert them that the body had been found? Like Glenn, he'd been in the area earlier that morning, at least according to Mellie.

Saffi stared at her sneakers, watching water seep into them, pressed out of the damp sand by her weight. Her feet went cold. It was time to replace the clogs she'd lost battling the tide as she crossed the creek to the body rocking against the shore. Saffi sighed. Instead of clearing her head for writing, as she'd hoped the beach would do, it simply reminded her of the unsolved mystery surrounding Linda's death.

She spotted a tiny ghost crab beside her shoe, bent down to pick it up, and placed it on her fingertip. At first, she'd thought the dime-sized crab was still alive. It was perfectly formed, its shell paper thin. The crab's four pairs of walking legs were still intact, as were its two pincher-tipped claw legs. One large black eye glistened at the end of each of two eyestalks that bulged from its head. Perfect. But perfectly lifeless. Saffi sighed. At the edge of the continent where land met water life could end instantly. A ghost crab... a woman, the sea's relentless tides did not discriminate.

A sharp bark brought Saffi's head up. She turned away from the estuary to see a scruffy white dog that looked like Archie racing onto the beach. The little dog sped toward the glistening puddle-dotted tideline where beach birds—tiny sanderlings and larger spotted sandpipers—pecked at breathing holes in the sand. Those holes revealed the hiding places of ghost crabs and lugworms, the birds' favorite treats. Just before the dog reached them, the sanderlings spread their wings and launched skyward in a rippling wave. The sand-pipers followed in a second perfectly choreographed wave. The dog stood panting, tongue out, as if satisfied with a job well done. Definitely Archie, Saffi decided, as he sniffed along her footsteps, a small scraggly sleuth in search of a scratch between the ears.

When he found her, Saffi obliged. "Where you been, little guy?"

As if he understood, Archie looked over his shoulder to the top of the berm where two figures sat in red folding chairs, faces hidden beneath floppy beach hats. "Are those your buddies?" Archie tensed, then barked twice toward the berm before racing back the way he'd come. Something had caught his attention, and now it caught Saffi's: the smell of smoke. An instant later, she spotted a wispy spiral rising from the park's center. Her whole body tensed. It wasn't the gray-white smoke of a campfire. The smoke was black. Something manmade was afire. As the smoke thickened, she realized it was something big—like an RV. *Not mine, not mine, not mine.* Saffi ran toward the path, shouting, "Fire! Fire!"

TWENTY

The figures sitting on the berm jumped to their feet. Saffi recognized Nicole and Casey, with Archie now barking at their heels. Casey started forward but Nicole caught her arm, holding her daughter at her side. She leaned toward Casey, mouth moving, then motioned her daughter toward their trailer. Saffi kept running, not stopping her headlong rush until she heard the whoop of sirens converging on the 101, wailing louder and louder as they approached the park.

Someone had already alerted the fire department. Saffi bent forward, hands on knees, to allow her heart rate to slow. *I'm getting too old for this,* she thought. Then she straightened and speed-walked in the direction of the smoke, which seemed to be in a center row, not in the outer loop where her Rambler sat. The knowledge slowed her heart rate a bit. As she got closer, the air tasted heavy, toxic. Her chest tightened and she coughed, lungs resisting the intrusion. A crowd had gathered at the end of one row, as if no one dared go closer. Saffi shouldered her way through. When a gap opened, it revealed the brown and tan Prevost engulfed in flame. *Jeff and Eliza!*

A chill passed through her body. She turned to a couple standing to her left. "Is anyone inside?"

"We don't know," the woman murmured.

"God help them if they are." The man put an arm around the woman's shoulders.

Saffi covered her mouth and nose with her hand, holding in her fear and keeping the acrid air out. In the minutes since she'd spotted the smoke, it had turned into a black column, billowing from the center of the Prevost's roof. Saffi watched in horror as fingers of fire clawed their way up the column and leapt skyward. The thought of someone being trapped inside was unbearable. Why were they all just standing there? Watching?

Just as Saffi started forward, a fire engine roared down the park road, horn blaring as it passed the office. It swung wide into the row behind the blazing rig, scattering Saffi and the other looky-loos in all directions. The second the truck braked, a firefighter wearing yellow gear and black rubber boots hopped off the side and waved his red helmet at the crowd. "Get back, everybody. Back!"

The crowd jostled backward a few steps, then coalesced. No one seemed to want to leave, not even Saffi, despite a vivid picture in her mind of the propane tank in the RV's basement blowing. If it did, the concussion would send them all flying. She crossed her arms in a foolhardy attempt to protect herself and stayed put.

Saffi turned toward the office as an ambulance sped into the park, followed by the fire chief's red SUV. The ambulance parked in the lane just beyond the office, but the chief braked in front of the office, the SUV's tires spitting gravel. When the door opened, the chief sprang out and hurried inside. Seconds later, Bill rushed out and loped across the grounds toward what looked like a power box. He took out a key, opened the box, pulled down a lever and waved an OK to the firefighters. With the park's power off, the area around the firetruck became a frenzy of action, the fire chief shouting instructions and fire-fighters rushing to carry them out.

Saffi noticed a strapping firefighter whose physique looked familiar. He hooked a prybar in the Prevost's front door and forced it open. As a wave of heat broiled out, he leapt back, turning away from the door to remove his red helmet and wipe his face with the back of his hand. Saffi startled. *Troy?* How was he here, fighting a fire, instead of offloading tourists and fish at the harbor? Her hands went clammy as her fears divided between the Carmodys and Troy.

A female firefighter heaved yellow hose from the rig's wheel jet, tucked the heavy-duty nozzle under her right arm, braced her feet and then pulled back a lever to release a gusher of water into the flames writhing inside. When the force made her wobble, Troy grabbed the hose a few feet behind her. Together, they kept the stream aimed toward the door he had levered open. Two more firefighters grabbed long-handled axes and started pounding the luxury RV's windows. With each explosive smash, Saffi jumped. Her nerves jangled and her heart thudded against her crossed arms.

Where were the Carmodys? From where she stood, she couldn't see the rental car. Maybe, just maybe, they weren't inside.

A stream of water gushed through the broken windows of the blazing RV, hissed and steamed as it hit the fire. As the blaze began to cool, the foul black smoke turned white. After a few minutes, the fire chief bellowed, "Hold!" The spray arcing into the rig stopped. Though flames still flickered from the roof, two firefighters headed toward the Prevost's open door. Saffi turned toward a person who'd pushed through the crowd to stand to her right—Bill, as it turned out. "They can't be going inside!"

Bill responded with a supercilious shrug. "Gotta see if anyone's roasting alive in there."

"What is *wrong* with you?" Saffi clenched her fists, her

heart pounding as if she was the one trapped in the conflagration while Bill made cavalier comments from a safe distance. For a few minutes, the yellow-clad firefighters attacked the center of the conflagration, which seemed to be just beyond the door. Then, through the broken windows, Saffi watched the firefighters' red helmets bob through the rig, first toward the front, and then into the back. Thinking about Jeff and Eliza who might, or might not, be Casey's grandparents, Saffi murmured an incantation: *Please don't be in there. Please don't be in there.*

After what seemed like hours, but was probably mere minutes, one of the two firefighters came to the door and twirled a hand in the air, as if signaling an "all-clear."

Saffi's breath burst free. Campers, clumped in twos and threes around her, clapped and whooped their relief. Bill shook his head. "Ten minutes. That's all it took. What a waste," he said as he walked away. The comment shocked Saffi to her core. Ten minutes? From a half-million-dollar luxury vehicle to a blackened gutted hulk.

As Saffi wove through the slowly dispersing crowd, she spotted Nicole at the back, edging her way forward as if to get a better view. Neither Casey nor Archie was with her. Saffi assumed she'd left both behind in the trailer. She glanced past Saffi to the ruined Prevost, shock freezing her in place. A few frantic yips from the direction of the berm turned Nicole's face deathly pale. Then she burst to life, sprinting back toward her trailer. Behind her, Saffi thought she heard Troy's voice calling, "Nicole! Wait!" But Nicole didn't wait. She ran. And Troy, held back by his fire duties, couldn't leave the scene of the fire to run after her.

Though the fire danger had passed, Saffi's body still buzzed with adrenaline. Since Troy was stuck on cleanup duty, she decided to follow Nicole. Her reaction to the Prevost fire seemed extreme, unless she knew whose rig had just gone up in flames.

Saffi had never been a runner, and she wasn't about to start now. Instead, she fast-walked down the lane toward the beach side of the park. Gravel crunched beneath her damp sneakers, the adrenaline spike fueling her speed. When she reached Nicole's trailer, the door stood open. "Nicole?" Saffi stuck her head inside the door. The trailer felt too silent to be occupied, but she called again, a bit louder. "Nicole? Casey?"

No one answered.

How had Nicole disappeared so fast, and where was Casey? Archie? She'd heard Nicole tell her daughter to go to the trailer when the fire started. Where had they gone?

As Saffi stood there, wondering what to do, the energy she'd felt sizzled out and her legs went noodley. Enough chasing clues. It was time to go home.

By the time she reached space 32, her thighs felt like lead weights. When she stepped inside her Rambler, she didn't feel the usual sense of calm, comfort, and safety. She felt vulnerable. Flames had consumed the Prevost as quickly as a child gobbled a charred marshmallow. A bite. A few chews. And the massive RV was gone. Her tiny Rambler would be less than a bite. A mouse-sized nibble.

Saffi wiggled her shoulders, hoping to shrug away her worries. Instead, she caught a whiff of acrid smoke lingering in her hair and clothes, a reminder she couldn't wait to remove. She pulled off her hoodie and turned the shower's hot water knob on full force. Once it warmed, she tempered the stream with a little cold water and stepped inside. As she soaped and rinsed her hair, water ran down her body, gray with soot. It circled the drain and swirled, disappearing down the pipe that led to the park's sewers. She wished the terror she'd felt watching the Prevost burn was as easy to wash away. Every fiber still thrummed with it. The thought of Jeff and Eliza being inside should have been unimaginable, but it wasn't. The theater of her mind ran a constant reel showing—in graphic detail—what it would have been like inside that inferno. Thank God they hadn't been there.

She stepped out of the shower, toweled dry, and snuggled into her terry cloth robe. There was no way she could write after what had happened. Her brain was too wired. So, she pulled an old friend from the bookshelf above her couch: *The Wind in the Willows*. Kenneth Grahame's classic story about Mole and Rat could always ease her mind, and, if she was lucky, send her to dreamland for healing.

The Mole had been working very hard all the morning, spring-cleaning his little home, she read. *First with brooms, then with dusters; then on ladders and steps and chairs, with a brush and a pail of whitewash; till he had dust in his throat and eyes, and splashes of whitewash all over his black fur, and an aching back and weary arms.*

TWENTY-ONE

Pounding. Someone was pounding. Firefighters with axes, pounding on windows, trying to smash them open. Saffi struggled out of the sleepy haze that engulfed her, striving to separate the sound from her dreams. "Saffi!" a voice called. "Are you in there?"

Saffi recognized the voice. She'd heard it before, along with a knock on her door. *Troy.*

"Just a... just a minute!" She untangled her robe from her legs and struggled to stand. For a moment, she swayed, trying to get her bearings. Then she tightened the sash on her robe and went to the door.

"What's going on?" She wiped sleep from her eyes and peered out, not into afternoon sunshine, but into the ruby tinge of twilight. She felt dull, disoriented, as she always did when a few minutes of shut-eye took her into deep sleep.

Troy, still dressed in firefighter's gear, pulled the door open and rushed up the stairs. "Have you seen her? Is she here?" He glanced around Saffi's living room as if there might be a place for someone to hide.

Saffi backed up and collapsed onto her couch. This was all

too much. "Number one, I don't know who or what you are talking about. Number two, you woke me from a sound sleep. Number three, what makes you think you can barge into my home uninvited? That is *not* OK!"

Troy ran a hand through his stubbled slate-gray hair. "I-I'm sorry. I just..." For a moment, his face melted. His gray-blue eyes shone with tears and his broad shoulders sagged. Then he squared his shoulders and set his lips in a grim line. "Casey's missing. Nicole went to check out the fire and when she got back, Casey was gone. Archie, too. We've looked everywhere."

"And for some reason you thought she might be hiding in a virtual stranger's RV?"

Troy looked her in the eye, then down at his mud-spattered boots. "I don't know what I was thinking. You found Archie. You found Linda. I guess I thought... you might have found Casey, too."

As Troy's words sank in, Saffi shook her head. Bewildered. He thought she had the mojo to find things, but that wasn't Saffi. It was Raven. And if Raven had called, she'd been too deeply asleep to hear. "Troy, I'm a writer, not a detective. If Casey's missing, you need to call the police." *And point them toward the Carmodys.* The skulking. The peering into windows. Grandparent kidnapping was a "thing" after all. And it was against the law.

Now Troy couldn't meet her eyes.

"Troy? Please tell me you've called 9-1-1? If someone has taken Casey, they can put out an Amber alert."

Troy toed the woolen rug at the top of her stairs with his boot. "If I tell you something, will you keep it to yourself?"

Saffi didn't even pause. "Ah, no. I don't think so. Since I've been here there's been a murder, a fire, and now, a what? *Kidnapping?* If Casey's in danger, it's time to stop keeping secrets and start telling the truth."

Troy sighed. "Fair enough." He backed up to get his muddy

boots off the mat and onto the entry stairs. "Sorry about the, uh, mess." He waved a hand toward the dark splotches. The woolen throw rug was washable, so she shrugged it away. "When Nicole told me about Casey, I lost my mind. If something happened to that girl..."

Saffi knew exactly what it felt like to lose someone you loved. "Sit. Explain." She nodded toward the couch, then thought twice, and held up a hand. "But, please, leave those boots on the stairs."

Troy turned awkwardly in the narrow stairwell, sat on the edge of the rug he'd muddied and tugged at his boots. Then he shook his head. "Space is tighter in here than on my boat! I'll just stay put."

Levi had found the Rambler a bit tight as well, but his lean body had been sculpted on racquetball courts and running tracks. Troy's muscle mass, on the other hand, had been bulked out and chiseled on decks and docks. Saffi positioned a cushioned dining chair to sit facing him, then tucked her hands under her thighs to stop herself from reaching out to see exactly how big the biceps bulging beneath his firefighter's gear might be.

Stop it! She shook herself. *The man is in crisis. Geez.* She put her elbows on her knees and leaned forward, forcing herself to listen, not look. By the time Troy finished explaining what had happened, she knew two things: one, there was a chance Casey wasn't in danger, and two, Nicole was in deep doo-doo.

As it turned out, Saffi's guess about Jeff and Eliza being Casey's grandparents was dead on. Nicole and her husband Roger, their son, were in the middle of a brutal custody battle which Nicole had little chance of winning. Like her mom, she had married a much older man. He'd left her when a newer model caught his eye—a college student he'd taken on as a veterinary assistant. A heartbroken and furious Nicole wanted to high-tail it out of the Lone Star State and never return. That had been fine with her soon-to-be-ex but not with his parents, who were determined to keep their only grandchild nearby.

"Nicole was too pissed off—excuse my French—to listen to reason. The Carmodys lawyered up." Troy shifted position on the step, hunching forward. "If Nicole wouldn't agree to stay in Texas and share custody, they would get a judge to grant their son sole custody." He glanced at Saffi, eyes glassy as the sea on a windless day. "Nicole was like a chihuahua up against a pack of pit bulls. I told her to stay put. Stand her ground. But she bolted. Took off with Casey in the middle of the night without telling a soul where they were going. Showed up at my boat with six pink suitcases and a niece I hadn't seen since she was eight years old."

Typical, Saffi mused, for a young woman who hadn't spent time living on her own to flee from one man straight into the protection of another. And her big brother had stepped right in to "save" her. Troy had loaned Nicole his camping trailer and explained the situation to Bill, who had taken one look at Nicole and offered her an oceanfront spot at the RV park, no questions asked.

The scurvy dog! Saffi sighed. He hadn't wiggled a mustache whisker to help *her* when she needed a space. If Nicole's life wasn't falling apart so spectacularly, she might have resented her for living the charmed life of the young, blonde, and beautiful. *OK.* She still resented her, but her heart went out to Nicole. Saffi had never experienced divorce herself, but a close friend once told her it sliced through you just like the death of a spouse. That pain was seared into every cell of Saffi's heart. But the threat of losing a daughter? In last year's *Bedside Reader*, Saffi had shared tragic tales of things mothers had done to protect their children. One mom had killed a man who attacked her daughter... during his trial... right in front of the judge. If fear or rage overcame good sense, committing murder was defi- nitely on the list of things a desperate mother might do.

Saffi was left with a single question. Although she'd seen Nicole and Casey on the berm when Archie started barking, she didn't remember seeing the pair on her way to the beach. Once on the beach, she'd spent most of her time staring across the water, birdwatching, brooding, and examining the tiny remains of a ghost crab. Nicole could have started the fire before she and Casey set up their red chairs. Motive, and opportunity.

Saffi looked Troy in the eyes. "Did Nicole start the fire?"

Troy put his face between his hands and squeezed. The resulting fish-face looked both humorous and haunted. "No. No. She wouldn't do that. I'm a volunteer firefighter. I've warned her repeatedly about the danger of fire in an RV. Unless she knew they weren't inside, she could have killed the Carmodys." He hesitated, his brows furrowing so deeply he clearly realized that what he'd said made Nicole *more* of a suspect, not less. He clenched his hands into fists, then seeming to notice, relaxed his fingers, rested them on his knees and let out a firm and final, "No. They're her daughter's grandparents, for God's sake!"

Saffi did not share his certainty, but the fact that Casey had gone missing during the fire could not be ignored. Once smoke started boiling out of the Prevost, every eye had turned that way. If Nicole hadn't done it, who would've had a motive? *The Texans, of course!* Had they set fire to their own rig? While everyone else was absorbed by the spectacle, they could have snatched Casey. When she shared the theory with Troy, he bolted to his feet. "I knew you could help!"

"Whoa! I'm just spinning ideas here. Would *anyone* destroy their own half-million-dollar RV to create a distraction?"

"They're loaded." Troy ticked off one finger. "They're insured." He ticked off a second, then a third. "And they want their granddaughter back in Texas. We need to find Jeff and Eliza."

Saffi cocked her head. "Find them?"

Troy rubbed his face. "No one seems to have seen them this morning."

Outside, Raven croaked, harsh and demanding. Saffi startled. A raven had led her to Jeff wrestling a giant box of potato chips from the trunk of his car. A chill washed over her. *The chips were a clue!* A clue Raven wanted her to share.

"Uhm, this may be nothing, but I saw Jeff on my way to the beach before the fire started. He was carrying this massive box of potato chips into the Prevost. I thought it was odd. It would take Jeff and Eliza a year to eat that many chips. Maybe he was stocking up for Casey?"

Troy jumped to his feet, nearly bashing his head on the ceiling.

"What the—?" Saffi pressed herself into the back of her chair.

"Chips? You saw him with a box of *potato chips?*"

For a second, Saffi felt silly, as if he was chiding her for mentioning something so innocuous, but he looked appalled, not amused. "Yes. A honking big one."

"That's it!" Troy slapped his thigh. "That's why the Prevost went up so fast."

He had to be kidding. "Because of potato chips?"

Troy bounced on the heels of his rubber boots. "Believe it or not, car thieves use bags of potato chips to destroy evidence when they abandon a vehicle. The oil in chips is a potent accelerant. It can set a car seat ablaze in minutes."

Saffi widened her eyes. "Or an RV," she whispered.

Troy nodded. "Exactly. I watched a ton of training videos before I was certified to go out on a fire. In one of them, arson investigators tested what happens when you set a chip bag alight. Not much for a few seconds, then, *Whoosh!*" He flung out his arms to grab Saffi's hands and give them a squeeze. "Without you, we'd have never found the cause. The fire would have obliterated every scrap of evidence. If we can find the Carmodys, we'll find Casey."

The potato chip factor certainly pointed to Jeff, as did the fact that the Carmodys were Casey's grandparents and now she'd gone missing. The hopeful look on Troy's face did Saffi in. Her declaration of not being a detective seemed trite, unfeeling. Troy saw her as someone he could trust in a crisis. That felt good in ways she couldn't even describe. It was time to put on her Sherlock Holmes deerstalker cap and start solving this mystery. Metaphorically, of course. In real life, a deerstalker would obliterate her curls.

So... where to begin? They had some information, but not enough. They needed more sources. More viewpoints. "With everyone watching the fire, who might have noticed what happened to Casey?"

"Bill! He's like a starving seagull when it comes to watching that entrance. Nobody goes in or out without him noticing."

Saffi shook her head. "The fire chief got him out of the office to switch off the power. He was standing right beside me when the firefighters gave the all-clear."

Troy focused on a point just behind her shoulder as if picturing the park in his mind's eye. "OK. Anyway, you'd need a bird's-eye view to watch the whole park. The office doesn't have that."

A bird's-eye view. Saffi scooched forward. "Mellie!"

Troy frowned. "The raven artist?"

Saffi nodded. "She seems to spend a lot of time at the overlook at Beachfront Park. If she was up there, she might have seen something."

Troy was on the bottom stair before he looked up at Saffi with a question on his face. "You're coming, right?"

"Sure," Saffi patted her terry cloth robe, "but it would probably be better if I put on more appropriate clothes."

TWENTY-TWO

By the time they reached Beachfront Park, the sun was an egg yolk sliced in half by the saffron-tinted sea. The benches lining the sidewalk that faced the horizon were empty.

"We're too late," Saffi said. "If she was here, she's packed up and headed home."

Troy hoisted himself out of the truck as if he hadn't heard a word she said. She caught up with him in the grove of trees where Mellie had parked her traveling art gallery the day Saffi met her. Troy seemed to be heading toward a hulking shape tucked inside the dense shadows. If not for the slight reflection of sunset off the box-trailer's gloss-black paint, Saffi would never have spotted it. Troy must have known it would be here. When he reached the trailer, he tapped on the back. "Mellie! It's Troy," he whisper-shouted.

After a few minutes rustling and squeaking, a door in the back of the box swung open, revealing a barefoot Mellie, tying the sash of a red silk kimono over loose black-and-white striped pajamas. Behind the artist, the pink glow of a Himalayan salt lamp washed across white walls, giving a rosy glow to the tiniest home Saffi had ever seen. For a moment, she imagined she could step straight through Mellie's box-trailer into Narnia, the fabled land of benevolent talking lions and fearsome white witches created by C.S. Lewis. She quickly took in the contents: a thick, tufted, rose-velour floor couch with matching backrest pillows propped against one wall; a wooden lap desk with spindly legs that seemed to serve as the artist's studio, its tray tilted to form an easel. Three wicker baskets—one for clothes, one for art supplies, and one for books—filled the front wall of the trailer. Probably not an entrance to Narnia then, Saffi decided, but just as magical. "Wow!" she whispered.

"I'd ask you in, but..." Mellie waved toward her cozy living compartment.

Troy ignored the niceties, cutting straight to the crux of why they'd come. "Look, Mellie, my niece has gone missing. Casey? Blond hair, so high?" He lifted a hand to just below his shoulder. "Saffi thought you might have, you know, seen something from... up here. During the fire."

"Ah." Mellie stepped down from the box and closed the door, shutting the rose-colored light inside. "Don't want 'you know who' to spot me."

It didn't take much to figure out that Mellie meant the police. Not only was she living off-grid, she was doing so inside a city park. Saffi gave her extra points for flouting authority in such a creative way.

"Casey?" Saffi encouraged, and Mellie turned toward her. In the fading twilight, Saffi watched thoughts shifting back and forth across the artist's dark eyes. After a minute, she seemed to come to a decision that left her eyes troubled.

"I didn't see a thing," she said. "Must have been napping."

Troy stepped backward as if he'd been slapped. "Napping? With every siren in town blaring?"

Saffi thought back to her first conversation with Mellie. Thanks to Raven, they'd made a connection, one she might be able to exploit now. "How about the ravens? No alarms?"

"They were... they were quiet." Mellie looked Saffi straight in the eye, but her voice dropped on the last word.

Before she left Temecula, Saffi had written a listicle for her next *Bedside Reader* called "Ten Ways to Spot a Lie." More meaty than a list, less detailed than an article, listicles made facts not only pop but stick in a reader's mind. Like the fact that Mellie's drop in tone, along with making direct eye contact—which 70 percent of liars actually do—meant the artist might have seen something she wasn't willing to share. But what? If she'd seen a stranger abduct Casey, surely she would want the girl rescued. And if she hadn't seen a stranger?

"If we're done here, I have a painting to finish." Mellie stepped toward her tiny abode and reached for the door.

Troy lunged forward as if to stop her, but Saffi hooked her arm through his. "We're done. Thanks, Mellie."

Though he tried to resist, Saffi tugged Troy toward his truck.

"What are you doing? She had to have—"

Saffi slipped her arm out of Troy's and strode toward the truck, guessing he'd be ticked off enough to follow. He was, though he still helped her into the cab after using his key fob to click the door open. Once he got behind the wheel, he turned a fury-reddened face toward her. "OK. What gives?"

After sharing her knowledge of how to spot lying liars who lie, Saffi told him what she thought might be going on. "I think Mellie saw someone with Casey, but I don't think it was the Carmodys. I think it was someone she knows. Someone she trusts."

Troy clutched the steering wheel and stared out at the blue-black cove. "Trust? Mellie? That would be a short list."

"Good!" Saffi pulled the seat belt across her body and buckled it in place. "That should make finding Casey easier."

The list was short, indeed. Glenn, who gave cookies to friends in need, such as Mellie; Delilah, who was willing to accept a used mug as a tip; Troy, who, he disclosed, sometimes shared home-canned jars of tuna and crab with Mellie; and—this one was a surprise—Bill, who had let Mellie camp at Last Chance Cove until Linda pulled the plug, proclaiming her box-trailer "not sanctioned by the city for camping."

Neither Saffi nor Troy had seen Glenn or Delilah at the park during the fire, but they could easily have been missed in the turmoil. Bill was there, right beside Saffi. She couldn't account for the time before he came out of the office or the time after she headed home, but as far as Saffi could figure, Bill didn't have a motive for kidnapping Casey. Defeated, they headed back to where they'd started: Saffi's RV. Troy centered his truck across the drive at the front of her Rambler and leaned back against the seat, shoulders sagging.

Saffi turned toward him. "There's something we're missing. As everyone ran toward the Prevost, what would someone who wanted to snatch Casey do?"

Troy scratched his head. "Get her out of the park?"

"Or hide her." Saffi ticked off all the possible places in the park. The office, bathhouse, or laundry room. All too public. Other than that, the only hiding places in the park were RVs, all of which were owner-occupied. Going door to door wouldn't do much good. They weren't the police, so they couldn't demand to search the premises if something seemed suspicious.

Troy clutched the steering wheel. "Linda's apartment!"

Of course. Linda's empty apartment would be the perfect place to hide Casey. And as far as Saffi knew, only one person Mellie trusted had access.

"Bill!" Saffi and Troy said simultaneously.

Saffi grasped the door handle to hop down from the truck, but Troy put a hand on her shoulder. The warmth of his touch seeped through her hoodie. She would have given a lot to sit there for a minute—or an hour—and soak in the steadying reassurance of his hand but Troy brought her back to where they were and what was at stake.

"Bill's off duty," he said. "If we go to his RV and piss him off, Smudge might go for our throats."

Was he kidding? Saffi wasn't sure. But she was sure of one thing: she wouldn't chance leaving Casey in Bill's clutches overnight, Smudge, or no Smudge. Troy decided to drive to Bill's RV, in case they needed to put metal doors between themselves and the canine's canines.

Not surprisingly, Bill lived in a bedraggled fifth wheel tucked behind a rusted, white, half-ton pickup. The cab-over trailer looked as if it hadn't moved in months. Even in the gathering dark, she could make out scraggly grass surrounding the trailer's wheels. Saffi wondered if Bill's truck bed had the U-shaped hitch needed to pull the fifth wheel. The paperwork he'd handed her after booking her monthly site clearly stated that all campers had to keep the means to pull their rigs out of their spaces. If Bill's spot was an example, park hosts weren't held to the same standards as regular campers. Monthly campers were required to keep their sites in good condition, but just outside Bill's RV, a weathered picnic table sagged beneath a jumble of planks. Saffi pictured Bill making them walk one of those planks, straight into Smudge's jaws. She wondered, for a second, why Linda had let him get away with it. She was, after all, the park manager. It would have been her job to make sure park hosts kept their sites ship-shape.

"Ready?" Troy interrupted her musing with a raised brow.

Was she ready to face a pissed-off pirate with a snarling German shepherd? Not really, but she *was* ready to help Troy find his niece. They grasped the truck's door handles at the same time and swung them open. Before their boots touched the ground, a growl rose from inside the fifth wheel, low and slow at first, but as they approached the door, the growl sharpened into a warning bark that became more and more frantic as

Troy reached the steps. Saffi couldn't help remembering an article she'd written about dangerous dogs. German shepherds were number three on the list, just behind pit bulls and Rottweilers. Despite being first choice as police dogs for their keen intelligence, work ethic, and control when well-trained, in the hands of a careless owner their aggressive, territorial nature could turn deadly. Saffi's hands went cold, and she tucked them under her arms. Troy's shoulders rose and fell as he took a deep breath and knocked.

"Smudge! Hush!" They heard Bill's rebuke through the thin RV walls. Smudge didn't hush, but he went back to the low and slow growl which sounded louder and scarier once Bill cracked open the door spilling light and the noxious scent of man cave into the night.

"Hey, Bill!" Troy lifted both hands in the age-old greeting that meant, "My hands are empty. I'm not a threat."

"Hey," Bill rumbled. "What's up?"

"Just wondering if you'd seen my niece this afternoon."

Bill went very still. Then he pushed the door open wider, giving them a view of Smudge, at heel but alert, ears pressed forward, teeth bared, and not—Saffi couldn't help noticing—on leash. The park host rubbed his scruffy beard with one hand as if thinking back over his day. "Saw her up on the berm earlier. With her mom."

Saffi frowned. "Weren't you in the office?"

"Yep. Got a fine pair of binoculars. Helps me keep an eye on the place." He winked at Troy. Saffi couldn't repress a cringe. Troy's jaw tightened. The idea of Bill eyeballing his sister and niece must be making him seethe but he managed to control his emotions. He'd been right about Bill. He was a watcher, and he'd just admitted watching Casey and Nicole.

"The girls set up chairs just after those Texans headed into the redwoods for the day."

The girls. Saffi stiffened. *What was it with this guy?* Troy glanced her way, holding her gaze until she pressed her lips together and lifted her chin. They needed Bill's information more than she needed to squash him like the cringey cockroach he kept proving himself to be.

"You saw the Carmodys leave the park?" Saffi asked.

"Yep."

If Jeff and Eliza had left for the redwood forest before Casey and Nicole went up on the berm, then they couldn't have taken her. But if Bill had his eye on the girl, the fire could have given him just the opening he needed to snatch her. He had, Saffi realized, left the fire scene just after Nicole arrived. The thought sent a chill across Saffi's shoulders.

"You seem to keep up with everyone's goings and comings." Saffi tried to sound admiring.

Bill grinned, showing his nicotine-stained teeth. "Part of my job. Advising tourists about local attractions."

"How about after the fire?" Troy pushed Bill back to his original question. "Did you see Casey after all the excitement?"

"Nopedy nope-nope-nope." Bill scratched his nose, then glanced down at Smudge. "Anything else I can help you with before I take Smudgie on his walk?" He reached to grab a long red leash off a hook on the stairwell wall. As he did, a red bandanna flopped to the floor. Bill snatched it up and stuffed it in the back pocket of his jeans.

"Is that Archie's bandanna? The one you were going to turn over to the police?"

Bill snorted. "What is it with women? You read a bunch of crap into everything, even a man's cleaning rag."

From the looks of Bill's site, he hadn't touched a cleaning rag since he'd been in the park. Before she could say more, Troy put a hand on her shoulder and gave a gentle squeeze, a reminder that their goal was to find Casey, not pick a fight with the park's resident misogynist. She squirreled away what she'd seen to share with Detective Richards. As for the red leash?

She'd seen Casey walking Archie on a long red leash, just like that one. Saffi knew she shouldn't read too much into it. Red leashes were common. But the leash was a flag she would not ignore, as was the suspicious way Bill snatched up the red "cleaning cloth."

"Thanks for your help," Troy said. "If you happen to see Casey—"

"Or Archie!" Saffi interjected, watching to see if Bill would react. He glanced up from hooking the leash to the German shepherd's collar, lips tight.

"Give me a buzz, OK?" As Troy finished his question, his eyes looked haunted. Clearly, he'd gotten just enough information to terrify him, but Saffi had a smidge more. When Bill left behind his usual gruff speech pattern for that bit of baby babble, he'd tipped his hand. She'd learned to pay attention to changes in speech patterns from that same listicle about recognizing lies. Bill had seen Casey. She was sure of it. The red leash might be a coincidence, or a clue, but the image of Smudge lunging at Troy's throat made her hold her tongue. She'd wait, and watch, because Bill wasn't the only one who could keep tabs on the park. She had binoculars, too, with military-grade night vision, and she wasn't afraid to use them.

Instead of getting into the blue pickup, she folded her arms. "I can walk back if you want to check on Nicole. She must be frantic."

Unexpectedly, Troy chuckled. "Frantic is my little sister's middle name. But you're right. If you don't mind, I'll head to her place. Let her know what we have, and haven't, discovered. Maybe try to talk her into calling the police. Casey would have come home by dark if she could. If her grandparents don't have her," his voice caught, "we need law enforcement on her trail."

Gravel crunched under Saffi's hikers as she headed toward space 32. She kicked her shoes off on the stairs then headed to the drawers beneath her closet to look for black clothes. She pulled out a long black turtleneck and thick black leggings. She bundled up in the warm clothes and grabbed her binoculars off the dash, then turned out the lights. Unlike Bill, she didn't want light spilling out when she opened the door. Instead of hikers, she slipped her feet into soft-soled moccasins to stifle her steps. Once outside, she lifted the binoculars to her eyes and scanned the rows nearest her space. *Nothing.* The park seemed strangely subdued after the day's calamity. No TVs blared. No flashlights bobbed along the rows. No country music bounced off the mist-soaked air. Even the sea had gone quiet, save for a soft *swish-shush* against the shore. No gulls cried. No ravens croaked.

Saffi stilled her breath and waited. Then, in the quiet between the mournful cries of the foghorn, she heard a single sound—a soft yip, coming from the direction of the bathhouse. *Archie?*

OK. Saffi inhaled. *Let's do this.*

A few seconds later, she was creeping along the side of the concrete building that housed the bathhouse, laundry room, and —on the second floor—Linda's apartment. Her ears were alert for the smallest yip or muffled cry, the kind reading too many mystery novels had led her to expect. She stayed in the shadows, avoiding the moth-haunted lights that illuminated the entrance to the laundry room on one end and the bathrooms on the other. Saffi was debating whether to dare the lights and take a quick look inside all three rooms when a raven's harsh croak made her jump so hard the binoculars flew out of her hands. Fortunately, she'd hung them from her neck. Unfortunately, they whacked her chest hard enough to make her cry out.

Not helpful, she sent Raven a mental rebuke. It took a few seconds to notice that the bird's rasp had stopped her just beneath the beachside window of Linda's second-floor apartment. Saffi stepped back from the building, hoping to get a look inside. Her timing could not have been worse. At the same moment, a hooded figure rounded the corner of the bathhouse and slammed into her. Before she could catch her breath, strong hands gripped her shoulders and pushed her into the light in front of the men's room.

In a split second, Saffi took stock of her resources. She knew enough tai chi to hurt herself, but probably no one else. Bizarrely, a refrain from a kindergarten exercise song blasted into her mind: "Head, shoulders, knees and toes." Head block. Shoulder slam. Knee lift. Toe tackle? *Oh, gods.* Why was she skulking about in the dark when she could have been home, curled up with a good book?

"Saffi?" The hands gripping her shoulders gave her a little shake. "Saffi!"

Someone was calling her name. She blinked, focusing for the first time on the person in the hoodie. "Delilah?"

Delilah let go and stepped back. "What the devil are you playing at? You nearly knocked me into next week!"

"I-I'm pretty sure you ran into me," Saffi stuttered. She leaned forward, hands on knees, giving her heart time to stop detonating behind her sternum.

"I wasn't expecting a ninja lurking outside the restroom, was I?"

Saffi looked down at her all-black garb. She couldn't blame Delilah for running into someone she couldn't see. What she could blame her for was the worn red leash clutched in her right hand which was attached to—

"Archie!" Saffi's chin came up and she gave Delilah a look of accusation. "What are you doing with Casey's dog?"

Delilah stiffened. "Whoa, Nellie. First, he's not Casey's dog, he's Linda's. Second, Bill found the little guy wandering alone in the park when he did his evening rounds. He had Smudge with him and the two dogs don't get along. Archie has some kind of grudge against that German shepherd. Whenever they get near each other, Archie goes bat-guano crazy. So, Bill left Archie leashed to the rail outside the men's room and asked me to take him home with me when I got off work."

Saffi clutched her binoculars. "That is the lamest story I've ever heard."

Delilah's eyes bulged. "Are you... are you calling me a liar?"

"I don't know. Should I?"

Delilah pushed her hood off her red curls, leaving them standing at attention. The knuckles on the hand clutching Archie's leash went white. "You should not! I don't even know why you would. I thought we were friends!"

By this time, Archie was whimpering. Delilah picked him up and tucked him into the crook of one arm. "It's OK, little guy. Saffi doesn't know she's being an old meanie." She kissed him on top of his scruffy white head.

"Sorry, Archie. I didn't mean to scare you." Saffi held out her hand for him to sniff. When he gave it a lick, she knew he forgave her. Would Delilah? "I'm sorry. Really. Of course, we're friends. At least, I hope so. Honestly, I'm a little freaked out right now, first the fire and now Casey's gone missing. It's a lot."

"Wait! Casey is *missing?*" Delilah's grip on Archie tightened and, when he squirmed, she set him down.

Saffi nodded. "She's been missing since the fire. Troy and I were at Bill's trailer no more than twenty minutes ago. He didn't say a word about finding Archie, even though I asked him to tell us if he did."

Delilah looked dumbfounded. "I didn't— I didn't know any of this." She raked her fingers through her hair.

"So, why would Bill ask *you* to retrieve Archie instead of taking the dog to Nicole's trailer?"

Delilah knelt down to give Archie a comforting scratch beneath the chin. "Well, I had told Bill I thought Archie should be with me, not a couple of strangers who'll be out of here sooner rather than later. Look, Linda could be the Witch of the

West when she wanted to be, but I was her closest friend in the park. And this place is Archie's home."

Archie cocked his head sideways to give Delilah more room for scratching and Saffi's stance softened. Obviously, the little terrier knew and liked the barista. It made sense for Delilah to keep him. Nicole had already told Casey they couldn't keep the terrier. But that didn't change what Bill had done. Passing Archie off to Delilah instead of telling them he'd already found the dog made her suspect Bill more than ever. Archie had been with Casey before the fire. If Bill had something to do with her kidnapping and Archie went nuts around Smudge, he wouldn't keep the little dog at his RV. If Archie started yapping his head off that would send an alarm through the entire park. Playing on Delilah's love of the dog must have seemed ideal. He could rid himself of Archie's telltale bark and hide what he was really up to.

Raven croaked nearby, reminding Saffi of what she'd been trying to do when the bird last alerted—she still needed to try to get a look into the beachside window of Linda's apartment. A featherlike idea tickled her mind. From what Delilah had just told her, she and Linda were closer than she'd thought. Maybe the barista had a key to her apartment.

TWENTY-THREE

Saffi thought hard about asking Delilah. She reminded herself that, much as she liked the barista, everything she knew about her could fit inside an oyster shell with the oyster still in it. She was relying on nothing but her gut. She cocked her head, hoping Raven might offer a low gurgle of encouragement or a shrill discouraging alarm. Raven stayed stubbornly mute.

Fine! Saffi took a deep breath and stilled her thoughts to check in with her gut. Her gut had gone to bed for the night and strongly recommended that she do the same.

"Hello?" Delilah snapped her fingers in front of Saffi's face. "Are you in some kind of trance?"

Saffi chuckled. "Something like that."

"So, should I take Archie home or what?"

Since none of her instincts disagreed, Saffi nodded. "I think that's a good idea. But first, uhm, I was wondering if you might have a key to Linda's apartment."

Delilah tightened her grip on Archie's red leash. "I might."

Saffi dared to reach out a hand to squeeze Delilah's shoulder. "Casey's missing, and there are only a few places on the grounds someone could hide her."

Delilah pulled a frown. "You mean, besides the eighty-odd RVs all over the place?"

Saffi dropped her hand. "That's why I like you. You have a way of pointing out glaring flaws in my theories."

Delilah blew on the bejeweled purple nails of the hand not holding the leash and then polished them on the front of her hoodie as if to say, *"Impressive, aren't I?"*

"Well, yes, except..." Saffi pointed toward the fake nail now stuck to Delilah's hoodie by one of the glimmering faux diamonds. *So that's how she changes her nail color so often.* Saffi let a grin spread across her face.

Delilah plucked the nail off her hoodie and stuffed it into the pocket of her jeans. "Yes, well, loose nails aside, what makes you think Casey would be in Linda's apartment?"

Saffi had to stop and think. She'd headed this way in the dark of the night because she'd heard Archie yipping from this direction. Flimsy, she now realized. Then Raven had croaked and she'd... OK, she'd jumped to a conclusion without any evidence whatsoever.

She gave Delilah a big toothy grin. "Raven told me?"

Delilah's eyes widened. "Dang, girl. Why didn't you say so. Let's get that key!"

As they walked Archie back to Delilah's tiny Terry trailer, Saffi tried to match the barista's determined stride but her soft-soled moccasins did little to cushion her feet from the gravel. She minced along a few steps behind, lips pressed together to keep from punctuating the park's brooding silence with "uffs" and "ughs" and "ouchies." As they slipped past Troy's truck parked crosswise of Nicole's drive, Saffi imagined him inside, trying to convince his half-sister to dial 9-1-1. Delilah set Archie up with water and dry dog food, which she kept on hand for the times Linda asked her to dog-sit. Though her trailer was tiny, Archie snuggled up beneath the dining table like he'd come home. The contented look on Delilah's face told Saffi she'd be the perfect new mom for the little terrier.

The park remained quiet as they headed back toward the bath-and-laundry house with Linda's key in hand. Saffi kept to the grass to avoid bruising her feet any more than she already had on the gravel. Last Chance Cove kept nighttime illumination to a minimum. Despite increasingly large and luxurious recreational vehicles, people who preferred camping to hotel stays wanted to feel like they were in the great outdoors, not the middle of a light-polluted city. At the moment, most of them had cozied themselves inside for the night with their blinds shut against stray beams of moonlight. The only lights illuminating their sites were the downward-streaming beams from the light-house-shaped power outlets. Helpful, when one pulled into the park after dark; however, right now at least a third of the bulbs seemed to have burned out. Not so helpful. The moon hadn't expanded much since Saffi arrived at the park, so they set their sights on the utility light above the laundry room door. When they reached it, Delilah slipped past and rounded the corner to a door Saffi hadn't noticed.

"Storage room," Delilah whispered. She unlocked the outer door, and then gestured Saffi inside. There wasn't enough light to make out what was stored in the narrow room, but the smell of mildewed mops and bleach made Saffi pinch her nostrils. She heard metal scrabbling against metal as Delilah tried to fit the key into the keyhole of an inner door Saffi could barely make out. After a few "Holy barking sea lions!" and "Blasted barnacles!" Saffi heard a click as Delilah turned the key in the lock.

"Let's go." Delilah tugged the binoculars still hanging from Saffi's neck, guiding her up one step, then two. Together, they crept up a steep, narrow—and very dark—staircase. The stench of mildew retreated slightly as they went higher, morphing into the sour reek of carpeting that had been shampooed sometime in the distant past and never quite dried out. She pressed a hand over her mouth, praying that a hacking fit wouldn't alert anyone to their presence.

Just as Delilah stepped into the room above, a fear-drenched voice squeaked, "Bill?"

Casey! Saffi took the last step so quickly she tripped. The threadbare carpet did little to soften the blow of both knees slamming into the floor. She bit her lip against the pain and let out a soft, "Ow, ow, ow."

Casey yelped and jumped to her feet. "Who's there?" she demanded.

"It's Delilah, sugar. And Saffi." The barista used the same calming tone she'd used on Archie earlier. "Can you flip on a light?"

Casey fumbled in the dark before her fingers found the switch on a lamp made from a green glass fishing float wrapped in knotted rope. Light flooded through the sand-colored linen shade, casting a warm glow on a room that looked as if it had been decorated in the 1970s and left to molder. Saffi hobbled over to a faded floral couch dressed in the ménage à trois of seventies' color: harvest gold, avocado green, and burnt orange.

"Casey," Saffi squeezed out as she eased herself onto the couch's flattened cushions. "We've been looking all over for you. What are you doing up here?"

Dark smudges shadowed Casey's blue eyes. They seemed twice their normal size, three times as haunted, and near replicas of the framed big-eyed girl reproduction on the wall behind her. She answered Saffi's question with a single word: "Hiding."

"Hiding? From *who*?" Delilah's voice edged into meltdown territory.

"My mom." Casey's answer was so soft Saffi struggled to parse what she'd said. Casey was hiding from her mother? Why?

A stair creak made Delilah whirl around. Saffi rose off the

couch, just enough for her knees to scream in protest, and then dropped back down. A blue wool Greek fisherman's cap bobbed above the half-wall, blocking her view of the stairs, but Delilah's face relaxed.

"Bill," Delilah acknowledged his presence. "What in the name of Davy Jones's locker is going on here?"

Bill cocked his hat and scratched his hairline, his eyes on Casey. "You OK, kid?"

"OK?" Saffi managed to stand without wobbling, but barely. "How could she be OK? You've squirreled her away in this moldy apartment while her family is going crazy trying to find her."

Bill tugged his hat back down. "Are they?"

Heat rose into Saffi's cheeks. "You know they are!"

"Then why haven't they called the police?"

Delilah looked from Bill to Saffi and back again. "She's been missing all afternoon, and they haven't reported it?" The barista's eyes darkened.

"Nope. Casey?" He lifted his chin toward the girl trembling in front of the couch. "Want to tell them why?"

Casey looked at the floor, then at her reflection in the picture window. Night had turned the glass into a mirror. Saffi could see the moment when the girl decided to share what had happened.

"My mom and dad are splitting up. She wants me to live with her. He wants me to live with him. They just kept fighting and fighting. And shouting! Every day. It was awful. I just... I just hid in my room." Tears caught in the girl's dark eyelashes. "So, when Mom asked me if I wanted to visit Uncle Troy out here on the coast to get away from the tension, I said yes."

"But she didn't tell you the whole story, did she?" Bill encouraged.

Casey shook her head. "No. She didn't."

"The woman kidnapped her own kid and swore her to

secrecy," Bill stormed. "Took away her cellphone so she couldn't call her dad or grandparents."

Casey's eyes regained a bit of sparkle. "I got some of those Last Chance Cove postcards from the office and mailed them to Grammie Eliza. Bill gave me some stamps." Her lips trembled as she shot him a small smile. "But I didn't know my grandparents were here. Not until Bill came by after the RV fire."

Had Nicole known that the Carmodys were in the park? Saffi tried to construct a timeline in her head. The morning Linda went missing, Casey had been out and about, helping with the search. The next day, when Casey and Archie stopped by Saffi's RV space, the girl had been out walking the dog. But, Saffi remembered, Nicole had told Casey not to leave their trailer. Motherly caution? Maybe. That evening, after the bonfire, Saffi had warned Nicole about the man in the Stetson peering into their window. After that, Nicole seemed spooked enough to keep Casey close. Until the fire lured her away.

Saffi shook her head. The timeline suggested that Nicole *could* have been frantic enough to set the fire. But Troy's potato chip theory and the fact that Bill had taken Casey during the fire pointed a finger at the Carmodys, not Nicole.

Saffi glanced at Casey. By this point, the girl looked like her own knees were about to give out. "Sit." Saffi patted the couch and Casey sank down beside her.

"Bill said—" Casey gulped down a sob. "He said my *mom* set that fire. She burned their bus, and sh-she didn't even know if they were in it or not."

Saffi stiffened. "Bill told you that?"

Casey sniffed. "Yes."

"And how would he know such a thing?"

Casey's eyes went from sad to confused. "I... Bill?" She turned toward the park host, whose eyes shifted away.

His shoulders hunched. "Saw her by the Prevost right before it started smoking, didn't I?"

Saffi shot to her feet, ignoring her stiffening knees. "You most certainly did not!"

Bill took a step forward. Looming over Saffi, he clenched his fists and glared. "I've had just about enough of you and your smarty-pants writer ways. Coming in here all uppity with your nose in the air like you're better than the rest of us."

Saffi forced herself to stand her ground. She hadn't told Bill about her writing, and she certainly held no illusions that her anthologies were more than recreational reading. How he knew, she could only guess. Park gossip? But his jibe told her one thing: the fact that she was a writer somehow intimidated him. Otherwise, why flip out about it?

Delilah wedged herself between them. "Back off, Bill." She stuck a long purple fake fingernail into Bill's chest and shoved it in like a dagger. Luckily for him, several layers of fluorescent-yellow park vest, zippered gray hoodie, and worn blue T-shirt protected his skin.

"Saffi? What makes you think Bill didn't see who set the fire?"

"He couldn't have. He was in the office, and you can't see the Carmody's RV site from there."

"And who told you where I was?" Bill glared.

"You did. And Troy was with me, so I have a witness. You told us you were in the office watching Nicole and Casey on the berm through your *binoculars*!"

"Ooh. Ick." Casey pressed her body against the back of the couch.

"What do you have to say about that?" Delilah squinted at Bill.

The park host had just opened his mouth to speak when footsteps pounded up the stairs.

"Casey!" Troy's frantic voice heralded his emergence from the stairwell. He pushed past Bill and headed straight for his niece, pulling her off the couch and into his embrace.

"You're OK. Thank God, you're OK. And you!" He whirled toward Bill. With one arm clutching Casey to his side, he thrust a rigid finger into Bill's chest. Unlike Delilah's soft poke, his shove was hard enough to shift the park host off balance.

A throat cleared in the stairwell. "That's enough, Troy. I'll take it from here." Detective Richards stepped into the dimly lit living room.

Delilah's right brow shot up and she turned on Bill. "Thought you said they didn't call the police?"

It took a few minutes to sort out what had led Troy and the detective up those stairs. Yes, Troy had persuaded Nicole to call the police. Just after Detective Richards met him outside Nicole's trailer, they noticed the light on in Linda's apartment, when the place should have been dark and deserted. Even with just a table lamp, they could see the scene unfolding behind the beachside window as if they were in a cinema watching a film. Detective Richards had told Nicole in no uncertain terms to stay in her trailer, but he couldn't stop Troy from racing toward the bathhouse and up the stairs—made easy by the fact that Delilah and Saffi had left both the outer and inner doors wide open.

"Mr. Kidd," Detective Richards stepped toward Bill, "I'll need you to come down to the station to answer a few questions."

Kidd? Saffi coughed into her hand to stifle a laugh. Bill's last name was Kidd? Had his parents really named him after William Kidd, the infamous Scottish pirate who inspired Robert Louis Stevenson's *Treasure Island?* Life in RV parks was informal. Exchanging last names wasn't common. Part of why Saffi offered her last name when she met new people was to make park life feel more like home. But she couldn't blame Bill for not owning up to that one.

Bill pulled her out of her reverie by rounding on the officer.

"I'm not going anywhere! I didn't do a thing but protect that kid!" He pointed at Casey.

Troy bared his teeth the same way Smudge had done when he growled at them earlier. Bill drew back his finger and stuck his hands under his armpits.

"Did you have her mother's permission to bring her here?" Detective Richards asked. His face remained calm, but his body was balanced, ready to spring into action if need be.

"Her mother is a lying conniving broad, just like that ex-wife of mine! And an arsonist to boot!" Bill's face had gone rage red, and he yanked the fisherman's hat off his head to slap his leg with it.

"My sister is not an arsonist!" Troy's hands clenched. "The *real* arsonist is—"

Detective Richards held up a hand. "The fire will be investigated by the proper authorities," the detective said. He gave Troy a look that told Saffi he'd already heard the potato chip theory and wanted to keep it quiet. "For now, Mr. Kidd, you need to come with me."

Bill shrank back. "I can't go with you! I have a park to take care of."

"I'll let the city manager know you'll be out of the park until further notice."

"Further notice? Why? I told you. I haven't done anything!"

"Mr. Kidd." Detective Richards' eyes darkened, and he pressed his full lips into a taut line. "You sequestered a minor in an undisclosed place without her mother's permission."

"The kid came up here of her own free will!"

"She's a *minor*." Detective Richards let the word hang in the air long enough to sink in.

Bill's ruddy cheeks went pale.

"While you have him, you might want to check his back pocket." Now seemed the perfect time for the detective to find Archie's bandanna. Proving he'd withheld evidence in a murder case would make it harder for the worm to wriggle off law enforcement's line. Detective Richards raised an eyebrow but checked both back pockets.

"Getting too familiar back there aren't you, Officer?" Bill sneered.

The detective's brown complexion went rosier than usual and the look he gave Saffi when Bill's pockets proved empty silenced her tongue. *Fine.* She'd caught him once; she could catch him again. Besides, seeing Bill perp-walked down the stairs gave Saffi more pleasure than it probably should have, given the situation.

"Delilah!" he yelled over his shoulder. "Take care of Smudge! He hates being alone at night."

"I can't watch Smudge. I have Archie!" Delilah yelled back.

"Troy! Troy! Smudge knows you. Watch out for him, would you? There's a key under the mat."

Troy's face went from shock to disbelief to anger to grudging acceptance. He might be furious with Bill for hiding Casey from her mother, but it warmed Saffi's heart to know he wasn't the kind of guy who would leave a dog alone and scared. Even one that might tear his throat out under the right—or wrong—circumstances.

Pain pulsed in Saffi's knees as she stepped up into her Rambler. They'd be the color of rain clouds by morning. She undressed without bothering to turn on any lights and eased into bed, trying not to set off a new round of throbbing. How could so much drama happen in one day? The morning was now a distant blur. She'd met with Val and learned that Linda hadn't drowned but had died from blunt force trauma. She'd tipped her hand to Glenn over Thai noodles. He now knew she saw him as a suspect and had warned her about the dangers of sleuthing. She'd seen a fire consume the most expensive RV in the park, then helped track down a kidnapper, or, at the very least, a misogynist who didn't have the sense God gave him. The one bright spot was watching Troy walking Casey home. His niece's head resting against his arm told Saffi that the girl had at least one person she could trust. Was there anyone at Last Chance Cove Saffi could trust? No. So far, the park at the edge of the continent seemed to harbor too much mystery and mayhem to engender trust.

TWENTY-FOUR

Saffi emerged one eyelid at a time from a dream in which she'd been captured by a gang of nine-year-old boys. Their leader, Billy the Kid, wore a red bandanna and sported a bushy mustache. He was demanding that she put on a bulky yellow safety vest, but she refused because it clashed with her hair which, somehow, had turned henna red, just like Delilah's.

She rousted herself out of bed and into the shower. Surprisingly, her knees were a bit sore this morning, but not bruised. The mildewed carpet in Linda's old apartment must have been thicker than it looked. She let the shower run as hot as she could stand it and stepped beneath the flow. It released the dream tension from her shoulders but did nothing to soothe her knees. For that, she'd need movement—a walk or a bike ride. Sitting down to write was out of the question. If she did that, she'd end up stiffer than a salt-crusted towel left on the beach.

She stepped out of the shower and swaddled her body in her oversized terry cloth robe, set water and oats to boil on her propane stove and opened the dining area window to let the gas fumes escape. Fresh sea air flooded the living room and she stood in front of the window, watching seabirds dip and dive as they fished for breakfast in the cove. Once her oatmeal had thickened and softened, she dished it into one of her two white ceramic bowls, then chunked it up with cashews, pecans, raisins, and blueberries. She sat down at her tiny table, sprinkled the hot oats with cinnamon and dug in.

"Breakfast with the birdies!" She saluted the window with her spoon.

After dressing in thick gray leggings and a long yellow tunic —disturbingly reminiscent of the safety vest in her dream—she stuck her feet into her sneakers. They were still clammy from being soaked at the beach the day before. She'd planned to head straight to Delilah for her morning coffee, but changed her mind.

"Time for those new clogs."

Hoping a bike ride into town wouldn't aggravate her sore knees, she turned left out of the park and pedaled at speed to Last Chance Mercantile, the quaint general store she'd noticed on yesterday's walk. The two-story building wore the same beach-blue shingles as its neighbors, but the architecture reminded Saffi of a Wild West hotel. A fancy facade extended above the gable roof and fat spindle pillars braced a balcony along the top floor. Saffi locked her bike to one of the ubiquitous wave-shaped racks and headed for the door.

The smells hit first: leather and wool and wood, chocolate and spice, pine and eucalyptus, overlain with a heart-tugging whiff of nostalgia. The massive plank-floored space was crowded with wooden shelves and glass cases crammed with everything from bags to boots, hats to hoodies, kitchen tools to kitsch. She skirted past wooden barrels overflowing with bags of licorice mix, Swedish fish, horehound candy, and dark chocolate caramels, but she kept going until she hit the clothing section. Despite her cozy yellow tunic, the wind coming off the cove had given her shivers the shivers. She picked out a soft gray hoodie with a black stylized raven on the front to block the chill. In the shoe section, she found sloggers, waterproof slip-ons that would be harder for the ocean to suck off her feet. She brooded over the colorful whimsical choices, narrowing it down to red shoes with yellow chickens or a light-blue pair with fat bees and perky daisies. The bees won. Before she went back outside, she slipped the hoodie over her tunic and pulled it down to her hips. The extra warmth made her ride to the harbor only half as chilling as it would have been.

"So, Bill has an ex?" Saffi murmured over the top of the oat-milk mocha Delilah set on the counter in front of her. Did the nugget he'd let slip last night explain why he hated women? At least—from what Saffi could tell—women of a certain age.

Delilah twisted her lips in thought. "He never mentioned one, but come on! Nothing unusual there. Most men like Bill have a string of 'em. Now that"—the barista gave a slight nod toward a table by the window—"is new."

Saffi twirled her stool to face an astounding vignette she hadn't noticed when she hurried into the café: Jeff and Eliza sharing a table with Casey and Nicole. A barrier of steaming mugs and luscious pastries separated them but, so far, no one seemed to have taken a sip or a bite. Casey leaned toward her grandparents, hands planted flat, eyes excited. The picture of a girl happy to be reunited with family. Nicole sat mannequin-stiff, face immobile, like a kid caught playing truant. Her flight to the cove had been a last chance to wrench custody of her daughter away from her soon-to-be ex-husband—a gamble she appeared to have lost.

Some might say Casey's grandparents had lost, too. They'd pulled into the park in a half-million-dollar rig that was now a gutted hulk encircled with yellow caution tape. Strangely, the look on their faces wasn't one of loss. Both grandparents looked like they'd been served fresh cream with their coffee: smug and satisfied. That made no sense, unless Troy was right, and Jeff was the arsonist. She'd detoured past their space as she rode out of the park this morning. Fire had turned the luxurious Prevost into a tangle of unrecognizable metal, its windshield black with char, the safety glass shattered and splintered in its frame. A miasma of chemicals still lingered in the air. If Saffi had lost a rig like that, she would be curled up in a fetal position, clutching her head in despair. But if she'd set the fire herself, she'd be as unfazed as Jeff and Eliza seemed to be.

Delilah scurried off to take orders and deliver food. When she made her way back behind the counter, Saffi turned to face her and leaned forward. "Those two don't look like they just lost a half-mil."

The barista swiped a towel along the counter as if trying to look like she was working instead of staring daggers at the Texans. "Honey, they didn't lose a thing. That bus would have been insured up the wazooni!"

Saffi had to agree. Troy had said the same thing. For people like Jeff and Eliza, the loss would be little more than an inconvenience. But what they'd gained? Their granddaughter? Priceless.

But what about Bill? She tapped a finger on the edge of her mug. "Tell me something. Is Bill the kind of guy who would risk getting arrested to protect a stranger's kid?"

Delilah harrumphed. "That man wouldn't risk a nail on his pinkie finger to protect anyone but himself, except Smudge."

"What if he had an incentive?"

"You mean, like cash?" Delilah rubbed two fingers together.

Saffi tilted her head. *Cash.* The elder Carmodys probably had barrels full of the stuff, and Bill had proven himself happy to pocket their money when they'd bribed their way into what should have been Saffi's monthly space. "So, for the right price, they could have talked Bill into helping them get their granddaughter away from her mother."

The barista slapped a hand on the counter. "They were in cahoots!"

"Sssh...!" Saffi put a finger to her lips and took a quick look over her shoulder. Jeff and Eliza were intent on something Casey was saying, but Nicole? Nicole was looking right at them, eyes widening as if the word "cahoots" told her exactly who and what they'd been discussing. When she turned back to the table her eyes had narrowed and her lips were set in a determined line.

"Oops!" Delilah grimaced. "Tell me I didn't just put frozen fries in a vat of hot oil."

Saffi pictured hot oil splattering in every direction and shuddered. The sudden screech of chair legs on tile brought the café's soft murmur of voices and Saffi's musings to a standstill.

"We're leaving!" Nicole's voice rose to a shriek. "Come on, Casey." Casey looked like a fish gasping for air. When she didn't move, her mother grasped her upper arm and pulled her to her feet. "Now!"

"Nicole, honey. Don't go and do something rash again," Jeff's rumbling bass cut across the café. His patronizing tone made the color rise even higher in Nicole's cheeks.

"Rash?" she shouted. "Like conspiring with that reprobate to kidnap your granddaughter?"

Delilah let out a low whistle and Jeff quickly scanned the café. Saffi wondered if he was calculating how much he'd have to spend to stop the rumor from spreading. Before he could pull out his wallet, Eliza hopped to her feet and the quiet bunny grew fangs. "Enough of this slander! If the police don't do their job and put you in jail, our lawyers will."

Casey's eyes widened. "*Jail?* You can't— What are you talking about?"

"Don't worry, dear. This won't affect you. Just your"—Eliza ran her tongue across her teeth as if clearing a rancid taste from her mouth—"mother."

"How does putting my *mom* in jail not affect *me?*"

Nothing says "I am so over you" like the look on the face of a teen who feels betrayed. Casey grasped her mother's hand and gave it a tug. "Come on, Mom. We're out of here."

Jeff's face looked grim as Eliza rejoined him at the table and took a prim bite of scone. He leaned toward his wife. "We came here to *keep* Casey in our lives. Not push her away."

Eliza waved a hand. "She'll come around, darling. Money *always* wins."

When Saffi turned back to Delilah, she saw the same shock on the barista's face that must be on her own.

"Wow," Delilah whispered.

"Hot oil." Saffi grasped her cup as if the dregs of her mocha could steady her nerves.

"Frozen fries!" Delilah put her hands together and shot them up and apart while making a splooshing noise. Discretion was not one of Delilah's virtues.

Saffi took a final sip from her mug, slipped a ten under it, and lifted a hand. "Gotta go. I'm off to the lighthouse to do some research. Then it's back to the grind for me. If I don't spend some time at my computer, my editor is going to sploosh *me.*"

"Back to the grind for both of us!" Delilah waved as she flipped a switch to pulverize more coffee beans.

Once outside, Saffi saluted the gulls pecking bread and French fry scraps off the pavement. She lifted her bike from the wave-shaped rack and drank in the morning air, freshening her lungs after the café's confinement. She cut across the marina parking lot toward the harbor trail, hoping to see Troy's boat in its slip. It wasn't. Seal barks competed with the rumble and swish of the bike's tires as she pedaled past row after row of boat slips, some empty—their boats having headed seaward before sunrise to reach fishing grounds beyond the horizon—some full. She hit the paved trail on the other side of the parking lot, feeling as if she'd found an old friend. Since she'd come to the cove, she'd spent more time on the trail than on the beach. It took her almost everywhere she needed to go. This morning, she would drop off her bike at home and walk the trail to the lighthouse, a comfortable distance of about a half mile.

When she wheeled into Last Chance Cove RV Park, the office was dark. Yesterday's "Closed" sign still hung in the window. Relief washed over Saffi. Bill was behind bars where he belonged. Saffi chained her bike behind her Rambler and hurried inside to change out of her damp sneakers. She put her new honeybee sloggers on the bottom shelf of her closet and pulled out worn rubber boots. Then she grabbed an apple from the fruit basket hanging beneath one of her kitchen cabinets, sat cross-legged on the couch, and pulled out the tide table and the lighthouse brochure she'd stuck into her bag at the visitor center. She crunched into the sweet firm Honeycrisp, brushing juice from the brochure. The tiny island on which the lighthouse perched, she read, was cut off from the mainland at high tide. Saffi unfolded the tide table. Today, that would happen around lunchtime. She took one more bite of apple, then put the rest in a reusable zipper bag and stuck it in the fridge. If she wanted to get on and off the island before the tide turned, she had to hurry.

Saffi stuffed her feet into the rubber boots. They were a bit clunky for a long walk, but they would keep her feet dry as she crossed the causeway. Rocky and slick with seaweed, the narrow gap between the mainland and the island was always damp and frequently flooded, even at low tide. At least, that's what the brochure had warned. If her boots didn't slow her down, she'd reach the island with plenty of time to explore.

Despite what she'd told Delilah about researching shipwrecks and ghosts, she planned a bit of sleuthing along the way. Uncovering the truth about any given story always required multiple sources. So did solving a mystery. The trail she tramped today conveniently wound past Mellie's hangout overlooking the beach. If Mellie had seen Bill with Casey yesterday, Saffi could use the fact that she already knew he had taken the girl to wrest more information out of the reluctant artist.

Fifteen minutes later, as she slogged up the slope to Beachfront Park, a chill ocean blast brought her to a halt. She zipped her hoodie to the neck and considered pulling the hood over her loose curls, despite knowing she'd spend the rest of the day with static frizz. Would it be worth it? By the time she crested the rise, she'd traded good hair for protecting her eardrums from the wind's piercing cold.

When she reached Mellie's usual bench, she was disappointed—but not surprised—to find it empty. The wind was too brisk for sea gazing. Saffi scanned the trees, hoping to spot the artist's gallery parked in the shadows. *Nothing*. Reluctantly, she gave up on her quest to squeeze information from her favorite raven artist and made her way toward the lighthouse. It was past time to buckle down and do the kind of research that paid her bills.

TWENTY-FIVE

By the time she left the trail for the narrow causeway separating the island from the mainland, her boots had rubbed blisters on both heels. The tide had already begun to rise and waves licked the island, making Saffi a tad less irritated with her waterproof footwear. She stumbled across uneven rocks slick with seaweed, then wobbled up a cement ramp. A set of concrete stairs led to the island's crest, topped by the lighthouse.

To her left, the puffy remains of the morning marine layer hugged the coastal headland. To her right, the Pacific rolled shoreward, the ocean's power unimpeded by land from this point to the coast of Japan. Frozen fingers of air slipped beneath her new hoodie's cotton drawstrings. She tugged them tighter as she took in the view. When a wave crashed against the island, a glorious white plume shot skyward. Saffi spread her arms and grinned as the spray splashed her face. She'd been in love with the Pacific since the moment she set eyes on it. No amount of cold, wind, or persistent cloud cover could dim her infatuation.

Saffi pulled herself away from the view to wander toward Last Chance Cove's famous lighthouse. It wasn't the typical tapered cylinder with a lens on top. It was a two-story Cape Cod-style whitewashed stone cottage with a weathered red roof. A central brick tower jutted from the roof's center, crowned with a glass-enclosed lantern room. At night, or in bad weather, the modern beacon it housed swooped outward in a circle every thirty seconds, warning mariners of dangerous rocks and reefs offshore.

A bell jangled as Saffi stepped through the front door into a narrow vestibule. As she eased the hood off her hair and unzipped her hoodie, footsteps rang on wooden floors, hurrying her way. A few seconds later, a tall thin man with a gray unibrow thrust a brochure toward her. "Welcome to Last Chance Lighthouse!"

Saffi blinked. "Martin?"

"At your service." The volunteer she'd last seen at the Historical Museum gave one of his signature eyebrow wiggles and sketched a tiny bow.

"What are you doing here? And where's Walter?"

Martin waved a hand toward a spindly table holding a guest book filled with scraggly signatures and dates. "If you're here for a tour, I'll be your guide. As for Walter, for the miserly sum of five dollars, I will not only show you through this historical treasure, I will reveal exactly why my illustrious compatriot does not volunteer his services here."

After Saffi stuffed a ten in the donation box, Martin wasted no time explaining what he was doing there. The town's Historical Society operated both the museum and the lighthouse. Volunteers split their time between the two. "Filled to the gills with history." Martin sniffed. "And mold. Both places, if you ask me. Still"—he waved a hand—"one must endure such things if one is to visit—or heaven forbid—live in this frigid watery terrace of Dante's Purgatory."

Walter, Martin told her, had only darkened the lighthouse door once before swearing never to enter again.

"Ghosts?" Saffi tried her own eyebrow wiggle.

Martin's lips skewed sideways. "If you really want to know why Walter stays away, follow me." First, he motioned her into a small gift and bookshop tucked into what once might have been a sitting room. When she shook her head at the shell-encrusted scented candles and windup plastic crabs, he led her through one room after another—the kitchen, the study, the living room, the bedroom—tolling out historical facts about when the place was built, how much it cost, how many keepers had manned the light, and which one played the piano that took up most of the living room wall.

When Saffi's head started to throb, she held up a hand. "If you don't mind, what I'd really like to hear about is—"

Martin cut her off with a slash. "Let me guess. Ghosts. Am I right?"

Saffi's face went hot. "Yes, well, that and—"

Martin lifted his eyes heavenward. "Sunken steamships."

Saffi lifted her hands and shrugged. "I did pay double."

Martin twisted his lips and slowly inhaled before bursting into story on the exhale. "Ship first, then ghosts. Since shipwrecks are the biggest reason why, according to local legend, every creak, crack, and pop this building makes can be attributed to specters."

As Martin related it, the alleged ghostly infestation started in 1865. A ship overloaded with passengers and gold steamed up the California coast on its way to Canada. When it reached Last Chance Cove, it ran straight into a monster gale.

"In weather that nasty, the reefs around here smoke like W.C. Fields on a bender!" Martin grinned.

When Saffi cocked her head, Martin's grin drooped.

"Walter warned me that my metaphors are getting dated. Fine. As I was saying, the gale whipped up a mist that was as thick as cigar smoke. The steamship captain tried to turn back to the cove, but he couldn't see the reef, or much else for that matter. And"—he clapped his hands close enough to Saffi's ears to make her jump—"*Bam!* Another one bites the dust!"

"The ship hit the reef?" Saffi widened her eyes. "How horrible."

"Dragon Rocks," Martin whispered.

The mythical name had Saffi scrabbling in her pack for a notebook and pen. She'd been so enthralled with Martin's storytelling, she'd forgotten she was here as a writer, not a tourist.

"Yes, do write that down." Martin pointed to her notebook. "It's catchy, is it not? Best of all, Dragon Rocks isn't just any old dime-a-dozen Pacific coast reef. It's the tiptop of a submerged volcanic mountain."

When she heard a story worth retelling, Saffi shivered. Martin's tale had just passed the chill test. "And the ghosts?" If Martin added ghosts to the story, it would be *Bedside Reader* gold.

Martin's face sagged. "Ghosts. Why not?" He cleared his throat to continue. "A mere nineteen survivors made it onto a lifeboat. The other two hundred or so souls drifted away from their drowned bodies as the ship went down. Some are said to have found their way here. The rocking chair rocks, all by itself." He nodded toward a spindly wooden rocker. "If you hear boots on the staircase? It won't be me. And should you feel a chill on your neck followed by a tap on the shoulder, whatever you do, don't turn around." His eyes went so squirrelly, the hair on Saffi's arms tingled. For a moment, she was convinced Martin believed the lighthouse was haunted. Then he chuckled. "But if you think that's why Walter won't work here, you're wrong. Come along!" He ushered her into a hallway. "And now, if you dare, the pièce de résistance!" Martin waved toward an open doorway.

If I dare? Peering inside, Saffi discovered a spiral staircase barely wide enough for one person.

"Up, up, up, my dear!" Martin crowed.

Curiosity trumped caution and Saffi went up... and up... and up. At the top of the stairs, she stepped into a tiny cylindrical room with a metal ladder bolted to one wall. Saffi craned her neck. At the ladder's top, a small hatch opened into what could only be the lantern room. "Please tell me I don't have to climb up there!"

Martin's unibrow did a little dance. "You do! Isn't it delightful?"

"Delightful." Saffi sized up the opening, unconsciously resting her hands on her bottom. "This is why Walter doesn't volunteer here, isn't it?"

Martin chuckled. "Kiddies love this part of the tour. But Walter? Can you imagine?"

Saffi did just that, picturing Martin's rotund companion at the Historical Museum trying to stuff himself through that hatch. "Wonderful." She sighed.

"You coming up?" She shot Martin a challenging glance.

"The space is quite... close." Martin actually batted his feathery gray eyelashes at her, and Saffi had to laugh. "Most visitors *do* prefer to revel in the majesty alone."

"Alone it is." Saffi put a hand on the lowest rung and started to climb.

Rubber boots had seemed like a good idea when contemplating wading through the onrushing tide, but for climbing? Big mistake. She was never sure if it was gumption that got her up the ladder and through the hatch or knowing that, if she failed, Martin would gleefully share the story with Walter—and all subsequent lighthouse visitors.

"Enjoy the view!" Martin called from below.

At the top of the ladder, Saffi peered over the edge of the hatch. Just inside the lantern room, she spotted a metal rail attached to the patched white wall. She clutched the rail with one hand and—with some very embarrassing wriggling and straining—managed to hoist herself through the hatch. When she stood, she found herself in a narrow walkway encircling a giant lens that glittered in the sunlight, the diamond in the lighthouse's crown. She turned from the lens toward the view and gasped. As she paced around the walkway, she had an unobstructed view of Last Chance Cove and beyond: the city's five squat commercial blocks, the harbor and the sheltered marina lined with fishing boats, the broad blue Pacific, and, to the north, she could just make out the pencil-thin silhouette of another lighthouse. She wondered if it had been built atop the infamous Dragon Rocks, a warning to ships of dangers lurking below.

Just on the other side of the narrow isthmus that separated the island from the mainland, she spotted the gloss-black gallery she'd been looking for earlier, parked in the graveled lot reserved for lighthouse visitors. The gallery seemed to be sealed shut. She didn't recognize Mellie among the salting of people nearby, but, from up here, people on the mainland looked like stick figures puffed out with chilly-weather gear. She spotted the Kevin's Kookies van in the same lot and a white truck with the city logo like the one the city manager drove. City vehicles were ubiquitous, she'd discovered as she walked or wheeled around town. Wherever she went, there they were.

A little south of the lighthouse lot, angled parking spaces lined the beachfront road. A black-and-silver Mini-Winnie parked parallel to the cove took up three parking spaces. The hooded figure slumped against its bumper seemed to be staring at the iconic lighthouse.

A lyric from Carole King's 1970s song, "Where You Lead," bubbled into Saffi's brain. Hinting that he was following where her blog posts led was one of her stalker's favorite intimidation tactics. She pressed her hands against the lantern room's glass exterior as a chill swept up her arms. She hadn't checked her blog for comments since she posted about Thunderbird. Had she revealed the kind of details that would let someone track her?

Get real, Saffi. The guy could be watching waves explode over the jetty or admiring his own boots for all she could tell from this distance. She tried to shake off the feeling of being watched by retracing her footsteps to the other side. Looking northward, the coast was a jumble of sea-washed rocks and bits of mainland broken off by time and tides. Waves swooped in to shatter against them, the last of their power eddying at their feet. Trees crowned some of the larger islets. Million-dollar homes clung to cliffs that looked fragile enough to break away at any moment. Would the risk be worth the view? From her perch at the top of the lighthouse she was pretty sure it would be. After one more long look, Saffi turned away. She'd dawdled enough. If she was going to get off the lighthouse island before the tide turned, it was time to go.

Saffi stepped toward the dark hatch and stared into it. *Great.* She'd forgotten how much harder it could be to go *down* a ladder than *up* one. There was only one thing to do: she grabbed the rail with her left hand for support and turned around to fumble for the top rung with her right boot. *Here goes nothing!* The first step made her heart galumph, but by the third rung it had steadied. Backing down the ladder turned out to be easier than she'd imagined. In fact, she was feeling quite proud of herself as she reached her right boot toward the bottom rung.

In an instant, everything changed. A cold chill washed across her shoulders, a hand clamped around her dangling leg... and pulled.

TWENTY-SIX

Saffi awakened with a jolt. When she tried to move, lightning forked down her hip and up into her ribcage. When she took a breath, a burst of pain made her wince. What had happened? She tried to remember. She'd felt a chill, then a tug on her leg. She'd turned her head, but she'd seen... no one, just as Martin had warned while sharing ghost stories.

Had she seen a shadow on the stairwell wall? Maybe, but she couldn't be certain. Had she heard the pounding of boots? No. She heard that now, and a voice calling her name. "Miss Graywood! Are you quite alright?" A moment later, Martin leaned over her, his gray unibrow creased with concern.

"I don't know," Saffi admitted. "Can you help me up?"

Martin put a hand under her left arm and eased her into a sitting position with her back resting against the wall. *Big mistake.* She clutched her side and tried not to breathe. "That-that's far enough!"

Martin ran his fingers through his gray fringe. "I should never have let you climb in those ridiculous galoshes!"

Saffi waved a hand. "I don't think my boots are to blame."

Martin quirked one side of his brow. "What are you implying?"

"I'm not implying. I'm stating a fact. My boots didn't trip me. Someone pulled me off the last rung."

"Someone, or some*thing*? Our resident spirit, perhaps?" Martin mused. "No one but you has toured the lighthouse this morning, which is why I'm so grateful for your large donation and that you're not sitting there contemplating a lawsuit. You're not, are you?"

Saffi snorted, then immediately regretted it when the lightning in her side sparked. "I'm not going to sue." She gasped. "But I *am* going to get to the bottom of what happened here. And you're going to help."

"Wonderful!" Martin smacked his hands together.

Saffi took a shallow breath and narrowed her eyes. "So, Martin. If no one else has been in the lighthouse this morning, that leaves only one suspect."

Martin's hands flew to his chest as if in protection. "*Moi?* What reason would I have to harm you?"

Saffi scrunched up her lips. "None that I can think of, but one tour guide, you, plus one visitor, me, equals—"

Martin held up his hands in defense. "OK, OK! I had a few visitors drop by this morning. Mellie, Glenn, and Randall come by for tea from time to time. Glenn always brings those scrumptious cookies." His eyes went dreamy.

"And you didn't mention them because…"

Martin looked guilty as a six-year-old boy caught with his hand in the cookie jar. "Walter doesn't know about our little repasts."

"And why is that?"

"You've met the man. Can't you guess?"

"Diabetes?" Saffi ventured.

Martin covered his eyes and shook his head. "Yes. He would kill and eat his own mother if she was sweeter."

"Were they still here when I arrived?"

Martin shook his head. "No, no. I shooed them out the back door."

So, Martin had seen them leave the lighthouse, but not the island. While Saffi and Martin had been talking, the stabbing pain in her side had devolved into a slow burn. She eased herself to her feet, using the wall as support. Glenn, Mellie, Randall, or Martin? Which one might want to harm her? And why? She'd pushed Glenn too far at the Thai restaurant, but *this* far? Doubtful. He'd warned her to be careful of others, not himself. As for Mellie, what reason could she possibly have? The artist might have lied about seeing Bill with Casey, but would Mellie give a flip if someone caught her out in a lie? Unlikely.

That left Randall and Martin. She'd barely met the city manager. He had no reason to harm her, unless fear of losing tourist dollars was enough to drive a man to mischief. Martin was also out of the question. The idea of the Muppet lookalike doing her harm would have made her chuckle if she wasn't in so much pain. Were the four of them really the only possibilities?

She looked up at Martin. "One more thing. Were you minding the entrance while I was in the lantern room?"

A blush shot up his neck, spread across his face, and made its way to the tips of his ears. "Uhm. No. I was... indisposed?"

"So, while you were in the—"

"Necessary." He nodded sagely.

"Which is where?"

Martin flapped a hand in the general direction of the back corner of the house.

"Anyone could have come inside and quietly made their way up the stairway and back down, without you knowing a thing."

"I regret to say that you are correct."

Saffi told Martin about the cold chill she'd felt just before the hand gripped her leg.

"The ghost!" He clutched his throat.

"Tour's over, Martin. Cut the melodrama."

Martin looked contrite for a fraction of a second, then his dimpled chin quivered with restrained laughter. After he got himself under control, he gave a one-shoulder shrug. "Cold air does tend to sweep up the staircase when the front door opens. Most visitors are too busy looking over their shoulders for ghosts to notice the correlation."

So much for the haunted lighthouse. "Then it's time to call Detective Richards."

Martin's skin bleached as white as a sand dollar left on the beach by the tide. "The police?"

Saffi nodded. She'd railed against Troy for not calling the police when Casey went missing. If her amateur sleuthing had led to an attack, putting the police on the scent might spook the pretend spook into leaving her alone. She fumbled in her pack for her phone, but it wasn't there. For a minute, she panicked, but then a picture of it sitting on her kitchen counter flashed into her mind. "I guess I left mine at home. Can you call?"

"Of course, I'll call," Martin assured her. "But he won't come—"

Saffi jumped in. "What do you mean he won't come? I was assaulted!"

Martin steepled his fingers. "If you'd let me finish, I was going to say he won't come until the next low tide."

Saffi clutched at the wall. "How long was I out?"

Martin drummed his fingers on the masonry wall. "Well, I spent a bit of time in the Necessary. And then I straightened the gift shop. I put the kettle on and—"

"How long?" Saffi demanded.

"Half an hour?" Martin's unibrow went up on one side. "A bit more?"

Saffi couldn't believe what she was hearing. "You heard me fall and you stopped to straighten mementos?"

"Of course not. Sounds get swallowed up by the tower's thick masonry walls. I didn't hear a thing. When I realized you'd been up there longer than I might have expected, I came to check and found you—" He wobbled a hand at the floor.

And while she was there, Saffi realized, the tide had turned. She was trapped. On an island. With Martin. And maybe... with someone who'd already attacked her once. Before grilling her tour guide further, Saffi asked Martin to help her down the spiral staircase. Her hip throbbed with each downward step, but she kept her hand on Martin's shoulder, closed her lips against the pain and kept going. Once they reached the hallway, Martin tucked an arm through hers and escorted her to the tufted fainting couch. She put out a hand to brace herself and sank toward a surface that might have been cushy a hundred years ago but felt brick-hard to her battered backside.

A reluctant Martin phoned Detective Richards, after which Saffi bullied him into searching every room in the lighthouse while she scooched back on the fainting couch for a rest. Once he declared the place "vermin-free, except for the mice," Martin brought her a stack of books to keep her company and headed to the kitchen to make lunch. After reading the back cover copy and first paragraph of each book—her usual strategy for selecting reading material—Saffi chose *Walk Across the Sea* by Susan Fletcher. It was a kids' book, but Saffi wasn't one of those readers who stuck her nose up at fiction for young people. In fact, too often, she found "literary" fiction for adults to be either pretentious, self-indulgent, leaden, or boring. Kids' books, on the other hand, had to compete with video games, twenty-four-hour-a-day streaming channels, and social media. They had to grab the reader on page one and hold on like barbed fishhooks. Fletcher's book did just that. It also sparked a *Bedside Reader* idea: the Chinese immigrant experience in the Pacific Northwest.

Saffi glanced around the museum-like room. What were the odds the lighthouse had a computer and internet connection? If she could work, she might not feel guilty about kicking back on a couch with ocean waves playing like a soundtrack in the background. "Martin!" she called. "Do you have a computer?"

He did, but he wasn't about to share it until after Saffi sampled the "little something" he'd put together for lunch: a watercress salad flecked with almonds, red onion, and Granny Smith apple bits, topped with smoked salmon, and sprinkled with shaved Romano cheese.

"Made locally," Martin declared.

He'd also loaded a lighthouse-shaped cutting board with sliced sourdough bread spread with goat cheese—the treat took her back to the trouble-making goat in the book she'd been reading. Maybe it was the adrenaline rush of falling or just the sea air, but she found herself pouncing on the food like a sailor whose ship had run out of grub a week before spotting land. After eating till her belly bulged, she gushed her approval. "Martin! You are a culinary genius."

He wiggled his eyebrows. "So I've been told."

Before she collapsed into a food coma, she reminded Martin of her computer request.

"Yes, yes. You can borrow my laptop. But for the love of all things civilized could we relax over a cup of coffee before you start pounding the keys?"

They could, and they did.

It took four more hours for the tide to clear the rocky path enough for Detective Richards—wearing rubber boots not unlike Saffi's own—to wade onto the island and begin a search of the grounds. Against his advice, Saffi joined him on a circuit of the island's outbuildings—a storage building, a defunct privy, and a generator house. She saw plenty of tools—both old and new—rusted cans filled with various nails and screws—and cobwebs, lots and lots of cobwebs. But the person who'd pulled her off the ladder had disappeared without a trace, just like, Saffi hated to admit, a ghost.

By the end of her interview with the detective, she was pretty sure he thought she had tripped on the bottom rung with the help of her boots and nothing else. Why, Saffi wondered, did men so often pooh-pooh women's accounts of their experiences? She was there. She'd felt the chill, the tug, the fear, and the fall. She endured the pain and she would be nursing the bruises for days. But, somehow, her firsthand report held little weight. If someone was stalking her steps with harmful intent, it would be up to her to sense their presence and turn quickly enough to catch them before they acted.

Detective Richards drove Saffi back to the RV park. Riding in the police SUV reminded her of the day she'd discovered Linda's body and been so shaken he wouldn't let her bike home. Somehow, she'd been dragged into a murder mystery that her aching side and hip told her she should never have pursued. After thanking the detective for once again rescuing her, she hoisted herself out of the SUV and into her Rambler, immediately spotting her cellphone on the kitchen counter. She snatched it up and collapsed into a padded dining chair at her tiny table. Before checking her phone for messages, she opened up her laptop to see if the day's writing she'd sent from Martin's computer had made it through the ether to her inbox. It had. She pressed the button to turn on her phone. As soon as it recognized her face, a string of messages she'd received from her editor while she'd been stuck on the island jammed the screen.

Here we go! Saffi straightened her shoulders and sent a silent word of thanks to the children's book author who'd set her on the trail of immigration stories. She could have wasted an entire day, but she hadn't. The messages were predictable, from the first "Just checking in. How's the writing going?" to "I could use some pages. Do you have any?" to "You're not ghosting me, are you?" The final message from her editor said simply, "Call me!"

TWENTY-SEVEN

After a cup of French press coffee and a banana chocolate-chip muffin, Saffi opened a video chat and dialed her editor. Since 6 p.m. in Last Chance Cove would be 9 p.m. in New York City, she was fairly confident that her workaholic editor would have long left her publisher's Manhattan office building and she'd have a full night's sleep before facing the wrath of Poppy Morales. She watched in horror as her normally video-perfect editor picked up the call with bedhead and eyebags puffy with sleep. Had she fallen asleep on her couch?

"Where in the name of Jack Sprat's wife have you been!!!"

Both Saffi and Poppy hated it when fledgling writers resorted to three exclamation marks to make a point instead of writing dialogue that did its own exclaiming, but Saffi heard all three "exclaims" in her editor's shriek.

A brief explanation of yesterday's misadventure led to a lecture she both expected and deserved. She listened, face frozen in contrition like a kindergartner who'd taken the tops off all the markers and hidden them in the Lego tub.

"Saffi! You can't let those amazing destinations you're determined to lord over me distract you!" her editor reminded her. "I know exploring is more fun than B.I.S., but think of me, would you? I'm cooped up in an eight-by-ten box in a Manhattan highrise for ten hours a day waiting for my inbox to ping!"

Saffi took a sip of coffee and nodded. She'd already beaten herself up about the fact that her butt had *not* been in the seat (B.I.S. being Poppy's shorthand for "sit down and write") for most of her time at Last Chance Cove. But, come on... *murder!* For the moment, visions of her editor having a stroke kept her mum about the ongoing investigation. What she didn't know couldn't kill her—at least, she hoped it couldn't.

"I need articles," Poppy's voice droned on, "and I need them regularly and on deadline."

Saffi knew the drill. Unlike other types of nonfiction, *Aunt Saffi's Bedside Reader* didn't have a single deadline. The content was written in batches of articles over a nine-month period. Articles varied from a single page to up to four pages long, and Saffi owed her editor about twenty of those each month. That led to a revolving door of submit-edit-revise that Saffi had to juggle while researching and writing *more* articles until she reached the magic number: 390 pages. Three hundred and ninety pages of content interesting enough that when a reader dipped into the book at any page, it would grab them and hold on, at least until their eyelids started to droop and they nodded off, drooling, with the book sliding off their belly.

When her editor's steam finally burned off, Saffi described the articles she had in process: haunted lighthouses, strange things found in shipwrecks, tragic tales of Chinese immigrants, world's weirdest tips and—one that had been buzzing at the back of her brain since the RV fire—tricks of the arsonist's trade.

"Oh." Poppy sounded contrite. "You *have* been working."

Saffi spurted out something that sounded halfway between a laugh and a cry for help. "I have. I have."

"*Saffi?*"

Shoot. Saffi sat on her hands. She should have skipped the second reassurance. It was one of the "tells" her editor had spotted years earlier. "Really." She pasted a grin on her face. "You can't walk out the door here without tripping over an idea." *Great!* Her grin wavered. Now she'd admitted she'd been out and about.

"Pages." Poppy's pointer finger loomed large as she tapped a nail on the computer screen. "In my inbox Monday morning. Ta!" She saluted just before her bedhead and eyebags disappeared.

Saffi ended the session and slumped in her chair. Monday. Three days. She could do it, but only if she left the mystery of Linda's death, and her own assault, in the hands of Detective Richards. Or... if she glued her butt to the chair right now and got the job done.

"Eleven pages!" If Saffi's shoulders weren't so stiff from hours in her chair without moving, she'd have patted herself on the back. The four articles she'd generated, two three-pagers, two two-pagers, and one single-pager, put her halfway toward completing this month's twenty pages. That is, if rushing to get them done didn't lead to page after page of blood-red "cut this" slashes or expletives—#$@!%—Poppy-speak for "I don't know what the hell you're talking about here." Oh, and the dreaded "MORE!" which meant, "You're on your way but you're not there yet."

She'd started writing last night after the Zoom call, worked till 2 a.m., and was snoring before her head hit the pillow. She got up with Raven's call just before sunrise to complete the pages she should have been writing since she pulled into Last Chance Cove RV Park five days ago. She hadn't bothered to shower or dress when she got up. She'd stayed in her red flannel pj's so she wouldn't be tempted to venture out for a walk. She'd even kept her curtains drawn to block out any distractions.

She'd gone through two pots of French press coffee and her body now buzzed like a beehive.

Shower, clothes, food, beach walk, she decided, in that order. Notably, she'd left questioning potential suspects off her list, and she planned to keep it that way. Whoever had pulled her off that ladder could have caused a broken leg or—God forbid—a concussion or a broken arm, things that could have wrecked this year's deadline. Poppy was right. She had to focus on her writing. That meant leaving Last Chance Cove's denizens to get into or out of trouble by themselves.

She turned the hot knob all the way to the "on" position and let steam fill the shower enclosure before she added just a bit of cold and stepped inside. Hot water cascaded over her shoulders, and she stayed there until the knotted muscles eased. Then she ducked her head under the stream, soaped her hair and body, and rinsed quickly knowing that the Rambler's twelve-gallon hot water tank would soon be empty. The last thing she needed was a cold rinse-off. Her shoulders would probably seize up again and she'd be forced to take ibuprofen to get them to loosen.

She'd just toweled off and was mulling over which color hoodie to wear with her jeans when someone pounded on the door. *No. No, no, a thousand times no!* She ignored the pummeling and concentrated on clothes. *Undies. Socks. Jeans. Yellow T-shirt. Green hoodie with Vermont College emblazoned in gold.*

"Saffi! Open up." Was that Mellie's voice? "I know you're in there! Raven sent me!"

Saffi yanked the hoodie over her damp curls. *Raven? Where was Raven yesterday?* she wondered. *For that matter, Miss Mellie, where were you! Skulking around a lighthouse, perchance?* She was suddenly gripped by an intense anger. What was it with these Last Chance Covers? Why couldn't they just leave her alone?

Alone, Saffi?

Saffi froze.

Is that what you really want?

The voice in her head was as familiar as her own, but it wasn't hers. It was Levi's. And he knew. He knew she didn't want to be alone. She wanted to be part of a community—always had. When Levi was alive, she'd melted as happily as cheddar on toast into the Vermont College community. His sudden death had snuffed her ties to the close-knit academic community as quickly and finally as a puff of breath on a candle.

She'd long since reconciled herself to life on the road. She loved traveling, meeting new people, seeing new places, spending a few months here and a few months there. She kept herself busy with research and writing, tai chi classes, books and bike rides and hikes. Those things kept her mind sharp, her creativity cranking, her body reasonably fit. Her rolling rambling RV had become her home. She'd learned to embrace, even relish, solitude, but she was an introvert, not a hermit. She needed people, and, it seemed, right now, Mellie needed her.

"Hang on!" she yelled. "I'll be there in a sec." She stared into the mirror, raking her fingers through her curls to give them some semblance of shape as they dried. Her face looked grim. Determined. Yes, she needed people. But she was done charging around town, as easily tricked as a bull by a matador's red cape.

A sudden silence alerted her to the fact that Mellie might have gotten tired of waiting. Saffi stopped fiddling with her hair and rushed to the door. The raven artist hadn't left. She was standing at the foot of the Rambler's steps with her arms crossed over her chest and one black Converse-clad foot tapping with impatience. Today's get-up was bright enough to wake Saffi from her post-writing fog—a traditional white cotton Mexican top with enough colorful embroidered flowers to put a peacock to shame. A swingy goldenrod skirt speckled with paint flared out beneath the top and, under that, a pair of artfully torn red fishnets.

Now that she'd opened the door, Saffi noticed the weather: blue sky, no marine layer. In most places that would have signaled warmth, but on the northwest coast loss of cloud cover meant any warmth the clouds had been holding against the shoreline floated up and away, leaving behind more, not less, chill. The skin Saffi could see between the mesh of Mellie's stockings reminded her of knees she'd once glimpsed between a bagpiper's tall socks and short kilt during a St. Patrick's Day parade in New York City. Red—the chapped tone of someone freezing their butt off. No wonder Mellie's arms were crossed.

"Come in and warm up!" She waved toward the couch. "Tea or coffee?"

Mellie curled up on the couch and draped Saffi's mottled gray-and-white Sherpa blanket over her legs. "Tea. Thanks."

Saffi boiled water in her electric kettle as Mellie took in her surroundings. For the first time, Saffi felt a bit self-conscious about her Rambler. She didn't know who designed RV interiors, but she pictured corporate teams choosing neutral colors that would offend no one. They didn't exactly *please* anyone either. They just... were. She'd added a few meaningful touches, including a pillow that featured a raven on a branch with the word "Nevermind" printed below. Mellie chuckled when she saw that one.

"Cozy. Minimalist. I like it." She nodded approval. "Could use some art though."

"I know," Saffi agreed. "But where would I put it?"

Mellie stood, tossing aside the blanket as she took the question to heart. "Something here and here." She pointed to the narrow wall spaces at either end of the couch. "Something on the dash. Love the raven, but what you really need are splashes of color. It's a bit tomblike in here." Mellie turned her penetrating stare on Saffi and the word "tomb" vibrated in the air.

The click of the kettle reaching a boil made Saffi jump. She set the stainless steel infuser into her glass teapot and scooped in a teaspoon of loose lemon balm and lavender tea. She drove away Mellie's gloomy evaluation by pouring boiling water over the tea and inhaling the heartening mix of citrus and flower. "Ready in three." She started to smile, but Mellie's next words stopped her.

"Raven says we need to talk."

Saffi took two cups down from their undercabinet storage hooks.

"You could start with those."

"Pardon?" Was Mellie still talking about Raven?

The artist nodded toward the white dollar-store mug in Saffi's hands. "I'll take you thrifting. There's a shop downtown with shelf after shelf of someone's granny's old china teacups."

"Mimi's Attic?" Saffi remembered the red barn of an antique store she'd passed on her way to the Historical Museum.

Mellie nodded. "That's the one. I spotted a set of teacups with purple and gold dragons in there last week. Gorgeous! I'd have scored them myself, but, as you saw, I have even less room that you do."

Saffi stared at the cup. She'd outfitted the RV with the cheapest dishes she could find for the cross-country trip she and Levi had begun. Then, when... Well, when she lost Levi, she'd put everything they owned into storage. She hadn't been ready to drink out of cups they'd shared or decorate with treasures they'd collected. Maybe Mellie was right. It was well past time to bring her rig to life with a few carefully chosen memory-free items.

Outside, a raven gave a low gurgling croak that rose to fill the space inside the Rambler. Saffi knew from her research that this was one of a raven's most common calls. It could be heard for up to a mile and was often used in response to another raven's call.

Mellie cocked her head sideways, listening. "Raven agrees. You need new cups. But it's OK to use those for now, so tea." She pointed her chin at the white mugs.

Saffi poured Mellie the first cup, and then filled the second for herself. She set oat milk and a honey bear on the counter and waved for Mellie to doctor her drink. The artist squeezed a thick stream of honey into her cup, along with a hefty pour of oat milk. "Out with the bitter, in with the sweet." The artist smiled, and then daintily lifted the chunky mug to her lips and sipped, pinkie extended.

Saffi took a seat on one end of the couch and Mellie settled onto the opposite end.

"So. Raven sent you?" Saffi prompted. "And probably not for decorating advice." She left the statement hanging in the air and waited. Whatever Mellie had come to tell her must be important enough to leave her gallery unattended.

"I heard about what happened at the lighthouse."

Saffi raised one brow. "Did you?"

Mellie took another sip. "Clunky boots. Bad fall. Looks like you're OK though, right?"

"Still sore, but, yes, fine." Saffi entwined hands and rested them on her knees. "But the boots had nothing to do with the fall."

"Yeah." Mellie nodded. "Raven told me. Said I needed to share some things I've been holding back."

Saffi stiffened. "About what?"

"About the day Casey went missing, for one thing."

And there it was. She'd been sure Mellie had seen something and now, thanks to Raven, she was ready to share.

"You've probably figured out that I saw Bill with her. I mean, the kid was found with him and all."

"Yes, she was."

Mellie stood and walked to the front of the rig. She set her cup down and drew open the light-blocking windshield curtains. Light streamed in, driving back the gloom. "You know the prissy lady and the hat dude?" Mellie pretended to tip a hat toward Saffi.

"Hat dude?" Saffi scrunched up her lips, then a memory cell pinged. Cowboy hat! Jeff was rarely outside without it. "The Carmodys. They're from Texas."

"Ah. Well, I saw Bill with them."

Had Mellie just confirmed her theory about Bill conspiring with the Carmodys? Saffi was so caught up in the question, she almost missed the artist's next comment.

"And there's something else, about the night Linda died." The artist glanced out the windshield and squinted into the sunlight for a minute. She froze, and then hastily retreated toward the shadows. "Can I, uh, can I use your restroom?"

"Mellie, what is it?"

The artist scowled. "Tea, OK? I gotta pee."

"Sure. The door slides out from the wall."

As Mellie vanished behind the bathroom door, Saffi hurried to the driver's cab and peered out. Mellie had seen something, or someone more likely, that spooked her. Saffi squinted against the afternoon glare. Sunshine on the coast inevitably brought campers streaming outside, most of them, like Mellie, optimistically dressed for a warm summer's day. A black and silver Mini-Winnie like the one she'd seen near the lighthouse lumbered along the lane scattering a group of unfamiliar campers headed toward the beach. She spotted Troy in their midst gripping Smudge's leash to keep him from lunging toward Bill's RV. Aaron—the widower she'd met the night of the bonfire—strolled arm-in-arm with, of all people, Delilah. Saffi shook her head. The age difference seemed extreme for more than just friendship, but who knew? Archie bobbed beside the mismatched

TWENTY-EIGHT

Soon wasn't soon enough. Something—or someone—had spooked Mellie. But what? Saffi jumped up and stuffed her feet into her sloggers to follow Mellie outside. She ran to the nose of her rig and shaded her eyes, hoping to spot the artist.

"Mellie? Mellie, wait!" The artist's outfit should have jumped out of the scenery, but Mellie seemed to have disappeared.

The estuary! Remembering the path behind her rig, Saffi turned just in time to see Mellie's head disappear below the berm as she bobbed down the trail to the narrow beach. Clearly, the artist wanted to avoid being spotted on the grounds. Saffi thought about going after her but stopped herself. Doing so might put the young woman's life in danger. She had to respect Mellie's decision to wait to share her secret until she felt safe.

Back inside, Saffi scrounged in the fridge for a container of hummus and grabbed a sleeve of brown rice crackers from the cabinet. She kicked off her honeybee shoes and plopped down on the couch, pulling the Sherpa blanket Mellie had abandoned over her lap. She crunched down the light lunch as she re-examined what had just happened. She had hoped Mellie would couple on the end of his red leash, triangular ears alert, carrot-shaped tail wagging, happy to be out and about, walking his humans. Jeff and Eliza stood outside the ruins of their RV with a young woman in a blue jacket and tan slacks who seemed to be logging information into an iPad. Insurance adjuster? Nicole and Casey fast-walked around the far side of the loop in the opposite direction of the beachgoers, arms pumping and blond hair swinging. They waved at Glenn as they passed the Kevin's Kookies van parked behind the office.

Which reminded her—tomorrow was the Saturday Market Delilah had told her about. Shouldn't Glenn be spending the day baking and packing cookies? Had his unexpected presence sent Mellie running to the loo? Saffi had grown fond of the British term for toilet after learning that it traced back to medieval times when those dumping chamber pots from windows called out, "guardez l'eau!"—French for "watch out for the water!" *Loo, bog, dunny, WC, John, privy, latrine, head...* Saffi counted off terms she remembered from a listicle she'd written as she waited for Mellie to slide open the bathroom door. She looked up when the lock clicked and smiled, certain that Mellie would sit back down and finish her tea when she came out. She didn't. She beelined for the door, calling back over her shoulder that she had to go but they'd talk again soon.

provide new leads. Instead, she'd confirmed what Saffi already knew or suspected. She'd seen Bill with Casey, and with the Carmodys. Even if he had conspired with them to snatch the girl, Casey had been found and returned to her mom. The Carmody family battle would end in a courtroom, not an RV park. Besides, whatever Mellie knew about Linda was big. Not custody battle big—murder big. Big enough to send the artist running like a ground squirrel with a wolverine on her tail.

So, who had scared her off? From the cab, Saffi had seen random campers, Troy, Aaron and Delilah, Jeff and Eliza, Nicole and Casey, Glenn. Almost everyone Saffi thought might have murdered the park manager was wandering around Last Chance Cove RV Park this afternoon. With a single exception: Bill, the last person Saffi wanted to remove from her list of suspects.

Saffi tossed off the blanket and paced the narrow living area. Over the years, she'd written about scores of murders. Murderers needed two things: motive and opportunity. Motives ranged from money to jealousy, revenge to rage, love (sadly) to hatred, fear to concealment. From what she'd gathered so far, at the time of Linda's murder, Nicole had the most to conceal and the park manager might have been blackmailing her. Nicole also had opportunity. Her trailer was close to where Linda had been killed. Glenn despised Linda for destroying his business and trying to wreck his reputation, but was he in the park when she died? She had no reason to think so. Bill hated Linda for everything from "stealing" his job to, basically, just being a woman. He'd been in the park the night of Linda's murder, but he was in police custody now. He couldn't have spooked Mellie.

Saffi shoved her fingers through her curls. She found it easy to figure out whodunit when reading mystery novels. Good writers salted in enough clues to make their books tasty. But in real life? Linda's murderer hadn't left a trail of obvious clues for her to follow. Saffi stopped pacing and clasped the back of the dining chair. Yesterday, someone had pulled her off a ladder, perhaps trying to scare her away from sleuthing. Surely that was a clue worth pursuing.

Who was on the grounds now and nearby before her lighthouse fall? Glenn and Mellie. Mellie seemed to be trying to help, not hurt, her. That meant, once again, Glenn rose to the top of the list. When she'd interrupted his lunch at the Thai restaurant, she'd all but accused him of murder. Saffi thought back to his reaction when he learned of Linda's death. Sheer shock. Could he have killed her and still reacted so strongly to her death? Maybe. If it had been an accident, he might not have known she'd died. A push, a pull, a fall...

Falling! If the murderer had pushed Linda and then yanked Saffi off the ladder, maybe it wasn't someone determined to kill. Maybe it was an accidental killer who had then tried to scare her away from the investigation. *Glenn.* Again, all fingers pointed to Glenn, and he was on the grounds right now. Saffi shoved her feet into her buzzy-bee sloggers, grabbed her keys from her bag and rushed outside, pausing just long enough to toss the hummus back into the refrigerator and lock her door. She loped toward the office as fast as her sore hip would allow. Just before she got there, she spotted Glenn sliding into the driver's seat of his van. "Glenn!" She waved. "Wait up!"

Glenn did not wait up. He slammed the door shut, cranked the engine, and shoved the van into drive so fast the gears ground. Gravel flew as he spun out of the space he'd backed into and shot around the corner of the office like a seal pup with a shark on its tail. Saffi put up an arm to shield her face from spraying gravel, wincing as bits stung her forearm, even through the thick cloth of her hoodie. A single rock glanced across her forehead, and when she tentatively touched the graze, her fingertip came away smudged with blood. Saffi rounded the office, staring open-mouthed at the retreating van nearly obscured by the dust cloud of a city truck preceding it out of the park.

"Surprised to see me?" A self-satisfied voice made her turn toward the office door where Bill stood, juggling a cookie box and jangling a ring of keys.

Saffi's mouth fell open. Bill *was* on the grounds! She clamped her mouth shut and pressed her hands against her hips. Surprise wasn't the half of it. What were the police thinking, letting a kidnapper walk free? They'd caught him red-handed.

"Speechless, huh?" He chuckled. "Looks good on you."

It was all Saffi could do to keep herself from jumping the rail and running him through with her house key. She stuffed down the urge and settled for stabbing him with an ice-hard glare. She needed him alive, at least until she'd unlocked the secret of his escape from justice.

"So?" She crossed her arms and waited, knowing Bill wouldn't be able to resist waving his freedom in her face.

"The kid put in a good word for me with the cops."

"Casey?" Saffi clenched her keys hard enough to make indentations in her palm. "Who talked her into that?"

Bill shrugged. "That cowboy gramps of hers, I suppose."

"The same cowboy gramps you were plotting with before Casey went missing?"

Bill bristled. "Who told you that?"

Saffi shrugged. "A little bird."

His eyes narrowed. "More like a raving lunatic."

Had he said "raven"? If so, that probably meant he'd seen Mellie. The chill shivering the back of her neck made Saffi keep pushing.

"And Nicole? Did she put in a good word for you? If Casey was my kid, I'd be pressing charges."

"You got kids, *Aunt Saffi*?" Bill gave her book name a prissy tone obviously meant to insult.

"No, Bill. Do *you?*"

Bill snorted. "That ex-wife of mine was too busy scheming and dreaming to have kids."

While they traded insults, Bill managed to unlock the office door and push it open with his shoulder. Almost against her will, Saffi followed him inside. "She live around here? Your ex?"

Bill whirled around, nearly whacking her with the cookie box. "That, missy, is none of your business. But since you asked, I'll say this—wherever she is, you can bet your bootlaces it's a better place than she deserves."

Bill's anger toward his ex was a fireworks finale waiting to explode across the sky. Saffi decided to defuse the situation before it ignited.

"What's up with the cookies?" She nodded toward the box Bill had set down on the counter.

"Gonna sell 'em in the office. My idea, which the city manager approved, since it's, you know, brilliant."

For once Saffi had to agree. Campers would be drawn to Kevin's Kookies like sand fleas to bare ankles. In fact, if she'd had any money on her, she would buy one right now. "So, Bill. Any idea why Glenn was in such a hurry to get out of here? I tried to wave him down but..." She held her hands out and shrugged.

Bill shrugged. "Don't know. Trying to catch up with Randall?"

"The city manager?" Saffi scrunched her face.

"Yeah. Nice guy, our city manager. Gave me a lift home from the hoosegow." Then he smirked. "Those two are thicker than thieves, if you know what I mean." He wiggled his bushy brows suggestively.

By now, Saffi was pretty sure she did know. Bill's smirk made her want to smack him.

"Back when Linda was throwing all that bull-pucky around, I figured Randall would dump him. But he didn't. Gotta give him that. Almost lost that fancy pants job of his, standing up for Glenn in front of the council."

Bill walked around the counter, opened the cabinet doors beneath it and started rumbling through the contents. When he came up for air he held a ratty driftwood basket, which he blew into, lifting what looked like desiccated bits of last year's leaves for the fraction of a second it took them to settle back to the bottom. "This'll do." He opened the box and transferred an assortment of individually wrapped cookies into the basket. "Glenn was in such a hurry to get out of here, he didn't even give me an invoice." He nodded toward the basket now filled with Kevin's Kookies. "Guess the first delivery's on the house." A yellow-toothed pirate's grin spread across his face.

Was Glenn trying to avoid Mellie? Or catch up with Randall? Saffi pondered as she rambled back to her RV. Either way, she'd missed her chance to rattle Glenn into spilling secrets. Still, the crumbs of information she'd collected might be enough to put Detective Richards on the cookie maker's trail. As soon as she got back to the Rambler, she phoned the station. The detective took her call but when she suggested that he might want to interview Glenn about the night of Linda's murder, he stopped her, his voice colder and more brusque than usual.

"Mrs. Graywood, I understand your interest in this case, given that you found the body. But this is an active murder investigation, not a story for one of your books."

Saffi stiffened. "I thought you hadn't read my books."

Detective Richards let out a disgruntled huff. "You gave me one, remember? Since you used your books as an excuse to pump my auntie for information, I thought I'd better see what they were all about."

What had she been thinking? Had she given him the volume with "How to *Not* Catch a Killer?" Her hands went clammy. He'd probably flagged page after page as he searched for clues to just how murdery the writer who'd found Linda's body might be.

"No. I, uhm, no. I only…" Saffi fumbled for an excuse but couldn't come up with one. She sucked in a breath. "OK. I might have done a little pumping, but your aunt's line of work is fascinating. I just finished writing an article based on some of her cases."

"If it's this case, you could be writing yourself into obstruction charges."

"Seriously?" Saffi let the question hang in the air for a second before assuring the detective that her article only covered cases that had been closed. "I'm not an ambulance chaser, Detective. I don't write for newspapers. I write books, every article of which has to be vetted by me, my editor, and a team of fact checkers."

"So, you're a pro?"

Even though he couldn't see her, Saffi squared her shoulders. "I am."

"Good. So am I. How about you keep writing those articles and I'll keep searching for the person who ended Linda's life. That way we won't step on each other's toes."

"But Glenn—"

"Lives in a house on Fifth Street, not in the RV park. Unlike you, he wasn't there on the night of Linda's death."

"Unlike me?" Saffi huffed. "You think *I* killed the park manager? Someone I'd never even met?"

"Who I do or do not suspect is police business, Mrs. Graywood. I'm just stating the facts: you were there. Glenn was not. Believe it or not, I have already questioned him about his whereabouts that night and have verified the alibi he provided. It is ironclad."

Something that sounded like a pen tap-tap-tapping on the detective's desk thumped in time to Saffi's rising blood pressure.

"Now, are there any other cove locals you'd like to accuse?"

"No. Not at the moment."

The pen tapped faster. "In that case, I'll get back to work."

"Wait!" Saffi stopped him. "Did Bill ever turn in that bandanna he found on the day of the murder?" Seconds passed. She could hear the detective breathing, so she knew he was still there. "Detective?"

"Do you have information about the bandanna?"

So Bill hadn't turned it in! Saffi bit her lip. The detective already thought she was an interfering nutcase, so why not? "I might have seen it in Bill's trailer when Troy and I asked him if he'd seen Casey. He took down a leash to walk Smudge and something red fell off the hook. He grabbed it and stuffed it into his back pocket as if he didn't want us to see it."

"Something... red?" He hesitated as if he might be about to say more, but, true to form, he didn't.

"Not just something. A red cloth that could have been Archie's bandanna."

"Ah. I see. Possible bandanna sighting. I'll make a note. Thank you for the information, Mrs. Graywood. Good day," he said, ending the call before she could say anything else.

Saffi slammed her cellphone down on the kitchen counter, grateful for the thick protective case that kept it from breaking. Before she could stew herself into righteous outrage, she headed back outside. The walk she'd intended to take earlier was long overdue and nothing could calm her better than strolling on the beach. As she locked the door of her Rambler, Raven squawked a warning.

"Oh, hush!" Saffi chided the hulking black bird pecking through the patchy grass in the empty space next to hers. "You've been nothing but trouble since I got here."

A few hours later, Saffi knocked on the door of Delilah's trailer, hoping to lure her out on the berm to watch the sunset. She held up a grease-smudged brown paper bag filled with calamari strips, coconut shrimp, and garlic cheese bread, freshly delivered from the brewpub opposite Beachfront Park. Delilah leaned forward and sniffed. Her eyes rolled toward heaven. "Blessed is she who brings the loaves and fishes."

"I also have these." Saffi held up a mesh bag dripping condensation from a chilled six-pack of Lost Coast Brewery's Citrus IPA.

"And turns the water into beer. Praise the Lord! Let me just grab a sweater."

Saffi unrolled the sleeping bag she'd tucked beneath her arm and spread it out a few feet away from the blackened remains of Tuesday evening's bonfire. Clouds had rolled in and, for the first time since Saffi arrived, the air was still, the breeze holding its breath as if to see what would happen next. She set out the food along with tangy tartar sauce and smoky remoulade for dunking while Delilah popped two beers and handed her one.

"Sisters of Seafood and Sand!" she saluted, tapping her beer to Saffi's.

The warm flush of fledgling friendship—boosted by six percent alcohol—washed over Saffi as she tipped the cold can and guzzled, long and slow.

They gorged themselves on cheesy bread and seafood, washing it all down with IPA. As they ate and chatted, the sinking sun gave the clouds an orange tang to match their beer. Saffi leaned back to stretch out her belly and enjoy the light show, glad she had changed out of jeans and into comfy drawstring beach pants.

"So, anything new on the Carmody clan?" Delilah's eyes reflected the sky's glow.

Should she tell Delilah what she'd learned from Mellie? If she'd built trust with anyone at Last Chance Cove, it was the barista. From the moment Saffi had found Linda's body, she'd felt the park manager's death as if it were a burden she alone was meant to bear. But was it? Delilah had been Linda's friend. She had real skin in this deadly game. And, unlike Saffi, Delilah had more than a passing acquaintance with everyone on her suspect list. They were all café regulars. She would make a great informant and ally.

As the setting sun sank below the cloud bank, a band of fire spread across the horizon. The atomic-white bulge at its center shot a laser of light across the cove, not stopping until it reached sand too dry to reflect its brilliance. The wonder of this place cracked open Saffi's guarded heart, and she turned to Delilah, ready to divulge what Mellie had told her, and hopeful that trusting her new friend would be a help, not a hazard.

TWENTY-NINE

Sharing with Delilah beneath the sunset had led Saffi to plan Saturday morning around the Farmers Market at the harbor. According to Delilah, both Glenn and Mellie would be there, selling their wares. As Saffi pedaled along the waterfront trail, she ran through her conversation with Delilah. When Saffi had set out her theories about who seemed most likely to have "dunit," Delilah had defended Glenn like he was her long-lost brother.

"Motive and opportunity aren't the only things you need to commit murder," the barista had insisted. "You need the stomach for it. And a guy who spills a mocha down his pants when his cousin dies doesn't have that. Besides, I've never seen Glenn as depressed as he is right now."

Saffi wasn't so sure. She'd researched accidental homicides for *Bedside Reader, #13* and learned that the guilt accidental killers felt could lead to memory lapses, nightmares, hallucinations, and depression. If Linda's death had been accidental, rather than intentional, Glenn's reaction made perfect sense.

Delilah wasn't buying it. She put Nicole at the top of her own list, sharing with Saffi that Linda had been frantic about money for the last few months. "She depleted her savings moving here. After the inheritance from Uncle Kevin fell through, she seemed desperate to get out of the cove, move on, or maybe move back to Arizona. Can't do that without the buckaroonies. It wouldn't be the first time she resorted to dirty pool to get what she wanted."

Saffi had to admit, if Linda was that desperate, blackmail was possible. And, clearly, Nicole would do whatever it took to keep Casey. What mother wouldn't? Besides, Glenn had an alibi. Ironclad, Detective Richards had assured her. Who would the detective trust enough to call an alibi ironclad? Randall? From what she'd seen so far, he was universally liked and respected. Still, he'd gone to bat for Glenn before and could be covering for the cookie maker now.

She approached the harbor from the north, passing the marina parking lot where vendors gathered to set up trailers and tents and tables. Custom banners waved in the breeze—red, green, blue, yellow—each emblazoned with a business name meant to catch the eye and stop the shopper. Ollie's Tamales, Huckleberry's Pies, The MicroGreenery, Kevin's Kookies, Seafood Sallie's, and—thank goodness—Last Chance Coffee Cart.

Saffi locked her bike in a wave-shaped rack just like the one outside the café and turned to scan the marina. A gentle breeze swirled her curls around her face, bringing with it the briny scent of ocean life and the bark of seals bobbing on their wooden platforms beyond the marina. A few fishing trawlers rested among the rows, their owners taking the day off, despite the calm weather. At the end of the middle row, the tall mast of a massive catamaran towered over the sport-fishing boats moored nearby. For a second, Saffi thought she saw Jeff, or at least a big man wearing a cowboy hat, skulking along the wooden dock in the direction of the cat. Despite being a likely accessory to kidnapping and possibly an arsonist, the Texan had fallen to the bottom of her list of murder suspects. Today, she'd concentrate on Glenn, but first, she would make him think she was just here to shop.

She turned without looking and stepped directly into the path of someone clutching a coffee cup in one hand and a bulging shopping bag in the other. The coffee went flying, up and over the rail, straight into the algae-green water at the edge of the marina.

"Oh, no! I'm so—" When Saffi looked up, the apology froze in her throat.

Troy had trapped his tousled slate-gray hair beneath a wide-brimmed cap and seemed to be dressed for a day at sea: a safety-orange waterproof anorak over a bright red hoodie. Gunmetal-gray sunglasses hid the expression in his eyes but she imagined something between annoyed and apoplectic. *Perfect timing, as ever.*

"Sorry?" she ventured.

He glanced over the rail to where the to-go cup bobbed in the backwash, clenched and released his jaw, then chuckled. "I was about to offer to buy you coffee, but now I think you're doing the buying."

How many men would respond to a klutz smashing into them with amusement rather than anger? It shouldn't have surprised her. Troy spent his days with the sea shifting beneath his boots. He had to be steady on his feet, and, since he dealt with tourists, cool as a cod on a bed of ice. She'd only seen him lose it twice and both times he'd been worried about his niece.

She smiled in apology. "Absolutely! Coffee is on me."

"Let's hope so." He grinned.

As they threaded between shoppers on their way to the coffee kiosk, Delilah spotted the pair and waved. "Hey!" She eyeballed Troy. "You swilled that one down fast."

"My bad." Saffi scrunched up her lips. "I barreled into him. Knocked his coffee right into the harbor."

Delilah snorted. "Knocked his drink into the drink. Wish I coulda seen that." She glanced at Troy. "Same again?"

"Nope. Something much pricier is in order." He nudged Saffi's shoulder.

His nudge made her feel warm all over but she hid her pleasure behind a look of contrition. "Whatever the man wants, the man gets."

Troy's whole face lit up and Saffi's temperature shot through the roof. *Hot flash?* Nope. It may have been three years, but she could still remember what sexual tension felt like.

"Now, now. Down, boy," Delilah flicked the brim of his cap.

Troy took it off, ran his fingers through his short curls, resettled it, then scrubbed the palm of his free hand across the peppery shadow of morning stubble on his chin. "How 'bout a red-eye?"

"Drip with a shot of espresso coming up! And you?" Delilah rapped her knuckles on the counter in front of Saffi. "The usual, or catch of the day?" She winked at Troy, then turned her shoulder so Saffi could see the chalkboard on the wall behind her. Someone had drawn a fishing pole, its line a swirl of movement as it pulled a to-go cup from a wave.

"Dark chocolate mocha with raspberry whipped cream and sugar sprinkles," Saffi read aloud. "Oh, yes! Give me one of those."

The barista ran an espresso shot for Troy's red-eye, pumped a to-go cup three-fourths full from the stainless steel Airpot on the counter, then splooped in the shot. Troy took a sip, declared it perfect, then—to Saffi's surprise and disappointment—announced that he had to be off.

"These groceries aren't going to put themselves away." He held his overstuffed bag high and walked toward the docks with a swagger in his step that said, *I don't need eyes in the back of my head to know you're watching.*

A few seconds later, he turned and caught her doing exactly that.

"Catch you later?"

Saffi lifted both hands, smiled and shrugged. Maybe he would. Maybe he wouldn't, but she had to admit, she wouldn't mind being caught by a fisher with glutes that looked like that in a pair of jeans.

"Nice trick. Knocking his coffee out of his hands," Delilah mused.

Saffi put her hands on her hips. "I did *not* do that on purpose."

Delilah chuckled as she pulled shots and frothed oat milk for Saffi's mocha. "Well, I wouldn't blame you a bit if you did."

Saffi turned away, partly to scan the vendors again, but mostly to keep Delilah from seeing her cheeks turn raspberry red. Mellie's Raven Mad art cart was still nowhere to be seen. Glenn was a few vendors away, lining a folding table outside his van with rows of bagged cookies. Like Saffi, he was scanning the crowd. She waved, to see what he'd do. He went still, hand poised above a bag until a customer walked up, blocking her view of the cookie baker.

"Catch of the day!" Delilah drew Saffi's attention back to the counter.

Saffi widened her eyes. "Seriously?" She licked sugared pink whipped cream from her mocha and groaned with pleasure. "This is magic. Really. Best mocha ever."

Delilah's cheeks flushed pink. "Thanks, hun." She drummed her nails on the counter. One eyebrow quirked upward as she nodded toward her hands. "Raspberry polish with rhinestone sugar sprinkles." When Saffi sputtered whipped cream, Delilah belly laughed. "I chose them to match today's coffee catch."

Saffi wiped her mouth on her hoodie sleeve, then glanced

over her shoulder. "Have you seen Mellie? I don't see her cart. Didn't you say she always showed up for the market?"

Delilah nodded. "Most weeks. It's the best place in the cove to tempt townies and tourists into buying things they didn't know they wanted and probably don't need."

Saffi sucked more whipped cream off her mocha, reducing the luscious mountain enough to squeeze on a lid. "Guess I'll stroll for a bit. Anything I shouldn't miss?"

"Seafood Sallie's. If it's not too early, try her smoked salmon skewers, or if you want something to take home, snag a jar of cream-cheese salmon spread."

"Thanks for the tip." Saffi smiled and lifted her coffee in salute.

"Here's another tip, for what it's worth, my sleuthing friend. Saturday Market is make or break for Glenn. So, please. Don't chase him away."

Saffi's shoulders sank. "If he's as innocent as you think, a few little questions won't make him run. If he's not..." She left the implication unvoiced.

"OK. OK. I get it." Delilah busied herself opening a fresh sleeve of coffee cups. "But Glenn's been through enough. I don't want to see him hurt by Linda any more than he already has been. Be kind."

Saffi thought back to her first meeting with Glenn. His floppy hair and smiling brown eyes. Green crushed-velvet top and bell-bottom pants. Tripping over himself to compliment her and failing like a true nerd. Why couldn't the clues point more clearly to someone despicable like Bill, or to the elder Carmodys with their entitled ways? "I will," she promised.

She unfurled the reusable bag clipped to her pack as she rumbled along the line of vendors. Organic vegetables drew her eye and fresh bakery loaves tempted her nose. She bought compostable baggies of alfalfa sprouts and pea shoots from a fresh-faced microgreens farmer, and a plastic pint basket of purple, green, and yellow grape tomatoes from a sun-baked hippie. By the time she reached the seafood stand, her bag bulged and her belly rumbled. She didn't even try to resist Sallie's smoked salmon on a stick. The smoky maple-glazed fish nearly melted on her tongue. At the end of the row of vendors, she turned on her heel and beelined back to Kevin's Kookies.

Despite her "I'm just another shopper" ruse, Glenn greeted her with stiff shoulders and a smile that didn't come close to reaching his eyes. Delilah's voice echoed in her head: *Don't chase him away.*

Sometimes when a jazzy slant for an article eluded her, Saffi had to sneak up on the information, hoping to catch a glimpse of something worth pursuing. Maybe the technique would work on the skittish Glenn. Cookies first, questions later.

"Luscious Lemon, Wedded Bliss, Busy Mama, Choco Cherry Oat, Cookie Monsters... wow! I didn't know you made so many kinds. What's your favorite?"

A hint of smile lit Glenn's eyes. "I love all of my cookie children equally."

Glenn's cookies didn't come cheap. Ten cookies per bag for fourteen bucks, but money loosened lips and Saffi needed Glenn to warm to her again. "I hate this kind of decision." Saffi bit her bottom lip between her teeth. "I'll take Busy Mama and... oh, this is too hard!" She glanced at Glenn for help.

The cookie baker's stance loosened, and he grinned. "OK. I lied. I am partial to Choco Cherry. It's my own recipe."

"Choco Cherry it is!"

Glenn nodded at her bag. "That looks a little... full. Want one of these?"

As Saffi scrambled in her sling for a twenty, a five, and three ones, Glenn shook out a recycled plastic grocery bag. "Perfect." She grinned. "I can hang it from my handlebars."

"Great weather for a ride." He returned her smile.

And there it was, the opening she'd been looking for. "It is!

I'm surprised Mellie didn't bike over. I've been thinking about buying one of her paintings. They're small enough for my tiny walls."

Glenn nodded. "She's usually the first one here. Thinks it's funny to snag my prime spot."

He had parked his van near the front of the line of vendors. A good strategy, Saffi decided, guaranteeing that shoppers would have room in their bags and money in their pockets when they reached him. Or, if they skipped Kevin's Kookies on their way in, they wouldn't be able to resist grabbing a bag on the way back to their cars.

A shadow crossed Glenn's face. "To be honest, I'm a bit worried."

"About Mellie?"

As Glenn lifted a hand to shade his eyes against the morning sun, his bottom lip trembled. "After Linda—" He put his hands on the table and took a long deep breath.

Saffi placed one hand over his, gave it a pat, and then stepped away. "I know. I feel it too. It's like a storm on the horizon. You know it's coming. You just don't know exactly when it will hit."

"Or who." Glenn looked up at her, face broken with worry. "Linda got whopped upside the head by a storm. But it was a storm of her own making."

Had Glenn just admitted knowing why Linda was killed? Saffi clutched the plastic bag filled with cookies. *A storm of her own making.* But what storm? The storm surrounding who should inherit Uncle Kevin's bakery? Or some other storm?

"Glenn, is Mellie in danger?"

Glenn's gaze turned laser sharp. "Why would she be? Has she said something to you?"

Saffi felt as if the pavement moved beneath her feet. Had Glenn seen Mellie at her RV yesterday? If he had, he could be the person who had scared the artist away. Saffi decided to go with the truth. If she could get Glenn to drop his defenses, he might let something slip.

"She did." Saffi nodded. "Apparently, the day Casey went missing, she saw Bill with Jeff, and, later, with the girl."

Glenn's brows shot up. "Why would Mellie tell *you* that?"

Saffi shook her head. She wasn't about to tell Glenn that Raven had sent Mellie to her. "You know her better than I do. What do you think?"

Before Glenn could answer, a customer sidled up to the table and reached for a bag of wedding cookies. "Eliza loves these things! How much?"

The thick drawl made Saffi turn. So, she *had* seen Jeff at the marina. "Miz Graywood." He tipped his Stetson toward Saffi. "I was wondering if I might have a word with you."

Saffi stepped back. "About what?" She hoped he hadn't heard what she'd just told Glenn.

"Hang on." Jeff pulled a monogrammed leather wallet out of the inner pocket of his cotton-cord deck jacket and pulled out two tens, motioning Saffi away before Glenn could give him his change.

"It's about that granddaughter of mine. I'm sure Troy has told you some cock-and-bull story about Eliza and me coming here to snatch her away from her mama. But you can't hang your hat on a word he tells you."

Saffi glanced at Glenn, who was clearly listening. The baker rolled his eyes and flamboyantly fanned his face with the bills that must have been Jeff's change.

Saffi bit back a laugh. "Mmm. And?"

"And, Casey trusts you. Something about rescuing a drowning dog?"

"Archie!" Glenn interjected.

Jeff turned toward the cookie maker as if he'd forgotten his existence. His face went from friendly to irritated and he snatched the bills from Glenn's hand. Then he grabbed Saffi's elbow, trying to guide her away from the cookie table. "The little lady's miffed, but I think you can help us get back in her good graces."

Saffi lowered her arm to pull her elbow out of his grasp and turned to face him. "Look, Jeff. Let's be honest," she said. "Your granddaughter has good reason for being upset with you. You collaborated with Bill to take her away from her mom."

"What in blue blazes?" Jeff spluttered.

Saffi held up a finger to stop him. "When that didn't work, you accused her mother of arson. And when that didn't work, your wife threatened her mother with a lawsuit. If you really want Casey to forgive you, you'll need Nicole on your side, not me."

The bewilderment in Jeff's eyes left Saffi feeling flabbergasted. Was he really so used to getting what he wanted that he didn't know what it felt like to reap what you'd sowed?

As he stormed away, Glenn waved merrily from the other side of the cookie table. "Good luck with that, cowboy!" Then he turned to Saffi with brown eyes that sparkled the way they had the day they'd first met. She'd accomplished her goal of warming Glenn up again. Unfortunately, she'd warmed as well and now found herself with Delilah, hoping against hope that those merry eyes weren't guarding a dark secret. Despite her gut telling her Glenn was innocent, she had to keep prodding.

"So, Glenn. Why *do* you think Mellie talked to me?" She still wanted the answer Jeff's interruption had kept her from getting.

The sparkles in Glenn's eyes stilled. He nodded toward Jeff's retreating figure. "There's something about you," he mused. "People trust you. Want to confide in you. Maybe it's your outsider vibe."

Saffi frowned. "People trust me because I'm not a local?" Her experience told her people tended to have the opposite reaction to outsiders. They weren't trusted until they'd been around long enough to become insiders.

"No. You're the other kind of outsider. Someone living life outside the norm. You're a wanderer and a writer. Artists, kids, middle-aged baristas, dudes selling cookies out of vans." He shrugged. "Like it or not, you're part of our tribe."

Part of a tribe? The idea made her smile. Levi had been part of the academic tribe. Her status as a professor's wife had allowed her into the college's inner circle, and the fact that she was a published writer had impressed Levi's colleagues. At least, at first. But at every cocktail party someone asked the question she came to dread: "What kind of books do you write?" Being the woman behind *Aunt Saffi's Bedside Reader* didn't have the cachet of publishing literary fiction or academic nonfiction. Once the professor or grad student or faculty member's partner who'd asked the question found out what kind of writing she actually did, they wandered away, leaving her spinning around the edges of the party, feeling as if she was about to be flung off into space. Having a tribe of her own sounded really good. Unfortunately, the guy welcoming her with open arms just happened to be a murder suspect.

Way to go, Saffi.

Her trip to the Saturday Market would fill her fridge with fresh food, but the information she'd gained wouldn't fill a sandwich bag. Glenn knew Mellie had talked to her, but he hadn't dropped any damning clues. Mellie hadn't shown up at the market and Glenn feared she might be in danger. Jeff was a Texas-sized jerk, but that wasn't news. After she dropped off the goods at her RV, she would head out to find Mellie. Then she would try again to pump Detective Richards for information. Find out who had given Glenn an alibi. If it was legit, she would gladly strike him off her list of suspects. After all, they belonged to the same tribe.

THIRTY

Back at her Rambler, Saffi unloaded her bags and scarfed down a salad before rewarding herself with one of Glenn's delectable Choco Cherry Oatmeal cookies. "Please don't be a murderer," she whispered as she picked chocolate crumbs off the front of her hoodie and popped them into her mouth. Anyone who could make oatmeal taste so good had to be innocent.

She locked up and then wandered around to the back of the coach. She'd stashed her bike there earlier, out of sight, not bothering to lock it up. Bike thefts were fairly common in RV parks, but they usually happened at night. The day had warmed enough to tie her hoodie around her waist rather than wearing it; she pedaled her cruiser onto the gravel RV loop with the pale rose T-shirt she'd pulled on that morning in full display. It sported her favorite writing quote: "I'm not quiet. I'm plotting." As appropriate, she realized with a shiver, for a killer as for a writer.

If this murder had been plotted, Glenn looked way too guilty to be the killer. Some secondary character like Jeff or Bill or Nicole—maybe even Mellie—would be the real villain. To figure out if one of them could be guilty, she had to answer the vital question: "Why?" Linda might have been blackmailing Nicole but, as far as Saffi could tell, Jeff hadn't even met her. And Bill? He resented Linda for taking his job, but killing someone over an RV park job? No mystery writer would hang a plot on such a flimsy motive. Still, Saffi knew from *Bedside Reader* stories that, in real life, people were sometimes killed for ridiculous reasons. A man killed for hogging a bag of Cheetos. A woman killed for making a fart joke. Apparently, humans could snap at any time, for any reason.

Saffi pedaled over the bike bridge, past the visitor center, and up the hill to the overlook above the cove, hoping to find Mellie in her usual spot. She wasn't. Saffi stopped long enough to peer into the trees, but Mellie's art cart wasn't there either. The only other place she knew to look was the parking lot near the lighthouse where she'd seen Mellie's gallery before. Saffi chewed her lip and straddled her bike, wondering if she should keep going or give up. Before she could decide, a shrill warning cry came from the trees and a raven burst from a branch in full flight. Terror surged up the back of Saffi's neck and into the roots of her hair. *Raven!* She'd heard the same call the night of Linda's murder. *Hurry!* It seemed to say.

Glenn was right. Mellie was in danger.

Saffi stood on her pedals, following the raven's flight path. Her calf muscles strained as she struggled to make the bike go faster and faster, fast enough—she prayed—to get her to Mellie before something terrible happened.

Moments later, Saffi reached the lighthouse lot. She braked hard enough to spin her back wheel sideways and spew gravel against the black and silver Mini-Winnie she'd seen from the lighthouse two days ago. Now that she thought about it, she'd seen a similar rig driving through the RV park. Coincidence? Stalker? Murder suspect? She braced herself for the hoodie-clad guy to jump out and either snatch her or yell at her for damaging his paint job.

When nothing happened, she relaxed enough to scan the lot and surrounding area. Seconds later, she spotted Mellie's sunflower-yellow trike unhooked from its companion gallery, sprang off her bike and let it fall.

"Mellie!" The Pacific blew her voice back into her face. "Mellie, where are you?" High tide had cut the lighthouse island off from the mainland, but the raven hadn't flown in that direction. It had flown just beyond the lot to a north-facing cliff and landed on the broken remains of a weathered fence, calling "Kraw, kraw, kraw!" The ruff of short black feathers around its neck expanded with each short burst as it repeated the call, its voice echoing Saffi's cry: "Where are you?"

Saffi ran toward the raven, through the wide gap in the broken fence, along a double line of wheel tracks in the wet grass, stopping at the crumbling edge of the cliff. She put her hands on her knees for balance and leaned forward, fighting against the vertigo that threatened to pitch her over. She spotted the debris first: bits and pieces of Mellie's beautiful gallery, her tiny home on wheels. Crumpled walls and wheels and ruined paintings were strewn down the slope below where she stood. Clothes and pillows and books and smashed mugs littered the crumbling cliff face. The twisted remains of the trailer had come to a stop against the wave-slapped rocks at the bottom of the cliff. A few feet above the debris pile, a lone patch of grass and dirt among the rocks made her breath catch in her chest. A poppy-red flower straight out of a Frida Kahlo painting bloomed in its center. "Mellie!" Saffi screamed.

She'd been here before. Eyes closed to block out things she couldn't bear seeing. Wrapped in a blanket that smelled vaguely of dog. Ocean-wet air weighing down her curls. Authoritative voices barking orders. This time, one voice stood out, calling her name. "Mrs. Graywood? Mrs. Graywood! *Saffi!*" She opened her eyes to see Detective Richards holding out a steaming cup of coffee. When she tried to take it, her hand shook so much that he put his palm beneath the cup until her grip steadied.

Somehow, after spotting Mellie, Saffi had managed to fumble her phone from her bag and call 9-1-1 before her knees collapsed. Last Chance Cove's rescue crew had seen this story often enough to know exactly what to do. Within seconds, sirens had sounded. Seconds later, the Mini-Winnie's engine had rumbled and the rig crept out of the lot, tires crunching gravel. The lighthouse parking lot had filled quickly. Firetruck. Rescue crew. Ambulance. Police cars. In the midst of the organized bedlam, Detective Richards had helped Saffi to her feet, walked her back from the edge, and sat her on the hard concrete bench of a cliffside picnic table. The dog blanket had come from his car, along with a thermos of coffee and two cups. The man was nothing if not prepared.

Side by side on the hard bench, they watched red-shirted members of the search and rescue team set up a complicated rope and pulley system. Two rescuers donned safety harnesses before being lowered down the cliff with a sturdily roped coffin-shaped basket on a separate pulley system between them. Saffi's gut clenched and she sipped the bitter black coffee, trying to stop her belly from heaving. As she waited, voices ebbed and surged around her.

"Must have been camping up here."

"Malarky. Mellie knew better than to camp on the edge of a cliff."

"I told her to put brakes on that ridiculous rig."

"Couldn't tell that girl a damned thing."

They were all talking about Mellie in the past tense as if the rescuers had already sent word that the artist had flown away on Raven's wings. Saffi refused to believe it. Mellie had landed on grass, not unforgiving rock. She could have survived. *She could have!* Something wet ran down Saffi's cheeks, flavoring her next sip of coffee with salt. And then a shout rose up the cliff. "She's alive!"

When the cup flopped over and hot liquid ran across the borrowed blanket and down the legs of her jeans, Saffi knew exactly how Glenn had felt when he'd learned of Linda's death. The shock of the unexpected news blasted through her and her muscles went completely limp.

Alive.

In this moment, that single word meant everything to Saffi. And then, the moment shattered.

"A bit of a miracle, was it?" Detective Richards leaned toward her. "Finding Mellie." He waited for her to fill the silence, but with what? "Like when you found Linda."

Was he accusing her of something? Saffi tossed off the coffee-soaked blanket and leapt to her feet. "No, Detective. It was nothing like that. Linda was dead. Mellie's alive."

He nodded. "Thanks to you, it seems."

Fury made Saffi's chest burn. "And Linda? Her killer is still out there somewhere. Is that thanks to you?"

Detective Richards stood and turned, eyes haunted as he looked toward the estuary where Linda's body had been found. "I'm missing something." He turned to look down at Saffi. "Maybe it's something you did."

Saffi stiffened, fists clenched, her whole body resisting the implication in his words.

"Or maybe it's something you know," he went on. "Something you're not telling me because, for some bizarre reason, you think a writer is better equipped to solve a mystery than a police detective."

The bubble of Saffi's anger burst and she sagged onto the bench like a popped balloon. Detective Richards sank down beside her. They waited in uneasy silence until the basket had been raised and lifted into the ambulance with Mellie's limp unconscious body strapped inside it. As the ambulance wailed its way to the hospital, Saffi broke her silence, spilling everything she'd discovered in her amateur sleuthing, holding nothing back—neither the guidance she'd received from Raven nor the fact that Mellie knew something about Linda's death. She gave the detective everything she'd learned about all of them—Bill, Jeff, Nicole, Glenn, even Troy—things she knew for sure and things she suspected. She told him everything because she was sure of *one* thing: if someone on her list of suspects sent the art cart over a cliff—with Mellie trapped inside—that person had to be found, and stopped, before anyone else got hurt... or worse.

THIRTY-ONE

Despite his misgivings, Detective Richards let Saffi accompany him to the hospital. After giving Mellie a quick exam, the ER doctor—apparently Chief Duarte's very eligible daughter—opened up like a happy clam when the detective locked eyes with her. Saffi thought Dr. Duarte was violating HIPAA rules to get closer to the handsome detective until the doctor turned toward her.

"We're allowed to divulge patient information to *law enforcement*," Dr. Duarte said pointedly.

Detective Richards bent toward the doctor. "If you don't let her stay, she'll stick around until she drags the information out of someone."

Before Saffi could huff out a denial, Dr. Duarte shrugged. "The cart took the brunt of the fall. The patient hit the ground on her left side. Dislocated left shoulder. Broken wrist, also the left one so she'll still be able to paint." Dr. Duarte shot a conspiratorial grin at the detective. "She's awake but bruised, confused, and most definitely concussed. They've taken her to imaging for an MRI. We'll check for internal injuries, but she's able to move so her spinal cord is intact. Probably thanks to that left-side landing. Her youth will help her heal. If she was older —" Dr. Duarte slanted her eyes toward Saffi as if in comparison.

Despite the dig, Saffi smiled as relief washed through her. Mellie's injuries sounded bad, but they were neither life-threatening nor disabling. She whispered thanks to Raven and to whatever blessed beings had been watching over the artist as she slept. Frida perhaps? The thought widened Saffi's smile. Detective Richards gave her a quizzical look, perhaps wondering why she'd be smiling after the doctor's unspoken jibe. Saffi chuckled. She let the doctor's ageism wash over her like waves over sand. She knew something the younger woman did not: aging didn't make a woman less. It set her free.

When Saffi didn't respond to her snide aside, the doctor encouraged Detective Richards to come back later in the day. "Mellie's tests will be finished. She'll be rested, so you can pepper her with questions to your heart's content. I'm off at five, so come before then!" She waved as Detective Richards ushered Saffi out of the Emergency Room's automatic sliding doors. Saffi wondered if he'd caught the doctor's thinly disguised wish to see him again before her shift ended.

The detective drove Saffi and the bike he'd loaded into his SUV earlier back to the RV park. He dropped her off at space 32 with a caution to stay out of the investigation. "No more amateur sleuthing. If we're dealing with the same perp..." He trailed off, shaking his head.

He didn't need to finish. If the person who'd killed Linda felt threatened enough to try to silence Mellie, he or she wouldn't hesitate to come after Saffi... again. She nodded her understanding. Seeing Mellie at the bottom of that cliff was all the warning she needed.

By the time she'd dragged her bike around the back of her Rambler and hoisted it into the bike carrier, a crowd of familiar faces had gathered, clamoring for information like gulls swarming a pile of fish guts. Delilah pushed her way forward, face pale, eyes hungry for good news.

Exhaustion weighed down Saffi's body. She didn't want to talk, not even to Delilah. She wanted to go inside and collapse or crank up the Rambler's engine and drive away. But running wasn't an option. For one thing, Detective Richards had warned her again that she was not to leave town without police permission. For another, a young woman was in the hospital, broken and battered. Whoever had done it had to be stopped.

"So, is she dead?" Bill demanded, bringing her attention back to the group of campers milling in her RV space.

"Is she *DEAD*?" Saffi's voice rose to its shrillest tone. "Do you want her to be?"

Behind her, someone gasped. Saffi whirled to face Nicole. "Or maybe you do?"

She flapped a hand at Glenn and then at the two Texans skulking at the rear of the crowd. "One of you, perchance?"

"Have you lost your damned mind?" Bill demanded. "Why would any of us want to kill Mellie?"

Saffi put her hands on her hips and speared Bill with her iciest glare. "I don't know. But whoever shoved her rig over that cliff had better enjoy their last days of freedom because Mellie's alive. And you can bet that as soon as she's able, she'll spill everything she knows."

She scanned the gathering, paying special attention to those on her list of suspects. She saw tightness around eyes, faces gone pale, hands jammed under armpits. Angry faces. Mulish faces. Nicole covering her mouth with her hand. Glenn taking shaky breaths. She zeroed in on Bill, who was looking around at everyone else as if checking their responses before figuring out his own. Suspicious? Maybe, but then Last Chance Cove's resident pirate always looked as if he'd just committed a crime or was thinking about committing one. Without waiting for the shocked responses she knew would come, Saffi unlocked her RV and escaped inside.

When the burst of anger passed, it hit her: by telling the crowd that Mellie was alive, she'd lit a fuse that could explode all over the artist. If one of them went after her, Saffi would never forgive herself. Her instincts told her to rush back to the hospital and stand guard by Mellie's bed. But Detective Richards' warning and her own gut-level knowledge that anyone who knew anything about Linda's murder was in danger —herself included—convinced her to stay put. To stop herself from doing anything rash, she put water in the electric kettle. Maybe a cup of tea would settle her nerves. In the meantime, she needed to get rid of the smell of wet dog and stale coffee. She stripped out of her clothes and sealed them in a kitchen trash bag before the smell could permeate her space. Then she slipped into her thick terry robe and tied it at her waist.

She tried to force down her fears by focusing on mundane things like the load of laundry she needed to do. It didn't work. Instead, it led her straight back into the mind-spinning morass. Nearly a week ago, she'd done her first load of laundry here. That evening seemed an eternity ago, but it wasn't. She'd over-heard Nicole and Troy's conversation. Watched him fold her laundry and come to the erroneous conclusion that they were a couple. From that moment, things had spun and tumbled until Saffi couldn't tell which way was up. She'd turned herself into a bumbling amateur sleuth, tried so hard to solve the crime, at first so that Chief Duarte and the city manager wouldn't label Linda's death an accident without turning over a single seashell on the beach. But she hadn't bumbled everything, had she? She'd found Casey before the Texans could spirit her away. And she'd found Mellie before she—

Saffi sucked in a shaky breath. She'd found Mellie... alive. She sent another silent thank you to Raven and promised to be a better listener in the future. When the kettle boiled and clicked itself off, Saffi took down a boring white cup from its hook with a twinge of remembrance. What she wouldn't give to go thrifting for beautiful cups with Mellie this afternoon. Her hand trembled as she spooned one of her favorite loose teas—Midnight in Paris—into a tea ball, nestled it into the cup and poured boiling water over it. Within moments, the scent of intense black tea with notes of bergamot, lemon, and anise filled the kitchen. Her shoulders relaxed and her hands stilled. She carried the cup to the couch and cozied up, tucking her chilled feet beneath her to take advantage of the warm folds of her robe.

Now that she was comfy and partially relaxed, she could consider the ramifications of what she'd done—spread the word that Mellie was alive. She'd been unforgivably reckless. She made a mental list of ways a clever killer could sneak into a hospital room. Fake an illness or injury and come in through the ER as a patient. Pretend to be a relative to gain access. Impersonate a police officer (although in a town this small that might not work). Steal scrubs and a clipboard and walk straight into Mellie's room. She'd seen that strategy on more than one TV series. There were so many ways to get to the artist. Detective Richards had told her in no uncertain terms to stay away from the investigation. Going to the hospital after being told not to would put her at the top of the detective's list of suspects.

Saffi sipped her tea and stewed, knowing that someone else was out there doing the same thing. Someone whose secrets Mellie had kept, who would feel even more threatened now that he (or she) had failed to silence the artist. She gripped her cup. If there was ever a time to leave things in police hands, this was it. Detective Richards would find the suspect. She didn't need to do anything but sit... and relax...

Stuff that! Saffi leapt to her feet so quickly tea splashed down her robe, but she was halfway out of it before she noticed. She needed clothes. Shoes. A hoodie. Her sling bag. And one more thing—transportation.

THIRTY-TWO

When Saffi decided to live and work in her RV, she'd chosen to go car-free. Her rig could have towed a small car, but once an RV had a "toad" attached, it became nearly impossible to back up. Saffi had opted for a bike instead. It got her where she wanted to go and kept her in shape. A win-win, as far as Saffi was concerned. At least, until she needed to get all the way across town before a killer could creep up on her friend. She couldn't exactly call Detective Richards for a ride. He'd told her to stay away. But she could hoof it over to Delilah's trailer and see if she could beg a lift.

A quick rat-a-tat on the side of the trailer brought Delilah to her door. Like Saffi, she was dressed in layers—jeans, T-shirt, hoodie—ready for anything the afternoon could toss her way. "I was just on my way to the hospital."

Oh, no! Saffi's mouth went dry. "To see Mellie?"

Delilah nodded. "I called to see if she can have visitors, and they said yes."

Saffi swallowed a few times, doing her best to convince herself that Delilah had only one reason to visit Mellie: they were friends. "Uhm, could I catch a ride?"

Delilah's eyes narrowed and she frowned. "You saw her earlier, right?"

"No." Saffi shook her head. "She was still being examined when I was there."

"Sure, hun. I'll give you a ride. As long as you're not going over there to finish her off."

Finish her off? Saffi sucked in a breath. "What? No, I—"

Delilah chuckled. "You were dangling Mellie like a worm on a line earlier. Was it that detective's idea? Or yours?"

Saffi blew out her breath. She was tempted to let Delilah think the detective had put her up to spreading the news. That he'd been setting a trap for a killer. But he hadn't. "I just lost it. Bill asking if Mellie was dead." Saffi shook her head. "I blurted it out without thinking."

Delilah's eyes bulged and she put a hand over her mouth. Then she lifted a finger. "Hang on a sec." She dipped back inside her trailer and came out stuffing a phone into a shoulder bag barely big enough to hold it. Keys jangled from her pinkie finger. "Off we go!" She stopped at the driver's-side door of the faded red VW Jetta parked in front of her Terry trailer. "Just don't go all murdery on me when we get there."

Suspicion, Saffi realized, was a two-way street. For a moment, she had feared Delilah had nefarious motives for visiting Mellie. The barista's offer of a ride had banished any suspicion. Someone wanting to harm Mellie wouldn't drag along a witness. Delilah had an equal right to suspect Saffi. Maybe more of a right, since the barista had been friends with both Linda and Mellie. "You have my word!" Saffi crossed her heart.

"OK." Delilah clicked the button on her smart key and the Jetta's lock release dinged. "Hop in."

Saffi hopped. The car's interior was worn but as clean as Delilah kept the counters at the café. A tree-shaped air freshener dangled from the rearview mirror. Saffi had a serious aversion to the chemicals in the fake pine scent, but she wasn't about to complain. A ride was a ride. "Mind if I roll down the window a bit?"

Delilah waved a hand, flashing the raspberry and rhinestone sugar nails she'd worn to match this morning's coffee catch. "Sure thing."

As the car rumbled down the RV park's gravel lane, Delilah shot a glance her way. "It must have been horrible. Finding Mellie like that."

Saffi linked her fingers together to keep her hands from starting to shake again. "I felt so..."

"Helpless?" Delilah clenched the wheel tighter.

"Yes."

"I remember that feeling. From the fire."

For a moment, Saffi thought she meant the Prevost fire at the RV park. Then she remembered—Delilah had lost everything to the Camp Fire in Paradise, California, then lost it all again a few years later. Saffi had written a piece on deadly wildfires for *Bedside Reader*, #14. The Camp Fire sparked when high winds downed a power line and ignited a long hot summer's worth of dead brush—dry grass, brittle leaves, desiccated needles, fallen twigs and branches. Strong winds spread flying embers from tree to tree and, once it reached Delilah's hometown, from house to house, business to business, growing at the rate of a football field every three seconds. As the fire spread, a town's worth of people threw valuables and important papers into their cars. Tragically, a single main artery led out of town. Traffic came to a standstill. The air went dark with ash. Trees along the road turned into flaming torches.

Saffi knew helplessness. She'd felt it when Levi died. But the kind of helplessness that Delilah must have felt, trapped in traffic that couldn't move as fire licked at the tires of her car, that was a helplessness she wouldn't wish on her worst enemy. She reached out and squeezed Delilah's hand. "I'm so sorry."

Delilah squeezed back. "Thanks. Some days I don't think about it at all. But most days, I do. And when someone I care about is a victim of violence, I just want to scream: Enough already!" The barista's voice rose straight out of her chest, vibrating through Saffi's bones. Eighty-five people had lost their lives in the Camp Fire. They were Delilah's friends, her neighbors. How the barista came out of that with a can-do attitude and cheerful demeanor, Saffi would never know.

The drive to the hospital passed in an eyeblink. Before Saffi had cleared her thoughts of smoke and flying sparks, Delilah pulled into a parking space in front of the squat rectangular building. The woman at the help desk gave them a warm smile which wavered and then set with far less warmth as she checked her computer screen for Mellie Blue.

"Second hall to your right," she said. "Room 137."

Springy, blue-marbled rubber flooring muffled their steps as they made their way down the main hallway. The artificially chilled air smelled of disinfectant and despair. When they reached the second double doorway to their right, Delilah stopped. Her face was flushed and the hand holding her keyring shook hard enough to jingle the keys.

"You OK?" Saffi reached out a hand, but Delilah pulled away.

"I'm fine. Just forgot to use the little girls' room before we came," she said. "You go ahead."

Delilah bolted back toward the women's room they'd just passed before Saffi could offer to wait for her. Inner alarms jangled. The little hairs on her arms tingled. What was that all about? Delilah couldn't possibly be up to something, could she?

Saffi considered her options. She could follow her friend, claiming she had to go, too. She could hide somewhere—behind the potted plant at the end of the hall, perhaps—and watch what Delilah did next. Or she could go straight to Mellie's room and lie in wait, terrified that she'd been horribly wrong about everything—everyone—since she arrived in Last Chance Cove.

She chose the latter, and it was much easier than it should have been. A call came in to the nurse's station just as she started down the hall. The duty nurse rushed away, leaving it unattended. Saffi passed room after room, all with their doors closed, including the one at the end of the hall: Room 137. She knocked softly, then opened the door and eased inside, letting it close behind her. The room went as black as a light-absorbing raven's feather.

Saffi blinked. Where was the patient monitor? She expected to see its familiar screen lit with green, yellow, magenta, and blue spiked waves busily tracking Mellie's heart rate, blood pressure, oxygen saturation, and temperature. As her eyes adjusted, she made out the shape of a white-sheeted hospital bed in the center of the room.

"Mellie?" she whispered as she crept toward the bed. "You awake?" Saffi heard soft breathing, as if someone was sleeping. Could that be why the room was so dark? "OK," she whispered. "You sleep, I'll watch."

The soft breathing caught for a second, then resumed its slow even pace. *Sorry,* Saffi mouthed. She felt her way to the foot of the bed and then around the other side, hoping to bump into the chair she was sure would be there. Her right slogger hit something, but it didn't have the metallic ring of a hospital chair leg. It thunked. And then... it moved. Saffi backpedaled until her rear hit the hard metal rails of the hospital bed. The figure in the chair stood, looming toward her. She sucked in a breath, readying herself to scream before she remembered. No one was at the nurse's station. The patients' doors were all closed.

"There's a-a guard outside," she bluffed. "If I scream, he'll be in here in a shot."

A deep voice chuckled with something that could have been menace, incredulity, or the beginnings of a bad cold. Before she could figure out which, the door behind her swung wide and light flooded the room. Saffi turned, blinking against the glare as Delilah strutted through the door.

"Delilah! Get help!" Saffi yelped.

"That won't be necessary." Saffi whirled around to find Detective Richards standing behind her. She looked from the detective to Delilah and back again. In the process, she took in the fact that the hospital bed poking her in the hip held nothing but a row of pillows draped in a blanket. Mellie wasn't even in the room.

"You... you—" Saffi blustered. "You set me up?"

Delilah pulled her phone from her bag and waggled it at Saffi. "I might have tipped him off that you were on your way."

Saffi flinched. So much for friendship. "Why would you do that?"

Delilah reached across the bed to squeeze her shoulder. "Don't fret, sugar. I just thought it was time *he*," Delilah pointed a raspberry fingernail at the detective, "eliminated *you* from his list of suspects so he can track the *real* killer."

"I need to sit down." Saffi brushed past the detective and sank into the chair he'd just vacated. She clasped her hands together to keep them steady. "And Mellie?"

"She's in a safe place," Detective Richards assured her.

Saffi skewered him with her fiercest scowl. "An *undisclosed* safe place, I hope?"

The detective nodded; his left brow quirked as if to say, *Only you would think I'd endanger someone who'd just been attacked and left for dead.*

"So, this whole thing?" She spread her arms to take in the room. "The nurse called away. Delilah"—she glared at her friend—"scampering off to the ladies'? To trap *me*? Why?"

Detective Richards took a small black notebook from the inside pocket of his jacket and flipped it open. "Let's see. You arrived the day of the murder. Mr. Kidd told me that you were very upset—'furious,' he said,"—the detective tapped the page with a finger—"when he couldn't give you the monthly space you claimed had been promised by Ms. Oates."

Saffi squinted up at him. "*Bill* told you? Bill the *kidnapper?*"

The detective glanced up, then back down at his notes. "That night, you showed up at Nicole's trailer with Archie, claiming to have found him on the beach. Then, the next morning, you just happened to 'find' Linda's body." He had the audacity to use air quotes and look her straight in the eye. "And today, you found Mellie, even though her gallery had plunged off a cliff."

He flipped the notebook shut. "You are, Mrs. Graywood, the only person who has been verifiably present throughout this case. Either you are poking around where you shouldn't, which makes you look guilty, or you are guilty."

"Congratulations, Detective. You've solved the case!" Saffi smacked her hands together, then rubbed them briskly. "I did it! I pulled into town just in time to kill a woman I'd never met because I didn't get an *RV space* and then I decided to push another woman off a cliff after she came to *me* as the person she trusted to tell whatever secret she's been hiding."

"So you claim."

Saffi nodded. "Right. No witnesses, so it didn't happen. And the person who yanked me off the steps at the lighthouse?"

Detective Richards slipped the notebook back into his inside pocket. "Rubber boots were not made for climbing ladders."

Saffi turned to Delilah. "What about you? Do you think I'm an opportunistic murdering klutz?"

Delilah put her hands on her hips. "Oh, come on. You should have seen the look on your face when I went to the restroom. You thought I was guilty as sin."

She hadn't exactly thought that, but she'd feared it. "Fair enough."

Detective Richards leaned forward and put a hand on Saffi's shoulder. "You asked why we put on this elaborate charade to trap you. You didn't ask if I thought you were guilty."

"And?" Saffi squeezed her hands together.

"I think what I've always thought. You're naturally curious —as evidenced by your *Bedside Readers*—and you are sleuthing your way into trouble. If the person who killed Linda sent Mellie over that cliff, we are dealing with a ruthless murderer."

"Or a fearful accidental killer," Saffi said.

Detective Richards raised both brows.

"Someone who didn't mean to kill Linda but is terrified of being found out?" The detective pressed his lips together as he thought through what Saffi had said. "Perhaps."

"Great! Now that we have all this pish-tosh out of the way" —Delilah's spangled nails sparkled in the light from the open door as she waved away their discussion—"can we visit Mellie?"

Detective Richards shook his head. "No. For the time being, she is under police protection."

"And you wouldn't want anyone to divulge her location?" Saffi bit her lip, still feeling guilty about alerting all the suspects to Mellie's vulnerable state.

"Has she told you who pushed her?" Saffi demanded. "Or who she's been protecting?"

Detective Richards had the grace to look a bit abashed.

"And she won't," Delilah informed him. "You guys have rousted her too many times for her to trust you now."

The detective set his lips. "That wasn't me."

Saffi wasn't surprised to hear that he hadn't been chasing Mellie from place to place. Enforcing city ordinances most often fell to uniformed police.

"So, if she won't talk to you, why not let us see her? Delilah's her friend, and Mellie tried to tell me what she knew before this happened."

"So you say."

Saffi stood and looked straight into the detective's serious brown eyes. "Yes. I do say, because it's true. It happened. And when it happened, Mellie ran and, from what I could tell, she ran because she saw someone who spooked her." Saffi repeated her list of the people she'd seen through the windshield of her rig—Troy, Aaron, Delilah, Jeff and Eliza, Nicole and Casey, Glenn. "And then there was Bill, who you released from custody, despite the fact that he'd snatched Casey and hidden her in Linda's apartment."

"No one wanted to press charges," the detective said, "not even Nicole. We couldn't hold him."

"Really?"

Now the detective looked sheepish. "And the city manager made a call to the chief. Said if we couldn't charge Bill, the park needed its manager back, pronto."

Saffi's belly clenched. "Manager? Since when is Bill the park manager?"

"Interim," the detective corrected. "Looks like Linda's death led to a promotion for Mr. Kidd."

Saffi tried to hide the wheels spinning in her head, but Detective Richards was good at reading faces. "I can see what you're thinking, Mrs. Graywood. In all honesty, I've thought it myself. But as far as I can tell, Mr. Kidd had no motive for killing Ms. Oates."

"No motive! Bill hated Linda for taking the job he thought should be his. He told me so himself."

Delilah clenched the metal bed rail so hard her knuckles went white. "What did you say?"

"That Bill had a reason for disliking Linda. He'd been at the park longer, but she swanned in and took the job he wanted."

Delilah tapped her nails on the rail. "Linda didn't take Bill's job. Randall hired her when she first came to town, months before Bill showed up begging for the park host job. She didn't want to hire him, but Randall said she needed to hire the candidate with the most pertinent experience."

The puzzle pieces in Saffi's head rearranged, leaving a question mark in place of the "fact" that Bill had despised Linda for taking "his" job. Clearly, the animosity he felt toward Linda was real. But what had caused it? And was the reason deep enough to be a motive for murder? In light of Delilah's revelation, that bright red bandanna Bill had "found" looked more and more like freshly spilled blood.

"Please let us visit Mellie," Saffi pleaded. "She may be protecting the person who pushed her. Give us a chance to find out."

"Pretty please, with chocolate sprinkles on top." Delilah batted her eyelashes.

Detective Richards threw up his hands in exasperation. "Fine. But I'll be posted outside."

Detective Richards led Saffi and Delilah out a back door and across a parking lot to a building labeled "Outpatient Services." Saffi spotted the detective's police SUV and, parked right beside it, the Kevin's Kookies van.

"Glenn is here?"

Delilah nudged her arm with an elbow. "Chill, super sleuth. The hospital's on his delivery route. Kevin's Kookies are better than a shot in the arm for what ails you."

As they walked toward the building, she heard the rumble and clunk of a truck going over one of the parking lot's speed bumps, but by the time she turned around, it had passed out of sight. Her mind flashed to the rattletrap truck she'd seen parked beside Bill's fifth wheel. Saffi shook herself. Her nerves were so on edge she was seeing—and hearing—suspects everywhere.

Detective Richards nodded at the admissions clerk at the front counter and the woman waved him in with a brief glance. Saffi hoped she wasn't as blasé about everyone who entered the building. If she was, Mellie might not be as safe as the detective claimed. Much like the hospital, Outpatient Services featured the neutral blues and creams of medical facility décor, all of which passed in a blur as they made their way through a maze of corridors to a room that seemed to be at the building's center. A uniformed officer rose as they approached. Saffi recognized the young woman from the day she'd found Linda. She was the officer who had covered the body with a tarp.

"All quiet?" Detective Richards asked.

"As a mouse's whiskers."

"Good. Why don't you take a break. I'll stand guard while these two visit their friend."

A look of intense relief broke across the officer's face. Without a word, she pigeon-walked to the ladies' room at the end of the hall and rushed inside. Detective Richards blushed while Saffi and Delilah bit back laughter. To cover his embarrassment, the detective opened the door and held it for them. "Ms. Blue, you have visitors," he announced. "I'll be right outside if you need me."

This time, Saffi found what she'd expected inside the room: a monitor lit up with Mellie's vital signs and the bruised but conscious artist propped up in a seated position on the hospital bed. Saffi flashed to a picture she'd seen of Frida Kahlo confined to her bed after the tragic trolley accident that nearly took her life. The parallel was jarring. Bruises beneath Mellie's dark eyes made her face look hollowed out. Her left arm was strapped across her belly, probably to stabilize her dislocated shoulder. A black brace supported her broken wrist. Luckily, the artist's right arm was free, and she gave them a sardonic wave.

"Oh, sugar!" Delilah hurried to Mellie's bedside. When a look of terror crossed the artist's face, Delilah stopped.

"I'm sorry." Mellie grimaced. "I was afraid you might try to hug me."

"No sorrys! If someone had pushed me over a cliff, I'd buy myself a shotgun and barricade myself inside my trailer."

"Remind me to stay on your good side." Saffi laughed.

Mellie started to join in, but a gasp of pain soon replaced her laughter.

"I know you probably don't feel like having company right now," Saffi went on, "so we'll make this quick."

Mellie's dark eyes clouded. "I've already been grilled by that detective."

Saffi nodded. "You and me both. In fact, the detective and this one," she jabbed a thumb at Delilah, "lured me into a trap to see if I planned to do you in."

The artist's thick brows joined in the middle as she scowled. "No surprise. We're vagabonds, you and I. That makes us suspicious characters to the police."

Saffi scrunched up her nose. "I think he's convinced now that I didn't kill Linda, or try to kill you, but someone did. Someone ruthless. So, please, tell me. Who are you protecting?"

Mellie flinched. Her gaze darted around the room as if she was searching for a way out. Then she shook her head as if to clear it, grimaced and put a hand to her brow. Her eyes glazed and lost focus. Then her head lolled back against the pillow.

"Mellie!" Delilah took her right hand and shook it.

Saffi glanced at the monitor on the other side of the bed. Mellie's oxygen saturation levels were dropping. "I'll get a nurse." She pulled at the door just as a nurse was pushing her way in, nearly slamming Saffi into the wall.

"Sorry," the nurse mumbled as she rushed to Mellie's bedside, pulled an oxygen mask over her face, and started fiddling with dials. She glanced back at Saffi and Delilah. "You'll have to go," she said briskly.

They went, stopping just outside the door. Detective Richards and the female officer stood against the opposite wall side by side, arms crossed. "Did you find out anything before you sent Mellie into a tailspin?" he asked.

Saffi looked down at her shoes. "No. She was about to—"

The detective cut her off. "I shouldn't have brought you here. Let's go."

"But Mellie!"

"Is in capable, professional hands, Mrs. Graywood." He nodded at the young officer, and she resumed her seat by Mellie's room. "Shall we?" He waved Saffi in front of him, and she went, with Delilah trailing silently behind her. Like Saffi, the barista must have felt chastened by Mellie's blackout. Clearly the young artist wasn't well enough to be quizzed by a couple of amateur sleuths.

As they strode toward the front door, Glenn walked in, a basket of cookies on his arm. Before Saffi could even react, the clerk at the front desk called out, "Kevin! Do you have any Hungry Mamas left? I could eat a dozen."

Glenn quirked a brow at Delilah, a shared acknowledgment of the fact that customers continued to conflate his name with his late uncle's. Then he plastered a smile on his face and strode to the front counter. "Lucy! I kept some just for you!"

"See." Delilah nudged Saffi as they walked out the door. "Told you. Cookies, cookies, nothing but cookies with our Glenn."

Saffi nodded. Her radar had turned from Glenn to Bill. And she couldn't get the look of panic on Mellie's face just before her blackout out of her head.

She looked up at the detective. "Did Mellie see who pushed her?"

After a dramatic sigh, Detective Richards stopped just outside the door. Hands on hips, he looked Saffi in the eyes. "No. She was sleeping and didn't wake up until her trailer hit the fence and broke through. Before she could get out of bed, it was in free fall."

Nausea twisted Saffi's gut. She didn't have to imagine what Mellie's fall felt like; she'd experienced free fall when someone pulled her off the ladder. And Linda had been through the same thing. Three women. Three falls. One person bent on covering up whatever he or she had done the night Linda died.

THIRTY-FOUR

In what felt like a déjà vu moment, Saffi woke after a night's sleep to pounding on the Rambler's door. *This has got to stop!* She tossed off the covers and struggled into her terry robe, cringing when she caught a glimpse of herself in her bathroom's mirrored closet. She cinched her robe around her waist and kept going. Anyone who would wake her from a sound sleep deserved the scare show he or she was about to get.

It didn't take her long to regret not stopping to untwist the snakes in her hair and wipe the sleep from her eyes. Troy stood at the bottom of her steps, hands stuffed in his pockets, fear furrowing his face.

"Oh, no. Please tell me no one's missing."

"Mellie. Fire and Rescue sent out an 'all hands' call for searchers."

Saffi put a hand over her mouth. Her legs wobbled and she sank to the floor at the top of the stairwell. "She couldn't disappear. She had a police guard!"

Troy shrugged. "It's an outpatient center. They lock the doors at night."

"They left her *alone*?" Saffi tried to keep her voice from rising into a shriek but didn't succeed.

Troy looked up at her from the bottom of the steps "No. Of course not. She had a private nurse watching over her and the police had a black-and-white parked outside all night."

"So, what happened?"

Troy rolled his eyes. "Call of nature. The outpatient center isn't set up for overnight stays, so no in-room facilities. The nurse went to the restroom down the hall. When she got back, Mellie was gone."

Saffi clutched her robe tight at the neck as if that could keep the chill she felt from settling in her chest. "And the officer parked outside?"

"Didn't see a thing. Parking lot was empty. Said it was as if she'd just got up and walked away."

From what Saffi had seen last evening, Mellie wouldn't have been able to walk anywhere, even if she'd wanted to. Someone had taken her, and, to do that, the person had to have known where she was. Who knew? Staff at the outpatient center. The police. Delilah. Did Glenn know? Just because he'd delivered cookies didn't mean he knew Mellie was there, did it?

Saffi's stomach clenched. He might not have known when he walked in the door, but he'd come face to face with two of Mellie's friends and a police detective. It wouldn't take a Miss Marple or Precious Ramotswe to figure out why that particular trio had visited the clinic.

"Glenn."

Troy's brows shot up. "What about him?"

"I think he took Mellie."

Troy pulled his phone from the inner pocket of his jacket. "We'd better call Richards."

"Call if you want, but he might not follow up. He's already told me that Glenn has a solid alibi for Linda's murder." Saffi tugged at the belt of her robe as she headed toward the bathroom. She slid the door shut behind her and started yanking layers from the drawers. Undies, T-shirt, jeans, zippered hoodie. When a fist pounded on the bathroom door, Saffi nearly jumped back out of the jeans she was stuffing herself into. "Hang on. Geez!"

Troy's steps thudded down the length of the Rambler, then back. "Hurry up. He's here!" Troy called.

"Who? Glenn?"

"Yes. He just pulled up by the office."

"I'm coming!" Saffi zipped herself into her jeans, then rushed to the bathroom sink. Teeth first, then hair. "Gimme jush a sec." She squeezed the words through toothpaste-coated teeth. She pulled her hair into a scrunchie and let the dark, silver-streaked tail of curls hang out of the back opening of a Vermont Lake Monsters baseball cap. By the time she locked her rig, Troy was behind the wheel of his blue truck with the passenger door open. Saffi climbed in, barely managing to shut the door before he hit the gas.

He glanced sideways, and barked, "Seat belt!" in a voice that told her he'd been driving a careless Casey around lately. She clicked her belt into the clip and chose not to point out that courteous drivers waited for that click *before* gunning the gas. But when she looked through the windshield, she got it. The Kevin's Kookies van was already headed out of the park. Troy followed at a more sedate pace, wanting to see which way Glenn turned while trying to avoid being spotted. Glenn took a right and drove toward the harbor. When the white van turned into Seal View Way, Troy followed.

"He's making a cookie delivery," he said as the van turned into the alley that led to Last Chance Café. He parked the truck in a space in front of his own business. As they waited, all Saffi could think was that she wanted one of Delilah's coffees so badly she could actually smell the brew. When Troy lifted one of the café's to-go cups from the console cup holder and took a sip, she understood why.

"You do know that qualifies as torture in some countries." She pointed toward the cup.

Troy grinned and took another long slow sip before nodding toward the second cup in the holder.

"Yesterday's dregs?" She shook her head. "No thank you."

"Please. I would never drink coffee without bringing a cup for my partner in crime-fighting."

Saffi touched the side of the second cup. Still hot. "A man who values his life." She picked up the coffee and took a sip. Mocha! A slow smile spread across her face. Tall, dark, thoughtful, and with lips that looked even tastier than the coffee she savored. "How'd you know?"

"Delilah!" they said at the same time, then burst out laughing.

A few sips later, Saffi felt warm and energized, ready for whatever the morning might bring. And a good thing. "Here he comes," she whispered, as if the man in the van could hear them.

They both ducked sideways, bumping heads. "Yowch!" Troy eased her head onto his lap and tucked himself behind her. Waves of warmth sent completely inappropriate zings through her body. She had to remind herself that Mellie was in danger to force herself back to a seated position after they heard Glenn's van pass.

Saffi watched the van rumble toward the stop sign at the 101.

"Let's hang back a minute. Glenn knows my truck. If he spotted me earlier and sees me pull out behind him, he might know we're following him." Troy turned his side mirror so he could see the van.

Saffi turned in her seat and got on her knees to get a better view through the truck's rear window. When the van turned left, she whirled around and sat back down, buckling her seat belt.

"He's heading toward town," she said.

Troy backed out so fast the shoulder strap tightened as she slammed into it, making her doubly glad she'd clicked the belt into place before he hit the gas. At the stop sign, he gunned the truck into a tiny break in the moving traffic. Saffi clasped the edge of the seat with both hands.

"Sorry." Troy glanced her way. "I don't want to lose him."

Saffi didn't want to lose him either, but she also didn't want to die an untimely death. Traffic streaming along both lanes slowed Troy down and gave her thumping heart a chance to slow as well. Even with a stream of cars between them, the van was easy to spot on the straight coastal road. Saffi lost sight of it for a second when Glenn hit the sharp right turn just past the RV park, but when they moved through the turn, she spotted the van heading along the road that paralleled Beachfront Park. One more turn and they knew where Glenn was headed.

"The lighthouse?" Troy glanced at Saffi. "Do they sell Kevin's Kookies?"

"I don't know if they sell them, but they definitely *eat* them!" She told Troy about Martin's morning cookie-and-tea parties with Glenn, Randall, and Mellie.

Troy shook his head. "I have to say, Saffi, so far it looks like Glenn's keeping to his regular routine. That doesn't seem like the behavior of someone who kidnapped a woman he tried to murder."

Saffi had to agree. "It doesn't." Not unless he'd taken her for tea with Martin, which was simply ridiculous. *Arrgh!* Detective Richards was right. Her sleuthing skills were rubbish.

"Fancy a visit to the lighthouse anyway?"

Troy shrugged. "We've come this far. We might as well go all the way."

The heat that rushed up Saffi's neck was such a giveaway

she turned to look out the window. *What are you, in high school?* She squeezed her hands between her thighs, then thought better of it and placed them demurely in her lap.

Gravel crunched as Troy pulled the truck into the parking lot next to the Kevin's Kookies van. Across the narrow rocky isthmus, they spotted Glenn carrying a basket as he hurried up the hill toward the Cape Cod-style lighthouse. He wasn't alone. Another man followed a few paces behind, one Saffi recognized. Short, pudgy, white poofs of hair above his ears lifting with the sea breeze blowing from behind the lighthouse— Walter, dangling a plastic grocery bag from each clenched fist.

"Looks like Walter discovered Martin's secret cookie binge." Saffi opened the truck door and hopped down. The sound of waves rushing toward the jetty that protected the harbor from the open sea made her body tense up. Waves slamming against rock. Against concrete. Against a cliff face. The sound she'd once loved so much now shot her back to scenes she would rather forget: a body shrouded in seaweed, a flower-shaped woman splayed in the grass. But she couldn't forget, not with a murderer on the loose. If Glenn was the culprit, maybe they could put an end to the fear and uncertainty that had surrounded her from her first night at Last Chance Cove. Maybe waves could be glorious waves again.

The causeway between the mainland and the island was as dry as it ever seemed to get. In other words—not very. The rocks were damp. Seaweed lingered, slimy and treacherous. Saffi picked her way from rock to rock, but a clumsy misstep sent her arms windmilling. Troy grabbed her hand and held tight, giving her time to regain her balance. He didn't let go until they gained the uphill path on the other side.

"Thank you." She looked up into those gray-blue eyes and tripped again.

"Maybe I should hold on until we reach solid footing?" he teased.

She laughed. "I might take you down with me."

"I'll take my chances."

His sinewy-strong fisherman's hand kept her feet steady and her heart rate high as they climbed the hill. Glenn and Walter had long since disappeared inside, and when Saffi tried the door, she found it locked. Troy checked a bulky black watch on his wrist with the most complicated display Saffi had ever seen.

"Is that the tide?" She pointed to a blue waveform that went from high to low.

"Tide graph. Moon phases. Altimeter. Barometer. Best fishing watch out there." Troy held out his arm to give her a closer look.

"Too bad it doesn't tell the time," Saffi teased.

Troy chuckled then double-pushed a button to reveal the glowing blue numbers of a digital clock. "Nine thirty," he noted as he turned to the sign on the lighthouse door. "Doors open at ten. Guess we'll have to crash the party."

Saffi hung back as Troy pounded on the door, worrying that Glenn would hide or flee before they could get inside.

"Come back at ten!" a voice Saffi recognized as Martin's called out. "When we're open. Like the signs says."

"Martin! We know you're in there!" Saffi hollered.

The voice came closer. "Who is this 'we' of whom you speak?"

Troy glanced at Saffi and put a gentle finger on her lips, then he turned back to the door. "Fire and rescue!" he boomed. "Open up!"

Behind the door, Saffi detected the scuffle of hastily vacated chairs and the thud of shoes on stairs. After the noise settled, Martin pulled open the door. "Ah!" He wiggled his gray unibrow. "The illustrious Aunt Saffi of *Bedside Reader* fame." He pinned Troy with an accusing stare. "I could have sworn you said, 'Fire and *rescue*,' not research."

Despite the scowl marring his face, Martin waved them

through the entry and up two steps into the living room. "Walter, we have guests."

Walter was perched on a spindly antique chair at a white lace-covered table behind the front room's roped-off area. He looked up from a copy of the *Last Chance Gazette* as if nothing at all could possibly be going on. Troy reached across the rope and turned the paper right side up.

"Better?" He quirked one brow.

"Thank you, but I couldn't find a thing worth reading today," Walter dissembled. He folded the paper and placed it on the table.

Saffi decided to cut to the chase. "We were actually hoping to catch Glenn."

Martin forcefully cleared his throat and Walter's bushy white mustache trembled.

"Catch?" Walter squeaked, his mouth pursed as if he'd sucked on a lemon. "Glenn?" He shook his head, and Saffi could see the denial forming before he opened his mouth. "Haven't seen him."

It was Saffi's turn for raised brows. "I'm afraid the evidence of his presence is all over your mustache."

Walter had the grace to blush before he began brushing crumbs from his whiskers straight onto the natty houndstooth vest straining against his ample belly.

Martin groaned and Saffi turned to see the tall lean man covering his eyes with a hand.

Saffi looked at Troy. "I'm beginning to think I was wrong."

"Good. Good. So, off you go." Martin stepped aside as if to let them pass. "Furniture to dust. Tours to give." Then he glared at Walter. "Crumbs to vacuum."

Walter looked sheepish.

"Sorry. I don't mean I was wrong about Glenn being here. He's here. In fact," she glanced at Walter, "we watched the two of you walk in together."

Walter rose from the table and inched his way behind Martin as if his tall friend could hide him.

"What I was wrong about was *why* he came here. I thought he'd taken Mellie from police protection to harm her. But a criminal conspiracy involving Waldorf and Statler?" Saffi shook her head. "Even I'm not that imaginative."

"Waldorf and Statler?" Troy asked at the same moment Martin clapped.

"You have a sharp eye," he said, "spotting the resemblance. And an even sharper mind for knowing that two aging gentlemen who modeled for a couple of elderly Muppets would be absolutely innocent of any crime. The only crime is that Mr. Henson never paid us a dime for using our likenesses. Walter thinks we should sue. Don't you, Walter?"

The face behind the bushy mustache had turned the color of a ripe eggplant.

Saffi put her hands on her hips. "Good luck convincing a lawyer that the two of you looked like Waldorf and Statler when you were, what? Thirty-something?"

Troy held up both hands. "I have no idea what is going on here, but you need to bring Glenn out from whatever rabbit hole he bolted into, right now."

Martin went to the door at the bottom of the winding stairs to the top of the lighthouse. "Glenn!" His voice echoed up the cylinder. "Come down!" The words bounced off the walls, merging into a ghostly swirl of sound. Once the echo settled, Saffi could hear two hushed voices going back and forth in a whispered argument which ended with the word, "Fine!" shouted by a voice that could only be Mellie's.

"Mellie!" Saffi tried to push past Martin to head up the stairs and Troy grabbed her elbow and held her back.

"Confronting a criminal in a stairwell is a very bad idea."

Given what had happened to her the last time she went up those stairs, Saffi knew Troy was right. She waited as boot-steps stomped around and around and down, followed by the soft slap of bare feet. Glenn emerged first, sporting a white crew neck sweater with blue stripes over navy bell-bottom pants. A few seconds later, a barefoot Mellie stepped into the hallway, her hospital gown engulfed by the folds of a zebra-striped silk robe that must have come straight out of Glenn's closet. The left sleeve hung loose to accommodate her arm and broken wrist, still in a sling against her chest to ease the weight on her injured shoulder. She lifted her right hand as if to wave then let it fall back to her side.

"You're just too good at this," Mellie mumbled.

"Good at what?"

Mellie's hand flopped out again. "You know, the whole sleuthing thing. Glenn thought I could hide here, but I knew you'd find me."

If Mellie had been kidnapped, she'd sound relieved. But "relieved" definitely did not fit the artist's demeanor. Resigned? Yes. That was the word.

"I don't understand." Saffi shook her head. "You don't want to be found?"

Mellie's eyes darkened. "If I wanted to be found, I would have stayed at the outpatient center. But you found me there, so I left. And now you've found me here." Mellie wandered over to the tufted fainting couch Saffi had used after her fall, flopped down on it, and then stretched out with her right arm resting across her eyes.

Saffi looked up at Troy, mouthing the word, "What?"

Troy squared his shoulders. "Mellie, the whole town is looking for you. Detective Richards called out Fire and Rescue. We *all* wanted to find you, and the best-case scenario is that we found you alive. You should be thanking Saffi."

Mellie lifted her arm off her face and sat forward. "For what? For all I know, *you* wrecked my gallery. Everywhere I go... there you are."

Saffi took a step backward, almost stumbling into Troy. All heads had turned her way as she blinked back the electric shock Mellie's words sent through her. A deep furrow turned Martin's unibrow into a grizzled "v." Walter's mustache twitched. Glenn's hands clenched into fists.

"I didn't. I wouldn't!" A steel band tightened around Saffi's chest. How could Mellie think such a thing? Did the others think so, too? She started to move toward Mellie, but Troy put a hand on her arm to stop her. *Et tu, Brute?* She knew just how betrayed Julius Caesar must have felt when the Roman senate, along with his good friend Brutus, turned against him. Mellie's blow felt almost as deadly. But she *hadn't* pushed Mellie. She knew it, and as Saffi stared into the artist's dark eyes and the artist looked away, she saw that Mellie knew it, too. That's when she remembered: Detective Richards had *told* her that Mellie hadn't seen anything. She'd been asleep in her trailer and woke up in free fall.

Saffi pulled her arm out of Troy's grasp, gave him a look that said, "Trust me," and walked slowly toward Mellie, palms up. *I mean you no harm,* the gesture said. When she reached the couch, Mellie tucked her feet so Saffi could sit.

"Mellie, please. Keeping quiet hasn't kept you safe. Neither has hiding, because you're right, I found you. And if I can find you, the person you're either scared of or protecting can find you. Last Chance Cove is too small to hide in."

Mellie leaned forward, cupping the arm bound to her chest with her right hand.

"As far as I know, there is only one person stalking me," she said softly.

"I'm not stalking *you*, Mellie. I'm stalking the truth."

Mellie drew in a long deep breath and her eyes shifted from accusation to acceptance. "Fine. It won't set anyone free," she said, "but here goes. The night Linda died, I was hanging with Bill in his RV."

"Bill?" Saffi tried to pull the shrill out of her voice, but she failed.

Mellie shrank back. "Yes, Bill. I know you don't like him, but he means a lot to me."

Disbelief must have shown on Saffi's face because Mellie scowled. "If you want me to talk, you better be ready to listen."

Chastised, Saffi nodded and cocked her head in her best "listening" pose.

"I first came to the RV park with friends from down South," Mellie went on.

On the West Coast, Saffi now knew, "Down South" meant southern California.

"They had this chill van conversion. We'd been traveling for like, a month, and having people around me all the time just made me... exhausted. You know? Every time I got back into the van to move to another place, I felt like ants were crawling all over my skin. I needed to be on my own for a while so I could recharge and create art again."

Saffi knew the creative introvert's dilemma. You need stimulation and new ideas to produce fresh work. You need to understand people at a deep level to have any hope of revealing the human condition through your art or craft. But people could be *tiring*. Saffi felt drained just thinking about it. In fact, sitting in this room surrounded by staring eyes while she interrogated the artist was sucking energy out of every pore. At some point, every creative yearned for some form of Virginia Woolf's room of one's own. In Saffi's case, the Rambler. In Mellie's case, the gallery. So how had Mellie gone from bumming it in a van to having that gallery? Mellie must have seen the question in her eyes.

"Bill came over to our campfire with his guitar and a twelve-pack most evenings," she said. "Those sea shanties of his got me right here." She knocked her right fist into the left side of her chest.

Saffi understood. Bill's booming voice had pulled her into the music at the bonfire, despite her resistance.

"One night he asked us where we were headed next and that's when it hit me. I didn't want to leave. I'd always dreamed of having a space of my own to crash in and sell my work. I don't know why, but Last Chance Cove seemed like the perfect place. I just didn't know how to make it happen."

A memory flashed into Saffi's head: the hodgepodge of lumber stacked on Bill's picnic table. Her mouth gaped open. "Bill built your gallery?"

Mellie grinned at Saffi like she was a six-year-old who'd finally learned to read. "You see it, right? Bill can be an arse but, deep down, he's one of the good guys."

Ah, to be young and naïve. Saffi shook her head. "Sorry. I haven't seen that side of Bill, but I'm glad you've decided to share it with us."

The rest of Mellie's story gushed out like waves washing over a jetty. When her friends left Last Chance Cove, Mellie stayed behind. One of her friends scribbled out the digits for the Mastercard his parents had given him so she could use his line of credit for as long as needed.

Ah! Trustafarians. Saffi winced. She'd run across a few of those while researching an article for *Bedside Reader, #10* called "Free Ride." Trustafarians were young adults from wealthy families who ditched their parents' posh worlds to live a nomadic lifestyle. The ones she had encountered spent their trust funds like tomorrow would pay for itself.

"The park let you pay that way?" In Saffi's experience, parks required a credit card in hand with a signature that matched the name of the person renting the space.

Mellie's dark eyes lit up. "Bill had no problem with it, but when Linda found out, she went gull-crap crazy!"

Much as Saffi liked Mellie, she couldn't blame Linda. Paying with someone else's card based on numbers scribbled on a piece of paper? Bill must have been out of his mind. Either that or blinded by Mellie's Frida Kahlo-esque beauty.

"Bill tried to get her to see reason, but she kicked me out of the park. I guess she still had the same stick up her ass she'd had when they were married."

The word shot through Saffi like a bolt from a crossbow.

Saffi didn't have to repeat it. The whole room rang with the word: "Married?" Martin, Walter, Troy, chimed the word, which Glenn echoed, as if Mellie had left him as clueless as the rest of them.

"Mells!" Glenn squeaked. "You've been sitting on an actual motive for murder!"

Mellie pressed her lips together and sank back against the head of the sleeping couch. "This is why I didn't tell anyone. So what if they were married? So what if she divorced him? None of that means he killed her."

Something else was off here, Saffi realized. If Bill and Linda had been married, why hadn't Glenn spilled the beans? When she asked, Glenn squeezed his face between his hands until he looked like an adorable otter. Saffi, who wanted to believe every word out of his mouth, steeled herself against the cookie maker's cuteness. She'd once read an article describing otters as "murderous, necrophilic aqua-weasels whose treachery knows few bounds."

Glenn released his face. "I mean, I knew she was married at some point but," he waved a hand as if swatting away a very annoying gnat, "we weren't close. Her parents moved to Arizona when she was a teen. She *never* came back to visit Uncle Kevin. That's why he cut her out of his will. So, no. I didn't know who she'd married. She did mention a divorce as her excuse for showing up in Last Chance Cove with her hand out." Glenn crossed his arms as if still trying to protect himself from his cousin's avarice.

The revelation that Bill and Linda had been married shook

Saffi, and Glenn was right. Since Bill hadn't revealed the relationship to the police, it made him look guilty as hell. Was that the big secret Mellie had been keeping? Or was there more? The way Mellie kept chewing her lower lip made her think Mellie was withholding something else—information she knew would further incriminate Bill, or someone else.

"Mellie, Bill is up to his eyeballs in this mess," Saffi said. "Why do you still trust this guy?"

Mellie sprang up from the couch, not at all like a woman who'd been laying at the foot of a cliff the day before. "Because *I* don't think he's done anything wrong, but I knew that *you* would, and you'd push and push until that detective had Bill in handcuffs again. Just like you did when that Texas lady paid him to hide Casey."

Eliza? Saffi had suspected Jeff of colluding with Bill, not Eliza, but the words Nicole's mother-in-law had spit out at the café the day after Saffi had found Casey thundered in her head: *Money always wins.* If Eliza was behind the kidnapping, Saffi had been missing clues big enough to drive a Prevost through.

"Mells..." Glenn eased the artist back down on the couch and knelt in front of her. "You're right about Aunt Saffi here." He turned to give Saffi an accusing look and she hunched into herself. "Have you read those books of hers? She's a pit bull. Bites down on a meaty topic and won't let go till she's wrung every bit of juice out of it. If she's determined to find Linda's killer, she'll find him. But before what you just told us, I don't think Bill was at the top of her list of suspects. I was. Me, Mells. Do you understand?"

Mellie's eyes flicked from Glenn to Saffi and back. "You?"

Glenn nodded. "She followed *me* here, sweets. Not Bill."

Tears welled in Mellie's eyes. "I hate this." She blinked and bit her lip. "But I hate whoever pushed me over the cliff even more, and it wasn't *Glenn*." She spat the name in Saffi's direction. "If it had been, he wouldn't have brought me here for tea and cookies. He'd have offed me in the back of his van and dumped my body off Last Chance Point." She gave Glenn an enigmatic Frida Kahlo smile. "Wouldn't you?"

Glenn returned her smile with a Davy Jones-worthy impish grin. "I would, indeed."

"Mellie!" Martin cleared his throat and shook a long, gnarled, pointer finger at her. "Stop soliloquizing and tell us what you know. If this ordeal isn't over soon, I fear poor Walter will have a stroke."

When they all turned to look at Walter, his face did, indeed, look apoplectic.

"Oh, Walter!" Mellie slid off the couch, guided Walter to the dining room chair he'd vacated earlier and took the chair next to him. "I'm sorry."

Martin held up Troy's arm so everyone could see the luminous blue digits on his wristwatch. "You have five minutes. Then I have to open the doors."

Walter moaned and Mellie stroked his hand.

"Sorry, Walter." She gave Glenn a long slow look. When he pressed his hands together in prayer position, she gave in at last. "On the night Linda died, Bill was worried about people going out on the beach despite the sneaker-wave alert. So, he went to check, and he took Smudge with him to stretch his legs and get some fresh air. They were gone so long I dozed off, so I was kind of hazy when they came back. But I remember a few things."

"Such as?" Martin nudged.

"Smudge went straight to his bed and tucked his head on his paws. Bill was clutching that red bandanna Archie wears. He didn't say a word. Just hung that thing on a hook in the stairwell, went to his room and shut the door."

"What did you do?" Saffi asked.

Mellie shrugged. "I went home. Man's got a right to his moods."

And there it was, the incriminating evidence Saffi had been

hoping to find, evidence that Saffi had already spotted but Detective Richards had failed to investigate with even the rigor she would have applied to a *Bedside Reader* article. Bill had Archie's bandanna the night *before* they went out searching for Linda. His story about finding it during the search was a lie.

One by one, the puzzle pieces of Linda's murder were clicking into place.

THIRTY-FIVE

Before they left the lighthouse, Troy called Detective Richards to let him know that Mellie had been found and that she had witnessed Bill's return to the RV with the incriminating bandanna on the night of Linda's murder, which meant he couldn't have found it the next morning as he'd claimed. For the time being, Mellie would remain at the lighthouse with Martin and Walter, the safest place in Last Chance Cove once the tide came in.

"We'll take excellent care of her," Martin promised.

Once Mellie had opened up, Walter's color had faded from "old man having a stroke" to "old man in need of a second cookie."

"We will! We will!" he gushed. "I've always wanted to sleep over here." His eyes sparkled like a kid's. "But Martin kept me away." He glared at his friend. "To save me from myself, so he said."

"Now that you're here, I can hardly wait to show you the view from the lens tower!" Martin wiggled his brow and Walter put his fingers in his ears and stuck out his tongue.

The elderly men's banter soothed Saffi like cold water on a burn. Soon, she hoped, this mystery would be solved. Soon, she could go back to her normal routine—researching, writing, revising—and leave the sleuthing to the pros. Soon... but not quite yet.

Troy peppered Saffi with advice during their short drive back to the park: "Let the authorities do their thing," he said. "Stay safe, so I don't have to be sorry."

Sweet, Saffi thought, but if he knew her better, he wouldn't have bothered.

"I'm headed over to talk to the fire chief," he told her as he swung the truck into the narrow road leading to the park. "He needs to know that Eliza was behind the kidnapping. Whoever planned that probably had a hand in the fire as well."

And I'm headed into the office to talk to Bill, Saffi thought, but she wasn't about to say that aloud. She did ask Troy to let her off at the park entrance, to "stretch her legs" a bit. He gave her a pointed look which she duly noted but chose to ignore. If Bill was in the office—a place too public for danger, she told herself—it would only take a word or two to get a reaction out of him, especially if he was guilty. With any luck, she'd have Bill on the ropes by the time Detective Richards arrived.

After the long stuffy stint inside the lighthouse, the fresh ocean air put pep in her stride. The salt-scoured blue office building looked almost cheerful in the afternoon sun. A gull swooped overhead, landed on the roof, and called out as if in welcome. Saffi wandered up the ramp, shielding her eyes to see inside. The lights were off, turning the window into a mirror that showed her curious frown, wind-pinked cheeks, and Vermont College cap as she tried to peer inside.

Saffi stepped back, hands on hips as her upper teeth worried her lower lip. The "Open" sign in the window meant someone was in there, or at least *should* be in there. The doorknob turned, so Saffi opened the door and strode inside. She blinked a few times. As her eyes adjusted to the dim interior, she spotted Bill, hunched in his chair in front of the computer, nose to the booking screen, spewing out a series of guttural expletives. Saffi cleared her throat.

Bill whirled toward the counter with a smile so big it had to be fake. The moment he saw Saffi, his smile drooped into a scowl.

"What do *you* want?" He glared.

Saffi raised her hands. "The customer service in this place has really gone downhill."

"Service shmervice. Look at this!" He flapped a hand at the booking screen. "At this rate, the whole park will go downhill, and I'll be out of a job." The screen showed a lot of green spaces that had been red when she arrived.

"Are the police still keeping the park closed?" *Ease into it,* she told herself. *Commiserate first, clobber later.*

Bill tugged his scruffy beard. "No. But who wants to come to the Murder Park? We're bleeding money here, and it's all your fault!"

Saffi rocked back a step. "My fault? How on earth could it be my fault?"

Bill jabbed a yellow-stained fingertip toward her. "If you hadn't stuck your nosy writer's nose into what happened, the cops would have ruled it accidental, and everything would be back to normal by now."

"But it wasn't an accident, was it, Bill?"

Bill jumped to his feet and loomed toward her. "It bleedin' well was!"

Saffi stiffened. The park host was much taller than she remembered. The burgundy T-shirt he wore beneath his safety vest didn't hide the bulging muscles in his arms the way his usual hoodie did. Clearly Bill had not been a desk jockey before he came to Last Chance Cove. Something in the building trades, she guessed, given that he'd built Mellie's gallery. She glanced at the office door. She'd left it open. Escape was just a few steps away. *Just get him to admit something and get out of here,* she told herself. She lowered her voice as if taking him into her confidence. "Look, Bill. Mellie talked. Detective Richards knows you and Linda were married. He also knows you were there the night she died, so stop the bluster."

Bill's face went as white as bleached whale bones. As Saffi shared Mellie's revelations, he reached back and pulled his rolling office chair behind his knees and sank into it. He pinched the bridge of his nose then smoothed down his mustache.

"Yeah. OK. Smudge and me did go out to the berm, mostly to check for tourists on the beach. No matter how many warning signs you hand out, some danged fool always heads out there."

"But you didn't find a tourist, did you?"

"Sure, I did. Saw that Texas woman, Liz, strolling toward the beach like she didn't have a care in the world. Dumb as a clod of dirt, that one, but more stuck up than a Rockiefeller. I delivered that wave warning to her door personally, then warned her again when I saw her. But did she thank me? Nope on a rope. She did not. Looked at me like I was some piece of crap she didn't want to step in. Till she needed me for her dirty work. *Hmph!*"

That sounded about right from what Saffi had seen of Eliza so far.

"Anyone else?" *Come on.* Saffi gritted her teeth. *Give me something here!*

Bill gave her a look that said she might be even dumber than Eliza.

"Linda? Did you see Linda?"

Bill stroked his mustache. "I hate writers. Damned nosy

busybodies with nothing better to do than muck out other people's stables."

Saffi put her hands on the counter and leaned toward him, pushing into his space the way he'd pushed into hers earlier. "You tracked her to Last Chance Cove, didn't you? Took the park host job to push your way back into her life?"

Poor Linda. She knew exactly what it felt like, the fear that someone had you in their sights and no matter how far you ran or how fast you drove, they might find you.

Bill's shoulders sagged.

"OK, OK. Yes. I came here to beg her to take me back. For all the good it did. I guess I thought—" Bill took a breath so deep it seemed to suck the air out of the room. "I thought she'd give me a chance, you know? One last chance to make it right."

"So, you did see her that night... on the berm?"

Bill closed his eyes and pressed his lips together. Saffi waited until he nodded, his gaze glued to the counter. "Smudgie sniffed her out. Nearly tore my arm off lunging up that hill." He absentmindedly rubbed his left tricep. "I told her I was sorry for all the... all the things I'd done to piss her off. That I could do better. Be better."

Just a few days' interaction with the gruff park host had given Saffi a taste of what he might have been like in a marriage. Misogynistic. Overbearing. Pushy. Abusive? From what she'd heard Linda didn't seem the type to take abuse, but over time abuse could either weaken a woman or harden her. The latter type was more likely to sue for divorce and get the heck out of Dodge. Still, Saffi had seen Bill upset, angry even, but not physically abusive. Verbal abuse, now that she could easily believe.

"Up on the berm, you asked her to give you another chance?"

He glanced up at Saffi, but his watery blue gaze seemed to be looking into the past. "Do you know what she said when I told her I wanted to try again?"

Saffi held her breath and waited.

"Said that mutt of hers had given her more love in the last year than I had in our twenty years together."

Ouch. Saffi grimaced. "That must have hurt."

Bill bared his teeth, sharklike. "Yeah, well. She got hers, didn't she?"

"When you pushed her?"

The park host's face slackened. The hands resting on his knees trembled. "I didn't push her. I would never. I just yelled a little, you know?"

Saffi could only imagine the kind of vitriol an emotionally wounded Bill would spew.

"Then that little ankle biter of hers went for me and Smudge lost it."

Saffi stiffened. "Lost it how?"

Bill smacked his palm down on a thick book sitting on his desk. *A Bedside Reader?* Saffi couldn't believe her eyes.

"Don't go writing some 'German Shepherd Goes Berserk' headline or nothing. Smudge didn't go after Linda. He went after Archie. Took hold of that bandanna around the scruff of his neck and shook him like the ridiculous ragamuffin he is. Tried to make him remember his manners. But the little doofus didn't yield. Gotta give him that. He tugged and tugged till his scrawny head slipped out of the bandanna and off he went. Down the beach like the hounds of hell were after him."

A memory clicked into place—what Delilah had told her about Archie having a beef with Smudge. If Smudge had attacked Archie thinking he was protecting Bill, that could explain the little dog's animosity toward the German shepherd.

After Archie ran, Bill revealed, Linda had started pounding his chest, demanding that he go after her "baby." Smudge's ears went up and he started growling. To keep the two of them from going after each other, Bill had tugged the German shepherd away and took off after the little terrier.

"An idiot's errand." Bill shook his head. "Waves were going crazy. Sneaker warning, remember? I wasn't about to drown for a woman who loved her dog more than me. Besides," he shrugged, "Archie was probably halfway to the harbor by the time we got down off the berm. No way were we gonna catch him."

"What happened next?" Saffi prodded. "What did you do?"

"Went back and told Linda her best bet was to just wait for him. He'd come back like the good little love slave she'd turned him into."

Saffi tucked her chin and shook her head. *Way to go, Bill.*

A grin that looked like a snarl quirked his mouth. "She was so mad she got the shakes. Going on about how I'd killed her dog, and she was going to fire my ass and chase me out of Last Chance Cove if it was the last thing she ever did. And I said she'd better not try, or I'd give Randall that list he told me to make."

Saffi lifted her brows. "List? What list?"

"Told you there was more than one way to get rid of bad management." His eyes were two angry blue-white marbles, glossy with tears. "A list of so-called 'fireable offenses.' Bit of insurance in case Linda went after Glenn again." He rubbed a hand across his glistening eyes, smoothed his mustache, and sniffed.

"And then?"

"Then? Then I left her there with her mouth hanging open. Went home to bed." He rolled his office chair back toward the computer table and started clicking keys. "Just left her there to die. No friggin' wonder she divorced me."

An unexpected wave of pity washed over Saffi. Linda had taunted Bill. Belittled him. Proclaimed to hold more love for her dog. Threatened to chase him out of town. The next day—if his story was true—he'd learned her fate. The woman who had been his wife for twenty years, the woman he claimed to love, had died. On top of it all, he'd felt compelled to keep silent to avoid looking guilty. How had the stress not broken him? Maybe it had. Maybe that was why he was doing stupid things like lying to the police and aiding and abetting a kidnapping. She could almost understand the crazy logic that would have kept his lips sealed, but if he didn't want to look guilty, why had he hung onto Archie's bandanna? She had to know, so she asked.

Bill's shoulders collapsed. "You're the sleuth. Why do you think?"

If Bill had really cared about Linda, he must be steeping in a bitter tea of his own making. Suddenly, she did understand.

"You kept Archie's bandanna to stay connected to Linda. To the last time you saw her."

Bill's beard dipped toward his chest.

"Wouldn't Archie have been a stronger connection? Why didn't you keep him?"

Bill turned from the computer and glared. "I told you the first day you were here. I'm allergic to the mutt."

Saffi didn't remember. If she had, she'd have puzzled over how he could be allergic to dogs and live in an RV with one. "What about Smudge?"

"I'm not allergic to *all* dogs. Just terriers."

"Bill, I don't think that's a thing."

"It's a thing, all right. Look it up. Put it in one of those books of yours if you want. Consider it a gift from me to you. Now do me a favor. Get out of here and let me figure out how to save this park."

Saffi started out the door, then turned. "Bill? Did you see anyone else out there?"

At first, she didn't think he'd answer. He rolled his chair closer to the computer station and clicked a few keys. Then he said something that rearranged the puzzle pieces to create a very different picture. "Saw Nicole coming out of her trailer.

Told her to stay off the danged beach unless she wanted to drown, so she headed up the berm."

Leave it to Bill to put Nicole—Saffi's original suspect—in the beam of the spotlight, right where Delilah thought she belonged. Saffi sighed. So much for getting closer to the hottest fisher*man* in the Pacific Northwest.

THIRTY-SIX

Saffi had promised herself that she'd call Detective Richards with the information Bill told her, so she did. *Sorry, Troy.* When the detective didn't answer, she left a message giving the details and letting him know she would stay away from Nicole's trailer and let him do his job. Trying to uncover a killer might be a job for an amateur sleuth, but arresting one? That was a job for the police.

Instead of going back to her Rambler, she crossed the gravel park entrance to the trail that led to the harbor. Hours had passed since Troy's wake-up knock on her door. She hadn't had a bite to eat and she'd burned off the coffee Troy brought her grilling Bill. The trail ran alongside a narrow access road that horseshoed off Highway 101 and was separated from the road by a wood-rail fence. It skirted past the park, ducked behind a hotel that had weathered too many winter storms, passed a dilapidated potter's gallery, and looped back to the highway a block south. As Saffi rambled along the trail, her thoughts rambled, too. How often had marriages gone wrong, shattering lives? Bill and Linda. Nicole and her cheating husband. Compared to the collateral damage surrounding those marriages—Casey pulled between two generations of Carmodys; Archie waiting for a companion who would never snuggle him close again? Losing Levi had been a brutal, almost surgical cut. Those, Saffi knew, healed faster.

Saffi drifted so far into herself she didn't notice a pickup truck roll to a stop beside her until a horn beeped.

"Hey, stranger! Thought you were headed home."

Saffi halted. Despite the fact that she'd just ratted his sister out to law enforcement, she turned like a sunflower toward the sound of Troy's voice. "I was until I realized that my brain was about to atrophy from lack of coffee and chowder."

"Need a lift?" He reached across and opened the passenger-side door. "I'm headed to the café. I'd love to buy you lunch."

Buy me lunch? Saffi couldn't stop the smile that spread across her face. Then reality hit and she froze. How would she get through a lunch without spilling everything she'd learned from Bill? She was still trying to get her head around what he'd told her. If Bill didn't do it, and if Nicole's presence on the berm was evidence of guilt, Saffi couldn't tell Troy. She had to give Detective Richards time to hear the message she'd left, locate Nicole and interrogate her. Troy loved his sister. If he knew what Bill had told Saffi, he wouldn't believe in her guilt. He would warn her, and she would run. For now, Saffi needed to keep her discoveries to herself. Still, keeping Troy at her side while she waited for news would be a lot more fun than strolling with the seagulls, waiting for one of them to drop a stink-bomb on her head.

"Lunch sounds great!"

Saffi ducked between the slats of the rail fence protecting the trail from the access road and stepped up into the pickup. She settled quickly: door closed, belt buckled, tummy rumbling.

Troy glanced sideways. "Sounds like I was just in time."

The guilt of not sharing what Bill had told her threatened to tie knots in her gut. Before they could tighten enough to force her to spill what she knew, she remembered where Troy had been going when he dropped her off at the park. "Did you talk to the fire chief?" she asked.

Troy nodded. "He thanked me for the information but, so far, the investigators haven't found a sliver of evidence to prove arson."

"Don't you mean a chip?" Saffi teased.

Troy chuckled. "Right. Chief says if all they've got is a witness who saw Jeff load a giant box of potato chips into the Prevost, they've got bupkes."

"Bupkes?" Saffi mused. "So, even if the Carmodys set that fire, they're not going to pay the price."

"Not likely." Troy tapped the steering wheel with his thumbs. "Unless... I put a bug in that insurance adjuster's ear. Even a whiff of suspected arson would merit further investigation."

Troy flashed a sharklike grin that reminded her for a second of Bill, but Saffi understood. The Carmodys were trying to rip his niece away from her mother. Who wouldn't want them to get their just deserts—as in "exactly what they deserved," as opposed to *just desserts* as in tiramisu or chocolate lava cake, neither of which the Carmodys deserved.

"Hit them in their bank account and they'll feel it. Especially Eliza. The woman's whole world turns on money."

Money, money, money. Bribing Bill to get Saffi's monthly spot when they first arrived. Paying him to hide Casey from her mother. Eliza's "money always wins" declaration to Nicole when she threw the "lawyer" threat at her daughter-in-law. Money kept popping up. Put blackmail in the mix and money might be the key to Linda's murder after all.

When Troy turned into the harbor road, Saffi started salivating. Coffee! And chowder! She hadn't had a bowl of creamy clam-filled goodness since her first day at the park. Just as Troy pulled into a parking space, his phone dinged. He glanced down to where it lay on the seat between them, frowning. Saffi could see that the message was from Casey and read the word "meet," but Troy scrolled the message away before she could read more. He drummed his thumbs on the steering wheel again, letting the truck idle instead of turning it off.

Saffi raised her brows. "Everything OK?"

Troy licked his lips. "I'm not sure. Casey's headed to my boat for some reason. I think I'd better zip over there for a sec. See what's up. But don't worry! I promised to buy you lunch, and I won't let my sleuthing partner down."

Sleuthing partner. Saffi sighed. So much for her lunch date. She patted Troy's leg and unbuckled her seat belt. "Better to let down a sleuthing partner than a niece."

Troy turned toward her, Montana-blue eyes sparkling. "Lightning-sharp mind plus a caring heart. Wow. You're a singular woman, Saffi Graywood."

Saffi wondered if he could hear how hard her heart was thudding. She could feel herself start to swoon toward him like her teenage self might have done, if she'd been lucky enough to be this close to Mr. Reel Sexy way back when. *Huh. Who was she kidding?* The teenage Troy would never have noticed the quirky bookish girl with the squirrel's nest of black curls. In high school, he would have been Jake, the heartthrob in John Hughes's *Sixteen Candles.* She would have been Hermione, the know-it-all witch who couldn't get the attention of the clueless red-haired Ron in the *Harry Potter* books.

"I might need to bring Casey back with me. If that's OK," Troy said.

"Absolutely," Saffi gulped out, hoping her eyes hadn't glazed over while her imagination tried—and failed—to cast her opposite him in a 1980s coming-of-age rom-com. Saffi opened the door and hopped down, turning to flash him a smile.

"Order me a drip!" Troy called as she started to swing the truck door shut. "Medium roast. I'll be back before it cools."

Troy reversed out of the parking space and whirled the wheel to point the pickup toward the marina lot across the street. The truck's wheels screeched as he hit the accelerator. She watched Troy race away, picturing those gray-blue eyes flashing with anger instead of interest if his sister was arrested because of the tip-off she'd left on Detective Richards' message machine. Saffi hurried toward the turquoise door, pouring her worries into pushing it open. Inside, she found Delilah behind the counter, taking an order from Jeff Carmody. The Texan's cheeks were ruddy, as if he'd stood dockside in the wind watching seals jostle for position on their floating platforms before coming into the café. Saffi exchanged a wave with the barista and slid onto the stool beside Jeff. The gentle murmur of conversation combined with the tantalizing smells of seafood and coffee settled her nerves.

Jeff twirled toward her, took off his cowboy hat and rested it on his knee. "Brisk out there, isn't it? I don't know how people live here. Even winter doesn't feel this cold on the Gulf."

Saffi didn't think she'd ever seen the Texan without his hat. Now she understood why. He wore his thinning white hair in a comb-over that did little to conceal that the top of his head was as bald and pink as a baby's butt. It made him look worn out. As if old age had caught up with him while he wasn't looking.

"Buy you a drink, young lady?" He winked, and plunked the Stetson back on his head as if the hat might bolster his swagger.

"Thanks, but I've got this." Saffi waved at Delilah, who gave her a nod and pointed toward the mug she was filling. When she brought Jeff his milk-white coffee he ripped open six sugar packets, one by one, and stirred their contents hard enough to make the spoon ring inside the ceramic mug. Finally, he took a long slow sip and then sighed. "Thanks, hon." He slid a twenty Delilah's way and told her to keep the change. Saffi thought back to the barista's claim that rich people were terrible tippers.

Delilah's effervescent personality must have inspired him to open his wallet.

"Thanks, cowboy!" Delilah fluttered taxi-cab yellow nails in the Texan's direction.

"Wow!" Saffi grabbed her hand for a closer look. Each yellow nail had a stylized raven plummeting toward the nailbed, a single tiny faux pearl where its eye would be.

The barista curled her fingers toward her own palm to admire them afresh. "Are they fabulous, or what?"

"Fabulous," Saffi agreed, "and a bit scary."

"Right? I love them SO-O-O much." Delilah flipped her henna-red curls off her forehead and gave Saffi a teasing stare. "So, did Troy rev you up this morning?"

Beside her, Jeff sat up straighter. Saffi felt an instant burn that she was sure showed in her cheeks.

Delilah chuckled. "With the mocha he bought for you, I mean."

Saffi clutched the counter. "Uh, yeah. He—I mean it, the mocha, that is—did. Rev me, uh, up." Saffi shook her head. Trying to get back into her full-on-adult-woman mindset, she ordered a caramel latte for herself. Hungry as she was, she'd wait for Troy before ordering food. But she did order his coffee as requested. "He's gone to meet Casey at the boat, but he'll be here soon."

Tension pulsed off Jeff like he'd grabbed a live wire and Saffi glanced his way. His hand wobbled slightly as he lifted his coffee to his lips, drained the mug, and sat it down hard enough to make the counter clang. "Gotta run, ladies." He tipped his Stetson and headed for the door, boot heels ringing on the black-and-white tiled floor.

Delilah's eyes widened. "You sure put a burr under his saddle. Order up, Buttercup, and get ready to shovel the shizzle!"

Speaking of shoveling, she leaned toward Delilah. "We found Mellie, and she finally spilled the beans."

Delilah's eyes widened, but Saffi set her lips and nodded toward the espresso machine. The barista got the hint. She hurried off to pull shots and pour coffee with a spring in her step. When she delivered the steaming mugs, she peered around the café. "Looks like they're all saucered and blowed."

Nostalgia washed over Saffi and she pressed a hand to her heart. She'd written articles about food idioms, but she hadn't heard this one spoken since she lost her dad. He'd perked and poured her first coffee when she was around eight years old. To spare her from a burned tongue he'd taught her to pour a little coffee into the saucer, blow on it to cool it down, then sip (or slurp) the cooled coffee right out of the saucer. Once boiled coffee became a thing of the past, the idiom came to mean "all taken care of," like the customers at the café's tables.

"So," Delilah rested her elbows on the counter. "Mellie spilled the beans at last. Tell me."

While she nursed her caramel latte, Saffi filled Delilah in on Mellie's explosive revelations about Bill. The barista responded with enough shock and awe to turn every head in the café their way.

"Ssh!" Saffi put a finger to her lips.

Delilah covered her mouth. "Sorry. Just... Linda never breathed a word about being married to Bill. Although..." She stopped tapping. "The way she wagged her tongue about him every chance she got, maybe I should have guessed."

"She didn't tell Glenn about Bill being her ex either, and he's her cousin."

Delilah's mouth sagged. "*Hmph!* Glenn wouldn't give that woman the time of day, cousin or not. She destroyed his reputation and cost him the bakery. Can you imagine what it's like to be gay in a town like this? And then someone insinuates you're a *pedo*? No. Glenn left those family ties behind like fish guts on a deck."

The raven on Delilah's right pointer fingernail pecked the counter three times. "Oh, what a tangled net we weave."

"Don't you mean web?"

The barista's eyes sparked. "Around here, it's a net. And Linda tangled hers up so bad she got caught in it."

Saffi licked a sticky bit of caramel off her thumb, wondering how it had gotten there. Delilah was right, and somewhere in that tangled net was a clue to why someone had murdered the park manager. But why Nicole would have wielded that net, she still didn't know. "That's not all," Saffi kept her voice low. "I cornered Bill, and he told me—"

Before she could finish, the door opened, followed by a chill wind off the harbor. A crewman straight off a boat plopped down a few stools away and the smell of fish quickly overcame the aroma of coffee. Delilah held up a finger. "Hold that thought. I'll be right back."

The fisherman jogged Saffi out of her memories. How much time had passed while she and Delilah talked? She glanced at the door, then back down at the mug of coffee cooling on the counter. When the barista came back, she looked up. "Troy should have been here by now."

Delilah drummed her nails on the counter making the stylized ravens dip and dive. The effect made Saffi's head spin. "Can you put that in a to-go cup?" She nodded at Troy's coffee as she slugged down the remainder of her latte.

"Tell me you're not gonna leave me hanging." Delilah glared.

"I'll be back," Saffi promised. "I just don't want Troy's coffee to get stone-cold before he can drink it." The word that often followed "stone-cold" rang in her head. *Dead. Stone-cold dead.*

Don't be ridiculous, Saffi. He's probably knee-deep in

preteen drama with Casey, and he's forgotten there's a woman with a caring heart and a cup of coffee waiting for him at the café. Delilah came back clutching Troy's lukewarm medium roast in its paper cup. "I'm not handing this over till you promise to come back and finish the story."

Saffi held up her right hand, three fingers straight, thumb over pinkie. "I promise," she swore like the Brownie Scout she'd once been. The moment Delilah handed over the cup, Saffi bolted for the door.

Clouds scuttled across the sky. Gulls argued over fish scraps. The marina's briny smell made her long for the chowder she still craved, but worry overcame the craving. She crossed Seal View Way and headed into the marina parking lot. The telltale wave-and-fish logo made Troy's boat easy to spot. As she scurried down the metal gangplank to the dock, it jangled and clanged in alarm. A sense of urgency shot through her, and she clutched the paper coffee cup between both hands to hurry her steps. A raven's harsh rasp drew her eye to its perch on the railing of Troy's boat. It wasn't alone. A second raven fretted along the same rail. When a third raven swooped over her head and landed beside them, Saffi dropped the coffee cup and ran.

"Troy?" she called as she grabbed the cold metal rail, hoisting herself over the gunwale and onto the deck. The ravens went silent as if they, like Saffi, listened for an answer from the bowels of the boat. She edged along the port side as she made her way toward the center of the boat. "Troy?" She poked her head into the steering console. The captain's chair sat empty. Where was he? And Casey. She should be here, too.

Saffi backed onto the deck and scanned the marina. Midday seemed to be a slow time. Boats that had gone out had yet to return. No one lingered nearby, conveniently placed to tell her if they'd seen Troy or Casey. Saffi took a deep breath to slow her pounding heart. Her belly roiled as air tainted with oil, diesel fumes, and fish guts filled her lungs. She bit her lip and turned her attention back to the boat beneath her feet. If she had been on one of Troy's tours, she would know the boat's layout. Since she hadn't, she had no idea if Troy and Casey could be on the boat but not able to hear her call.

A quick glance around showed an open door near the steering console with steps leading belowdecks. Saffi ducked her head to look inside. "Troy?" She crept down the three steps into a cabin feebly lit by afternoon sunlight filtering in from outside. To her right, cushioned benches ran along either side of the hull toward the bow. After the brisk ocean breeze, the cabin air felt close, as if holding its breath waiting. To her left was a mini-kitchen. Was that peppermint tea she smelled? Why would Troy make tea when he'd asked her to order a coffee? On the other side of the cabin a closed door led to what could be the head—the mariner's term for *toilet*. Beyond that, in a dark alcove at the stern she made out a rumpled bed. At the end of the bed—Saffi blinked to let her eyes adjust to the darkness—the soles of two shoes poked out beyond the mattress.

"Troy!"

As Saffi rushed past the head toward the bedroom, her shoe caught on the edge of a woven rug in front of the mini-kitchen, and she stumbled. She heard a door slide open and a hand grabbed her left shoulder, pulling her backward. At first, she thought someone had rescued her from a fall but a second later, the cold tip of what could only be a knife bit into her neck. The searing pain shocked her into stillness.

"Troy said you were waiting for him," a soft voice wrapped in warm breath whispered past her ear, "and that you weren't the type to wait too long. Unfortunately for you, he was right."

THIRTY-SEVEN

"Eliza?" Saffi gasped out the Texan's name. "What are you doing? And what's wrong with Troy?"

"He's just taking a little nap. He needs to be rested for our fishing trip, you see."

Saffi opened and closed her hands, then gulped, trying to stay calm. "You're going fishing?"

"Oh, yes. As soon as Casey joins us."

"And why would she do that?"

"What girl wouldn't want to go fishing with her uncle?" Eliza whispered into Saffi's ear as she pressed the knife against her throat. The cut Eliza had already made burned beneath it. She had to do something. Casey was about to walk into real danger. But if she moved... Saffi didn't want to think about what Eliza might do, so she moved the only thing she could: her eyes. The cabin was neat as a pin. No books she could smash into Eliza's face. No tools lying around she could grab and slam into a knee. Of course, either of those actions would probably result in having her throat slit. *Think, Saffi. Think!*

Saffi did the only thing she could think of: she prepared. She reached back to her tai chi training, imagined roots growing from her feet and spiraling down through the water, down into the earth to twice her height. Barely moving, she bent her knees and let her weight sink into her heels, grounding her for whatever might happen. She'd made the mistake of letting Eliza sneak up on her, get close enough to put that knife to her neck. She couldn't control what the Texan did next, but she had a few tricks she could try. The first was to keep her talking.

"I'm guessing you have a reason for putting a knife to my throat. Want to share?"

Eliza's chuckle chilled Saffi to the bone. "If I do that, I'll have to kill you, won't I?"

Saffi's guts wanted to liquefy, so she turned her attention to the energy of the earth. She channeled chi—the vital force of all things—up through her heels and into her legs, her thighs, her belly, her arms, her hands. Warmth rose along with it and, Saffi hoped, power, at least enough to overwhelm a woman twenty years her senior. Besides, Saffi was sturdy. Eliza looked like she existed on nothing but the smell of salads.

"Let me guess. You cooked up a fake fishing trip to lure Casey here. She messaged Troy that she'd see him at the boat, and he came over to find out why. Then you, what? Walloped him over the head with a tackle box?" She was dangling bait, hoping Eliza would bite. She did.

"Nothing so gauche as a blow to the head," Eliza said. "I simply slipped a few of my favorite little sleep enhancers into a pot of tea and offered him a cup to drink while we waited for my granddaughter."

A lot of words for "heartless, terrible female" shouted in Saffi's head, none of which she dared say aloud to a woman with a knife at her throat. All she could do was pray that Eliza hadn't misjudged how many pills it would take to put Troy down for a nap. At least Saffi's plan to keep the Texan talking seemed to be working.

"Will it be a cup of tea for me as well?" Saffi almost hoped the answer was "yes." Being drugged seemed a lot better than having her throat slit.

"Don't blame me. If that silly granddaughter of mine hadn't texted her uncle, we would be out to sea by now."

"I've written about people like you. Grandparents who snatched their own grandchildren. It rarely ends well." At this point, she was babbling, but Saffi didn't care. Anything to keep that knife from digging deeper.

"That idiot of a park host told me about you and those, what are they... Bathroom Readers?" Eliza scoffed. "Seems a fitting place for books someone like you would write."

Saffi sniffed. "*Bedside* Readers, if you please."

"He advised me to either stay off your radar or pay you off."

"The way you paid him?"

Eliza laughed. "Mr. Kidd was quite pleased with the pin money I keep in my purse. I doubt you could be so cheaply bought."

Pin money. It seemed to be a day for idioms. Saffi barely stopped herself from shaking her head and sinking the knife into her own skin. This particular antiquated saying once referred to the small amount of money a man gave to his wife for personal expenses. In Eliza's case that probably meant enough to get her hair done, buy clothes, shoes, and jewelry, and, apparently, hire a kidnapper.

"I wish you'd asked, instead of..." She flapped her right hand toward the knife. Had things already gone too far? Or could she convince the Texas nutcase she'd take a payout?

"I considered it," Eliza admitted. "But then I looked you up. You've sold millions of those readers. Heaven knows why. If you cost me more than my lawyers would charge, what's the point?"

Saffi had been standing in "mountain pose"—knees bent, weight sunk earthward—for so long her thighs were on fire. She began to worry that her limbs would go past burning to numb before she could make a move. But, with the knifepoint still against her skin, talking remained wiser than moving.

"You told Nicole you'd let your lawyers handle this whole thing. I heard you, at the café. Why get blood on your hands?"

Really, Saffi could only think of one reason for a woman like Eliza to resort to violence instead of lawyers: she'd already gone too far. Arson. Kidnapping. Murder? Bill had seen the Texan headed toward the beach before Linda died. If blackmail had been on the park manager's mind, the Prevost rolling into the park could have added a few decimal points to the dollar signs in her eyes. If she'd shifted her scheme from Nicole to Eliza, she could very well have made a fatal mistake. Clearly, Eliza intended to take her granddaughter back to Texas, no matter what she had to do. Was she insane?

"You'd kill Troy—and me, it seems—to take Casey away from her mother?"

"Ah, yes. *Nicole*." Eliza sneered. "Can you imagine the agony she'll go through? Losing both Casey and her beloved stepbrother?" The knife in Eliza's hand trembled against Saffi's throat. "The same agony she put me through when she took Casey away from *me!*"

No thought of Casey's feelings if she was taken from her mother. No mention of her son, Casey's father. Just me... me... me!

Above decks, the ravens cried out—a series of shrill warning calls. Someone was coming aboard.

"Uncle Troy?"

Saffi recognized the eager young voice immediately. Her heart fluttered its distress. *Don't come down. Don't come down,* she pleaded to every entity she'd ever heard of that might come to her aid, including Raven. On the deck above, the ravens squawked but Eliza's syrupy grandmother voice rose to block it out.

"Down here, sweetheart!"

She pressed the wrist of her knife hand into Saffi's clavicle, pulling her backward between the cushioned benches at the tip of the bow, perhaps hoping Casey wouldn't see them until she'd come down the steps. "Not a word," she seethed.

Saffi stared toward the stern, hoping against hope to see Troy's feet move. They didn't. No one was coming to the rescue, but within seconds, Casey would come down those steps to face something no grandchild should ever have to experience. Saffi couldn't let that happen. Talking time was over.

Eliza's attention shifted to the door as she watched for her granddaughter and her knife hand relaxed away from Saffi's neck. Was it enough? Saffi didn't know, but it had to be. Before she could think herself out of it, Saffi grasped Eliza's thin wrist with both hands, twisting it outward and down with every ounce of fear thudding through her veins. At the same time, she ducked through the opening she'd made between Eliza's arm and body, bringing the arm down with her in a twist so severe the older woman screeched and dropped the knife.

Only then did Saffi scream, "Run, Casey!" at the top of her lungs.

But Casey didn't run. She rushed down the stairs into the cabin, drawn by her grandmother's painful scream. Her wide eyes took in her grandmother clutching her wrist and grimacing in pain while Saffi loomed over her with the knife she'd grabbed before Eliza could recover.

"Grandma!" Casey rushed toward Eliza.

"No, Casey!" Saffi held the knife behind her back. "It's not what you think. Your grandmother—"

Before she could finish, a figure loomed outside the door, blocking out the sun's light and darkening the cabin. "Casey, come to me." Jeff's deep drawl boomed down the stairwell. Casey looked back and forth from her grandmother to her grandfather, wanting to stay but equally drawn to Jeff's command. Footsteps pounded across the deck and another voice screamed Casey's name.

"Mom?"

Then a third voice, brisk, commanding. "Police! Move aside!" Detective Richards stepped gun-first through the door, edged down the stairs and into the cabin. "Hands up!"

Casey's hands went up first, then Saffi raised her hands, still clutching the knife.

"Drop the knife!" He motioned with the gun and Saffi complied.

"Detective Richards. Thank God!" Eliza took a step toward him, arm clutched against her chest. "I think that woman broke my wrist!"

All eyes turned toward Saffi. She hadn't realized that the knot of fear in her belly had been the only thing holding her upright until it loosened. Her legs and knees went with it, and it was all she could do to back up against the cushioned bench before they decided they were done with standing for the moment, thank you very much.

Detective Richards holstered his gun and unhooked handcuffs from his utility belt. He gave Saffi a long slow look. She met his eyes, then pulled her dark curls away from her neck and leaned her head sideways.

"Jesus, Liz!" Jeff scowled at his wife.

"Broke your wrist, did she?" the detective mused, head turning toward Eliza. "Was that before or after you tried to slit Mrs. Graywood's throat?" Without waiting for an answer, he grasped Eliza's uninjured arm, hooked one cuff around her wrist and the other to a metal grabrail beside the stairs.

The rest of Saffi's muscles melted, and she collapsed against the back of the bench, but as her body relaxed, her mind sharpened. "Troy!" She lurched off the bench and pushed past Detective Richards to get to the bedroom. She nudged Troy's feet aside and crawled to the head of the bed, putting her ear to his lips. Soft puffs of warm breath blew against her skin. She let her cheek rest against his as relief surged through her. Then she sat back on her heels, fists resting against her thighs. "He's alive," she said. "But she drugged him. Sleeping pills."

Detective Richards' handheld radio crackled to life. "Richards? Report."

"Ten seventy-eight," he barked into it. "Send ambulance my location."

Saffi rested a hand on Troy's shoulder, taking comfort every time it rose and fell. "Help is on the way. You're going to be OK." If he could hear her voice, maybe he would be reassured. Either way, her words sent a message to the universe. Troy would be fine. He had to be.

THIRTY-EIGHT

A hot shower soothed some of the stress of yesterday's ordeal from Saffi's body but the spot where Eliza's knife had serrated her skin stung whenever the spray hit it. Hours of interrogation had left her exhausted as Detective Richards tried to understand how she'd ended up at the point of that knife. The answer was simple, yet complex. Since she'd arrived in Last Chance Cove, she'd run into trouble the way she ran after every exciting story—by following the most intriguing facts she found in her research until her article reached a satisfying (shocking, unbelievable, or astounding) conclusion. That worked well on the page—the bigger the "wow" factor, the better. True crime stories and unsolved mysteries had helped make her books bestsellers. But yesterday, her instinct to run toward dangerous stories could have ended her life.

Of course, she'd also saved a life—Troy's. With any luck, Delilah would give her a lift to the hospital so she could see for herself that all was well. She'd just struggled into a fresh outfit—a swingy rose tunic over flowered leggings—when a meaty knock thudded on her door.

"Just a sec!" She ran a detangling comb through her curls, then leaned over and shook her head to fluff out her hair.

When she opened the door, her mouth fell open. Nicole stood at the bottom of the steps, elbow to elbow with her father-in-law. Behind them, the Pacific sighed against the beach, breathing in and out as if impossible things weren't happening right on Saffi's doorstep.

"Uh. Come in?" she mumbled. The invitation came out as a question because, really, she wasn't at all sure she should let Jeff, of all people, anywhere near her. On top of that, she didn't dare ask him to remove his cowboy boots, even though he'd probably collected a beach-worth of sand on the soles.

"Thanks." Nicole took the lead up the steps, slipping off her white sneakers on the mat at the top. "We just wanted to stop by and update you on Troy."

Jeff took off his Stetson as he ducked through the door frame, but she was right about the boots. They stayed on his feet, although he did kick the riser of each step to knock off sand as he climbed them. "I'm probably about as welcome as a porcupine on a nudie beach, but that sleuthin' nose of yours stopped my wife from destroying our lives. I want you to know I'm grateful. Mighty grateful."

Apparently, Jeff had come—literally and metaphorically—with his hat in his hands. Saffi pressed her lips together, then let out a sigh. "Have a seat." She gestured toward the couch. Jeff and Nicole sat side by side, somewhat uncomfortably, but far from the enemies Eliza had tried to turn them into.

Saffi turned the passenger-side captain's chair around and sat as far from them as her tiny living room would allow. "Is Troy awake?"

Nicole nodded. "He woke up so groggy and frantic he didn't see Casey sitting on a chair beside the bed. Demanded to know if she was safe. He only noticed her when she started giggling."

"Does he remember what happened?"

Nicole clasped her hands together. "Some. He remembers Eliza being on the boat. She told him Casey was on her way to join her for a family fishing trip. He was pretty sure no one had talked to him about taking the boat out. He drank a cup of tea with Eliza while they waited, then... nothing."

"Can he have visitors?"

Nicole shook her head. "If he rests today, the doctor thinks he can go home tomorrow." She glanced at Jeff, then back down to her hands. "Poor Troy. I dragged him into my mess and look what happened. If it wasn't for you—" She leaned forward and grabbed Saffi's hands. "Thank you, Saffi. Thank you so much. For saving Troy and-and Casey. I would just die if I lost her. I would. I should never have come here." Nicole drew in a breath. "I was so... so scared of losing Casey. I just... *ran.*"

Nicole's hands went limp, as if she really was as powerless as she imagined herself to be. Saffi thought back to what Troy had told her the day of the fire: Nicole had followed her mother's lead into a May–December marriage. Her husband had education, money, a career. She had youth and beauty. Early on, that would have given her enough power for the relationship to feel balanced, but it probably never had been. As she'd aged, become a mom, whatever power youth and beauty had given her had diminished. Like many trophy wives before her, Nicole had found herself replaced by the next pretty young thing. Saffi's heart went out to her, but at the same time she wanted to smack Nicole for the turmoil she'd brought into so many lives. They'd all paid the price of her immaturity.

"If your husband was unfaithful, I doubt a judge would grant him full custody of Casey." Saffi tried to bring a little reality into the room.

Nicole's gaze shifted to Jeff. "Eliza was the one pushing for full custody. Roger was so ga-ga over his latest conquest he probably would've signed anything."

Jeff's face sagged. "You have to understand. Casey is like a daughter to Eliza!"

Nicole stiffened. "But she's not, Jeff. She's *my* daughter."

"I know. I know." The condescending knee pat Jeff gave Nicole made Saffi want to slap his hand away. She had to clench every muscle in her body to keep still. "If Roger could just keep his zipper—"

"Jeff! Please." Nicole's cheeks went sunset red.

When Jeff chuckled away her plea, Nicole turned toward Saffi and mouthed "Sorry."

"Look." Jeff paused to rub his chin. "Roger's last wife, Stella — No, Stella was number two. Cherise. That's the one. Anyway, Cherise concocted a scheme to drive up the coast from San Francisco to Seattle to celebrate their tenth anniversary. They'd made that drive on their honeymoon, and she thought it would rekindle their marriage. Something kindled alright, the minute Roger set eyes on Nicki." He squeezed Nicole's knee and Saffi gritted her teeth. "She'd just graduated from high school and was waiting tables at that little café at the marina."

Last Chance Café? Had Saffi's humdrum existence turned into an episode of *Days of Our Lives?*

"Whooee!" Jeff patted his daughter-in-law's knee again. "She was the prettiest little pony Roger ever laid eyes on." This time, Saffi didn't have to react. Nicole lifted his veined hand like it was a dead fish and placed it on the couch between them. Oblivious, Jeff just kept talking. "Kid was so young when Casey came along, she didn't have a clue what to do with a baby, so Eliza took over. Cared for that baby girl like she was her own. Didn't she, Nicole?"

Nicole's eyes blazed the brightest blue Saffi had ever seen. "She took over, all right. At my elbow night and day as if I didn't have the sense God gave a female dog. She'd have nursed her if she hadn't been dried up as a year-old prune."

"Nicki!" Jeff slid down the couch so he could turn toward his now furious daughter-in-law. "What in God's name has gotten into you lately?"

Nicole rose to her feet, hands clenched. The chihuahua had reached her limit. "I'm not that gullible girl anymore, Jeff. I'm a grown-ass woman. And I'm plumb sick of being belittled and manipulated, and-and fondled. Yes! That's what you were doing, you old fart. So cut it the heck out! And as for Eliza, she tried to *take my child* from *me!*" Nicole slapped her chest with each word. "And *that* is *not* happening, you hear me! I'll see Eliza rot in jail before that happens."

Here, Saffi realized, was the mother who had left it all behind rather than let someone else raise her daughter. It wasn't fear that had put her on the road with six pink suitcases and a twelve-year-old daughter. It was fury. *You, go, Nic!*

"Looka here, young lady." Jeff whipped off his Stetson and smacked his knee with it. "When you spirited that girl away, Eliza fell apart. Wouldn't eat. Couldn't sleep. Just walked the floors fretting and carrying on. Doc put her on these little blue pill thingies. They were supposed to help, and they did, till we got that postcard from Casey. '*Greetings from Last Chance Cove.*'" Jeff made air quotes. "Had this whiskery seal grinning in front of a humpback-whale-shaped hill. Even without the greeting, we'd have known where she was." Jeff glanced at Nicole whose face had gone rigid. "Liz started yammering at me to come get the girl." He rubbed a hand across his mouth. "She's my wife. What was I supposed to do?"

Saffi gritted her teeth. *So many things. Let your son face the karmic result of his own actions. Stop using money to make things go your way. Notice that your wife is popping more blue pills than her doctor prescribed.* Given the absolute craziness of Eliza's actions, Detective Richards had her taken to the hospital for evaluation. She had enough anti-anxiety meds in her to trigger dangerous side effects, such as irritability and behavioral changes. Apparently, she wasn't the first person to commit violent acts after gobbling too many little blue pills.

Saffi glared at the Texan. "You weren't supposed to aid and abet a murder, that's for sure."

"Murder?" Jeff scrambled to his feet. "Eliza didn't kill anyone. And I wasn't gonna let her. Why do you think I skedaddled out of the café when you said Troy was meeting Casey at the boat? I called Nicole straight away, but Casey had already left. Lucky for all of us that detective feller was with Nicki. They rushed right over, and, well, you know what happened next. Nobody got murdered. Not even close."

Anger surged through Saffi making her whole body boil and her hands shake. "So, Linda Oates doesn't count?"

"Now just a dad-gummed minute." Jeff waved the Stetson in Saffi's direction. "We came over to extend a hand of friendship. Not to git accused of murder. Nic, let's go."

Nicole hesitated, glanced at Saffi, her eyes clouded with indecision. "No. You go ahead. I'll meet up with you later."

Jeff's face said he didn't want to leave his daughter-in-law behind, but Nicole patted his shoulder in reassurance, took the Stetson out of his hand, sat it on his head, and adjusted it to cover his thinning hair with more affection than Saffi would have expected. "I'll be fine."

Once Jeff was out the door, Nicole pulled it shut. Then she whirled around to face Saffi. "I know you never met Linda, but believe me, she was *not* a nice woman. She was a scheming, backstabbing money grubber."

A cold weight settled in Saffi's gut. Was Nicole saying Linda deserved to die? Was she about to confess to the murder? God, she hoped not. Troy would be devastated. She clutched the arms of the captain's chair, ready to vault to her feet if needed. All along she'd suspected Linda of blackmailing Nicole. Before Eliza had put that knife to her throat, she'd been convinced Nicole was the killer. Saffi licked her lips, ignoring the voice pleading with her to stay silent.

"My first night in the park, I heard you and Troy arguing. In the laundry room."

Nicole's face went rigid. Her fingers curled into fists.

"You were talking about paying someone off. At least, that's what it sounded like."

Instead of attacking, as Saffi half expected, Nicole deflated. She collapsed on the couch and put her face in her hands. "Troy was right," she mumbled through her fingers. "I should have stayed in Texas and dealt with the divorce. Instead, I shoveled up a pile of manure and stepped right into it."

Colorful metaphors aside, Saffi was tired of being put off. She needed to know the truth. "Nicole, was Linda blackmailing you?"

Nicole picked up the Raven pillow from the end of the couch and squeezed it against her chest. "Linda came by my trailer, the afternoon before she... before she was killed. She said Bill had rented your space to a couple from Texas." Nicole blinked rapidly, as if she were reliving the moment. "I didn't want Casey to overhear, so I asked her if we could talk outside. Once we got out there, she said, 'Funny how those Texans have the same last name as you. *Carmody.*'" Nicole locked eyes with Saffi. "She gave me this look that was—I don't know—predatory? Like I was a chipmunk, and she was a kai-oat looking for a meal."

It took Saffi's brain a few seconds to translate "kai-oat" to "coyote."

"And?" Saffi prodded.

Nicole's eyes filled with tears, and then she started to sob. Compassion overcame fear and Saffi went to the couch to put her arms around the young woman. It took a box of tissues and a cup of camomile-lavender tea to finally get the rest of the story out of her. Linda had offered Nicole a deal she didn't dare refuse. For five thousand dollars, she would tell the Carmodys that Bill had made a mistake when he gave them Saffi's site and send them on their way.

"So you met her on the berm that night to pay her off?"

Nicole blew her tear-reddened nose into a tissue. "You mean, did I go up there with an envelope filled with cash?"

The look on Saffi's face must have told the younger woman that she had been imagining exactly that.

Nicole let out a shaky burst of laughter. "Course not. I transferred the money to her bank account and texted her a 'done' emoji. She texted THX and a smiley face."

"Nicole, Bill saw you head up the berm that night."

The young woman screwed up her face. "That's right. I saw Linda up there. Told her she'd better make good on her promise to send the Carmodys packing. When I saw the Prevost sitting there the next morning, I was fit to be tied." Her chin wobbled. "If I'd seen her right then I'd have pushed her off that berm myself."

Nicole looked as wrung out and miserable as Archie had when Saffi found him on the beach. Her blue eyes were so red they looked burned. But Saffi couldn't let her empathy blind her to the fact that Nicole had both motive and opportunity for murder.

Saffi chose her next words carefully. "Why didn't you tell the police any of this?"

Anxiety furrowed Nicole's brow. "I'd have to be nutty as a koo-koo bird to do that. They'd have locked me in the slammer and the Carmodys would have hauled Casey back to Texas before I got my one phone call."

Despite learning that Linda had blackmailed Nicole, Saffi found herself not wanting to believe that Troy's sister was a murderer. She put a gentle hand on Nicole's shoulder. "You're going to have to tell Detective Richards what you told me. You know that, right?"

"Saffi." Nicole huffed. "Sometimes I wonder if you're as smart as that brother of mine thinks you are."

Saffi sat back, trying not to take offense. "OK. I've sleuthed myself into enough dead ends over the last week to deserve that, I suppose."

Nicole turned her tear-reddened eyes toward Saffi. "You sent that detective to grill me, remember?"

So much had happened, Saffi had almost forgotten. She'd left Detective Richards a message about Nicole before she'd headed to the café... which was before she'd followed Troy to the boat... which was before Eliza nearly slit her throat. It all seemed so long ago.

"I told the detective the same thing I just told you."

"And he believed you?"

Nicole threw up her hands. "I don't know. If Eliza hadn't gone stabby as a hat pin on you, he probably would have put *me* in jail, not her. But neither one of us killed Linda."

Saffi chewed her bottom lip. If Nicole had paid Linda off, killing her would be self-defeating. She needed Linda alive to get the Carmodys out of the park. "You really don't think Eliza did it?"

Nicole snorted. "Why, Saffi? Why would Eliza kill a woman she'd never even met?"

The air went out of Saffi. Nicole was right. Eliza had no motive for Linda's murder. No motive for pushing Mellie's gallery over the cliff. No history with any of the townspeople. The Carmody family feud had clouded the waters like an algae bloom, making it hard to see anything else. Linda's killer would not be found in those murky waters. The murderer would be found among those who knew Linda well. At least... well enough to be familiar with her poison tongue and pernicious ways.

Only one person remained on Saffi's list of suspects. A person who had been publicly humiliated by Linda, his business crushed. A person who had a solid alibi, according to Detective Richards. If the detective thought he had the murderer in custody, would he loosen up enough to tell her what that alibi was? Probably not, but with Linda's murder hanging over the park like a death shroud, she had to try.

THIRTY-NINE

No matter how many strands a *Bedside Reader* article had, Saffi knew that her readers would not be satisfied until the fibers had been woven together into a net tight enough to hold a conclusion. All the questions posed at the beginning, or along the way, had to be answered, especially the question first posed to the reader. The first question was clear: "What happened to Linda Oates?" Saffi had chased down answers to the surge of questions that rolled shoreward from that first question. Linda Oates was murdered. But why? And... by whom?

Nicole had paid off a blackmailer, but, in the end, immaturity was her biggest crime. Bill had tried—and failed—to win back his ex. He was guilty of being an abysmal husband, but not of murder. The elder Carmodys were guilty of everything from arrogance to arson to assault but, Saffi now believed, not murder. Answering the most important question—"Who killed Linda?"—was like looking for a boat lost in a fog bank. She could see something, vague and blurry in the distance, but every time she waded forward, it retreated, remaining just out of sight.

After showing Nicole to the door, Saffi dug her cellphone out of her sling bag and punched in a now-familiar number.

"Detective Richards."

"It's Saffi."

Silence.

"Graywood?"

A drawn-out sigh breathed into her ear. "Believe it or not, Mrs. Graywood, I know your first name."

"Right. Well, I just need to know one thing about the night Linda died."

"This is still an open investigation, Mrs. Graywood. Even if we have arrested the perpetrator."

"Yes, but..." Saffi hesitated. "Are you... are you sure? I mean, that Eliza killed Linda as well as attacking me and Troy?"

Saffi heard the cellphone clunk to the desk, then fumbling, then Detective Richards' irritated voice as he spent five minutes recounting how many of Saffi's "suspects" he'd chased after and how many police hours he'd logged for the case. "But that's OK, because, this time, you handed me the culprit, the weapon she used in an assault, and a victim she drugged. You've done your civic duty and more. The town of Last Chance Cove thanks you."

"I don't want thanks!" Saffi huffed. "I want to know why."

"Why?"

"Why would Eliza kill Linda?"

"After interrogating her, I would say because she thought she was entitled to do so. Entitled to kidnap her granddaughter, to drug Troy, to attack you. Entitled."

Saffi nodded, feeling a bit silly since the detective on the other end of the cellphone couldn't see her. "But for each of those despicable deeds, the one thing Eliza felt *most* entitled to was her granddaughter."

When Nicole asked why her mother-in-law would have murdered Linda, she'd reminded Saffi of how critical it was to know what was at stake. What could have been at stake? If Linda had died the next morning, after she'd told the Carmodys to move on, the pill-addled Eliza might very well have been the culprit. But Linda hadn't made it till morning. In most murders, something vital was at stake—a marriage or a career or a secret that could ruin lives. Linda had specialized in ruining lives, and the one life she'd most wanted to ruin was Glenn's.

"So, about that airtight alibi? I have one final question. Is there anything at stake for the person verifying the alibi?"

Detective Richards paused for so long Saffi wondered if he'd hung up the phone. When he did speak, his "yes" carried a bone-deep weariness.

Saffi and Detective Richards met at City Hall, a wood-shingled building with a colorful hand-painted sign above a periwinkle-blue door. The sign featured a seal perched on a rock. Vibrant blue sea surrounded a lighthouse island in the background. It was a happy sign, bright and colorful. No slate-gray sea. No hint of fog or chill. No bodies rocking in the tide. The office closed at 5 p.m., but Detective Richards had phoned ahead. Randall Bevins—the city manager and Glenn's partner—as Saffi had suspected and the detective had confirmed earlier—had stayed after hours to meet with them. When Saffi knocked on the locked door, Bevins opened it and ushered them inside. They followed him down a carpeted hall to an office just big enough for a wide mahogany desk, a wooden file cabinet, and a barrister's bookcase, the kind with glass-fronted doors that opened outward.

A single antique armchair sat against the wall and Detective Richards pulled it forward, gesturing for Saffi to sit. She waved away the offer, opting to lean against the wall and let him do what only he could do. He didn't waste time with gentlemanly arguments but perched on the edge of the faded, floral-cush-ioned seat and got down to business.

"Thank you for meeting with us," Detective Richards began. "I just have a few questions."

Bevins waved his thanks away. "The sooner we put this case to bed, the sooner the park can go back to full capacity."

As Bill had told her repeatedly, Last Chance Cove RV Park was owned by the city. The city manager had an even bigger stake in keeping the park full so the city's coffers would be, too.

"You may have heard that we have a suspect in custody in the Linda Oates case. She's been charged with two counts of assault but we're still gathering information before bringing more serious charges."

Serious enough. Saffi squirmed, reaching up to touch the spot where Eliza's knife had chafed her neck.

Bevins nodded, licked his lips, then pointed at Saffi, who gave a little wave. "And she's here because...?"

Detective Richards twisted around to look at Saffi, who tried her best to disappear into the wall. "She's like a tick. Can't shake her."

In a city, that explanation wouldn't have held water, and she'd have been asked to leave. Last Chance Cove was a different animal. Bevins laughed, shook his head slowly, and spread his hands in welcome. Though she'd been in town for just over a week, Saffi had seen firsthand the way law enforce-ment intertwined with the fire department, city employees, and elected officials. They were all well-oiled gears in the machine that kept the town running. As a tourist destination on the edge of the mighty and merciless Pacific, the town must, Saffi real-ized, see more than its share of accidents, weather events, and violent acts, many of them involving—or caused by—tourists. Most incidents needed the know-how of more than one of the city's departments.

Randall Bevins rested his elbows on the blotter protecting

the polished mahogany desktop, leaned forward and folded his hands together. "How can I help you?"

Detective Richards opened his notepad and flipped through the pages until he found what he was looking for. "I need to confirm the alibi you gave early in the investigation."

Bevins stiffened and pushed himself upright, splaying his hands on the desktop. His nails, Saffi noticed, were manicured. His shirt bleached white, his tie alive with colorful swirls in green, blue, yellow and red. A fastidious man, Saffi decided, careful, career-oriented, but his tie hinted at passion pulsing beneath the suave surface.

Detective Richards looked up from his notebook. "You stated that you and your partner were asleep by ten p.m."

"That's right. Monday morning comes early." Bevins leaned back and smoothed his tie against his shirt.

"And nothing happened to wake you before morning?"

Bevins thought for a moment. He started to shake his head but the cellphone resting on his desk seemed to catch his attention and he reached instinctively to cover it with his hand.

"A call?" Saffi interjected. Cellphones had done a lot to make law enforcement jobs easier. Calls made and received. Location data. Internet searches. All helpfully logged on one handy device.

Bevins shifted his eyes her way. She could almost hear the precision gears of the brain that ran the city clicking.

"Oh, right. Sometime after we went to sleep, the phone rang. I mumbled something like, 'Don't you dare answer that.'" He chuckled. "Then I fell right back to sleep."

Saffi leaned forward. "Did you notice the time?"

The city manager's eyes narrowed. "Why do you ask?"

"Mrs. Graywood heard a scream at midnight," Detective Richards interjected.

Randall Bevins adjusted the knot of his tie and cleared his

throat twice before answering Saffi's question with a voice deepened by emotion.

"Eleven thirty."

"At which time your partner took the call and you fell back to sleep." Saffi met the city manager's cool blue eyes. He did not look away.

"That is correct."

As they left the city manager's office, weariness settled on Saffi's shoulders. Murder mysteries weren't supposed to end this way. They were supposed to end with a high-speed chase or a struggle for a gun or someone tied to a chair in an abandoned warehouse that had been rigged to blow. They ended with the sleuth in mortal danger from a perpetrator the author had made it easy to despise. Someone sneering. Obnoxious. Deserving of the fate his or her actions all but guaranteed.

Not this mystery.

"Want a lift?" Detective Richards asked as they left City Hall.

Saffi shook her head. She wanted to walk and keep walking until the clues added up to somebody, anybody besides the person whose alibi had just fallen apart. The person Detective Richards was on his way to detain: Glenn. She fast-walked, drawing ocean-moist air into lungs dried out from sighing. Her mind kept trying to create a different picture from the puzzle of clues she'd gathered over the past week. One puzzle piece still didn't fit: the attempted murder of Mellie. At the Saturday Market, Glenn had seemed genuinely worried about her. Then he'd spirited her out of Outpatient Services to hide her, not hurt her.

She barely noticed the shuttered shops and offices as she passed through the small downtown area. When the side street she'd taken from City Hall dead-ended in a small park, she looked up, disoriented. Should she turn right or left? As her thoughts stilled, she heard the growl of semis and the roar of massive RVs. She followed the noise away from the park to a traffic light at a busy intersection with Highway 101. She paced —unable to stand still—as she waited for the crossing sign to turn from a red-orange hand to an illuminated walker. As soon as the sign changed, she stepped into the crosswalk.

She knew better. Far too many drivers paid absolutely no attention to walkers, but the one who turned from the side street onto the highway and nearly hit her should have. The careless driver was in a city vehicle, a white truck emblazoned with the same lighthouse and seal logo she'd seen above the entrance to City Hall. She jumped back, heels hitting the curb hard enough to make her windmill to stay upright. Fury rose like high tide. She turned toward the speeding truck, fist raised, but something she noticed on the truck's back bumper made her lower her arm. The clues she'd been thinking about moved like one of those plastic sliding puzzles she'd played with as a kid.

A van—or a truck—had rumbled through the RV park the night Linda died. *Click.*

Mellie had been targeted because she saw the killer. *Click.*

That person had everything to lose. *Click.*

Just like that, a different picture appeared. Once Saffi's heart stopped thudding, she picked up her pace.

FORTY

As she reached the RV park, the evening sun sank toward the coastal head. A soft pink glow ghosted across the cove and shimmered off the metal roofs of trailers and coaches, their noses pointed toward the sea as if taking a last look before twilight dissolved the view. A city truck just like the one that had almost hit her sat in one of the parking spaces beside the laundry room. She walked close enough to touch the hood. *Warm.* That didn't prove the driver was the person who'd almost run her down. The city had a fleet of vehicles. She'd seen them all over Last Chance Cove, driven by maintenance crews of all kinds. This one, however, bore the mark she'd seen only minutes ago. If the driver was nearby, she needed to know.

She circled the two-story concrete-block building hunched beside the office. First, she checked the laundry room. A wave of musty humid air engulfed her when she opened the door, but the room was empty. Next, she checked the storage room that led to Linda's old apartment. Locked. She rounded the end of the building and stepped into both restrooms—women's and men's. Both smelled of disinfectant, as if recently cleaned, but whoever had done the cleaning was gone and silence echoed off the concrete floors. Finally, she crossed to the office. A "Closed" sign hung in the front window. The door was locked.

Saffi stood in the gravel lane, shielding her eyes from the sinking sun as she scanned the rows of RVs. The truck's driver could be anywhere on the grounds or even inside one of the RVs. If she spotted the driver, it would be dumb luck. Squaring her shoulders, Saffi bypassed the lane that would lead to the safety and seclusion of her Rambler. At the moment, seclusion was the last thing she needed. She needed a friend to talk to, someone who knew the cove and its denizens far better than she did. She needed Delilah.

Saffi spotted Delilah sitting at a weathered picnic table outside her small Terry trailer. Two figures sat on the opposite side. With the blazing sun setting behind them, both were in silhouette, but as she walked toward the tableau, a shiver of recognition started at the back of her neck, intensifying as she got closer.

"And here she is! Aunt Saffi!" Glenn raised his beer bottle in salute. "Randall's been telling me about your little visit to his office with Detective Richards. Solved the mystery of my dear cousin's untimely demise, did you?" As he spoke, an ocean breeze puffed his silky brown bangs off his forehead, revealing deep worry lines that belied his carefree sarcasm. Glenn looked doubly adorable in a double-breasted black shirt with big white buttons, a patterned cream and crimson ascot knotted at his neck. She wondered if he'd dressed for the man seated beside him.

The setting sun washed the scene with a rosy contented glow but the people around the table looked far from content. Saffi stepped over the picnic table's bench one foot at a time, and sat beside Delilah, studiously avoiding her friend's eyes. Across the cove, seals barked good evening. Gulls pirate-walked atop the berm, stiff-legged and jaunty. The briny smell of sea life suffused the air. Saffi drank it all in, pushing away the thought that this glorious evening might bring heartbreak to some of her favorite Last Chance locals.

"Randall," she nodded toward the man at Glenn's side. The city manager looked down at the Harbor Citra IPA in his hand. Was he thinking about taking a sip or slamming it against her head? Either could be possible.

Delilah popped the top off a bottle. "I don't believe it. Not for a minute," she said, as if the conversation had started long before Saffi arrived. When Saffi turned to meet the barista's eyes, they were hard as fingernails. The barista's lips tightened into a thin line that barely kept her anger inside. Her hand shook as she handed Saffi the sweat-beaded beer.

Throughout the investigation, Saffi had convinced herself that Glenn could not possibly be guilty. The clues kept pointing his way—his clear animosity for Linda, a hatred he didn't even try to hide. The heavy rumble of tires on gravel the night she died coupled with the van he drove. His outsized reaction when he'd heard of his cousin's death. His presence at the lighthouse when someone pulled Saffi off the ladder. Spiriting Mellie away from the outpatient center and hiding her in the lighthouse. Glenn's hands in prayer position as he urged her to throw Bill under the bus to keep Saffi off his trail.

Saffi didn't know where Detective Richards had gone when they'd parted outside City Hall. To the station? To the house Glenn shared with Randall? All she knew was that the detective wasn't here. She was. So, she had to take charge. She slipped her phone out of the front pocket of her sling bag. Both Glenn and Randall tensed, but Saffi smiled and pointed behind them. "Look at that sunset!" She snapped a few shots of the pair, making sure to get the berm with its saucy seagulls into the photo. "My editor has been begging me to send photos. Hang on." She forwarded the photo to the last number she'd called on her phone then slid the device back into the pocket of her sling and grinned. "She'll love those."

Randall lifted his beer to his lips and drained it, then started to rise. "Thanks for the drink, Delilah. Glenn, shall we?"

Saffi could not let them leave. Not before she got at least one answer. "Glenn? Randall told Detective Richards that you got a call the night Linda died. Around eleven thirty? Who was it?"

"Here we go." Glenn closed his eyes and rubbed the lids. When he opened them again, they were filled with despair, and resignation. He glanced at Randall. The city manager shook his head and held out his hand to help Glenn to his feet.

"This is absurd. Don't humor her."

Instead of taking his partner's hand, Glenn licked his lips, took a deep breath, and then looked straight at Saffi.

"Linda called. She wanted to meet. I asked her if hell had frozen over, because, if it had... sure. I'd come out in the middle of the night and meet her."

Delilah choked on the slug of beer she'd just inhaled. Saffi slapped her on the back until she stopped coughing. "You OK?"

"Heck no, I'm not OK. This is ridiculous. You're not a cop. You need to stop this nonsense."

Glenn offered a shrug and a sardonic grin. "Come on, Delilah. Don't you want to see into the mind behind *Aunt Saffi's Bedside Reader*? I, for one, am intrigued by the way Saffi's brain works. The twists. The turns. The way she ties herself, and everyone else," he paused to offer another beer-bottle salute, "into knots."

Delilah put her hands over her ears as if she couldn't bear to hear something she couldn't unhear. The barista was right. Saffi shouldn't be asking questions. Detective Richards should. But he wasn't here, and if she didn't ask, if Randall led Glenn away, the answer would go with them to... who knew where?

She turned her attention back to Glenn. "What did Linda say? When she called."

"Glenn!" Randall interrupted. "Don't do this. Please."

Glenn patted the bench beside him. Reluctantly, Randall sat, not with his legs tucked beneath the table as before, but sideways, crooked elbow resting on the table, poised as if ready to flee. Before Saffi could prod Glenn further, a raven swooped up from the beach. A big one, tall as her knee, like the one that had alerted her the night Linda died. It landed just to Saffi's right, shuffled closer, then leapt to the tabletop, like Super Raven, in a single bound. Randall shoved to his feet. Delilah covered her mouth with her hand. Saffi saw four shocked faces reflected in the raven's mirror-black eyes. Head cocked to one side, it gave a gurgling croak that rose in pitch, like a question.

Glenn cleared his throat and gave an uneasy chuckle. "Mellie told me you'd get to the truth. Not because you're smarter than the police, but because Raven has your back. Looks like she's right."

Saffi hoped so. With the massive bird's beak and claws mere inches from her face, she really wanted Raven to have her back, not go for her eyes.

Delilah's eyes had gone so wide Saffi thought she might be having a stroke. "Glenn? Could you... could you tell Saffi what she wants to know? Please?"

Glenn glanced back at Randall, who stood a few paces from the table. "Why not? Linda told me to get my tush over to the park, that Randall had been plotting against her and she had proof." His gaze flitted to Randall, who sank back down on the bench as if drowning in the tsunami of Glenn's words. "The thing is, when the council went after me, they cautioned Randall. If he retaliated against Linda in any way, he'd lose his job." He reached for his beer to take a sip. His hand shook hard enough to clink the bottle against his teeth. "She told me to meet her on the berm behind the RV park."

"You went." Saffi raised her brows.

"Duh. She cost me my bakery. I wasn't about to let her destroy Randall's career!"

"And you didn't hear him go?" She nodded toward Randall, whose face settled into a mask-like stillness.

Glenn glanced at Randall, eyes pleading. For what? Confirmation? Silence? "Don't be silly. I slipped out as quiet as a little mouse."

The rest of Glenn's confession came out in fits and starts. He'd parked the cookie van in an empty space near the berm and picked his way through stubby ice plant to where Linda told him she would be. He'd learned what set her off: the list Bill had been keeping and his threat to turn it over to Randall. "Linda wasn't about to let Bill have that kind of power over her. She searched the office until she found it. Underneath the cash drawer." Glenn shook his head. "Not the brightest starfish in the sea, our Bill."

"If she had the list, why did she need you?"

Once again Glenn's gaze flitted to Randall. The city manager's face was tight. Unreadable. "She wanted to send Bill packing, but she couldn't fire him without Randall's sign-off."

Saffi leaned forward, then quickly pushed back when the raven turned its fierce black beak toward her. She clutched the tabletop and squinted at the raven. "I think you've made your point." Her face—pale with fear—stared back from its eyes. The raven gave a shrill *caw* then pushed off with both legs, the sharp tips of its wing feathers scraping her face as it launched itself skyward.

"Ouch!" Saffi rubbed the sting from her cheek, hoping the wingtips hadn't broken skin.

A whistle of relief went round the table. Shoulders relaxed. Glenn took a long slow sip of his beer, then nodded, ready to continue his tale as if some supernatural creature hadn't scared the truth out of him with its presence.

"If I could convince Randall to fire Bill, she'd keep the list to herself. "

Saffi could picture the scene. Linda and Glenn wrapped together in a cloak of darkness. Waves crashing against the berm as she threatened to crash Randall's world the way she'd crashed Glenn's. The offer Linda had made would have put a noose around Randall's neck, one that she could loosen or tighten at will. *Oh, Bill. What did you do?*

"I lost it. I-I reached out and grabbed her by that bug-ugly yellow safety vest she always wore." He stared down at the sun-scoured tabletop. "She pulled away, demanding that I get my hands off her." Glenn stopped, his gaze lost its focus, as if he looked into the past. "So, I did. I let go, just as she stepped back-ward. She lost her balance, and before I could react, she—" He glanced at Randall again. "She fell."

Delilah looked up, eyes wide. Then she reached toward Glenn. "If that's true, honey, it was an accident. Not murder."

Glenn slammed his bottle down on the table so hard Saffi thought it might explode. "Of course it was an accident! But that's not what people will say. Is it? They'll say maybe it *wasn't* an accident. Maybe my hatred for Linda finally boiled over." He pointed an accusing finger at Delilah. "*You* of all people know how quickly gossip spreads in this town."

Delilah had the good grace to blush. "I would never. Not about something like this. About you? No."

Glenn's eyes softened. "Of course not. You may be the Mouth of the Cove, but I love you. Just the way you are.

"After Linda's head hit the concrete, there was no going back. If I'd called the police, they would have grilled me like a tuna steak. Next morning, the *Last Chance Gazette* would have run a godawful picture of me on a bad hair day under the head-line, *City Manager's Pedo Partner Commits Murder*."

"Oh, come on, Glenn. You don't really think that, do you?" Delilah's nervous nails clicked on the tabletop.

"Small towns, small minds," Randall murmured.

Delilah stood up and rubbed her hands on her thighs, drying off the condensation left by the beer she'd finished. "Small towns can also have big hearts, Randall. That's the Last Chance Cove I know. A few knuckleheads on the council made a big mistake. They wronged Glenn, but most folks stood by him. Me included."

She walked around the table and put a hand on Glenn's shoulder. "Maybe you haven't noticed, but half the town has gained weight since you opened that cookie cart. Just look at my thighs." She slapped her lean legs with both hands, making Saffi roll her eyes. "People don't just buy cookies week after week because they're irresistible. They buy them because *you're* irresistible. They buy them because they care about *you*.

"If you believed in yourself half as much as this town does, you would have walked away from Linda's threats. The next morning, you'd have come into the café to gossip about your vile cousin over a four-shot sixteen-ounce mocha with extra whipped."

Delilah was right. If Glenn had walked away, he could have shrugged it off. Glenn was right, too. Once Linda went over the berm, things changed. The history the two of them shared would have colored any investigation. And, sadly, statistics showed that gay people were more than three times more likely to be incarcerated than straight people.

Saffi could hardly bear to look at Glenn's face. He hunched into himself, his brown eyes shining as tears spilled down his cheeks. "I wish that had happened," he whispered. "I really do."

Saffi believed him. Linda had been caught in the net of vitriol and self-interest she'd woven, but so had Glenn. Trapped, not because of something he'd done, but because of who he was. Different. Vulnerable. Caring. Too caring, Saffi suspected, for his own good.

It was time to slide the last puzzle piece into the opening

she'd seen when the city truck almost ran her over. "So." She rapped her knuckles on the tabletop, grimacing when a splinter jabbed into her skin. She plucked it out and sucked away the sting before continuing. "I just have one more question. This one"—she turned away from Glenn—"is for Randall."

FORTY-ONE

Glenn stiffened. "You, uh... what?" He looked from Saffi to Randall, confused.

Delilah put her hands on her hips, curling her long nails into her belly as if wishing she could sink them into Saffi. "What in the name of all the seaweed in God's green ocean is happening right now?"

Randall crossed his arms and squeezed his hands beneath his armpits. "I, for one, have no intention of being questioned by anyone without the presence of an attorney. Least of all some-some *writer* trying to dig dirt for her next book. And, just so you know, nothing Glenn just said can be used in a court of law."

"You're right. It can't." Saffi bounced her thighs, waking her legs up in case she needed to move quickly. "It's just, I was wondering if the city truck parked by the laundry room is yours?"

Glenn scrunched up his face in confusion. "Of course it isn't Randall's. By virtue of being a city truck, it belongs to the city."

"But you drive it." She nodded at Randall.

"Sometimes."

"Like today?"

This time, Randall nodded.

Delilah came back to Saffi's side of the table. "You're making my brain hurt." She plopped down on the end of the bench, jolting Saffi enough to make her clutch the table.

"If you'll all humor me, I'd like to show you something." Saffi stood and motioned in the direction of the park office. She forced herself to smile as if sandflies weren't swooping in her stomach, as if she wasn't walking herself—and other innocents—toward a possible "knife at the throat" moment like the one she'd faced the day before.

Randall was the first to stand. "We'll humor you as far as the truck. Then we'll be leaving."

Glenn glanced up at Randall, and then nodded. Delilah shrugged and stood as well. The four of them wandered in a loose knot down the gravel lane toward the front of the park. A pair of poodles swept past them, tugging a woman with two pink leashes looped around her waist in their wake.

Delilah nudged Saffi. "I can't tell who's walking who."

Saffi coughed out a chuckle.

The Mini-Winnie Saffi had seen three times before rumbled into the park, stopped for just long enough to spot the "Closed" sign on the office door, then headed down the lane as if searching for an empty space to settle for the night. A squirm of unease passed through her but she brushed it aside. Linda's murderer wasn't behind the wheel and her Thunderbird post hadn't elicited a single stalkery comment. It was not at all unusual to see an RV free-park for a few days and then rent a space to refill water and dump. As the quartet stepped aside to let the Winnebago pass, its tires kicked up sand, coating their clothes with a fine layer of dust. Randall unbuttoned his jacket, took it off, gave it a shake, and then tucked it over his arm.

As they passed Bill's fifth wheel, sea shanties soared from the open window covering up the sound of the van rumbling into the park. Even if he hadn't pushed his ex-wife, the list he'd made and the taunt he'd delivered had set the fatal moment in motion. How would he feel when the truth emerged?

Saffi kept her steps slow, measured, hoping to spread a sense of ease through the group. By the time they passed the office, Glenn had relaxed enough to take Randall's free hand. When they reached the city truck, Saffi kept walking until she'd rounded the back. The others followed.

"Check this out." She pointed at the bumper. Daylight had lingered long enough to reveal what she had seen as the truck swept past her: a grim streak of gloss-black paint. She looked up, not at Randall, but at Glenn. Her eyes challenged him to see what she'd seen, to deduce what she had deduced. "A perfect match for Mellie's gallery, wouldn't you say?"

Randall put an arm around Glenn's shoulder. "That's a stretch, even for Aunt Saffi, wouldn't *you* say?"

Glenn kept his eyes glued to the graze of black paint. "A stretch. Yes." He clutched his ascot.

Saffi folded her arms. "Well, no need to guess. There's enough paint for the police to see if it's a match. Because if it *is* a match, the person driving this truck shoved Mellie off a cliff with a clear intent to kill her."

Delilah gasped. She backed away from the truck as Glenn stepped out of Randall's embrace and turned toward him.

"Glenn. Sweetie." Randall's voice went soft, like a trainer trying to gentle a spooked horse. "Lots of people drive this truck. You know that."

Glenn moved toward the bumper, trailed a finger along the black streak. His breath turned ragged. "I do know that. I do. I also know that Mellie saw you at the RV park that night. And I know that I *told* you she saw you because I *trusted* you!" He turned toward Randall, his body shaking so hard Saffi feared he would collapse. He didn't. Instead, he chan- neled his rage into a shove that sent Randall reeling backward. The jacket that had been draped over his arm went flying.

"Glenn, no! It wasn't me. She's-she's a *writer*. She makes this stuff up for a living."

"She's a *nonfiction* writer!" Glenn glared. "She has fact checkers!"

If the situation hadn't been so dire, Saffi would have laughed out loud. Instead, she asked the questions she'd been wanting to ask since Glenn proclaimed his guilt. "Did you really go to the berm that night, Glenn? Did you grab Linda's vest? Did you let her fall?"

Glenn's expressive face went through a series of emotions: from shame to remorse to despair then, finally, to his jaw set in determination. "No."

Randall scooped up his jacket and pulled a key fob from the left pocket. "I've had enough of this. I'm going home. Are you coming?" He quirked an eyebrow at Glenn.

Glenn pointed straight-armed at the gash of gloss-black paint across the truck's bumper. "I thought I was protecting your *career* when I offered to take the blame for Linda's death. Not protecting a-a serial killer!"

"We've talked about this, you know. Public histrionics." Randall shook his head. "Not your finest quality." He clicked his key fob to unlock the truck and stepped into the cab. Then he buckled himself in and turned the key in the ignition before rolling down the window. "Linda's death was an accident, Glenn. You know that. And Mellie? Mellie is fine. We'll be fine, too." Randall revved the engine and shifted the truck into reverse. "Come on, sweetheart." When Glenn didn't move to join him, he locked eyes with Saffi in the truck's rearview mirror and smiled.

Saffi had seen her share of sharklike grins since arriving in Last Chance Cove, but this was the first time she'd been sure the shark's bite would kill.

"Run!" She grabbed Glenn's hand and yanked him out of the way a split second before Randall hit the accelerator. The truck sped backward. Randall slammed on the brakes, shifted into drive, hit the gas and fishtailed. Sand and gravel spun from beneath the tires as Saffi, Glenn, and Delilah scattered, running for their lives. The truck's engine whined as Randall ignored the other two and aimed its nose toward Saffi.

She ran. Full out, as she'd done the night of the sneaker waves with Archie clutched to her chest. She darted between the office and the concrete bathhouse, praying the gap was too narrow for the city truck. It wasn't. The truck was so close she could feel the heat coming off the engine. She did the only thing she could think of—as she reached the back of the office, she threw herself behind it. She hit the ground with a sickening thud. Pain exploded through her body. As the truck's brakes squealed, she struggled to her feet. *Come on, Saffi! Get up, get up, get...* Up! She was up, limping but lumbering around the corner of the office. She thought she heard the truck behind her, its hot grate sniffing at her heels. She was wrong. When she came around the front of the office, there it was sliding sideways around the back of the bathhouse and straightening out to ram into her.

Saffi's head pounded. Her heart thrummed like the wings of a gull caught in a gale. Something wailed. *Was it her?* Then a single whoop sounded, a siren's frantic blast as an SUV with reds and blues flashing skidded between Randall's oncoming truck and Saffi. The door burst open, and Detective Richards jumped out. Without stopping, he raced toward Saffi, hooked his left arm around her, and pulled her up the ramp to the office just as the city truck rammed into the police SUV and plowed it past the spot where Saffi had just been standing.

Detective Richards shoved Saffi behind him and drew his service revolver. "Turn it off, Randall! And get out. Slowly."

After Detective Richards loaded Randall into his police

SUV to take him downtown, Glenn collapsed onto a bench outside the laundry room like a laundry bag emptied of its contents. Saffi sat down on his left, Delilah on his right. Like mourners at a wake, they kept vigil, allowing him to process what had happened in a silence broken only by the foghorn's mournful cry. Dark draped itself over their shoulders and the dusk-to-dawn outdoor light above their heads came on. Moths and other flying insects swarmed toward the light, not attracted by the light itself, as had been believed since the invention of artificial lights, but confused by it.

Insects—Saffi knew from an article about odd animal behavior (*Bedside Reader*, #12)—fly so fast they can't tell up from down. For 370 million years, they had solved the up/down problem by keeping their backs to the brightest source of light in the sky—the sun, moon, or stars. Then... mankind invented porch lights. From that day forward, insect kind had been doomed to either orbit ceaselessly around artificial globes until overcome by exhaustion or flip over in futile attempts to point their backs toward the sky whereupon they tumbled, crashed, and died. By morning, Saffi knew, many of the insects whirling above their heads would have perished, along with Randall's career and Glenn's belief in the love he and his partner had shared.

<h1 style="text-align:center">FORTY-TWO</h1>

Once in a great while, when conditions were just right, Last Chance Cove offered up a brilliant blue-diamond day. A blaze of sunlight shot between the rose-colored curtains in Saffi's bedroom. She woke with a smile, soaked in the warm rays for a few minutes, then stretched catlike and bounced out of bed.

"Owie, owie, owie!" Saffi hissed. Her body ached in places she couldn't even name. But she'd awakened to too many foggy mornings over the last week to miss seeing the glorious Pacific naked, its deep-blue body sparkling with diamonds.

She went into prep mode like a kid on the first day of school. Face. Teeth. Hair. Clothes. She shoved her feet into her almost-new light-blue sloggers whose fat bees and perky daisies never failed to make her happy. Ready in record time, she locked the Rambler and brisk-walked the gravel lane toward the beach, waving at any camper who looked at all familiar. Today, those who had griped about being trapped at Last Chance Cove could pack up and pull out. Those who planned to stay could finally relax and enjoy their stay, which was exactly what Saffi planned to do.

She quick-stepped along the narrow beach trail between

Delilah's and Nicole's trailers but when she hit the deep sand at the edge of the beach, her shoes dug in, straining her thighs. She slogged toward the dark, damp, firm sand at the tide's edge and picked up her pace, enjoying the crunch of wave-broken shells beneath her shoes. The morning smelled of salt, seaweed, and hope. With Linda's killer in jail, she could stop sleuthing and settle into the writing routine she'd imagined before her arrival. Wake up. Walk or bike ride to a café for coffee. Revise and write. Practice tai chi on the beach or scout out a pickleball court. Research and write. Sunset walk. Leave the cozy comfort of her RV to spend time around campfires drinking wine and chatting. If she was lucky, someone would dish about something that would make a perfect *Bedside Reader* article. Read. Fall asleep... and repeat.

To Saffi's right, wave-polished pebbles rolled in the surf. To her left, sand disappeared beneath wind-sculpted bushes, reminding her of the night Archie made his escape from Bill and Smudge. The night she found the white terrier bedraggled on the beach. The night that began a nightmare from which the cove had finally awakened. Overhead, gulls rode the cross-winds, rising and dipping then swooping seaward, their raucous cries mingling with the honks, groans, and growls of harbor seals sunning on the abandoned docks at the edge of the harbor.

She walked the length of the beach from RV park to harbor and back twice before the coffee jones hit hard and she turned toward the trail to the marina parking lot. As she crossed the lot, she spotted yesterday evening's Mini-Winnie. Neither a murderer nor a stalker, she decided. A stealth camper. Most parks had them, RVs that snuck in after hours to hook into services then jetted before the park awakened to keep from paying a fee. As she passed the dock where Troy's boat strained against its moorings, a chill shuddered her shoulders. Troy should have been guiding a tour today, not recuperating in a hospital bed. Saffi would have been aboard, doing her best impression of someone who knew how to bait a hook. She touched the sore spot where Eliza's knife had scraped her neck, then straightened, banishing the memory as she marched toward the familiar turquoise door of Last Chance Café.

A wave of coffee-scented warmth steamed her face as she pushed inside. The smell of fresh-baked scones made her salivate. She'd arrived at the height of the early-morning coffee rush, so she waved toward Delilah and eased herself into the turquoise-and-white armchair beneath Troy's photos, smiling as she noticed that he had added a few RV-sized eight-by-tens to the wall. Some local scenes were now familiar: the lighthouse with its beam sweeping the rocks, a conspiracy of ravens perched on a gnarled tree limb. Some she hoped to discover: the knobby toes of a giant redwood, an elk drinking from a stream in a fern-draped canyon.

Once the rush cleared, Delilah slid a mocha with a heart-shaped foam swirl onto the glass-topped table. She held up a finger. She'd switched out yesterday's ravens for blue nails tipped with rhinestones that glittered like the ocean outside the café's window. "Scones!" She winked. "Back in a sec."

When the turquoise door washed in a new wave of customers, Delilah's second stretched into fifteen minutes. Most of the newcomers grabbed to-go coffees and left. A few scattered among the tables, heads bent toward companions or cellphones. Saffi savored her mocha, smiling as Delilah bustled behind the counter, red curls bouncing with each step. The barista had added a dash of cinnamon and a peppering of cayenne to Saffi's mocha. The spices woke up Saffi's tastebuds and put a smile on her face.

When the final newcomer had been served, Delilah placed a sign on the counter that read, "Don't be depresso-ed! I'll be right back." Then she carried over a plate of warm Marionberry scones and slid it onto the table. She sat in the armchair opposite Saffi and crossed her arms over her chest as if expecting bad news.

Saffi snagged a scone from the plate, sliced it in half and spread whipped butter across both surfaces. She let the butter melt before taking a bite, then chewed slowly.

"Well?" Delilah demanded. "What have you heard? Is Randall in jail? Is that aggravatingly adorable detective going to arrest Glenn, too?"

Saffi held up a hand for Delilah to wait till she'd finished the bite.

"Nobody chews that slow." The barista glared. "You're just stalling."

Saffi licked crumbs from her lips and took a sip of mocha. "I'm not stalling. I don't know anything. I don't even *suspect* anything." Saffi grinned. "I can't tell you how good that feels."

The barista pulled the corners of her eyes downward and then out, doing her best to keep tears from falling in front of customers. "Glenn didn't do a thing but cover for that lousy boyfriend of his. If there was a law against falling for an a-hole, half the country would be in jail." Her eyes begged Saffi to confirm her hope.

"True that." Saffi put another bite into her mouth, enjoying the buttery berry burst. She rolled her shoulders to dislodge the kinks from hunching over the table, not to mention throwing herself to the ground and being virtually tackled by Detective Richards.

When Delilah started biting a thumbnail, Saffi raised a brow and shoved the plate of scones toward her. "These taste better. Believe me."

Delilah stopped biting and reached for a scone. Saffi settled into the armchair, the same one Troy had filled with his manly bulk the first time she'd visited Last Chance Café. She could feel Casey's grin shining from the photo behind her as Delilah speculated on what might happen to Glenn, to Randall, to

Mellie, who had lost both her gallery and her home, to Nicole, Casey, and the elder Carmodys. To Bill.

Delilah pursed her mouth. "They all lied. Every last one of them. Since the minute Linda disappeared, if their lips were moving, they were lying."

No matter what role they'd played in the puzzle of Linda's death, these people were no longer strangers. They were a part of her life she'd never forget, even if she left the cove after three months as she'd planned. But Delilah was right. They had all had a hand in casting a net of confusion over the investigation.

Delilah brushed crumbs off her turquoise Last Chance Café T-shirt. "If I had Linda in front of me right now, I'd snatch her bald. All the trouble she's caused." She shoved her fingers through her short, hennaed curls then shook them loose.

Saffi had to agree. She hadn't even met Linda, but the woman had caused her problems and pain from the moment she drove into Last Chance Cove RV Park. Despite it all, she pitied Linda. Her untimely death had cut short her chance to grow, to change, to become a better version of herself. Saffi tasted Marionberry at the corners of her mouth and licked away the remains. "She didn't deserve to die."

Delilah sighed. "No. But as my mama would have said, she needed a good talking-to."

Saffi tugged the tail of the Bigfoot T-shirt she'd put on in her hurry to greet the day. Crumbs went flying. Even upside down she could read the T-shirt's anti-littering slogan: *Be like me. Leave no trace.*

"Sorry." She gave Delilah a penitent smile. "And not just about being messier than Bigfoot. I'm sorry that Glenn got dragged into this whole mess. I never wanted it to be him, and I'm so relieved it wasn't." She bit her lip and lifted one eyebrow, hoping Delilah wouldn't hold her responsible for what Glenn was going through.

Delilah reached out for her hands and gave them a squeeze.

"What would you have to be sorry for? Being smarter than the rest of us?"

Saffi laughed. "Not smarter, not by a long shot. Just insanely curious and stubborn. Detective Richards said I was a tick he couldn't shake off."

Delilah threw back her head and roared. "A tick! That's you with a capital *T*. Maybe it can be your sleuthing name: The Tick!"

Saffi snorted. "Having written about the weirdest of weird comic book characters, I can tell you that *The Tick* is already taken."

"Shame."

When Delilah grinned, a sense of relief washed over Saffi. Delilah was the forgiving kind. She lifted her coffee mug to the barista's. "Friends?"

Delilah smiled so wide her dimples showed. "Friends!" She clinked her mug against Saffi's.

Troy had been released from the hospital and was home by lunchtime. "Home," Saffi discovered by stopping at Nicole's trailer, was a cottage tucked into a redwood grove on a hill above town. After calling to make sure he hadn't already eaten and would be home, she picked up a fisherman's platter from Beachfront Brews. The owner—Troy's fishing buddy, as it turned out—loaded her up with beer-battered halibut, buttery scallops, and juicy clam strips. "Better hang on tight to that one," he told her with a wink. "He's escaped a lot of hooks."

She backpedaled out of the shop before her whole face could turn red, and then tucked the warm bag of food into her rear bike basket. She swung a leg over and scootched onto the large, padded seat, pedaling away as fast as she could pump. The sea breeze cooled her flushed face as she passed the RV park, but she heated up again—this time from exertion, not embarrassment—after turning left then right onto the winding lane that led to Troy's cottage. Ten minutes later, her calves and lungs were begging her to turn around and coast home. But when she reached Troy's yard and dismounted, gasping for oxygen, she was glad she hadn't. She wobbled off the bike, legs shaking, planted the kickstand and marveled at the view.

Unbelievably, Troy's tiny homestead overlooked the cove and the marina. Just beyond, the blue Pacific blazed as far as her straining eyes could see. Saffi inhaled the intermingled scent of forest and ocean. If she hadn't known a few things about his family—including the nutty Eliza who'd drugged him with a cup of tea—she would have thought Troy led a charmed life.

As she approached the cottage, lunch bag clutched in one hand, she saw that the redwood shake siding was real, not vinyl. The front door, also redwood, was carved with a fish jumping above a cresting wave. She thunked the anchor-shaped knocker against the thick wood and clutched the still-warm bag of food against her belly to quell her nerves.

The quirky welcoming smile Troy gave her when he opened the door reminded her so much of Levi, tears stung her eyes. He wasn't Levi, of course. He was someone completely different, and that was completely OK. As he led her through the house to a cobbled patio outside his back door, she had just enough time to take in a built-in bookcase filled with a hodge-podge of books, a cozy armchair flanked by blue-glass Japanese fishing floats, and a redwood coffee table with a pile of fishing magazines tumbling off what looked like a brand-new copy of *Aunt Saffi's Bedside Reader,* #19. She was glad she was behind him so he couldn't see the goofy grin that spread across her face.

Once outside, Troy tugged the bag from her grasp, unrolled the top, and inhaled. "Oh, man! I'm so hungry I could eat a whale."

"That is not PC," Saffi chided.

"I said 'I could.' Not 'I *would.*'" His gray-blue eyes twinkled with mischief.

"Ah. That's OK then."

Saffi arranged the seafood on a bistro-style table centered on a brickwork patio. She added the sides she'd chosen—onion rings and coleslaw—and fished in the bottom of the brown paper bag for the small round containers of tartar sauce, remoulade, and ketchup. Troy ducked into the cottage. He came back out juggling plates, forks, napkins and two sweating bottles of Lost Coast Brewery's chocolatey Downtown Brown ale. They ate in silence, relishing every bite with the occasional moan of pleasure from one or the other. Hers drew grins from Troy and his coaxed giggles from Saffi. She wasn't usually a giggler but when the beer made him belch, she realized that sharing a near-death experience had pushed them both back to high school lunchroom behavior.

Once the feeding frenzy slowed, Saffi filled Troy in on what had happened while he was unconscious as well as while he recuperated in the hospital. He was devastated to learn of Randall's role in Linda's death, not to mention his near-fatal attack on Mellie.

Troy drew in a sharp breath. "Did Randall try to kill you too? That day at the lighthouse?"

A shudder of fear passed through Saffi's body. "I did see a city truck parked by Glenn's van when I was up in the beacon."

"I can't believe the killer is someone I *like.*" Troy scowled. "And Glenn! Why would he cover for him?"

The things people did for love never ceased to amaze and bewilder Saffi. "Have you ever trusted someone enough to give them your heart?" she asked, holding her breath as seconds ticked by.

Troy folded his hands over his belly. "I have."

Saffi smiled her relief. After all, as she'd discovered while writing *Bedside Readers*, men who never truly loved sometimes turned out to be serial killers.

"Then you know why Glenn did what he did. He trusted Randall. But after the way he lost his bakery, he no longer trusted Last Chance Cove. Small towns, small minds?"

Troy shook his head but finished chewing the clam in his mouth before speaking. "Small people have small minds. Not small towns."

Wow. Saffi set her beer on the table. *Could this guy be more irresistible?* "Can I steal that line?"

"For one of your *Bedside Readers*?" He grinned. "I'd be honored." He cleaned his hands with a napkin, wadded it up, and tossed it on his now-empty plate. "So," his Montana sapphire eyes teased, "now that you've solved the mystery, what shall we do with the rest of our day?"

Saffi quirked an eyebrow. *What, indeed?*

FORTY-THREE

As June ran headlong into July, rumors swirled around Glenn like early-morning fog over the headlands. If he was really innocent, why would he take the fall for Randall? Delilah steamed lattes, swabbed counters, and smacked down every slur she heard. "Tell me with a straight face you've never been a fool for love, and I'll pay for your coffee myself." Since they all dished dirt on each other on a regular basis, Delilah had a "What about that time you...?" for the ones brazen enough to take up the challenge. With the "Mouth of the Cove" behind the counter, they all ended up red-faced.

The city started a search for a new "non-murdery" manager, and Glenn kept Kevin's Kookies rolling. The only hint he gave that his heart had been crushed was a new cookie creation: Baker's Tears, bittersweet chocolate sprinkled with sea salt. Saffi became so addicted to them that Glenn threatened to cut her off.

With the city's permission, and to Saffi's surprise, Bill put out a jar in the park office to collect donations to rebuild Mellie's gallery. It filled to the brim within a week. The piratical handyman had already purchased a trailer and framed in the structure. Another jar went up to predict how long it would take him to complete the build. If anyone guessed the exact date, they'd win a free week's stay at the park. Poppy had reminded Saffi of her book's deadline so often, it was the only date she could think of, so she tucked a slip with September 1 written on it into the jar. Meanwhile, once Dr. Duarte pronounced her shoulder and wrist mended, Mellie volunteered at the lighthouse, keeping the place ship-shape. She also helped Martin give tours and badgered Walter about eating too many cookies. The gig came with free lodging and ended in October, but at the rate Bill was building, she'd be rehoused long before then.

The elder Carmodys had their claim on the Prevost rejected due to Troy's potato chip tip-off. The fire had burned hot enough to destroy all evidence, so arson could neither be proved nor disproved. That created enough suspicion to deny the claim. Predictably, Eliza hired a hotshot San Francisco attorney who blamed the little blue pills she'd been taking for her erratic behavior. He'd plea-bargained her out of the assault charges then sued the pharmaceutical company.

Had money won after all? Saffi didn't think so. Jeff and Eliza flew home a half-mil short and estranged from not only their daughter-in-law and granddaughter, but their son as well. Nicole's soon-to-be ex-husband was furious with his parents. He'd become contrite, apologetic, and willing to work out a custody agreement that was in Casey's best interests. Then he'd signed over the house they'd shared to lure them back to Texas.

Nicole stayed long enough to celebrate July 4th with a beach bonfire bang, then loaded her pink suitcases into her car to head home. She had plans for a podcast that would empower trophy wives to reach their full potential, before, during, and after marriage. As Nicole and Casey buckled themselves into the green Subaru, Archie danced at the end of his leash. He demanded so many doggie kisses Delilah had to pick him up before Casey could close her door.

"Don't be a stranger!" Troy called as his sister and niece drove away. The telltale shine in his eyes told Saffi he feared he wouldn't see his niece again until her high school graduation.

Saffi squeezed his hand and whispered, "You don't have to wait for them to visit you. A day and a half of driving gets you to Texas, and if you're in a pickup truck, the Lone Star State will welcome you with open arms."

"How are you so wise, Saffi Graywood?" He kissed the unruly curls on the top of her head.

As for Saffi? She had a lot of reasons to want to extend her stay in Last Chance Cove and only a single reason to go—a blog comment: *Solved any murders lately?* The minute the murder investigation was put to bed, a steady stream of campers flowed into the RV park. Gossip pinged and ponged between sites and some found their way onto the internet, including one about Saffi's role in finding the killer. Anyone could set a Google alert for a name, including her stalker, but Saffi wasn't about to let one comment drive her away from the first place she'd felt at home since Levi died.

Even though she had almost two months left on her stay, she'd begun to consider asking Bill for an extension. Would he give her one? Probably not. Unless...? The memory of a flyer about park hosts posted in the office window the day she arrived popped into her head. Linda's death—horrible though it was— meant the park needed new hosts even more than it had on the day she'd pulled into its potholed driveway.

The morning after Nicole and Casey left, Saffi waited till Bill had done his morning round of the park to see if anyone had pulled out early or snuck in after hours. Then she slurped the last sip of the London Fog she'd made herself (Earl Grey with steamed oat milk and a dash of vanilla syrup), finger-combed her morning Medusa curls and headed to the office. Her guess had been right. The flyer was still in the window. Bill had written URGENT in red felt-tip at the top of the flyer. PARK HOSTS was circled in red and red exclamation marks sprouted like porcupine quills from the circle. Saffi grinned. Bill was desperate. She marched inside and tugged the flyer off the glass.

"Hey, now, missie. What do you think you're doing?" He scowled beneath his grizzly mustache.

"Applying for the job." Saffi plunked the flyer down on the counter. "Tell me how it works."

Bill went from ornery to obsequious in an eyeblink. "The famous Aunt Saffi working for me? Now that's something to write home about."

He opened a filing cabinet, pulled out four sheets of paper from four separate files, and stapled them together in the top left corner. "Fill out the top sheet, read the rest, sign and date everything and get it back to me asap. You'll have to talk to the gal in HR but, right now, she'll hire anyone who's breathing."

Saffi ignored the dig and scanned the pages, her eyes stopping on the paragraph about compensation. *The sole compensation for this volunteer position with the City of Last Chance Cove consists of one free RV space of the park manager's choosing to include water, electricity, cable, and Wi-Fi.*

Saffi looked up at Bill, who was nervously chewing a yellow thumbnail. "Space of the park manager's choosing?"

Bill's eyes narrowed. "Still don't trust me, eh? OK. Here's what I'll do. I'll keep you in space thirty-two. Another monthly camper reserved it after your three months were up, but I can put them in thirty-one. It has a better view of the lighthouse anyway."

Saffi tapped the paper. "In writing."

Bill circled "one free RV space" and drew an arrow to the margin where he hastily scribbled "space 32" plus the date and his initials.

Saffi turned the paperwork around that afternoon. By the

end of the week she'd been interviewed, drug tested, and cleared for duty. Really, she could hardly believe her luck. Free water, free electricity, free cable, free Wi-Fi. Spotty at times, she'd already discovered, but free. Access to the twenty-four-hour laundry. Not free. But at a buck-fifty a load, close enough. From the RV park, she could walk or bike to restaurants, a natural food store, the library, downtown shops, the harbor, and—of course—her favorite destination: Last Chance Café. In exchange, she'd work eight-to-five, two days a week. Two on, five off. Plenty of time to stay on deadline. Even Poppy, her skeptical editor, thought she'd have enough time to write.

"But if pages start to slow down, I'll come out there and drag them out of you," she declared.

That had made Saffi laugh. Maybe she'd slow her output on purpose. There was nothing Poppy Morales would love more than a trip to the West Coast at the publishing company's expense.

The biggest drawback to hosting was Bill. As the most experienced employee in the park, he'd finagled his way into Linda's old job. The badge on his yellow vest now read *Park Manager*. Sure, Saffi had reservations. A laundry list of them. But if putting up with Bill meant more time to explore Last Chance Cove and her blossoming friendship with Troy, she'd do it.

At 8 a.m. on the second Monday in July—a month after her arrival in Last Chance Cove—Saffi sauntered into the office wearing the bug-ugly yellow safety vest Bill had given her over a comfy pair of jeans. She'd already taken a long beach walk to get her steps in before she sat down at the computer. It would take time to learn the booking system, Bill had warned. She anticipated spending her first few days doing just that.

She should have known better. Instead of ushering her behind the counter, Bill gave her a wily, yellow-toothed smile and handed her a plastic cleaning caddy.

"You'll need to check both bathrooms three times a day. Women's and men's."

Saffi stepped back. "Wait! You want me to clean toilets?"

Bill nodded. "Give everything a basic spray and wipe. Counters. Door knobs. Handles. Whatever gets touched a lot. A crew comes in at night for the heavy cleaning. If you find a clogged toilet, plunger's in there." He nodded toward the caddy now clutched in Saffi's right hand. Blue latex gloves. A spray bottle half-filled with all-purpose cleaner. A toilet brush, well-used. *Ugh.* A plastic canister of disinfecting wipes guaranteed to eliminate 99 percent of all common household germs. A peeling laminated sign that read *Closed for Cleaning*. These would, apparently, be the tools of her new trade—at least three times a day.

Bill hadn't said a word about toilets when he'd given Saffi the rundown on park host duties, but the devious pirate had apparently prepared for pushback. He held up the work exchange agreement she'd signed the week before. There it was, in black and white, near the bottom of a bulleted list of duties stapled to the back of the agreement. No wonder park hosts came and went with the tide.

Saffi set the cleaning caddy on the counter. "You added that page after I signed!"

"You wish." Bill tapped a tobacco-stained fingertip on a line that bore her scribbled initials. "In time, you'll learn to pay attention to details. Like I do." He gave her his sharkiest grin. "That's why they pay me the big bucks."

If she'd been alone, she'd have done a face-plant. She prided herself on being detail-oriented. How could she have missed that detail? Maybe she could back out. Tear up the paperwork and find someplace else to camp after her three-month stay ended.

The road is calling, Saffi, the inner voice that sounded like Levi's whispered, but it was wrong. For the first time in three years, the pull to stay was stronger than the pull to go. Saffi straightened her shoulders, grabbed the cleaning caddy, and turned to go outside.

"Be sure to knock on the Men's and give a holler. Wouldn't want you to walk into anything unsavory." Bill's chuckle followed her out the door.

As Saffi stepped into the sunshine, Delilah trundled past in her faded red Jetta. She rolled down the window and waved. "See you at lunch?"

"You bet!" Saffi called.

Gulls soared above, their wings spread to salute the morning. In the distance, seals barked an early-morning hello. The mighty Pacific shushed against the shore and the clearest air she'd ever breathed filled her lungs. As she stood there wondering what to do, a raven landed in the gravel-and-sand drive a few steps away and cocked its head as if to say, "Well?"

Well, indeed. Would a few toilets scare her away from her new friends? From the *Reel Sexy* man with Montana-sapphire eyes who'd promised to grill fresh tuna at his place this evening? From the natural wonders she encountered every time she stepped outside her RV door? And most of all, from the sense of finding home she'd begun to feel in Last Chance Cove?

No, Saffi decided. They would not.

A LETTER FROM THE AUTHOR

Miles and miles of thanks for reading *Murder at Last Chance Cove*. I hope Saffi reeled you in with her first Rambling RV Mystery. Saffi's future holds friends and foes, twists and turns, coffee and conundrums. If you're ready to buckle in for more mayhem along the "drop-dead" gorgeous Pacific Northwest coast, join other readers in hearing all about my new releases and bonus content by signing up for my newsletter!

www.stormpublishing.co/kim-griswell

I don't know about you, but I've discovered SO MANY good books by reading reviews. If you've fallen for the cove, the coast, and the characters, I hope you'll introduce other readers to Saffi and friends. Even a short review can make all the difference in encouraging a reader to discover my book. Thank you so much!

Like Saffi Graywood, I'm a rambling RV writer. The highways and byways of the Pacific Northwest inspire me every time I travel them in my 35-foot RV. The views are dramatic, the curves... terrifying! I can't help wondering what other terrors might befall the hardy, quirky, rambling people who camp in the RV parks I visit.

If you stay in an RV park for months, as I have, you see a constant stream of people come and go. Lives that would never have touched intersect for a moment, a day, a week. Personalities mesh or clash. Unexpected things happen. Sneaker waves surge. Ravens croak warnings. Mysteries ghost into shore on the morning marine layer. Saffi wandered into my writing at a campground very much like Last Chance Cove RV Park. I followed her over the sandy berm on her first sleuthing adventure and I am beyond delighted that you decided to come with us.

I raise my coffee mug to the baristas of the world and to you, the amazing readers who support my writing and coffee habits. Thank you for being part of this amazing journey with me. I hope you'll stay in touch—I have so many more stories and ideas to entertain you with!

Kim

www.kimgriswell.com

 facebook.com/kim.griswell

x.com/kimgriswell

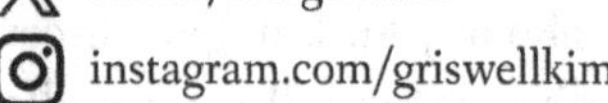 instagram.com/griswellkim